The Persolus Race

Volume One

Alex O'Neill
with Rachel Shipp &
M.M. Dixon

Cover art courtesy Simon Hill: www.simonjthill.co.uk
Art for The Placebo Effect courtesy Gabe Attano:
                                        twitter.com/GabeAttanoArt

Acquisitions Editor: Alex O'Neill
Additional Editors: Rachel Shipp, M.M. Dixon

Find out more about this anthology at www.thepersolusrace.com

ISBN: 978-1-7374683-0-1 (paperback)
           978-1-7374683-1-8 (ebook)

For my mum and dad.
Without their support, this book would not have been written.

Contents

Contents

Editor's Preface

Please enjoy my first book, *The Persolus Race: Volume One*. This book is the result of a combination of efforts from people brought together by the power of the internet, never having met each other in person. I was assisted by two other editors, and along with fourteen authors, we have put together this book during the COVID-19 crisis.

The initial premise, when I thought of it in Spring 2020, was "What if the human race traveled out into the stars, and they never found any aliens? What would that mean for humans then?" This takes the Rare Earth hypothesis—the idea that the conditions to create life are down to an extremely improbable set of factors—to its absolute limit. The stories are in chronological order within this book.

I hope you enjoy,
Alex O'Neill
Acquisitions Editor

Foreword
By George O'Neill

Science fiction (or sci-fi) often looks to the future, but the genre itself has actually been around much longer than most people realize. The epic anthology, *One Thousand and One Nights*, also known as *Arabian Nights*, is a compilation of tales written around the eighth to tenth centuries AD. It is mostly thought of as fairy tale and fantasy, but it also included stories which fall firmly in the sci-fi genre, such as *The Adventures of Bulukiya*, in which Bulukiya embarks on a quest for immortality and, along the way, visits many places and worlds filled with fantastic creatures. In another story in the collection, *The Ebony Horse*, a Persian sage presents his king, Sabur, with an ebony horse. It turns out the horse is a magical flying machine controlled by dials.

Many sci-fi stories involve extraterrestrials, a term coined during the Golden Age of Science Fiction in the 1950s, which we of course know more commonly as aliens. By including aliens, authors can explore the nature of humanity and can generate stresses and contrasts to provide a canvas for the development of their human characters, central to almost all sci-fi stories. Even if there are no humans, aliens allow authors to construct situations which examine the human condition, maybe from an "alien" perspective.

The earlier aliens in fiction are human-like, such as Edgar Rice Burroughs's Martians (*Mars* or *A Princess of Mars*), which vary from humans mostly in color, size, and their number of limbs. Over time, aliens in sci-fi have become more and more bizarre, such as the intelligent ocean in Stanislaw Lem's *Solaris*.

As well as providing a rich environment for character development, aliens are supported by the long-established concept of Cosmic Pluralism, in which the universe comprises many worlds with many creatures. As early as the seventh century AD, Imam Muhammad al-Baqir wrote: "Maybe you see that God created only this single world and that God did not create humans besides you. Well, I swear by God that God created thousands and thousands of worlds and thousands and thousands of humankind."

French astronomer Camille Flammarion was a proponent of Cosmic Pluralism, and during the late nineteenth century, his book, *La pluralité des mondes habités*, was a best seller, printing thirty-three editions in its first twenty years. Flammarion hypothesized that extraterrestrials were genuinely different to humans and not simply variations of creatures found on Earth.

Much less popular with sci-fi authors is the Rare Earth hypothesis, which is the idea that intelligent life is possible only because Earth has a rare set of factors, including having a large moon, oxygen, and tectonic plates, which, taken together, are uncommon in the universe. The term "Rare Earth" was coined by Peter Ward and Donald E. Brownlee in their book *Rare Earth: Why Complex Life Is Uncommon in the Universe* (2000). Ward and Brownlee are not sci-fi authors, but a geologist and paleontologist, and an astronomer and astrobiologist, respectively. Indeed, it almost seems like they have set out to undermine the basic ideas on which much sci-fi is built.

However, it is this Rare Earth universe which we find ourselves in with this anthology, *The Persolus Race,* with *Persolus* being Latin for solitary or lonely. The stories in the anthology have a common setting: a universe where humankind has been around a long time, long enough to establish with some certainty that the phenomenon of intelligent life is not only rare but unique to humankind. This scenario has provided a backdrop for twelve different sci-fi authors to use their imaginations to generate a gripping set of stories.

I am a longtime reader of sci-fi, particularly classic authors such as Jules Verne, Isaac Asimov, and Philip K. Dick. When I was a teenager, I was particularly taken with Arthur C. Clarke's *Tales of the White Hart* short-story collection. Inspired by that book, I have held an idea for an original short story in my head for many years, but never put pen to paper. When my son, Alex O'Neill, told me he was bringing this anthology together, I was more than happy to donate that story idea to him, which he has now brought to life as *The Man in the Mountain*.

Modern technology has provided the platform for this anthology to come together. Under the shadow of the Coronavirus pandemic in 2020, the authors, editors, proofreaders, and illustrators have collaborated via social media to create this anthology and have never met each other in person—a process which earlier sci-fi authors may have considered too outlandish to have even included in their stories! It seems that even if science removes some of the foundational tools of the sci-fi author, their imaginations make up for it in other directions.

I hope you enjoy this anthology and look forward to further work from the authors, as I shall.

Thanks,

George O'Neill

Prologue: We are Alone

By Alex O'Neill

In 1969, the human race, found on Earth, sent a man to the moon.

In 2029, they landed on Mars.

In 2036, they built great geoengineering projects to slow the effects of climate change, allowing the economy and, therefore, scientific research to grow without further worry.

In 2040, the Integrated Space Agency, or ISA, was created by the space agencies of countries within the United Nations.

The human race advanced and reached into the stars, developing the first hyperspeed engine. Earth's best scientists set about understanding atmospheric science, botany, and soils. They put together terraforming engines, known as Edens.

By the end of the 26th century, most of the Milky Way had been explored, and many planets in nearby systems had been terraformed for humans. Despite hopes, no alien life had been found.

In 2949, the human race developed its first faster-than-light-speed engine.

By 3462, the human race had traveled to the edge of the Virgo Supercluster.

They did not stop there. The human race carried on expanding, landing on planets, using up their resources—water, fuel, and air—to power their ships; to power their Edens; to run experiments.

In 3999, the ISA made an announcement. Despite the expansion, despite searches, despite attempts to make contact, no intelligent life had been found anywhere within the Virgo Supercluster.

The human race must face the very real possibility that they are alone in the universe.

The Man in the Mountain

By Alex O'Neill

(Based on an original idea by George O'Neill)

Date: 2450

The University of New Aberdeen was a truly sensational place to learn and work.

Everybody said so.

Voted best new university of the twenty-fourth century.

It was a place to be respected, and a place where the best and brightest came to test their mettle.

New Aberdeen was a quickly developing city built on the southern border of the Cairngorms National Park, intentionally built to be an economic hub north of Glasgow and Edinburgh.

The university sat right in the middle of the city and boasted a huge dome based on St. Paul's Cathedral from London. The main building was a bright white, rather than a drab gray like the Cathedral. Behind the main building lay a maze of science laboratories and cafes. The whole place looked so clean one could eat their dinner off it.

It was no lie that the original Goliath robots were designed and tested there.

Or that the science behind creating cybernetics for human longevity was first formulated there.

It was an icon, a shining star.

And, for Lab Assistant Adam Rehange, German-English theoretical physics student, it was the place he called work. Sometimes, when deadlines were due, it was also home—mainly because he slept there; not because he liked it that much. He did really like it, though. He liked to think that he had made it.

Adam was studying towards his PhD when he landed the research placement of a lifetime: working in a top-secret lab with Dr. Jodie Connors, renowned physicist, and author of the books *How to Build an Eden in Your Back Garden* and *25 Rules for the 25th Century Physicist*, both excellent books that had sold very well. Adam, of course, had his copies signed.

Dr. Connors had landed tenure with the university as one of their resident semi-celebrities; however, she still taught one module of Adam's undergraduate course, about contemporary issues within the scientific community. It was in that class Adam first made contact, and over the next couple of years of loose face-to-face exchanges and via online communications, he had managed to secure his placement.

He'd worked hard, and fast, to get to where he was. And he'd never looked back.

***

It was a gray, midweek morning, and a weak sun penetrated the huge, double-glazed windows found across the University.

Adam sat alone in the university cafeteria, working a marble between his fingers. He was a lanky, young, blond man in his mid-twenties; that never stopped him from getting asked for ID in the university bars. He wore a baggy green hoodie and skinny black jeans, a red cap and large black-rim glasses. Between taking sips of his coffee, he placed the small marble under his thumb. As he pressed down, the marble went spinning out from under his thumb, across the table, and then onto the floor.

It moved almost faster than Adam's eyes could follow, but as soon as it hit the floor, he leaned over and scooped it up. His eyes darted around to see if anyone had spotted him; the cafeteria janitor—a squat middle-aged lady with curly hair—frowned at him, shook her head, and carried on cleaning.

Adam sat back up and placed the marble back under his thumb, and then heard, "Blondie! Heads up!" Suddenly, a small plastic box came flying toward his face. Adam quickly grabbed the box and smoothly placed it on the table. The voice came from one of the few people he ever spoke to around the university, one of his research partners, Maria Smith. Maria was a chubby woman, perhaps a couple of years older than himself, with thick brown hair, big eyes, and an even bigger voice.

She sat down opposite Adam, her arms spreading to more than half the small table.

"What the hell is this?" Adam asked, squinting at the box which Maria had launched at his head.

"It's a digital versatile disk."

"No, it's a box."

"No, dumbass, it's inside. That is the casing."

"I see," Adam muttered, flipping the box over to read through the front cover. "The…Prestige."

"Early twenty-first century movie," Maria stated.

"What's it about? I never really liked films. I was too busy growing up for these sorts of things."

"Two competing magicians…both hoping to pull off the ultimate trick. Eventually, their ambition proves their undoing."

"How does that work?"

"Well, they both become so desperate, and their tricks become so elaborate, one of them loses their life," Maria said.

Adam blinked, breathed in slowly, and then back out. "You're showing me this because?"

"I don't really know. It just made me think of you. You'd like it. You're always reading those classic books," she pointed out.

"Those are novels. You know I don't like films," Adam reminded her.

"Will you watch it?" Maria asked. "I mean, it's based on a novel."

"Yes." Adam smiled, his stiff frame relaxing a little. "For you, Maria, of course I will." For a moment, the two of them locked eyes, and Maria put her hand through Adam's hair. "My sister used to do that," he said and pulled Maria's hand away. "Which means please don't." The two locked eyes again, and Adam paused. *That didn't come out the way I meant*, he thought.

"Come on." Adam stood up. "We've got work to be doing."

"You know, we could do with some time off, Adam," Maria stated, standing up too. "You especially. When was the last time you had eight hours sleep?"

"I don't know," Adam stated, "I don't remember the last time I had *five* hours sleep."

***

Adam and Maria clocked in for the morning. Roger, the gentleman who operated security, buzzed him in and handed him a locker key. Adam had always thought Roger looked like the human version of a pug: small, with thin brown hair and large, dark eyes. Maria followed quickly after, smiling and winking Roger, who smiled back and handed her a key too, as he buzzed her in.

Maria followed Adam into the elevator, and as they descended, she smiled at him. Adam looked ahead, and then caught her eyes, then looked away again.

"Do you ever think about the fact that no one has a clue what we do here?" Maria asked.

"I think it's best that way. Not many high and mighty academics would like to know we're building a time machine down here."

Adam thought slowly about the situation. The experiment had been self-funded by the head of their project, Dr. Connors, who had handpicked Maria and Adam from PhD programs she taught on. Adam was brought on to support with the research, and Maria as a practical lab technician. Their world, overnight, had changed. That said, Adam had never looked back, never questioned why he had been chosen. He had known—he had always known—that he was going to do something special with his life.

The elevator finally reached its destination, and Maria and Adam stepped out, Adam allowing Maria out first.

Adam smiled, nodded at Maria, and headed into the changing rooms. He put his bag away, removed his jewelry, and replaced his thin reading glasses with prescription safety goggles.

Dr. Connors met him as he entered the lab. She was a tall, thin woman with small, brown eyes and wiry brown hair. She looked like everyone's marmite, firm-but-fair schoolteacher. Despite being tiny in comparison to Maria or Adam, neither one of them questioned her intellect or ability to run the experiment. Adam had found her very affable and well-humored, as far as genius scientists went. He had read all her books and had picked New Aberdeen (amongst other reasons) because he knew she worked there.

"Big day," she said with a smile. "Our first living subject."

"You got it?" Adam asked, glad to see his mentor so upbeat.

"I had to sneak it out of the environment study building last night," Dr. Connors stated, "But if anyone had challenged me, I would probably just ask if they knew who I am."

Adam laughed. Dr. Connors was not a complete egomaniac, but she certainly knew she was famous and would not be afraid to flaunt her fame if it helped. Adam believed, passionately, that she wanted to make the world a better place, and therefore he didn't mind.

***

They approached the machine together, as Maria moved around, placing reflectors in position. They had found that to use the time machine created an enormous amount of excess energy, some of which converted into light that they had to reflect away from themselves to prevent blindness. This was something Dr. Connors and Adam knew they had to iron out before running a demonstration for the entire faculty.

Maria joined Dr. Connors and Adam, giving a quick thumbs-up. She passed a big cardboard box to Dr. Connors, who pulled out a large black rat.

"Right," she said, smiling. "We shall call you…Rattus?"

"I think it looks like an Adam," Maria stated.

Adam shook his head, looking at Dr. Connors.

"You know," Adam stated. "I'm happy to try it. I really don't see why the animals get to go first."

"Too much paperwork," Dr. Connors said firmly, a twinkle remaining in her eye.

"The first living creature to travel in time is a stinking rat. It won't sound particularly good when I tell this to my grandchildren," Adam said, looking at Dr. Connors, who then turned away to look at the rat, giving it a gentle stroke.

"I think I'll name him Michael, after my ex-husband," she said, and Adam had to smile.

"Okay. So, Maria, get ready." Dr. Connors waved her right hand. Maria rushed to power up the machine.

"Adam, get the video recorders ready." Due to the light, they wouldn't be able to record much, but they needed everything they could get, should there be testing issues, some teething problems with the machine for example.

Adam set up four video cameras facing into the machine, and then, using a sliding ladder, switched on a fifth camera that looked directly down. Dr. Connors placed Michael into an open box, and then inside the time machine.

The three of them stepped inside a control room, as the time machine powered up.

"Godspeed, Michael-the-rat," Maria said, her accent barely separating the words.

Dr. Connors leaned forward and sorted out the settings. "Okay, let's start small, with one centi-second. It won't mean much to us, but we can use the cameras to observe any change. We don't want to put Michael through more than we need to in case the experience is painful."

"Are you sure you want to go with a jump that can't be observed by the naked eye?" Maria asked.

"I do." Dr. Connors nodded. "Let's not run before we can crawl." With that, she pulled the switch, initiating what they had coined "the jump."

There was a huge flash of light, which was successfully reflected by the mirrors. Almost as soon as it had started, it was over. The time machine powered down, a deep hum resonating through the entire spacious laboratory. It wasn't to worry; they had the finest sound-proofing that Dr. Connors's considerable wallet could supply.

Adam smiled when he saw all the cameras and mirrors remained unharmed.

Dr. Connors was the first to step out. She moved quickly toward the box, almost at a trot. Adam was close behind her, while Maria hung back. Dr. Connors and Adam peered into the box.

Michael was missing.

"What?" Dr. Connors asked no one in particular. "Was he vaporized?"

"Vaporized?" Adam was confused.

"Get the video footage now!" Dr. Connors's voice was suddenly raised.

Adam scrambled to the top of the sliding ladder, unplugging the camera before coming back down. He turned to Dr. Connors, about to speak, when she nodded behind him. "I see him!"

Adam turned to see Michael pressed up against the inside of the time machine, well outside his box, uncomfortable but alive. Dr. Connors picked up Michael once again, stroking him to calm him.

"He's very startled," she stated. "But I don't think this caused him any physical harm. Mental, maybe, but he's not exhibiting any unnatural behaviors."

"Do you think he actually time traveled?" Adam asked.

"I don't know, but he couldn't have climbed out of his box. It's far too large."

"Then maybe…maybe the machine affected his mass?"

"It's not impossible, but this is conjecture. We don't know, not yet." Dr. Connors stated. "You know what I'm about to say. Play the footage, Adam."

A few moments later, Michael had been placed safely within the control room, and Maria was left to attend the lab. Adam and Dr. Connors headed into her research office down the hall.

Adam connected the chip from the video recorder to the computer, while Dr. Connors set about making them both a coffee.

As Dr. Connors came round, she allowed Adam to sit in her swivel chair to operate her computer and stood behind him, looking over his shoulder.

"Okay, this is at a fiftieth of normal speed," Adam said as he hit play. The footage played slowly, the light present to a degree, though dimmed using Adam's editing skills. Michael-the-rat sat nonchalantly in the box, positioned in the middle of the screen. Suddenly, as the video played frame by frame, Michael vanished.

"Stop the recording!" Dr. Connors exclaimed. "Where did he go?"

"I don't know."

"Play the next frame," Dr. Connors ordered, and Adam hit play again. As soon as Michael disappeared, he reappeared in the corner of the camera, pressed up against the inside of the time machine, right where they'd found him.

"Damn," Adam swallowed. "He didn't climb out of the box."

"No, Adam," Dr. Connors shook her head. "It would appear that he teleported."

"Did we—did we just invent the teleport?" Adam asked.

"No," Dr. Connors stated firmly. Her usually approachable demeanor dropped, and she became instantly sterner. "But we might need to look at the drawing board again."

Adam and Dr. Connors headed out of the office. For the next few hours, Dr. Connors returned to her laboratory and poured over the recording, noting, slowing the footage down again and again. Adam was sent away to the library to do some reading, and then the pair of them attended a meeting with the dean, where Dr. Connors continued with the lie that their work involved testing power cells for Edens. She sent Adam away to update their costing sheets to help cover the lie; everything they did had to help cover the lie, down to making the laboratory look like it was made to test power cells.

Adam headed downstairs, back into Dr. Connors's office, and began filling in sheets and sheets on his laptop, the bags under his eyes increasing.

"Adam," came a loud voice, and he looked up to see the curvy outline of Maria filling the doorway, her lab coat removed, just wearing a-white shirt and gray suit trousers. "Are you okay, pal?" she asked.

"I feel like a failure…Dr. Connors picked me for this project, and I can't even get it right. I can't even figure out why it's not working."

"You're being hard on yourself," Maria stated. "Too hard on yourself. For god's sake, Adam, Dr. Connors can't figure out why it's not working either, and she's like the Einstein of our times."

"I suppose," Adam responded, smiling slowly.

"You look tired," Maria said.

"I am tired."

"Go home. Watch that film. Get an early night. I'll finish this off."

"Yes, ma'am," Adam said, standing up and smiling to himself. *Maybe there was something to Maria*, he thought. *She was certainly a good person.*

"I know you like being told what to do. Otherwise, you wouldn't have put up with Dr. Connors for so long," Maria stated, blushing ever so slightly. "You know, maybe Friday night, I could come home with you?"

"You wish," Adam smiled, and stopped as he passed Maria. The two exchanged a brief hug, which was warm and momentarily fulfilling, then Adam cleared his throat and headed out of the door.

"You still got that movie on you?" Maria asked, and Adam turned, reached into his pocket, and waved it at her.

"Still on me," he smiled.

Adam headed out the door, up to the changing rooms, and picked up his stuff, placing his jewelry back on. Then, before going out of the building, he quickly opened the lab door, and saw Michael-the-rat in his box, squeaking away. Adam nodded at Michael, quickly looked around the lab to make sure that none of his stuff was left inside, and then closed the lab door and went out of the building, back to his home.

***

The following morning, Adam swept into the lab with a new vigor.

"Morning, sunshine," Maria said.

"Morning, dear," Adam responded.

"Good film?"

"It was. I found it very compelling. Those men…would have done anything to impress."

"I'm not sure that's the takeaway I had," Maria stated.

"I just thought it was all so intriguing. I guess, it's not far from what we're doing here, you know? A lot of people might think what we're doing here is like a magic trick. Seemingly impossible, with a pledge; we have a rat, then a turn; we make it disappear, and then a prestige; it reappears in a different place and time."

"You know, while we made this machine work, we haven't worked out its prestige. Why it works, as it were," Maria said. Adam looked away for a moment, and then back at Maria.

"You still look tired," she said.

"Thanks, mom. I tried to sleep, but it didn't really happen."

"Well, at least you tried," Maria replied. "Maybe I could buy you a meal, some drinks? Or cook you something? Put you into a food coma? That'll make you sleep?"

"Fuck off." Adam smiled. "Well, maybe actually." He then looked over to the observation room. "How is our favorite rat this morning?"

"He's content," Maria said, as she pulled the veils off the main pillars of the time machine. "He could do with a feeding himself?"

"On it." Adam headed into the observation room, pulled some feed from a small Tupperware box on the side, and ran his hand under Michael's nose. Michael sniffed it, and then quickly began to gobble it up. Adam smiled. While he'd never been a biologist, he found animals very easy to get on with, almost always more often than he did people.

***

"Maria," Dr. Connors said as she entered the lab suddenly, and without any notice to either of them. "We're going to run another test this morning. Is Michael ready?" Adam noted a nervousness in Dr. Connors's voice that had not been there before.

"He is." Once again, Maria moved forward with the box containing Michael and placed it in the center of the time machine. Adam switched the cameras on.

Dr. Connors moved swiftly into the control room, followed by Adam and Maria.

Dr. Connors's hands hovered above the control board. "We need to put Michael's destination in to match his current location."

"In terms of longitude and latitude?" Adam asked.

"No, er... no, that doesn't matter. The landing destination needs to read 'same as starting position.' See, look—we didn't put anything last time. That must be where we went wrong?"

"You think?"

"Yes," Dr. Connors replied, "and the small jump in time was mirrored with a small jump in space. We've got to manually take out the jump in space. You know, ask the machine not to do it."

"And if you're wrong?" Adam raised an eyebrow. "That's a theory. We've got no evidence to support it."

"Then we've invented a teleport device, not a time machine."

"Michael disappeared. For a frame of that recording, he was gone; no puff, no bang, just gone," Adam said nervously. "He no longer existed."

"That might be the effect of a teleport. The atoms that formed Michael temporarily disappeared and then reappeared elsewhere."

"Maybe. But we ought to increase the time jump to be certain."

Dr. Connors nodded. "Good idea. Maria, increase the jump time to a second."

"Putting it up to a second, Dr. Connors."

"God, I hope you're right, Adam. I want you to be right."

"Me too, boss."

"Hit it, Maria," Dr. Connors ordered, and Maria flipped the start switch.

The time machine flickered into life once again, roaring and ready to go. There was the same flash of light, shining only for a moment, then flickering away.

When it was completely gone, Michael had disappeared. He did not reappear.

Adam and Dr. Connors ran into the lab, as Maria scrambled to power everything down. Adam looked round the inside of the time machine, while Dr. Connors looked under every box and into every nook and cranny within the entire lab. Maria soon joined her.

"He's not here," Dr. Connors said after a couple of minutes.

"Shit." Adam groaned and sat down on the inside of the time machine, just next to the box.

***

A few minutes later, Adam and Dr. Connors were back in her office, with a recording of the most recent test. Adam hit play. Just like last time, Michael disappeared. But then, even playing at reduced speed, he did not reappear. He was just...gone.

"Adam, what the fuck? Tell me you're seeing this, too."

"We teleported him."

"We did not teleport him! That machine is not set up to be a teleport. It sends objects to one of two places: the same destination as it set off from, or nowhere, in which case the machine reverts to sending to where the object set off from. Either way, it seems to want to teleport the object somewhere else."

"Then maybe...maybe we should specifically put in coordinates. Longitude and latitude, like Maria suggested."

"We could put in the longitude and latitude of right here, but to put in the coordinates of anywhere else on the globe, to jump the object in space and time simultaneously, would require a redesign and a rebuild of the existing machine. We don't have time for that. I don't have the patience." Dr. Connors was firm. "I have spent too much time on the exact details of the post-build theory to be looking at a physical rebuild."

"But we are already jumping objects in time and space," Adam stated. "Somehow."

"What do you mean?"

"That first jump, with Michael, he moved in time and also in space. It was minuscule, but it was still a jump in both dimensions," Adam explained.

"Go on."

"And perhaps the second jump was too big. Machine couldn't handle it. Vaporized the rat," Adam explained.

Dr. Connors' eyes widened. "And maybe the two don't exist without one another. Maybe we can't jump things through time without also jumping them through space. And because we didn't set the location, it tried to jump it in space while getting it as near as possible to the original destination. Second time round, when we asked it to stay in the same place intentionally, the machine vaporized the rat."

"It's possible." Adam nodded. "All we need to do is improve the machine, and theoretically, we could do bigger jumps?"

"Exactly," she smiled. "Maybe we're getting somewhere."

"Perhaps it needs a more considerable subject," Adam stated, "I'm happy to be the first human subject if that makes any difference."

"Possibly, Adam, quite possibly a larger organism could make a difference to the machine's processes. But I want to try the rat again first."

"The offer is still there." Adam nodded. "The sooner we put a person through the machine the quicker we'll get a first-hand account of what it feels like, and we'll begin to understand it better."

"I accept your point," Dr. Connors agreed. "But this is all a lot to think about. I need to go over the math again. Look at the footage—from every angle. We won't do another physical test today, but I need you to get this written up, beat by beat, into some form of report."

"I can do that." Adam nodded before turning from the office.

"I want them done before we start tomorrow," Dr. Connors stated loudly, but Adam didn't respond; he was already out of the door.

***

It was several hours later, and Adam sat in the university cafeteria, eating some cheap chili con carne served on a plastic plate. All that money and the catering was shit. He turned the food around on his plate, and then flicked out his phone. Messages from Dr. Connors and Maria, both work-related. Nothing else. He dismissed the notifications and stared at his phone background, a picture of himself, his sister, and his parents. He looked so young.

Out of the huge, glass pane windows that surrounded the cafeteria, the sun was sinking just below the horizon. There were a few kitchen staff moving around behind the serving stations, clearing away the cooking trays and vats that had been used that day.

A plump, young janitor moved between the tables with a mop and bucket. A pair of undergrad students sat far away from him—a couple ogling each other while they pushed their chili meals around on their plates, letting them run cold.

Adam recognized them; they were physics students who had been in a module he'd lectured on earlier in his PhD. He was unsure whether to make eye contact.

One of them, the lad, smiled and waved. The girl followed suit.

Adam looked up from the unappetizing food, smiled, nodded, and looked back down. It was getting late. There was a moderately comfortable bed waiting for him at home.

As the young couple left, the janitor went over to clear the mess that remained on their table. Adam was in the middle of the cafeteria, completely alone.

Suddenly he heard a scream and his head snapped toward the kitchen. One of the staff dropped a pot of boiling water, and in the confusion, a black rat with no tail ran out from underneath the serving stations.

It was Michael.

"Pass me that pot," Adam exclaimed, and the kitchen worker threw the small pot to him. Adam caught it and chased Michael between the tables, keeping his eyes focused on the small rodent.

Michael dodged and dove, but the janitor turned to face him, which caused the rat to double back on himself, right into Adam's path. Adam slammed the cooking pot on top of Michael, trapping him inside.

"Got you," Adam grunted. "Slippery bastard."

"Keep an eye on the rat," Adam ordered the janitor and headed into the kitchen. A couple of the staff were still shaken. Adam turned to them and nodded at a big man, the sous-chef.

"Where did it come from?" Adam asked.

"He popped out from that ventilation shaft." The man pointed at the bottom of the wall where a small ventilation shaft had been popped off its hinges. Adam crouched down and inspected it. The inside of the ventilation shaft had claw marks on it, as if Michael had struggled. Really struggled. And trapped within the ventilation shaft entrance itself was Michael's tail. It lay there, lifeless.

"Anything?" The sous-chef asked. Adam pulled Michael's tail from the ventilation grate and stuffed it into his breast pocket.

"Nothing. Poor thing had got caught, had to ram its way through, tail came off in the process," Adam said.

"Is that normal?" the sous-chef asked.

"I'm no biologist, but I believe so," Adam hedged. "It's probably just a stray, nothing to worry about, no lawsuits, I'd say. I'll take the thing to the lab and destroy it humanely."

But Adam knew the truth. They must have teleported Michael into the grate by accident earlier. He had struggled, for potentially hours, before finally pulling his own tail off and breaking out of the ventilation shaft.

Adam walked over to the pot and picked up Michael. It was almost nine in the evening, but his work was not yet finished for the day. Adam headed back to the lab with a spring in his step. He knew what to do. It was one of the rare instances in his life where everything aligned, and he knew *exactly* what to do.

***

Adam entered the lab, flicked the lights on, and set Michael down inside his box in the control room. He knew that this machine wasn't a teleport. It couldn't be.

He thought that, possibly, maybe, it was confusing space and time. Adam struggled to work it out; he knew he almost had it. He picked up a nearby piece of paper and scrawled some notes.

For a brief moment, Adam's hand hovered over his mobile phone. Should he call Dr. Connors? Should he wait?

Or should he leap now at the opportunity to make history?

The wind was taken from his sails, and suddenly a huge knot built in his stomach. If he called that number and brought Dr. Connors in, this discovery might never be his. Then again, he owed it Dr. Connors, in a professional capacity, to even be there. He picked up the phone and dialed her number.

"Adam," came a tired voice. "Are you okay?"

"Jodie," Adam said solemnly. "Why did you pick me?"

"Can this wait until morning?"

"Why did you pick me?" Adam asked again.

"Because you were the right man for this job," Dr. Connors said. "I saw determination. A sensitive, intelligent young man, who was going to keep pushing, and keep pushing to get my idea working."

"You saw desperation," Adam responded. "And obedience. A person who would put up with your secrets and your caginess."

"Adam," Dr. Connors said, her voice giving no ego, no arrogance. "Please let us discuss this tomorrow. Put the phone down, tap out, and go to bed."

"Did you ever read my file on the university intranet?" Adam asked.

"No, I don't want to know who you were before I met you. I know the Adam Rehange I know now, and I like him."

"I was obsessed with rugby. I had all the makings of the next big thing. I liked to think I was the full package. And you know, I put my time, and my time again, into the sport, training every single day, never giving myself the time off. And then, two nights before my first national match, my sister called me to tell me her boyfriend was attacking her. It was late, and I headed across the city to get to her, running like I had never run, until I took a wrong turn into the dodgy part of the city. I got stabbed in the leg by some crackhead, tearing my calf muscle. It never fully healed, there's now a twist in that muscle that can't be fixed. I was just in the wrong place at the wrong time. I was so close to being famous, to doing something good with my life. Something meaningful."

"There's more to life than being famous," Dr. Connors responded. "Trust me. What you do here is meaningful."

"That's easy for you to say," Adam spat. "My sister died. Her boyfriend got life. She could have had a life that was meaningful if I'd run a different way or faster. Or slower. Or hell, if I'd gotten a taxi.

"Please Adam," Dr. Connors cried, "don't do anything rash. Go home, get some sleep."

"You know," Adam said, "I used to think you were the greatest living scientist. You and I met; you know, before I came here."

"I think I would remember. I have a memory for those sorts of things."

"I know. But still, I doubt it. I had just finished key stage three, and I'd read your second book. I was captain of my year's rugby team, but my parents were still determined to get me into university to do physics.

My dad took me to a book signing at our local store, and you were there. I still remember what you put into my copy of the book, it said 'Make a life you will remember.'"

"Why have you never told me this, Adam?"

"Because you never asked," Adam replied. "In fact, you never ask anything about me."

"Adam…please," Dr. Connors begged.

"Goodnight, Jodie," Adam said, hanging up and then flicking the phone into his pocket.

***

Adam took a swig from an old whiskey bottle he had kept in his locker, set up the controls for a ten-minute jump into the future, removing longitude and latitude and landing back in the same spot. He didn't need the rat.

Adam adjusted the cameras, stepped back into the control room, and set the machine in motion. Then he hopped out again with enthusiasm and stepped into the time machine. The machine began to whir into life and hummed with noise. Slowly but surely, light began to surround him.

Michael-the-rat squealed from his box, panicked and unable to understand what was going on.

Adam looked up, embracing the light. The feeling of energy enveloped him, like a solid coating. It tingled every skin particle, like nothing Adam had ever experienced.

Adam felt it burning up, the heat increasing. What seemed like a moment in the control room was an eternity inside the machine.

Adam closed his eyes and began to smile. His feet began to lift off the ground; he felt entirely weightless.

This is what they had worked for all this time—to jump a living human being through time. And he, Adam Rehange, was the first.

He felt the energy, the sound, the temperature increasing all around him, and he embraced it.

"This is my prestige," Adam whispered to himself.

The burning brilliance increased and increased, with what must have taken a second from outside the machine seeming to take an eternity from within it. Just when it became too much for him to bear, he heard a jagged ripping, and everything went black.

***

The following morning, Dr. Connors and Maria entered the lab, almost simultaneously, to find the cameras set up and still running.

Dr. Connors searched the control room and found a terrified, tailless Michael running in circles inside his box. The control panel reading showed a planned ten-minute jump with no change to the location.

"What the hell? What happened here? Where is Adam?" Dr. Connors asked.

"There's footage," Maria shouted. "It's still recording—almost thirteen hours of it."

"Switch it off," Dr. Connors ordered. "Load it up on my computer now."

"It won't be fast," Maria said.

"I know. Just get it done. Was this Adam?"

"Either that, or we had an intruder."

"No, there's no sign of a forced entry. And apart from us, Adam was the only one with the code to the doors. We left together yesterday, so unless you snuck back in, this was him."

"This was him, then." Maria headed out to upload the file to Dr. Connors's computer.

"Please tell me he didn't get in that thing without supervision," Dr. Connors whispered.

Dr. Connors searched the control room and spotted a piece of paper with Adam's scrawled handwriting: "Michael travels 1 centi-second—jump across the machine. Michael travels 1 second—jumps into the green cafeteria."

Dr. Connors read it, and then read it again.

"Ah, shit," she whispered to herself and began to panic. Adam must have come across Michael after she'd left. The machine had jumped the rat in space; if Michael had landed in the green cafeteria, he'd jumped almost three hundred meters.

Dr. Connors frowned and headed out of the lab. She swung into her office, where Maria sat at her desk, uploading the video file.

"Which way is the green cafeteria from here?"

"West," Maria said.

"On the first jump, Michael was pressed up against the machine on our left, from the control room, which is…westerly?"

"That's right," Maria confirmed. Dr. Connors handed her Adam's note.

"Oh my god. What does this mean?"

Suddenly there was ding, and Maria checked the computer. "The video. It's ready to watch."

Dr. Connors and Maria sat side by side, watching the video screen intently, unsure of what was about to happen. They watched as Adam stepped inside the time machine. Everything seemed normal. The time machine flicked into life, then Adam was surrounded by light and disappeared. Gone.

They fast-forwarded ten minutes, but he was still nowhere to be seen. They waited another minute. Dr. Connors hit the fast-forward, and they sped through the recording at about fifty-times regular speed. After another few minutes, there was still nothing.

Dr. Connors and Maria slowly turned to look at each other and then back to the screen. Dr. Connors cut to the end of the recording, where the lab looked exactly the same.

They sat in their seats, not saying anything, for quite some time.

After a while, Dr. Connors spoke. "I have had an idea, but the ramifications are not pleasant. We programmed the machine to ignore latitude and longitude, in order to not confuse it. Even to the same measure, the subject could end up in a slightly different spot. You follow?"

"Yes," Maria replied.

"So, to avoid that, we wanted the subject to end up in exactly the same spot in space, yes? The issue is the Earth is always moving. It's always spinning on its axis and it's always rotating around the sun. The machine calculates not to throw objects into space due the Earth's orbit; it might fail to factor in the Earth rotating on its axis. That means whatever's west of us is coming toward us at an incredible speed."

"Okay...."

"About two hundred eighty meters per second, if my memory serves me correctly," Dr. Connors said. "So, when we jumped Michael across the time machine floor, he landed in the same place he set off. But everything else on Earth had moved two-point-eight meters due to the rotation."

Maria nodded.

"And then when we jumped Michael for a full second, he might have been gone for that second, but he landed in the green cafeteria, which is two hundred eighty meters west of the lab. So, when Adam jumped ten minutes, it would have landed him—"

"Landed him west of here," Maria finished. "But wait, you're saying he's, okay? That the time machine works?"

"It works," Dr. Connors smiled.

"Then...where's Adam?" Maria asked.

"He'll be wherever's one hundred seventy kilometers west of here." Dr. Connors searched on her laptop to work out exactly where that was. But when she saw where, her face dropped.

"Oh, shit," she whispered. "He might be dead."

"What?" Maria asked, moving closer to the smaller woman.

"I knew Adam was brash...but I never thought he'd do this," Dr. Connors stated.

"You picked him for a reason?"

"I picked him because he was desperate, and he was bright," Dr. Connors admitted, her eyes barely meeting Maria's.

"You picked him because he was vulnerable," Maria said, disgusted.

"I'd kept my eye on him ever since he got here. He stood out to me. His conviction."

"He was a person, Jodie," Maria responded. "He was a good man, and you contently led him to his death!"

"I didn't mean to," Dr. Connors replied. "He did seem out of sorts last night."

"What do you mean?"

"He called me, and I think he was drunk. Asking me why I chose him for this. I had an inkling he was going to do something awful to himself," Dr. Connors admitted.

"You...You knew he was going to do something, and you didn't come in?" Maria exclaimed.

"When you put it like that, it sounds bad...but as he hung up, I thought that maybe now we know what Adam did wrong...we can carry on testing, improving the machine. This is my moment, yours too, Maria," Dr. Connors explained.

"Fuck you," Maria snapped, "I quit. I am taking this to the dean. Don't worry, Jodie, everyone will know what happened here today." With that, Maria turned and left the room, closing the door behind her. On the way out, she popped her head into the laboratory, scooped up Michael-the-rat and looked into his beady black eyes.

"You, Michael," she said, "you're coming home with me." As she headed back into the corridor, Dr. Connors rushed to stand between Maria and the elevator.

"What are you going to do now?" Dr. Connors demanded.

"I'm going home," Maria informed her, "Then I'm going to get a map out and find Adam, and call search and rescue. Wherever he is, he can be found!"

***

Ben Nevis is the tallest mountain in the United Kingdom, located in the county of Inverness-shire in Scotland. This natural beauty, composed of thousands of tons of metamorphic and igneous rock, sits at the very edge of Loch Linnhe and near the town of Fort William. It stands a fine 1,345 meters above sea level and is what remains of a Devonian volcano. One of its sides, Glen Nevis, is the steepest hill slope in Britain. It is visited by thousands of tourists every year, prompting the opening of a pub at the mountain's summit in 2039.

In English, its name is Venomous Mountain.

Underneath all that rock, all that wildlife, all those people, in the base of Ben Nevis, a man appeared.

The man appeared from nowhere and all he could see was blackness. The weight of the mountain pressed upon him, the stone running through his legs, where two objects were attempting to fill the exact same space. He was bleeding out, running out of oxygen, deep in the base of Ben Nevis.

He tried to reach down to his pocket for his phone, but he couldn't move.

He tried to work out where he was, but with the lack of oxygen, his head began to pound. He had been in a lab...somewhere...somewhere that must have been far away. But now he no longer knew where he was.

He gritted his teeth and tried to remain calm, thinking about his friends, his mom, his dad, his sister. Trying to fight through the pain, he focused on his happiest moments. He would not go calmly into the darkness. Recent memories rose up, and he clung to them. A machine, a machine that had puzzled him beyond belief, that he had spent his academic life working toward, from school through to doctorate.

That was it—a time machine. Memories started to come back to him. He wanted to invent time travel; and he had done so. He was the very first person to travel in time. He'd certainly go down in the history books, that much he knew. He could just see himself, standing on a plinth, holding a Nobel Prize in Physics, where he would join his childhood heroes— scientists like Curie and Newton, Einstein, and Hawking—on the next generation of physicists' bedroom walls.

The man smiled. He had made it. He'd worked hard, and fast, to get to where he was. And he'd never looked back.

Then the man in the mountain, whose name was Adam Rehange, closed his eyes, rested his head on a stone, and smiled no more.

The Snake in Eden

By Josh Whittle

Date: 2550

The man sat in the dark room where shadows danced in the soft blue light from the monitor. He half-heartedly looked at the images on the screens, a tumbler of whiskey in his hand, his legs crossed.

"What am I looking at?"

"These people are at the top of your threat list, sir," his assistant said in a British accent as she refilled his glass. "The number one threat is Link Norton."

The man looked at the photo of Link, a young handsome man with long blond hair, and grunted. *Who the hell has cybernetics in only one eye?*

"He graduated from MIT with a degree in environmental engineering. He comes from money and has bankrolled at least two environmental paramilitary attacks on a mine on Io."

The man stroked his chin, then sipped his drink. "Known associates?"

"His girlfriend, Ocean Miller."

"Hmm," he said, bored.

She smiled. "Stay with me, sir, it gets exciting from here."

He looked at her. Then to the side-by-side pictures of an attractive woman. In one, her face was covered in piercings with a tattoo along her cheekbone and a huge pile of blue, dreadlocked hair. In the other picture she had a buzz cut and her dark skin was clear of piercings and tattoos.

"Gunnery Sargent Ocean Miller was honorably discharged from the Jupiter Planetary Defense Force four years ago. She was trained as a military marksman. She earned the Thunderbolt of Zeus for conspicuous bravery and extreme devotion to duty in the presence of the enemy in the Ganymede Uprising. She still holds a record for the most kills of any one soldier in the JPDF."

The man nodded. "Cybernetics?"

"Extensive, military-grade."

A new image came up, a hulking man with a dark, scruffy beard. "And rounding out the trio is Ben Jones. Sargent Major Jones was also honorably discharged from the JPDF. He received the Jupiter Fist for being injured in the line of duty while fighting in the Ganymede Uprising. He received extensive training as shock infantry. Jones specialized as an explosive ordnance specialist. He also has extensive cybernetics."

"Norton has quite the team around him."

"Indeed, sir, and there is one more."

He nodded.

She continued, "This one is a strange one."

A blurry picture of a young woman flashed up. He took an impressive sip of whiskey.

"Three weeks ago, Norton started meeting with this woman. The system says she is 107 years old and called Merry Joe, which has to be a fake identity. Other than that, there is no record of her anywhere. She is a ghost."

He frowned and leaned forward. "Cybernetics?"

"No, sir, none."

He snapped, "Not just military."

She gave a little cough. "Sir, I mean no cybernetics at all. She's never had them."

"Well, bugger me. That explains your fake identity comment." He sat back in his chair. "Do we have a potential asset available?"

A picture flashed on the screen, and he laughed. "Oh wonderful."

***

"Hello, I'm Arlo Remington with TRC Evening News, in front of the Australian ISA Center, where we are into the fourth day of this peaceful protest." The reporter walked to a nearby protester and yelled over the chanting mass of people. "Excuses me, sir, but can you show the camera your sign please?"

"My sign says, 'Fuck ISA, Fuck the Eden project!'" The handsome man with long blond hair was in his mid-twenties.

"But, sir, you have to agree that the ISA has advanced the human race more than any other time in history?" Arlo asked.

"That's fucking bullshit!"

"Please not so much swearing," Arlo chided.

The man shook his head. "I'm sorry, man. Yeah, you're right; but at what cost? They say—" he made quotation marks with his fingers "—that they have not found life. But, like, there was a time when there was no advanced life on this planet. Would we be alive today if the Earth had been terraformed? Remember the Charon incident? They had proof of life but killed them all."

"Come on, sir, the moon of Pluto was terraformed one hundred thirty years ago. If you still believe that conspiracy, how do you feel about chemtrails?" Arlo joked.

The man's one cybernetic eye focused on Arlo while his mud-brown eye became a slit. "Sure, a member of government-funded media trying to discredit the truth. TRC is the bitch of the ISA."

Arlo rolled his eyes. The man screamed his slogan into the camera, then pushed it away and walked off.

"Well folks, you heard it here first."

***

Scout leaned into the wind, her mouse-brown hair whipping out behind her as she tried to keep from flying off the top of Ochre Tower. "It's kind of ironic that we're going to topple one environmental criminal from the building of another environmental criminal."

"Yep, Ochre Mining is next, for sure!" Ocean tied her thick, blue dreadlocks back, and Scout admired how they contrasted with her dark skin. Scout then watched Ocean double-check the BAX-R8 sniper rifle.

"Hey, Ocean, how are your new cybernetics? What did you go for?" asked Ben.

"Full upgrade—full set of Týr cybernetics. Even splurged some more and got the Fenris optics. What did you end up upgrading?"

"What! Why did you spend that much for? You should have got Aries implants as I did—they're half the price!"

Scout rolled her eyes and mumbled, "If cybernetics are that important, why am I here?"

"Fuck you, Scout." Ben scratched at his beard and turned back to Ocean. "I don't trust the clean-skins. They're unnatural." He stood tall and strong, his cybernetic legs holding him to the roof.

"What do you mean 'it's unnatural,' you idiot? *Not* having cybernetics is natural," snapped Scout.

What is the point of being muscular if it's not even aesthetically pleasing anymore in this age of cybernetics? Scout thought. Even her slight frame was thought to be overly developed. *What a stupid vain ass!*

Ben turned his angry cybernetic eyes to Scout.

"That's enough. Both of you," Ocean snapped. "The ISA has cutting-edge security. It focuses on electronic currents, targeting cybernetics. We need a clean-skin. No cybernetics means no security forces."

"No shit, it's my plan, Ocean. Remember who your boss is. It's not like the JPDF days."

"You better remember that as well, Ben." They all spun to see a tall thin man with long blonde hair and one cybernetic eye.

"Hey Link, you're back. How was being famous?" Ocean grinned.

"Fucking Arlo but he is the best reporter out there." Link squatted down next to Ocean, resting his hand on her ass.

Scout looked away from them, giving them some privacy. She noticed Ben's face and giggled at his look of suppressed rage and jealousy.

Link looked up at Scout. "What's up?"

"Oh, nothing. Just thinking about poor old Arlo; he must have flipped after what you told him," she lied.

She walked to Ben, who was watching Link and Ocean kissing now. "So, which is it—jealousy or anger?" Scout asked softly.

"Wh-what?"

She casually nodded at the entanglement of limbs and whispered, "Those two. That must be hard for you, with your feelings for her. You must hate having to watch this. It's near porn!"

Ben's fist flashed out and he grabbed her by the neck. "Fuck you."

Before he started squeezing, she mouthed, "Temper, temper."

"We ready to go or what?" Scout gasped as Ben's hand dropped. His face still showed anger, and she backed across the roof. She checked an antique pistol and slid it into a thigh holster. Then she pulled a fake skin over her face. She blew Ben a kiss.

Link disentangled himself and checked the time. "Oh, yeah. Let's go now."

Scout sprinted off, activating her boost pack and shooting across the roof. She planted her foot on the edge of the roof, then jumped and dropped the boost pack. She spread her arms and legs, and as the wingsuit caught the wind, she whooped and screamed with joy. "This is the best!"

Ocean followed Scout with the scope of her rifle, both to keep an eye on her and to provide cover. *I would have hated being a sniper back in the day*, she thought as her cybernetics worked out the wind speed and the trigonometry of the shot for her.

Ben tested his boost pack and checked his VXSS-02 anti-personnel railgun. *I don't trust that bitch Merry Joe, Scout, whoever she is. She's not one of us*, he thought.

Link counted down as Scout approached the ISA building. "Well, it worked," he said as she passed through the shield.

Scout leaned back and pulled her parachute. She slowed down to an almost complete stop, cut the chute cord, and as it was whipped away, the sudden change in momentum spoiled her aim. "Oh fuck," she screamed as she dropped through space, flailing her arms as the ledge rushed up at her.

Thank God, she thought as her hand hit the ledge and she bore the brunt of the impact in her tucked legs. She puffed her cheeks, pulled herself up, and rolled over the edge. She was breathing hard as adrenaline coursed through her but gave her team the thumbs-up as she stood.

"Well, she's made it over. Let see if she can get in," said Link.

"Doubt it," Ben grunted.

Scout quickly stripped off the wings of her suit and tossed them over the ledge. She walked past windows, counting until she found the one, she was looking for. She pulled a roll of detonation cord out of her pack and made a big X on the window. She dropped the remainder back in her pack and jogged along the ledge until it opened to a roof. She found a fire escape door and went to work unlocking it with a tool from her pack.

"How the hell can the ISA make a mistake like this? I don't understand—not everyone has cybernetics," grumbled Ocean.

"As Ben said, she's strange; cybernetics is an everyday thing. Scout is the only person I have ever met who has nothing. Shit, babe, I had like four cybernetics given to me before I was born." Link watched Scout work.

Scout opened the security lock and gave a wicked grin. "I love this part."

"Hey, the security guards are checking the floor now," said Ocean, following the two guards with her cybernetic eyes.

"Come on, Scout, hurry up," muttered Link. In a louder voice he said, "Ben, get ready."

"Yeah, Link." Ben bent into a sprinter's stance.

Scout pulled a rubber glove and a can of water from her pack. She tossed the water on the electronic circuits. *Boom!* Sparks shot from the lock and the building went black. "Dumb asses! This would never have worked four hundred years ago," she laughed.

Ben sprinted and jumped, his cybernetic legs launching him into the space between the buildings. As he dropped low, he hit the boost pack and shot forward again. He landed running on the roof, his legs taking the impact. He nodded to Scout and moved quickly through the door. He lifted the VXSS-02 and pressed it to his shoulder, locking the smart sights with his cybernetic eyes. Scout drew her antique pistol and followed the former soldier.

"Report," said Link into his communication implants.

"Making our way to the guards. Repeat rule of engagement," Ben replied.

"Contact if necessary. We don't want the law here, and I don't need two martyrs, either."

Ben used his smart sight to find the CEO's office. He could see the two guards and gave Scout a grin as he knelt low and leaned around the corner. He fired twice in quick succession, making fist-sized holes in the back of the guards' heads.

"Fuck, Ben! What did I just say?" screamed Link.

Ben smiled. "Link, it's fine." He walked over the corpses and opened the door for Scout.

She shook her head, and ran into the office, stopping at the big wooden desk. "Holy shit! I think this is real wood!"

"The power will come back on in three…two…one."

As Ocean counted down, Ben took out three black boxes the size of his fingers, hit the big red buttons on top, tossed them into the corners of the office, and shut the door on Scout trapping her with the micro-EMPs. The lights began to flicker as Ocean finished her countdown, then the micro-EMP grenades popped, and the office went black again. By then, though, the security system had found Ben's cybernetics.

Red lights flashed and a siren bellowed. Scout opened the door and gave Ben a look that could kill as the now harmless, optics-destroying chaff billowed out of the office.

"What the actual fuck?" Scout blew glittery chaff from her lips.

"What? It won't hurt you—you're a clean-skin!" Ben smiled as he threw her the spare boost pack and a set of electronic tools. "Get to work, Scout."

"You're an ass Ben, just watch the door," snapped Scout as she put a communications earpiece in. She was going to say more, but her mouth snapped shut as a security ship roared past.

"Security has arrived," said Ocean.

"Do not contact until they enter the building," said Link. "Get to work, Scout."

Scout walked to the back of the room and knocked a picture from the wall to reveal a safe. *Wow, this is some old-school shit*, she thought.

She pulled a small box out of her lead-lined case, then opened it. She lifted a cybernetic lens and, using her other hand to open her eyelid, put it in. She gave a few blinks, then quickly made a hole with her drill, revealing a glowing blue wire. Using the cybernetic hacking tool in her lens, she sunk into the internal system of the safe and ran her program.

"The door will be breached in three…two…" Ocean began.

Ben grinned and launched three more micro-EMPs from his position at the bend in the hallway.

"One," finished Ocean, looking away so the chaff from Ben's EMPs wouldn't damage her optics.

The door blew off its hinges and security threw their own EMPs. As soon they did, though, Ben's blew. The security team's EMPs harmlessly hit the ground, and their weapons short-circuited. Ben made the most of his short advantage and used his VXSS-02 to fill the hallway with a barrage of fire.

Link kissed Ocean on the cheek and stood up. "Moving to second position."

"Confirmed," called the team.

Scout smiled as she opened the safe door and downloaded the damning evidence. "Ten seconds then I'm done."

"I'm moving to second position." Ben ducked back around the corner. A micro-EMP grenade landed next to him. Bang!

"I'll give cover, Ben," said Ocean as she started firing her BAX-R8, which sounded like a thunderclap.

"Woo hoo, hell yeah! I love that sound, Ocean!" Scout laughed.

Ben peeked around the corner to see the BAX-R8 launch three security guards backward. He quickly opened his VXSS-02 and removed the burnt firing circuit, then took a fresh one from his lead-lined pouch and reloaded the weapon. He then rebooted his cybernetics, and not for the first time, he was glad they were military-grade kit and not civilian. "Locked and loaded."

"I'm reloading. Start running, Ben," said Ocean.

"I'm done here as well," said Scout, walking to the door.

Ben charged down the hall with security guards on his tail. Scout raised the antique pistol, shot twice, and was surprised as a shell flew out of the gun. Ben slid down the last few meters, rolled onto his stomach, and fired back the way he had come.

"I'm getting out," said Scout.

"Confirmed," called the team.

Scout activated the detonation cord to blow out the window, while Ocean shot at the building's security team. Scout, keeping low, sprinted and jumped out the window. Ben tossed the last of his grenades and ran to the ledge, letting his cybernetic legs launch him out of the window and into the night. He found Scout boosting off toward the extraction point and went after her.

Ocean watched Ben and Scout jump. "Great, now for the bit of the plan I hate," she mumbled to herself. She switched her rifle from semi- to full-automatic and rained hell into the security forces. Then a security ship roared around the ISA building in a whoosh of wind and the spotlight found Ocean.

Ocean screamed and her comms cut to static. Scout looked over her shoulder to see the Ochre Tower explode. Scout started to hyperventilate. She could not see Ocean anywhere. "Ocean! Oh no, oh no, oh no!"

"Calm down, Scout! Finish the job first, mate," said Ben.

Scout was shaking violently when she landed. She fell to the ground, hyperventilating. Ben hit the roof next to her, picked her up, and held her close.

"Shh, Scout, it's alright," he softly comforted her. "Link, where the fuck are you, bro?"

Scout screamed as a ship roared up next to them. "It's just Link," soothed Ben.

"Okay. I'm okay," said Scout as she disentangled herself from his embrace. She unzipped her jumpsuit and stepped out of it to reveal crumpled, sweat-soaked street clothes, then peeled the fake skin from her face, looking like an actress. She put the jumpsuit, skin, tools, and even the priceless pistol in a bag along with a grenade on a one-hour timer, then zipped the bag up. When Ben had done the same, they both tied the bundles to their booster packs and launched them off the side of the building.

They watched their packs fly away until Link said, "Come on; let's go see what Ocean died for."

***

An hour later, sitting around a table in Link's apartment in the Yaninee Tower, they all watched a TRC live news stream coming from the ISA building. Arlo's somber face filled the screen.

"Ah-ha. Bingo, I'm in." Scout finished hacking the intelligence she'd extracted earlier and started to read. The more she read, the more her mouth fell open.

"What is it, Scout?" asked Link.

"Um, just look." Scout sent him the documents.

Link started reading. Ben looked over from where he was lounging with a beer. He gave a look of disgust and went back watching the news.

It's like they don't even care about Ocean.

"It's not just Charon. There are hundreds of instances when the Edens destroyed life," said Link.

"Oh shit! Read this one!" spat Scout.

Integrated Space Agency

Department: Exploration, Research, Resources.

Case report: 23,867,123

Officer: G.R. Charles, Head of ERR in Fornax

Constellation: Fornax

System: Helmi stream

Star: HIP-13044/ F-type Red Giant

Planet: HIP-13044b

The opening opinion is that oxygen levels are not adequate but could be so with minor terraforming. Multiple elemental scans have all come back as rich. In addition, an extensive deposit of **RETRACTED** has been found. Further testing has found large ice deposits. There are multiple signs of life, although most are little more than bacteria, and some are believed to be unintelligent lifeforms. One species uses tools and has an advanced language system. They seem to be hunters and gatherers.

My final opinion is that, despite the wealth of minerals, we should not risk the native population. Furthermore, I hold the opinion that given their level of intellect, we should not disturb the population of HIP-13044b.

"What the fuck! They found life in Fornax?" Link's mouth hung open.

"Hey, what did you say about Fornax?" Ben looked up from the news.

"They found life there, Ben. Come quick!"

"Bullshit. I'm from Fornax," said Ben as he stood up.

"Really. Hang on." Scout opened her star chart and found Fornax, then the Helmi stream.

"They changed the names. Hang on a sec." She worked quickly. "Yes, I've found it! HIP-13044 is now called Koyash. What is HIP-13044b called?"

"No way. It's Planck." Ben was horrified.

"Hey, isn't that where you're from?" asked Link.

"Yep." Ben ran his hand over his face. "What do you think was retracted?"

"Fucked if I know, man," said Link.

***

"Coming online now. Three…two…one. It's now live!"

"Good. let's get this done." The man walked close to his assistant, and she could see his bright blue eyes.

In another part of the city, a slow-blinking blue light became solid red.

***

Link kept reading and shaking his head. "This is so messed up; there are so many cases! Hey, Scout, have you managed to find Mr. Charles yet?"

"Nope, no record of him being employed—or even being born." Scout ran her hands through her hair. "But I did find this spreadsheet. It says the ISA owns a controlling share in Ochre Mining and a company on Mars called Paulum and Malum Co."

"Hey, isn't that a conflict of interest—them having shares in mining?" asked Ben.

"Yeah, you idiot." Scout stared at Ben for a moment. Then sighed "Sorry, Ben it's just, you know. Ocean."

"Yeah, it's hard to believe," said Ben as he looked away.

Scout saw a tear ran down Link's face, she said softly. "You heard of Paulum and Malum Co., Link?"

Link wiped his face and shook his head. "That means nothing to me." He looked to Ben, who just shrugged.

"Look into that, too, Scout," said Link, and she nodded.

There was a clap of thunder as Ben stood up. The wall was ripped apart and Ben was flung across the room in a spray of blood, cybernetics fluid, and detached body parts. Scout screamed as gore rained down on her. Three more thunderclaps boomed in quick succession. Link dragged her to the door.

"Move it, Scout! Get your ass in gear!" Link screamed as a volley of fire ripped into his living room. One shot screamed close enough to singe his hair. A moment later he heard a terrible keening sound and felt wetness on the side of his face. He reached up and touched it; his hand came back covered in blood.

There must have been more shots, he thought. *The sound keeps on going.*

He looked at Scout's wide-open eyes. She was screaming, but he couldn't hear her.

Scout looked up at Link, his face confused, blood dribbling from his ears and dripping off his chin. The smell of gore and burning hair filled her nose.

His head exploded. One moment his handsome face was there. The next it was not.

He dropped onto her. Blood pumped out of the ragged stump of his neck. She put both of her hands on his shoulders and pushed, frantically kicking at the dead weight.

Boom! Boom! Boom!

Scout squealed and slid out from under him. Keeping low, she tried to run, but the floor was thick with blood. She slipped and stumbled out of the apartment as the sniper rounds punched holes behind her. There were screams of fear from people, young and old, in other apartments and the hallway, all trying to flee the destruction.

***

"Civilians have been shot by the agent, sir. Your instructions?" said a female voice.

In the dark room, the man smiled. "Fire at will! A few lives are worth keeping this from the public."

***

The assassin saw the target in the mass of bodies in the hallway, clicked the rifle into full-auto, and moved to a better firing position along the arm of the crane. Cybernetic eyes didn't leave their prey. Resting the barrel on a booster pack, the assassin fired.

Scout tried to push her way through the mass of bodies, but a huge man knocked her to the ground. She screamed and curled up as people stepped on her. The floor shook like an earthquake with the sound of rolling thunder. Heavy weights landed on her, and she peeked up to see people getting cut to pieces around her. The huge man toppled onto her, and her bladder gave out.

"Fuck, fuck, fuck!" Scout screamed as she was being crushed and drowned in gore. "Oh please, God, please!"

The assassin looked into the hallway, cybernetic eyes flicking through infrared, thermal, and motion-capture filters. The sheer number of bodies and carnage negated both the thermal and infrared data, so the assassin relied on the motion-capture vision, flares lighting up at any movement.

The assassin clicked the selector on the weapon back to semi-automatic and shot into the flares. After a while, movement stopped. The assassin stood, slung the rifle over one shoulder, and launched into the air. At the ark of the leap, the assassin activated a booster pack, entering the Yaninee Tower through the hole in the wall and drawing a Manta-98 tactical pistol upon hitting the ground. The assassin moved with purpose into the hallway and froze. There was a gap in the bodies that shouldn't have been there. The assassin resumed walking and turned the corner at the end of the hallway, finding a pile of vomit and a bloody handprint. The assassin scanned the print; it came back as Merry Joe. The assassin sighed and followed the bloody boot prints.

***

Scout ran along the sidewalk with her head down, moving through the denizens of the night. As traffic roared above her, Scout looked over her shoulder to see a hooded person burst out of the Yaninee Tower lobby.

Oh shit! As Scout turned forward, she ran into someone, and they both fell in a heap.

"Oh damn! What the hell? Watch where you're going!" Then the cop she'd run into noticed all the blood.

"Are you alright, miss?" he asked. "I need backup ASAP, as well as an ambulance. We have one woman covered in blood."

"Please help me! I'm being chased!" Scout sobbed as she looked back to the hooded assassin. "Oh shit! There!"

The cop looked up, one hand on his service weapon, to see the assassin raise a pistol. The pistol boomed, and the cop's chest was ripped open.

Scout sobbed as more blood sprayed on her. "Not again."

The assassin fired the pistol. Scout quickly pulled the cop's gun and rolled away as the path burst into sparks. She shot behind her without looking, hoping she didn't hit any innocent bystanders. She kept running.

The assassin ran past the cop, shooting him twice more in the chest, then took aim at the target and fired. Scout tripped, and the shot missed its mark. The assassin swore and re-aimed but was forced to move as Scout shot behind her. The assassin ran after her, around a corner, and onto a busier street. Cybernetic eyes scanned the people and located the target running down the stairs into Penong Subway Station. The assassin leapt and hit the booster pack, making huge ground on the target, and charged down the stairs five at a time, cybernetic legs preventing a fall and broken neck.

Scout ran down the stairs, gasping for breath. She felt a huge impact. The assassin landed at the top of the stairs, then bounced down. Scout stopped and pivoted, shooting twice. The assassin dropped hard and fired back. Scout hid behind a wall as the assassin's rounds blew away the ground behind her. Scout moved fast, trying to increase the distance between them, and then saw two guards running to the stairs looking down the sights of their VXSS-02s.

"Hey, you! Stop! Gun down!"

Scout looked up and saw a lone guard walking toward her, a VXSS-02 pointed at her own eyes. The guard's eye flashed away at a burst of fire from the stairs. Scout knocked the guard's gun arm to the side and shot her in the leg. Kicking the guard's arm, Scout ripped the gun from her grasp. Scout bent down to pick it up and saw two more guards covering each other as they constantly fired at the assassin. Scout sprinted to the subway platform, going faster when she heard the subway car coming. The guards' near-constant fire was replaced by the rolling thunder of a long gun on full-auto, and Scout stumbled at the deafening reports.

I know that sound. That's a BAX-R8! Scout regained her footing and ran.

***

The assassin shot twice more, launching the guards across the floor, then shouldered the BAX-R8 and sprinted to the platform to see the end of the subway car speeding away. The assassin charged after it, using the booster pack to go faster. At the last minute, the assassin jumped and drove one fist into the back of the car, splitting skin and ripping flesh from the bone. The cybernetics held and the assassin was on the subway car.

Scout let go of the breath she was holding as she watched the assassin hit the subway car. She scratched at the drying blood, and it cracked as she moved. She ducked into the women's bathroom, looked at herself in the mirror, and peeled her blood-stained clothes off.

"Fuck, it's even soaked into my bra and panties," she mumbled as she attempted to wash her face, arms, and hair. A woman wearing a trench coat and holding a suitcase stepped out of a stall, then squeaked and went for the door when she saw Scout.

Not taking her eyes from the mirror, Scout whipped her VXSS-02 up and pointed it at the woman. "Do not move a muscle."

The woman froze. Scout walked to her, wearing nothing but blood-stained shoes and underwear, bloody water dripping from her hair.

"Please don't kill me," whimpered the woman.

"It's okay. I only need some clothes." Scout pointed to the woman's bag.

Moments later the woman walked quickly out of the bathroom. Scout followed after, in a long gray trench coat, wet shoes, and only underwear underneath. Her light brown hair was stained dark with blood, even though she had washed it twice.

***

In the dark room, the female voice said, "She didn't get the subway car."

"What?" barked the man. "Where the fuck is she?"

The woman showed the man live feed from the subway security system.

"Fuck! Get our agent back on it and get more of them!"

Three more flashing blue lights turned solid red.

***

As the subway car raced along, the assassin smashed a window with the other fist and climbed in.

"She's still at the station," said a voice over the comm, and footage of the target walking in a gray trench coat flashed in cybernetic eyes.

The assassin swore and looked around, smiling at the sight of a panel. Moments later the subway car was rocketing back the other way.

***

Okay, Scout, now what the hell are you going to do? She walked out a different subway station exit, security and police running past her. She looked up and saw a billboard for TRC news with Arlo Remington's handsome face staring at her. *Take it to the media. Arlo seems like a trustworthy guy despite what Link said about the media being state-run.* She kept her head down and walked fast.

"Hey you, stop!" called a fat woman. Scout pretended not to hear and sped up as she slid her hand into her pocket to hold the grip of the police-issue pistol.

"Hey, you! Stop fucking now!" called the woman again. Scout turned and saw the woman's pistol come up.

Scout shot twice from inside her pocket and the woman chest was ripped apart. Scout ran away, but this time she had a plan.

I hope Arlo is in his office. She ran through the confused and scared crowd. Looking over her shoulder, she gave a sigh of relief. The police and three bots were caught up in the confusion. *Right, got to get off the main road and away from the police. With my record, they are more likely to just shoot me than let me explain.*

Scout cut down a dingy alley. As she moved away from the main road, she slowed down to conserve energy and to think about what was going on.

"What's that?" she said to herself as she looked over her shoulder and saw a man running at her. "Oh no, not again!" She turned and ran.

The man tackled her to the ground, knocking the wind out of her. She gasped and wrapped her legs around him, looking up into his dead eyes. He moved his fist back, and she threw her arms around his neck, limiting the space for his punch, but his cybernetic arm still hurt. She could smell his bad breath as he tried to bite her.

"No way!" She sunk her teeth into his nose. He screamed as hot blood flooded her mouth.

Yeah, bleed, you bastard. I need my gun! But each time she reached for it, a crushing punch smashed into her.

He grunted and jammed his fingers into her eye. She spat blood onto his face and grabbed the hand that was trying to poke her eye out. She pulled his arm across her body, uncrossed her legs from behind his back, and swung her hips around, putting her leg over his head. Catching him in a tight arm bar, she squeezed her knees and pulled hard on the arm. She chopped her leg down, and he fell over. She pulled hard on the arm again. But he just laughed and lifted her with one arm, as he got back to his knee. They came eye to eye again, and it was her turn to smile as she jammed the VXSS-02 into his laughing mouth and fired.

"You shouldn't have kept laughing, asshole." She stood up just in time to see another man charging at her. She just sighed and emptied the VXSS-02 into him.

***

In the dark room, the man swore. "Get our agent after her!"

"Yes, sir," said the female voice.

***

Scout continued down the ally, and as she came to each corner she slowed down and peaked around. Then it started—her hand was visibly shaking.

Come on, Scout, keep moving, one more step.

There was a sound behind her. She spun, pulling up her VXSS-02, but there was nothing there. Her breath came in ragged gulps, and her knees started to shake as well.

"Come on, come on, come on, damn it," she whimpered.

But her body betrayed her she backed up to the wall and slid down as her knees knocked and her teeth chattered. She hugged herself and tried to rub warmth into her arm. *Get up! I need to move. Come on.*

She huddled against the grimy wall and shook as her mind was assaulted by everything she had seen that night. *Poor Ocean and poor Link.* Her mind drifted back to his head exploding.

She tried to shake the memory from her mind. *Even Ben was killed. He hugged me after Ocean was killed.*

Scout gulped in air as she was hit with a new wave of regret and remorse. *I was so mean to him.*

She tried to take calming breath. *Right. I need to move. There is still one chasing me! I hope it only one! Calm down, Scout. We have got to go.*

Scout fell to her side and vomited. *Too much blood, too much gore. I should have asked for more money for this damn job!* She spat and retched some more, then pushing herself up started walking on shaky legs. She then came to another road and looked for more attackers, but instead saw a taxi glide down and land near her. She ran to it and all but dragged a man out before climbing in.

"The TRC building, please," she said to the driverless taxi.

She slid down into the footwell of her seat and sighed. Then she noticed the ads on a screen on the back of the seat in front of her. "Are your cybernetics letting you down? Do you need something stronger in your life?" The video showed a man unable to climb stairs or do a box jump. "Do you want to try something more extreme? Are you worried your old cybernetics won't cut it?"

Scout snorted with derision and mumbled, "I do fine without them."

"Then you need Týr cybernetics! For the first time, you can get the same cybernetics as the military." The clip then showed the same man doing extreme jumps and lifting heavy weights. "Týr cybernetics brought to you by Quilpie Manufacturing."

As the ad ended, she noticed some small writing at the bottom of the screen: Quilpie Manufacturing, a subsidiary of Paulum and Malum Co.

"Hey, hold on, what was that?" she said, eyes wide open.

She quickly hacked the screen with her cybernetic lens and searched Paulum and Malum Co. Even with her advanced skills, she couldn't find anything. On the other hand, Quilpie Manufacturing produced heaps of hits. She read quickly, taking in the new information. She closed her eyes once she had finished.

So Quilpie Manufacturing has won every cybernetics contract for the police, military, everything, for, like, thirty years. They are owned by Paulum and Malum Co., which must be a shell company—there's just no information about it. But why does the ISA need a shell company to own Quilpie Manufacturing? And why is it so hidden? Scout chewed her fingernail until she tasted the blood, then spat. "What does it mean? Damn it!" She punched the seat.

"Spitting and hitting this taxicab has added $100 to your fare. Please refrain from doing this in the future."

"Fine," snarled Scout.

She continued her search and found a news report about Paulum and Malum Co.

"Fuck me, they've hidden this well," she said, hitting play.

"Today, Paulum and Malum Co. CEO, Dylan Taipan, was convicted of privacy crimes in the criminal court of Mars," said the newsreader. Scout watched the footage of an older man with bright blue eyes and white-blond hair wearing a beautiful black-and-white pinstriped suit.

"Bingo!" Scout searched Mr. Taipan, but after few minutes her grin had turned to a frown. There seemed to be even less information on Taipan than Paulum and Malum Co.

Then she found a comment on a forum that stopped her: "Dylan Taipan didn't get into trouble just because of installing hidden trackers in cybernetics. He was adding a control switch." The commenter's name had been removed. Scout shook her head.

"We are arriving at your destination." The taxi came to a stop and Scout paid, her mind spinning. She looked up at the beautiful building, glass elevators gliding up and down its side, and suddenly felt self-conscious with her hideous shoes, blood-stained hair, and now-filthy coat. *What if they don't let me in? I look like a homeless person.* She walked through the door.

The clerk at the front desk asked, "How can I help you today?"

"I'm here to see Arlo Remington. I have a story for him."

***

The assassin looked at the building the target had entered.

"Do not damage the building. You need to do this clean," said the woman in the dark room.

The assassin sighed and tossed the BAX-R8 into a dumpster. "I'm going to regret having to lose this."

***

"Look, Scout, I'm very busy," said Arlo over the commlink, flicking through a porn site.

Scout looked around the lobby, then whispered "I was at the ISA break-in tonight."

"Yep, sure you were. Why don't I call the police?" Arlo yawned.

"For fuck's sake, Arlo! I have secret documents that criminalize the ISA. I have proof that they own Paulum and Malum Co."

"Yep."

"Please, Mr. Remington. Have you heard about the shootings at Yaninee Tower and Penong Station?"

Arlo started paying attention. "You mean the terrorist attacks. What about them?"

"What? No! It's ISA—they were attempting to kill me."

Arlo sighed, put his hands behind his head, and thought about what the woman was saying. *What was her name?* "Alright, miss, come on up. You have ten minutes."

The clerk at the front desk told Scout to go to the two hundred forty-fifth floor and follow the signs to Arlo's office.

Scout grinned to herself and walked quickly to the elevator, keeping her head down. As the doors closed and the elevator took off, she looked out of the glass walls at the city. She rested her head against the glass, closed her eyes and tried to put the carnage of the night out of her mind: the blood, the smells, and Link's head disappearing in front of her. She swore, turned, and slid down the wall. She started to shake. She tried to run her hand through her hair, but it was too stiff. She swore again. She punched the floor.

The elevator pinged. Scout stood on shaky legs, took a calming breath, and went to Arlo's office.

***

The assassin walked into the beautiful TRC building and strolled to the front desk. "Hello. My friend was just in here, and I have some important information for her. Can you tell me where she went?"

"Why certainly. What was her name?"

The assassin used a finger to tuck a blue dreadlock behind one ear. "Scout Amaya."

***

At the knock on his door, Arlo closed the website, sanitized his hands, and used the walk to the door to catch his breath.

"Welcome, Miss Amaya." Arlo stuck out his hand.

"Yeah, hi." Scout looked at his offered hand, then around the glass-walled office with its curtains drawn. She jammed a chair under the door handle, then looked out the big window.

Arlo let his hand drop, walked back around his desk, and sat in his chair. "You know, this building has a good security team—fifteen battle androids armed with Manta-98s."

Scout smiled over her shoulder and pulled her VXSS-02 out from under her trench coat. She walked to the bookshelf, taking the best cover available. "Yeah, I saw how good ISA assassins are against security at Penong Station. Let's cut the bullshit. Look at this."

"Okay." Arlo stared at the rail gun.

She hacked his computer with her cybernetics lens.

"Hey, what the fuck are you doing?"

"Shut up and look at this." Scout showed him the case report she'd found earlier.

Arlo read it through. He shook his head and read it again, more slowly. "Where is this?"

"Planck."

"Oh shit, no fucking way! What else do you have?" Arlo put his hands behind his head. His eyes were wide.

"Heaps. I haven't even seen most of it. I found this ledger, though," she said as she sent it to him.

"Oh wow, they have a controlling share in Ochre Mining. That is bad of them!" Arlo laughed.

"It has to be a conflict of interest, right?" asked Scout.

"Yep," Arlo kept reading, shaking his head. "I don't get it. Paulum and Malum Co.—who are they?"

She sighed. "I'm not sure what this means either, but the ISA owns Paulum and Malum Co. and Quilpie Manufacturing. Then I found that the former CEO of Paulum and Malum Co. was called Taipan or something and was doing some crazy shit with trackers."

Arlo shook his head. "And that doesn't mean anything. It's hearsay at best. But I have heard of Taipan—he was supposed to be doing mind control shit with cybernetics, but there was no proof and he ended up getting a fine for tax evasion. That's it."

He tapped his lips with his fingers. "But this case report and the mining stuff, that's what we are talking about. Do you have anything else?"

Scout puffed out her cheeks and sighed. "I have no idea what else is in here." She rested her head against the wall and closed her eyes.

There was a crash of glass.

"Hey! Who are you? And what are you doing here?"

Scout's eyes flicked open, and her heart started pounding. She looked at the assassin, and when the hood slipped down, she saw something she couldn't explain.

"Ah, Mr. Remington. I'm here for Scout," said Ocean as she pulled her Manta-98 from behind her back and shot Arlo.

Scout couldn't compute what was going on.

Scout shot at Ocean with her VXSS-02, but shock threw off her aim and she only hit the Manta-98 which was flung from Ocean's hand. She aimed again, but Ocean had already jumped back out of the office. Scout stayed low, firing where she had last seen Ocean and walking backward to the window. She quickly turned to shoot out the window behind her, then continued firing at glimpses of blue hair. Scout looked out the broken window to the elevator stopped at the floor below, her trench coat whipping in the night wind. She jumped from the window, and as she fell, she shot out the elevator's glass roof. She reached out to hit a button to go down, but the elevator was called to the top floor.

The door opened and Scout knocked two men to the ground as she raced out. Over the top of the office cubicles, she saw blue hair leaving the elevator across the room. As Scout whipped up her gun, an older woman walked of her cubicle. The woman's eyes widened. Scout pressed a finger to her lips, and the woman backed into her cubicle. Scout smiled at her, then fear shot down her spine as she looked around. *Where the hell did Ocean go?*

Scout saw something out of the corner of her eye and turned, but it was too late. The small micro-EMP grenades blew up in her face, and as chaff billowed around, her cybernetics lens shut down. She pointed the VXSS-02 in the general direction the grenades had come from, but the trigger was locked. She looked around and saw Ocean charging down the cubicle aisle. Scout turned and ran toward the fire escape dead ahead. She hit the door open, knocking two cleaning androids to the ground. They blocked her path down, so she ascended the stairs two at a time. She burst out onto the roof.

Ocean hit the stairs at a full cybernetics-enhanced sprint. By the time she reached the top, the door was swinging shut. She slowed and pushed the door open, her eyes flicking through the different filters.

"Hey, Scout, where are you? Come out, come out, wherever you are." Ocean checked her other enhanced senses, but the screaming wind of the night hurt her ears. She took a deep breath. *Ah-ha!* Ocean smelled blood, sweat, and fear.

"Ocean, I saw you die." Scout clutched the useless gun, thinking she could use it as a club.

"No, I jumped on the ship, then they fired. I told you, Scout, Ochre was going to get theirs as well." Ocean crept toward Scout's voice. She jumped around the corner of an air conditioning unit, but there was no one there.

"But you hate the ISA."

Ocean ran around to the other side, where Scout's voice had come from. "Well, I did hate them? They killed my family." Ocean said to herself, confused.

***

The red light electronically connected to Ocean's new Týr cybernetics flickered blue.

"She is regaining control, sir!"

"Get her back online, damn it!" yelled the man.

"Yes, sir."

***

Scout dropped from the top of the unit, creeping behind Ocean as she shook her head and stopped mumbling. She quickly wrapped her arm around Ocean's neck and began to choke her as she kicked the back of her knees. She dragged Ocean backward, not letting the stronger woman gain any purchase on the ground, effectively negating her cybernetic legs. Ocean's fingers tore painfully at Scout's face and arms, but this meant life or death for Scout, and she grunted with the pain and effort. Ocean's arm slowed then stopped.

Ocean was out. Scout let go and rolled Ocean's body off her. As she climbed onto the unconscious woman to hit her with the VXSS-02, Ocean's hand flashed up and closed around Scout's throat, squeezing. Scout slammed the gun down, but Ocean's other hand caught it. Scout noticed Ocean's blank, unconscious eyes and began to panic.

I don't understand. What's going on? Scout looked around wildly and scrambled to her feet just in time to see Ocean pull a knee to her chest, then shoot out a kick into Scout's chest. Scout was hurled back and off the roof. She frantically grabbed at the ledge as it whistled past, but it was too far away. Then the wind ripped her away from the building and into traffic. As she fell, the wind roared in her ears, and she saw a kaleidoscope of flashing lights.

Watching Scout fall, Ocean scratched her head and tried to remember what happened. *How did Scout get over there and on the ground? Last thing I remember she was on my back.* Then with a sigh, she saw Scout slam into a taxi.

"Well fuck!" Ocean spat.

***

She awoke in pain; a constant beeping made her want to cry. She slowly opened her eyes, the light stinging until they adjusted. She looked around the room. She was in a hospital bed with a nursing android hovering over her.

"You're awake? Hello, my name is Asha. I'm a nurse with the Dunlop Hospital. Could you please tell me your name?"

"Um...no. I don't remember." As her heart raced, the beeping got faster. She touched her face. "I don't remember who I am. What the fuck? Why can't I remember?"

"It's okay, miss, you were in an accident. Your memory will come in time."

"Who am I?"

"Your name is Scout Amaya, and you're twenty-two years old," said Asha.

"Do you mind if I have a word with Miss Amaya?"

Scout moved painfully to look over Asha's shoulder to a handsome older man with bright blue eyes and white-blond hair, wearing a beautiful cream, three-piece suit and a crimson silk shirt. Behind him was a woman, her dark skin contrasted with her electric blue dreadlocks.

"Yes, sir, she has woken, and her vitals are steady."

"Thank you, nurse. Please leave us." The man's voice was deep and rich.

"Yes, Mr. Taipan, but be gentle with her. Her memory is fragile."

The nurse left the room and there was an uncomfortable silence.

Scout looked from one to the other. "Well, Mr. Taipan, who are you? And who is she?"

Taipan gave a little cough into his hand. "Ah, Miss Amaya, I'm your boss. Do you really not remember anything?"

Scout shook her head and it hurt. "I don't remember anything. Well...your friend looks oddly familiar?"

"That makes sense. Ocean here is your supervisor." Ocean gave Scout a smile and small wave.

"Oh. Well, what happened to me?" Scout's voice was small.

"You were doing maintenance on one of our buildings and were blown off by the wind. You fell and were, oddly, saved by hitting a taxi." He chuckled. "It's not every day you can tell someone they were saved by being hit by a taxi."

Scout gave the joke a halfhearted smile. "What about safety measures? That seems, well, extreme. Blown off a building."

Mr. Taipan looked at his feet. "You're right, Miss Amaya. It was a freak gust, and your harness was faulty. It's amazing that even now we can't stop faulty equipment from slipping through." He took a shaky breath, and Scout felt for the man. He cleared his throat. "Miss Amaya, we have paid all of your medical costs, and I have given you the cybernetics that you have been saving for. Free of charge and with our best wishes."

Scout's mouth fell open. "I didn't have cybernetics? That seems weird." She shook her head. "Shit. I'm sorry, Mr. Taipan. That's kind of you. Thank you! I'm incredibly grateful. Confused, but very grateful."

Mr. Taipan smiled at her. "Can we expect you back at work when you recover?"

Scout almost agreed but hesitated at the way he said it. She looked at Ocean who was staring at her.

"Um, Mr. Taipan. I'm very grateful for everything you have done, but sorry, I can't? I was thrown from a building, and I can't remember anything except that I'm scared of Ocean. I don't know why, but she sends a chill up my spine. I think I need to find myself...or maybe become someone new? I'm sorry, sir," Scout said quietly.

Mr. Taipan's kind eyes turned mean, and he crossed his arms. "Well, Miss Amaya, I can understand where you're coming from. I'm sorry to hear it." He stood up and Ocean opened the door for him. As they walked out, he called, "Good day!"

Scout watched them walk away, and then Asha came back in.

Scout said to the android excitedly, "I have cybernetics!"

"Yes, you do. The very best there is." Asha fussed around with the monitors.

"Really?" Scout was surprised.

"Yes. You got a full set of Týr cybernetics, with their new Fenris optics!"

***

In the back of his limousine, Dylan Taipan was angry. He turned to Ocean. "Fuck you! You should have fucking killed her!"

"I wanted to smother her in the hospital! You're the one who fixed her!"

Taipan pointed a finger at Ocean, his face turning blue with rage. Ocean regretted saying anything. He turned to the other person in the limousine, a female staff member. "Bring Scout online. Now!"

In a British accent, the staffer said, "Yes, sir."

Deep in the muscles at the base of Scout's skull, a small blinking blue light turned solid red.

Oisettio

By Jess Milner

Date: 2623

Chapter 1

Forbes lived on the planet Urayso, in the Tenth District of The City's outer circle. He was typical of a Skreek—messy hair, long ears, and no money. A thief, probably; most certainly a vagabond.

Skreeks were usually unemployed and, as such, were unwelcome in most districts. They were not entitled to pod-car or dome licenses. They lived in underground rentals if they were lucky, or on the streets if they weren't.

Forbes's dirty black cloak was drizzle soaked as he walked quickly down the dark street, unnoticed by the pod-cars, their hover zones splashing through the flooded gutters as they zoomed past. The Pleebs looked the other way or even crossed the street when they saw him as they tramped through the bad weather on the way home to warm beds, hot dinners, and family arguments.

Over a hundred years had gone by since the Pleebs and their Univi forces had invaded Urayso. You know, mass murder, lands sold, cities polluted. Skreeks had been dispersed about the planet—a species to be used and controlled, no longer in command of their own lands, lives, or anything at all.

Back in the days of Earth, before Urayso was even colonized, the early Skreek Experiments had been wildly unsuccessful. The ISA scientists were growing human fetuses in laboratories and injecting them with Krem-knows-what. The people of Earth, or Pleebs, as they were known, rallied in mass protests, fighting for this injustice to stop.

But, of course, it didn't.

The scientists were so full of it they had started experimenting on the local fauna. Twisting genetics and splicing them together. Injecting and filling test tubes. Until one day, the first Skreek was born. The protesters quieted. It was exciting, unnatural, frightening. Then, a few generations in, they saw that the Skreeks could breed. That was too much for them.

The Pleebs of Earth shipped off the Skreeks to this barely terraformed planet and dumped them. The Univi government enforced the move, making sure that the early Skreeks had no pod-ships or space travel technologies. That was over three hundred years ago.

Forbes stopped. He'd reached his destination. He pulled down his hood to reveal a huge, fanged grin and two bright eyes. His tall, jet-black ears unfurled as he tried to shake himself dry. Something was afoot. He tugged open the door to his right and strode into the booming establishment.

Forbes leaned across the bar and motioned to a nearby barmaid.

"Is Debbie in?"

The young girl nodded and ran off, returning a minute later with a disgruntled-looking Pleeb woman.

"What the Krem, Forbes? I was having a snooze. This had better be good."

"It is, Debbie." He grinned, knocking back a bracer of Perlite liquor. "Have I got news for you!"

"How many times have I heard that?" Debbie smiled warmly and pulled up a barstool.

"It's the Warblers; they're on the move again. News of it is all over, and they've got it spreading. This ain't like last time, Debbs. They're pushing a mass recruitment! It's all over the underground. Any able-bodied man or woman can join up—Pleeb or Skreek, all expenses paid. I came for the address. This time I won't miss out..."

***

Alice moved away then, unsure if the pair had seen her watching. After all, she was "just a barmaid" and not to get involved in business. She walked round back, grabbed the bar phone, and called them. This was news she knew they would love to hear. Five minutes later, she tugged on her oversized jacket and picked up her last paycheck, before she sidled out the back door of Debbie's bar, into the damp evening streets. It was time to reconnect a little.

She reached the Warbler offices quickly, shuddering as she entered the door. As she approached his office, she realized the light was on.

Her Pleeb father stood by the door. His round, sagging stomach supported his gun in its holster. He was staring at her.

"Hey, Alice. Long time, no see, sweetie." His smile, as always, didn't reach his eyes.

Chapter 2

Forbes was on a one-man mission to join the Warblers. They were the main united renegades against the oppressive Univi government. They were adored in the Skreek underground, and they were growing stronger. So many fellow Skreeks had joined in recent years that it was hard to find a guy around his age who wasn't either already a Warbler or avidly set on joining up. It wasn't just Skreeks in the Warblers, either. The Pleebs were sick of the Univi government too. They ruled with an iron fist. Whatever they said went, a dictatorship of wills. Even the head honcho of the Warblers was a Pleeb.

Forbes wanted to fight for his freedom, to have his day in the sunlight. To save the planet. For himself and for his ancestors.

The Warblers stood for everything he believed in. Peace on planet Urayso. A united front against the tyranny of the Univi government. Pleebs and Skreeks finally living as equals.

He cut his hair and sold it to a wig guy for a few quid. He exchanged this and the little savings he had for a pulsar pistol; well, it didn't look like it would do more damage than a potato gun, but it was a start, at least.

"One must be armed!" sang Forbes, as he whisked himself out of the gun shop and down the quiet, empty streets.

Forbes reached his destination faster than he'd expected. His excitement overtaking his evening fatigue, he'd half-run through the four districts it had taken to get there. He looked around the high-ceilinged Warbler building with wild adrenaline as he headed confidently through the double doors, straight for the steel-clad reception desk.

The circular room was impressively decorated with holo-photos of famous Warblers and renegades. Two tall staircases fanned each side of the room, with large, fancy airlifts behind the reception. Above, he could see a wide balcony, full of troops and secretaries rushing around. The light breeze of giant air conditioning units gently brushed his hair as he looked upward.

"Krem, these guys must have gone up in the world!" He laughed out loud.

"I wanna speak to your head guy; I'm here to join up." He beamed at the bored-looking receptionist.

The receptionist looked back at him with a turned-up nose and pressed some buttons on her receiver. A shrill secretarial tone on the other end gave a few blasts.

"Right this way," she pointed to a staircase, "Floor 19."

***

Alice shivered slightly in the waiting room outside her father's office. He'd dismissed her several hours before, but she had decided to wait around to try and listen in on some business. She could hear him laughing loudly on the phone.

"Yeah, we dispatched 'em earlier today! Yes, all of them—stupid idiot had three fully manned ships in our district, full of 'em dirty dogs. Boom, gone. Boom! All gone!" He laughed.

She pressed on the air conditioning to drown out the sounds of his murderous boasts. She hated him and every part of this syndicate, but there was no escaping a father like hers. Her mother lived on a farm in the Outer District somewhere, or so she was told. She knew better—but she wouldn't tell him that. Her father saw Alice as a mistake, something to be hushed away, but used when necessary. She was his dirty secret, a half-blood Skreek from her mother's side. He'd had her ears and hair follicles surgically altered when she was a child. This was not an uncommon decision made by high-flying Pleebs to minimize societal outcry amongst their business and golf buddies.

Alice was shaken from her train of thought by a tapping on the glass of the waiting room door.

"Oh. It's you." She pointed with a chewed fingertip at her father's office. "He's in there."

Forbes gaped at her by the glass door.

"Yeah, it's me, the barmaid. We've been watching you for months." Alice smiled a little at his shocked face. "Anyway, you'd better get in there. My wonderful father, the all-powerful Captain John Ereys, has been expecting you. Go on. In you go." She rolled her eyes sarcastically and, with trained apathy, relaxed into her chair.

***

Forbes stepped tentatively toward the office doors. He wondered for an instant if his big idea hadn't been his at all. The door swung open and revealed an insanely terrifying-looking chunk of a man. Forbes stepped backward before being physically pulled into the room.

"Welcome to the Warblers," Captain Ereys boomed as spit hailed on Forbes' face.

Alice switched off the air conditioning and began listening intently while chewing on what was left of her fingernail.

An hour later, Forbes edged out of the room, the lightness in his step temporarily eradicated. As the door slammed behind him, he stumbled, and someone caught his arm. It was her.

Alice gripped his elbow as she led him down the long, brightly lit corridor.

"I'll show you to your quarters," she said.

"Weapons training starts tomorrow."

Chapter 3

Forbes was given everything except permission to leave the building. His quarters were huge, with two white rooms and a double bed, and food in the mess halls three times daily. It was more than he had ever had. They gave him generous rations of booze and cigarettes and provided all the latest entertainment tech. He met a bunch of other guys, both Skreek and Pleeb, who all sang the praises of the whole Warbler outfit. He didn't see much of Alice, or anything of the big boss man, but he felt they were both watching him, each in their own way, each for their own reasons.

He did well in training. The fitter he got, the better he was at the athletic stuff, obviously. But the clever bits, like bomb detection and deployment, math and logic, he excelled at. He enjoyed all the guns too, of course. Anticipation for that day when he would be sent with his crew of Skreeks and Pleebs to attack the Univi stronghold mounted within him with each new skill he honed.

After four months of guerrilla-like training, Forbes was given his first deployment. Some guy from the Univi was the target: one Colonel Gama A big-shot in the world of the far-right Pleebs.

What an honor for a first assignment. Forbes stared at Gama's photo in the auto-logbook. He was a tall Pleeb guy with blonde hair and pumped muscles, in his 50s maybe. Shouldn't be too hard.

Forbes's platoon was to hunt and dispatch Gama and his battalion by any means necessary. The day after notice was sent to his station, Forbes and the rest of the platoon headed out in the back of a pod-car to the Ninth District, where the Mid-Autumn Festival was about to take place.

Chapter 4

Colonel Gama's Univi ship descended on the Ninth District in mid-autumn as planned. He and a few crew members took a small pod-car down to the festival. The sun was shining. Empty, dilapidated tents littered the surrounding grasslands. There was an eerie quiet about the place. Someone must have come and shut them down already. There were no bands playing, no Pleebs in sight. Gama shrugged and called into the head office to report that it seemed the whole place was empty. No one had heard of any festival shut down. Strange.

He was turning back toward the pod-car, ordering his troops to leave, when he heard gunshots. One, two, three shots, three of his best men dropped around him like flies. The two others were close by with weapons ready, spinning around, trying to take aim, but there was no one to shoot at.

He ducked just in time as a bullet whistled over his head. Snipers, miles away. Their best bet was to crawl back to the pod-car.

On his stomach in the dry earth, Colonel Gama lay as flat as possible. Several shots sang above his graying blond hair as he quickly rolled his body into the pod. His two remaining soldiers were close behind him. They leaned backward in their chairs and zoomed away above the long grasses. As he drove, he radioed for reinforcements. There was a whistle through the air, louder than last time. He opened the window and looked back.

Bad move.

Boom!

Oblivion.

***

Forbes flicked back the safety on his panzer, gazing as the embers glowed on the grass under what had just been a state-of-the-art Univi pod-car. He could just discern the smoldering remains of what looked like three dead men. He felt utterly sick as his platoon drove him away from the festival.

What have I done? His throat tightened, and he gripped his hands together as he tried to turn from the other troopers.

He could hear whistles of Univi reinforcement pods rushing to the area. The pod-car raced along, splashing into the rain-swept streets.

***

Alice watched from above as Forbes shakily ascended the stairs back at the Warbler building. She felt somewhat to blame for this, but she knew it wasn't forever. She looked at his familiar ashen face as he headed toward his rooms. She'd seen them all go through this so many times before…a lost soul, a hunter, a killer, a slave.

***

Forbes awoke the next day to the sound of birds outside his quarters. His auto-logbook was still open in his palm, showing the bright photo of the blond man he'd shot the day before. With the sunrise came more orders, another target next week. New, more intensive training. A uniform fitting. Forbes clutched the logbook hard in his hand, and swiped it left to record the death. There was no going back. He sat up in his bed, his mind drifting as he stared hard out of the foggy, sunlit window, trying to push Gama out of his mind. He watched as Pleebs rushed around on the streets below. The early morning taxi-pods were collecting commuters as they grabbed breakfast from smoking street vendors.

The idea of Edens was in the far distant past for the citizens of Urayso. The air here was hot and acrid. Air conditioners hummed from every building and windows were firmly bolted closed. In true Skreek style, Forbes's ancestors and the hundreds of thousands of other Skreeks dumped on the planet had made the best of it. They had built up the cities and formed societies and families. They had put their own mark on it and even farmed the bare volcanic countryside for hardy crops like maize and potatoes. The planet Urayso had enough natural resources to sustain a few hundred thousand humanoids for a fair while. Nowadays, it was overloaded. Tower blocks full of apartments stretched out into the polluted skies. There were citizens bursting out of the metro-pod, rushing to overcrowded schools and office buildings. While underground, the Skreek lodgings spread throughout haphazard tunnels like a drunken spider's web.

He heard a rap on the door, Alice strode in before he could answer and brandished a plastic tray.

"I got you some stuff from the kitchen. You weren't back in time for mess yesterday, and I thought you might be hungry."

He rolled out of bed and slumped into a chair. She noticed he was still wearing his muddy boots from the night before. She placed the tray on the table beside him.

"Eat something. You'll feel better if you eat something." She turned to leave.

"Cheers."

He pulled the tray over. "I guess this is it, then."

She turned to face him and stared for a second, like she wanted to say something, but then left without so much as a whisper.

From early on, Forbes looked forward to Alice's company—her wide amber eyes, the rare, sparkling smiles. She was clearly half-Skreek, but he never broached the subject. He saw how she pulled a cap over her eyes and instinctively went to brush the area her ears would have been when she was deep in thought. It was clearly something she didn't want to talk about. She was serious, but not averse to a flutter on a game of cards or a chilled few hours gaming on the Realitron headsets in the holo-screening room. She got on well with the others in the barracks, too. Forbes noticed she never spoke about herself much, or her father. Again, he put this down to a security thing. He wasn't willing to open that particular can of worms anyway. He had only just recently become comfortable with murdering people he'd never met. A man should know his limits.

Several years went by and Forbes carried on. Each day he grew less daunted by murder. Each day he felt more at one with the cause. Until finally, he didn't even question it anymore. He threw himself into weapons training, spending hours in simulations. The lines between what was real and what was not became so blurred he could cross them with barely a wince.

There was no leaving the Warblers. He hadn't heard of anyone even attempting it. It was like this—you were with the Warblers or an enemy of the Warblers. There was no in-between.

He relaxed into his role as a soldier and, after a time, started to train new recruits. He had a certain sympathy for their nervous wild faces as they entered his training sessions, but he left no room for error. It was kill or be killed. He pushed new soldiers as hard as he could, making them take aim at the same holo-targets again and again until they could get a perfect head shot, before moving them on to the next target and doing the same again, this time while he was running at them firing a hail of holo-bullets.

He took his missions in stride, and soon he had completed so many he found it hard to remember the faces of the men he had shot down. His auto-logbook front page glittered with the images of shining stars. Medals he had collected for the number of kills he'd made since joining up. A record of his weekly exploits. He carried on and worked hard, anticipating the day that this would all come to fruition, the day the Warblers would take on the Univi.

Chapter 5

It was a rainy Sunday afternoon when the call came resounding through the tower, shaking the men and women inside awake with fear and anticipation.

This was it.

Finally.

After all this time.

The call to war.

Forbes leapt up and dashed from the room, strapping his holster around his waist. He saw Alice on the way to the stairs, and she grabbed his arm.

"This way," she ordered, as she led him down the front steps and outside. He caught sight of Univi guards and a group of Warblers battling it out on the street corner. Something whistled in the skies overhead, and with a deafening sound, knocked out six of them. Heavily armed pod-cars were zooming across the streets. He couldn't see who was driving them, or even what side they were on, just bullets hailing out like rain.

"Come on!"

Alice tugged on his wrist to make him move. Screams of rage and agony engulfed his ears as they ran. Pleebs and Skreeks dove at each other from every angle, aiming blindly to the left and right, seemingly unconcerned about who they were firing at. He saw two Warblers he knew running to help a Skreek Warbler trapped in a smoldering pod-car. A Univi soldier came running in, and Forbes dispatched him with a round from his gun. The Skreek Warbler in the pod-car had managed to shove the door open and was climbing out to make his escape. The Pleeb Warblers didn't change course. They ran, shooting in the direction of the Skreek. They weren't helping him at all—they were killing him.

Shocked, Forbes shouted out; he saw the man's knees buckle as he fell to the ground, his blood seeping and shimmering beneath him. The Pleeb Warblers smiled manically at each other and ran off in the other direction before Forbes could think of how to react. They'd just murdered someone on their same side, right in front of his horrified eyes.

Forbes willed himself back into some form of alertness and focused on the carnage in front of him. Univi and Warbler Pleebs were massing in a circle around the center of a nearby plaza, within which were a terrified huddle of Warbler Skreeks. "What the Krem!" he called out. Forbes started to run toward them. He had to do something.

Alice spun round and leapt at him as he rushed forward, pulling him to the ground. "You can't do anything!" she screamed into his face.

"They're as good as dead. Come!" Her eyes were bulging with fear and determination as she unrelentingly dragged him away from the plaza.

Forbes pulled back as he heard a familiar whistle above. *Boom!* the plaza rattled with the sound of it as the Skreeks were sent into eternity. The laughing Pleebs had already pulled away and spread out to continue their massacre.

He looked at Alice up ahead. He saw her narrowly miss a wall of bullets from an oncoming Warbler. What was happening? He rushed to catch up with her. He had to get her to safety.

A nearby explosion caused them to veer off to the right, and they crouched, panting, against the wall of a deserted carpark. Alice pushed her hair from her ash-covered face.

"My father. He's actually done it." She wiped the sweat from her eyes as she clicked on some old-style phone.

He noticed how her hair had fallen back into place, and how her hands had stopped shaking. She was really something. He stared at her.

"What the Krem are you talking about?"

Alice wasn't listening; she was staring at someone on the far side of the carpark. A Skreek woman came striding confidently toward them. She paid no heed to the raging battle, and her eyes shone with determination. Forbes was taking no chances. He reached for his gun, but his holster was empty. Alice had it aimed straight at his forehead.

Chapter 6

"The pod-cars are on the way," Alice told the confident woman.

Just as she said this, two old-school-looking pod-cars came from the right-hand side.

"Get in," shouted the woman.

Alice shoved Forbes through the open door into the back and clambered in after him. They were racing through the streets at an inhuman speed. These cars must have had some work done, Forbes thought, as the buildings beside them became gray blurs.

"Right. What's going on? This is crazy...who the Krem *are* you?" He stared at Alice.

"I'm the daughter of John Ereys, head of the Warblers, of course," Alice said, "but also of Claris, the leader of the true resistance." She gestured to the Skreek woman from the carpark who had buckled herself into the front passenger side of the pod-car. "My mother."

"Nice to meet you, Forbes." Alice's mother reached round to grasp his hand. "As my daughter neatly put it, I lead the resistance known as the Oisettians. I believe you already know my vile ex-husband, Captain John Ereys, your boss in the Warblers. It's time to relearn a little of what you know about the situation. The Warblers and the Univi—they are both part of the same thing. You must have noticed, growing up as a Skreek, how difficult you had it. There's something more to all these planetary takeovers, to the lack of Edens here. It is all intentional.

"They want to slowly eradicate our kind from existence. In their eyes, we are toys. Something they have grown out of. They think of Skreeks as less than human, and they're more than ready to throw us away. As the resistance, we are making a stand. We already have over five hundred thousand warriors and agents, not to mention over a million citizens, and are claiming our planets back from the inside out. As you know, Urayso is thought of as the major Skreek home planet. It is the original place we were shipped off to when Skreeks were evicted from Earth and denied their human rights. From what you have seen today, I'm sure you realize that the Univi and Warblers are fighting back. That's what you were trained for as a Warbler. My ex-husband is using you and others like you to do his dirty work for him. The Warblers are just a faction of the Univi government, being used to eradicate our kind and anyone with an inclination to protect us."

Forbes saw his time in the Warblers unfold like a storybook before his eyes. All those late-night deployments, the look in the eyes of the colonels and Pleebs as he'd gunned them down, just blindly following orders. He remembered back to the late-night conversations with Alice. She had never touched on the subject of his missions but focused on anything else. He remembered how her eyes had met his all that time ago on the night after his first deployment in the Ninth District; how she had cared for him.

"Alice has been doing a little intel on you all these years. She assures me that you will be a perfect fit into our syndicate." Forbes turned to Alice.

"I couldn't tell you." She looked at him with honesty. "I had to wait, to show you, or you might not have believed me. You were so dead set on the Warblers, and then so hypnotized to stay there. Think about what you've seen today. They weren't aiming at each other. They were aiming at the Skreeks."

The scenes from earlier played out in Forbes's mind. He saw again the shocked and terrified faces of the Skreeks in the plaza as they were surrounded by Warblers and Univi alike, and their confusion as they looked to the sky before being blown to smithereens.

"So, are you with us?"

Forbes slowly nodded.

"I don't think I have a choice."

The pod-cars sped up even more until Forbes's head felt pinned to the headrest. He felt bile rising inside him, and it became like a mantra to keep it down. It no longer felt like they were traveling in the city but were airborne. The windows of the pod-car were shrouded in the deep, inky blackness of space. There was no sound—just the continuous thundering pressure that he felt all around him. Alice had leaned back in her seat, eyes closed, like she was used to this crazy method of space travel.

As soon as they began to descend, the sound came back, and the pressure lifted. They were thundering toward some other planet. This definitely wasn't Urayso. As the place came into view, Forbes could see a meadow. Rabbits were hopping around nibbling on green grasses, and flowers littered the ground sporadically. The blue skies, which were now above them, stretched for miles, with clouds fanning the corners. One giant sun shone so brightly that he had to half-close his eyes from the light. The windows of the car slid down, and a warm breeze floated in. *It's like breathing gold*, thought Forbes. No pollution, no cities. It was fresh, clean, oxygenated air. He could see several Edens in the distance.

They came to a stop by a large group of ambi-tents, the kind that explorers and maintenance guys used.

"Welcome to Oisettio." Claris smiled as she stretched out of the pod-car and walked toward the people who had begun emerging from the tents.

Forbes saw more Skreeks in one place than he had ever seen before. They were healthy and strong, not malnourished like the ones on Urayso. One came forward and firmly shook his hand.

"Good to see you!" The man smiled. More started forward, patting his back and fist-bumping him. Men, women, children, even elderly Skreeks.

All smiling, and all healthy.

Alice was grinning beside him as she watched him take it all in.

"Right, time for a drink." She winked at Forbes as barrels of Glee-Juice were rolled out of one of the nearby tents.

"I reckon you need it," she laughed.

Chapter 7

Sitting in the breezy tent, Claris, Alice, and Forbes pulled up chairs to a large table. The Glee-Juice was better than on Urayso, thought Forbes, or perhaps that was just the idyllic setting of Oisettio. He turned and noticed a vaguely familiar face heading toward him. The blonde-haired, thick-muscled man nodded briskly at him before taking a seat at their table.

"Hello, I believe you owe me a pint."

Colonel Gama, the guy from the auto-logbook, stared at him from across the table. The first man Forbes had been deployed to kill.

A man Forbes had believed dead.

"Gama is one of ours," explained Claris. "We pulled him from the burning pod-car just in time, after you left. Captain Ereys found out Gama here was an Oisettian spy hidden inside the Univi military. That's why he had you target him."

"And I'm glad I was your first deployment; it looks as if you're tougher than that now, boy." Gama reached a hand across the table. "All is fair in war and rebellion." Forbes took his hand and felt rattled as he shook it. He forced his eyes to meet Gama's and nodded.

"I am indebted to your forgiveness." He hit his chest in the traditional show of respect for an older, more experienced soldier.

Claris indicated for a round of Perlite liquor and several more pints to be passed around the table before she began to expand on the situation.

"We have given solace to over eight hundred thousand Skreeks over the past forty years. The Pleebs on Earth were only the first to start to play with genetics. Pleebs around the galaxy have been doing much the same thing, sometimes even with positive outcomes. I heard of some planets where all Pleebs have opted to add Skreek-like traits to enhance their abilities, usually on those planets that have a higher topography or stranger living conditions. Mostly, though, the news is bad. All over the known universe, we have humanoids punished for being different, punished for being made into half-human, half-animal creatures. Punished simply for existing. We didn't ask to be created and spliced together, and we should not be treated differently because of their emotional reaction to us. We have as much right to live, and to live well, as any Pleeb." She brushed back her hair. Something was troubling her. Or perhaps she was just working out how much to tell him.

"As you can see," she held a hand up to her long brown ears, "Alice is a little more than your average Pleeb." She flashed an amber eye at Alice, before relaxing into her chair, seeming to disappear into her own thoughts. She took a deep sip of Glee-Juice.

It was a while before she spoke again.

"The resistance is older than me," continued Claris. "My predecessor started the movement. It was his aim to solidify the nations of Skreeks. He brought some from each of their home planets to meet here on Oisettio. That was the start of it. They placed the Edens here and set up many camps. This is one of the older, more established areas, but we have them all over the planet. We choose not to build, as we want to leave as little an impact on the nature of the place as possible. Plus, technology is how the Univi find you. That's why we use the old-type pod-cars. Their tracking signals are easier to scramble. We are protected via other means, of course, but it always pays to be discreet. We have medical help and rehabilitation for those who need it, and of course, we are centered around training for war. That's where you come in. From Alice's observations, we believe you have the skills needed to help us to return your planet, Urayso, to its natural beauty and to reclaim it as a peaceful nation, free from the overbearing far-right Pleebs."

Forbes realized that the whole bar had stopped to listen, and everyone was looking at him. He laughed at the seriousness of the situation, feeling drunk and totally out of his depth. This was like some kind of fantasy. He thought about what he'd learned that day. This certainly seemed like his calling in life. It was like everything he had been doing was linked to this moment. He felt like this was less of a coincidence, and more to do with the deft life-orchestrating abilities of Alice.

He turned to see her smiling face, her hand gripping the Glee mug firmly. He would give the people what they wanted.

He pushed back his stool and got up. He held out his hands.

"I accept!" he roared. "I will do my best for you, Claris, and the best for Oisettio."

His cheesy Warbler-taught mentality and the several pints he had just swallowed allowed him to fist-punch the air and raise a resounding warlike cheer from those around him.

Chapter 8

In the weeks that followed, Alice noticed just how perfect a man for the job Forbes really was. He'd taken the whole idea in stride and didn't seem overwhelmed or unsure of himself in the situation, like other recruits often did. She had been right to wait, to show him the truth back at the plaza. Several other recruits from the Warblers had been picked up that day by other Oisettian platoons and were all making great progress too, though they would have to work their way up before they met her mother and learned the full truth.

Forbes already had the confidence from others that comes from being a good leader. He even had the trust of some of the more difficult Skreeks in the camp. He was good at passing on his knowledge and taking control without being overbearing, and his relaxed attitude made him easy to get along with. Alice's mother was impressed with her find. Alice could see that by how much work had already been sent Forbes' way.

She knew the war was looming. The big one—it wasn't just Univi or the Warblers. The Pleebs had vaguely been ignoring the Oisettians up until now. They'd thought they could control them with underhanded attacks and contrived government and social structures, like those they had in place on Urayso. But it was becoming hard to hide just how much the resistance in Oisettio was growing. Every day, they had more recruits coming in from other planets and deployed back to their home planets for undercover operations post-training.

It wasn't just Skreeks, either, but also Pleebs who had seen the injustice and wanted to make it right. Freedom-fighter types and those who had been brought up alongside Skreeks were coming forth to lend a hand and to train for war. Others simply wanted to be a part of the start of a new civilization. Signals were being drip-fed down through encrypted news-tab articles to all Skreeks and sympathizers of the cause on Oisettio, Urayso, and the neighboring planets, showing the injustice of the Univi and the need for the people to awaken and start a movement.

Alice thought of her father. It was as though evil had ruptured his very soul. He hadn't always been that way. Her parents split when she was just a little kid, but even after that, he had a passion against the Univi, against the oppression. But then, back when he joined the Warblers and later became their leader, he'd changed. Like some terrible super villain, the power got to him, along with the money, the control, and the deep-seated corruption. She had seen him order killing after killing.

It wasn't until she was fifteen that her mother had secretly visited her. Just as she'd taken Forbes to Oisettio, her mother had shown her the truth. Alice had found it much harder to take in, being so much more personal. But once she had met the people there, and gotten to know and trust her mother, she saw that she had found what she was looking for. That she was fighting for the righteous side.

Chapter 9

The resistance continued to grow over the next year, and tensions on planet Urayso were growing, too. More Skreeks were killed, and the Warblers were losing their mask. Whispers of the atrocities they had committed were spreading around the districts. The Univi seemed to have stopped caring about being caught. Daily reports were in the news-tabs damning the Skreeks and blaming them for any and every problem in society. Many Pleebs had stopped socializing with Skreeks at all.

On the planet Oisettio, Forbes and Alice were training hard.

"We need to come up with a game plan—something big that the Univi can't back away from. We need to expose them and the Warblers as one group. And we will need more than just Skreeks on our side to win this war."

Alice looked over at Forbes. "I know, honey. Don't worry. I've made some calls and gotten back in touch with Debbie."

Forbes jokingly winced as she called him honey, but he loved it.

Later that week, Forbes and Alice were back in the souped-up Oisettian pod-car, hurtling through space toward Urayso and back to The City. They then walked down the same rain-swept streets Forbes had danced down on his way to join the Warblers, and right into the bar where he and Alice had first met. The thought seemed to dawn on them both, and the seriousness of the situation was temporarily eradicated as they realized the romantic feel of the place.

"It's been a while." Forbes smiled as he scooped up Alice's hand in his and gave it a squeeze.

"Alice! Forbes!" Debbie, the bar owner, swooped toward them, her gaze lingering on their enveloped hands for a moment. Her cheeks went red, and her eyes danced with mild amusement.

"So, the rumors are true then—you two are finally an item." She laughed and grappled them both into a crunching embrace. As she pulled away, Forbes saw that Debbie looked down.

"What's up, Debbs?" He'd known her for years, and she was always the happiest of people.

"Ah, you know." She wiped at her eyes. "Life has been pretty tough these last few months. They've got me down as a Skreek sympathizer. It looks like I'm losing the club."

Forbes took a moment to follow her gaze as she looked around the establishment. It was empty except for them and a few regulars on the barstools. It used to be packed this time in the evening.

"I'm so sorry, Debbs." Alice touched her arm. "Don't worry. We will help any way we can. On that note…do you have any information for us?"

The three sat down at one of the empty tables and began to quietly discuss the comings and goings of the Warblers. Debbie was a direct link to them, as Alice had previously explained to Forbes. That was how Alice's old barmaid job had started. Her father believed she was in a Warbler-based club, looking out for new recruits. However, Debbie was an old colleague of Alice's mother and a firm believer in the resistance.

She was going to help them get a message to all the Skreeks in the Warblers to try and turn their heads.

"We need to get people moving—protests, upheaval. Once we open their eyes a bit, it will be easy."

Debbie had sent out notices across the net to any Oisettians listed as being on Urayso. Skreek and Pleeb alike, they had all received the call. She had plans in place for mass Skreek protests that would be formed mainly of those in the know.

"As soon as the others see it, they'll join in." She grinned. "My rumors have been doing wonders. There isn't a Skreek in any district now that will just sit on their butt and do nothing. They're ready and waiting. You mark my words."

Forbes laughed. "Brilliant, Debbie. I'm glad you're on our side!"

Just as Debbie had predicted, the next few weeks showed massive upheaval. Protests were in full swing across most of the major districts. Skreeks were bailing from the Warblers quicker than they could be captured. They were forming their own groups and factions protesting the Univi government. The Warblers were shown to be a corrupt organization, and their "secret-location" buildings were graffitied, and windows smashed. Univi patrols were chased out of the Skreek territories, and anger and violence paraded in the streets. Alternative net-stations were played out with messages of the Resistance, while kids in garages uploaded constant video streams of Oisettian slogans and ideals. It was too hot to handle. It couldn't be covered up.

The Univi were forced to pull back. They stopped their arrests and hid within their iron buildings, posting news that all the citizens could clearly see was fake. The Oisettians had an opening, but they knew it wouldn't be for long.

Colonel Gama and Forbes were rallying the troops on Oisettio. They had struck up an excellent relationship, considering Forbes had tried to kill him. But Gama wasn't one for grudges, and it would have been seen as losing face for him to continue the feud. Besides, Gama liked the guy. He reminded him of a skinnier, rattier version of himself.

Gama took the initial battalion down to Urayso to hide out in one of the far districts under Forbes's orders. He was to send out recruiters to the protests under the cover of chaos and bring them under the wing of

Oisettio. Other factions were doing the same across several of the districts.

Back on Oisettio, Forbes had thousands of men and women on constant training regimes and in grueling meetings. Nothing got past him. Everything was organized and militant. Everyone was focused on their duties. With their total trust in Forbes and faith in the cause, they were pumped for war.

Chapter 10

The day came rapidly. The hot sun rose across the rabbit-filled fields of Oisettio. The dawn chorus of birds rang around the planet like an alarm bell. The ground seemed to vibrate as Oisettians of every shape and size rose from their ambi-tents to join the lines of warriors forming in front of the giant domed stage that had been erected in the center of the meadow. Pleebs and Skreeks from all over Oisettio had arrived for the cause.

Claris stood in the center of the stage, with Alice on her right and Forbes on her left. It took almost two hours for the Oisettians to line up in formation. Claris stood taller and pulled on her headset to face her warriors. "Within just a few short hours, on this longest day of the Solarstice, we will be fighting to return these men and women to their rightful home, the planet Urayso, the homeland for Skreeks everywhere." Claris's clear voice attested through her headset. Silence fell across the rows and rows of Oisettians.

Forbes felt the hairs rise on his neck.

"We are not only fighting to oust the far-right Univi, but all those who have oppressed us, all those who have deemed us as unworthy humans. We will not bow to those who believe that those space agency scientists can play with life. We will not become martyrs to their ideas. We will not stand and watch as our people and those we love are de-humanized and turned into criminals! As our once-golden lands are smeared with concrete and glass. I have fought alongside many of you before, and we have won. I have fought alongside you, and we have also had our defeats. This time, we will not fail. We have more strength, are more in number, and this time, the *people* are with us! We will defeat the Univi, and we will WIN!" Her voice echoed across the meadow and into the trees.

The sound of the troops was deafening as they burned for the battle to come, sending gun shots into the air, and shouting war cries that hadn't been heard in centuries. Alice and Forbes screamed with them, their feet rattling the wooden stage beneath as their rage erupted.

Chapter 11

The first group of old-looking Oisettian ships descended on the First District in the early afternoon, their worn-out bodywork covering fully automated systems, sonic engines, and heavily fortified antidetection fields. They snuck past the Univi space-tracking systems and scrambled the headsets of the unsuspecting sergeants and colonels in the barracks and offices surrounding them.

The large doors clattered open, and the otherwise-silent streets echoed the footfalls of the Oisettian warriors as they took to their positions. Forbes led his battalion to the barracks on the far side of the district, while Alice took another to the Univi head offices in the center. The Univi saw them, and tech-messengers sounded on the telescreens across the district, but they were too late. Several other battalions, led by Forbes's handpicked men, surrounded a further two barracks on the northern and eastern side of the district.

Forbes and Claris had chosen this timing, as they knew the majority of the Univi soldiers would be at lunch in the barracks mess halls. It was the day of the new year, the Solarstice, when the light would be in the skies the longest. They would have twelve hours to complete their mission. Other Univi employees who worked in the hundreds of smaller offices around the district would be mostly unarmed and unprepared. The element of surprise would be their most useful tool.

Colonel Gama and other Oisettian spies in the Univi had designed maps and info-leaks that had been distributed at Oisettian meetings months ago. These detailed the times of expected meetings and where they would be held. They showed the placement of all major offices, mess halls and habitation rooms, the times of weapons training, court cases, and even which officers had holiday booked that day. Nothing was left to chance.

The surprise tactic worked like a charm. The Univi had no time to react. When they tried to communicate, they found their headsets jammed and playing the Oisettian war jingle–a comic touch from Forbes, designed to mock and anger the Univi and give the Oisettians the upper hand. Of course, they had drills for surprise attacks, but everything was slower as they were preoccupied eating lunch. By the time they realized anything was happening, their respective bases were surrounded.

The sheer mass of Oisettians came like one huge wave. They were all side by side, a wall closing in around their targets. Women, men and even some children were bearing down on the Univi. Worn-out looking weapons hid state-of-the-art killing mechanisms. The few external Univi guards were killed instantly or scattered. The battle screams were consistent and terrifying. Noises of those being gunned down were drowned out by the screeches of rage and determination from the Oisettian warriors. None were spared. It was a total massacre.

Alice was the first to breach the glass doors of the Univi head office she had been deployed to. She made her way with her squad to the room on the sixth floor where the head of the Univi was supposed to be, but no one was there. He must have escaped. She shot three guys she found in the adjoining room, but none of them were worth anything—just paper-pushers and caretakers, all stinking Pleebs.

Throughout the building, the rest of her battalion had split up and taken a floor each, storming the stairs and cutting the solar supplies to the lifts. There really was no escape. Terrified soldiers and office clerks jumped from windows and hid under tables as the Oisettians barraged through every room like a systematic machine. They took no prisoners, killed all Pleebs, and indeed any Univi Skreeks they saw. All Univi had to die.

As Alice made her way up to the next floor, a member of another squad caught her attention.

"He's gone. Somehow managed to get to the pod-copter on the roof."

***

The faceless leader of the Univi on Urayso had left without so much as a backward glance at the planet. He had launched a pod-copter and headed directly to Krem knows where. Alice knew he would return with reinforcements, and she knew they had to be ready when that happened.

But that was a battle for another time. She had to focus. Her next mission entirely took over her thoughts.

Massing her squad and a few from other floors, she left the building and headed to the smaller neighboring Univi offices. On the way, she radioed Colonel Gama the signal to start the pincer movement from the outer districts.

Gama got the call at one o'clock, earlier than expected, but he was ready. He gave a nod to his comrades, and, with a few swipes on their logpads, bombs were triggered in offices throughout the five outer districts. Skreeks who had deserted the Warblers and others from new rebel factions had planted the bombs over the past few months. *That sound is almost festival-like*, Gama thought, as explosions rattled the buildings for miles around, like giant fireworks. Glass shattered into streets below as hundreds of buildings collapsed within minutes. Waiting for the ground to stop trembling, he crouched low, suddenly realized the enormity of what was happening.

How many civilians would die?

How many Pleebs would be burned to the ground for the sake of victory?

He gathered himself, as he had been taught in the forces.

"OK, guys," he bellowed. "It's time to go." A familiar manic feeling swept through his soul as he headed inward to take the outer districts.

Thousands of deserters, renegades, and spies began to mass. From under the ground in the Skreek tunnels, the inhabitants launched themselves into battle, using whatever weapons they had against the Univi troops and any Pleebs they could see. Untrained men and women attacked with such ferocity that they could be mistaken for soldiers, sweeping buildings and tearing down monuments across the city.

Forbes by this time had taken two barracks on the western side of the First District. His men worked fast and efficiently, trusting in their leader. They took each room and killed every occupant, barely losing even five percent of their own warriors. As they took each barracks, they brought the weapons outside and left them in piles for Claris and the second wave of Oisettians to collect. After the fourth barracks was taken, Forbes called the order over his speaker phone to his ship on the ground. It launched and headed into space, where Claris waited.

Forbes amassed his warriors.

"It's time to go and pay that lying bastard a visit!" He called above the ringing carnage and explosions from the outer districts.

"I know a lot of you have been waiting a long time for this—let's not screw it up." He laughed then, leaning his head back to show his sharp fangs, his eyes wild with the taste for battle. He and any other pilots in the area headed to abandoned Univi ships, and the Oisettians boarded. They were on their way to the Eighth District. The Warbler building was still standing. No one had dared to plant a bomb here, fearing the detection systems were too advanced. The building stood, looking empty, but strong in its silence. As Forbes and several leagues of Oisettians surrounded it, it seemed somehow more daunting than the barracks or Univi offices. Those who had deserted the Warblers looked on with a trace of fear in their eyes. They had no element of surprise now. The Warblers knew they were coming.

The decision to attack the Univi offices first had weighed heavily on Forbes's mind, but it was the only chance they'd had of catching and killing their elusive leader. Besides, he knew that without the Univi, Ereys and the Warblers had little or no real power. Death was all that faced them.

He attached a mega-synth to his speaker phone and turned to face the hundreds of warriors in front of him.

"The time has come to take your vengeance, on not just the Univi, but this vile syndicate that made you turn against your fellow Skreek. That made you slaves to their lying ideals. That took so many good people from us and turned lives into empty graves. Now is your chance to inflict the suffering on them they have inflicted on all of us! Let's burn this place to the ground!"

A war cry sounded as the warriors stormed forward. The cry rapidly turned to screams, as suddenly before them, a great jet of fire streamed out of the building. Oisettians lay squirming on the ground, screaming as oil and fire enveloped their bodies. A hum sounded from inside, as the Oisettian forces dropped back. The hum grew louder and louder, like a huge generator was revving up.

The hum stopped.

A sonic boom ripped through the crowds. The sound was piercing. Stunned Oisettians fell hard to the ground, their ears ringing and bleeding from the force of it. Forbes was on the ground, too. He had managed to cover his ears, but still, he could not move or think. The pain seared through his skull like a hot knife.

"Get up," he said from the ground as he tried to push his legs into action.

"Get up. GET UP!" he screamed, though he could still not hear his own voice. His warriors were watching him heave himself from the ground. Fear and determination shone on their faces as they forced themselves to get up. The ringing began subsiding in his head as Forbes signaled his troops to mass again. "Forward!" He motioned them onward, and they charged at the building. The doors splintered glass as they pushed through.

Inside, the Warblers were waiting. They were so equipped with guns that they were fearsome to look at. Lasers and panzers blasted into the Oisettians as they charged forward.

"Stay together. Keep advancing!" Forbes called, unsure whether anyone could hear him.

Blood smeared across the tiled floors as Pleeb and Skreek fell. Forbes swung himself over the reception desk for cover and shouted commands to regain order and trust amongst his warriors. It was working. He could see they were back in action. They edged along the sides of the room, closing in on the Warblers, forcing them into the center. Scenes of the plaza all those years ago flashed into Forbes's head. He smiled at the sweet irony of it. They had this covered.

He called to a few of his squadron to follow him and gestured for some to take the side stairs as he careered up the right main staircase to the office on floor nineteen. Sure enough, as Forbes knew he would be, Captain John Ereys was there. He sat in his wide leather chair, smoking a stench-filled e-cigar. The plumes of vapor filled the room, the air conditioning turned off.

"Well done, kid." Ereys stared at Forbes with the dead eyes of a dangerous man who knew he was beaten. He lifted his hands in surrender.

"Take me in," he said.

Forbes hesitated before he lifted his gun.

Some moral duty tried to stop him as he pulled the trigger, but the day was too long, and his hatred too complex.

Ereys lay slumped on his Earth-wood mahogany table. His blood streamed to the floor, adding to the many liters of human blood that had flowed on the streets that day. By evening, the battle had quietened. Oisettians and rebel Uraysions picked their way through buildings and down alleyways, finding Univi and Warbler troops. They searched anywhere they could be hiding or attempting last-minute fortifications. Like ants of one mind, they ransacked the city. Every district was alive with makeshift hunters tracking and erasing their prey any way they could. Buildings that had not exploded in the Gama attacks were set on fire as symbols of victory and dominance by the Skreeks.

By midnight, exhausted, most of the first wave of warriors were flagging. Either catching moments for water and to tend to superficial wounds, or simply collapsing where they stood from fatigue and pain.

Claris and the second wave had infiltrated most of any leftover Univi buildings and had set up medi-stations in all the inner districts. She herself was walking amongst the injured to calm and congratulate them on their successes, to whisper words to the dying and give water to the shaken. Citizens that had not been fighting stayed hidden in their homes or lay dead in the rubble from the explosions.

"A necessity of war," breathed Claris as she stepped over the corpse of yet another mother clutching her unmoving child.

The dawn rose over the wasted city. The longest night of the year had ended. The dust settled on the battle as pieces of broken glass and debris from buildings cracked underfoot. The Oisettians—those not being treated for wounds in the medi-stations—stood in groups, leaning to catch their breath. Those people staying hidden in their homes waited in silence, afraid of the carnage the day before had brought. Children who'd been screaming for safety were now sleeping soundly for a few eerie hours, as the daylight washed away the sounds of the battle. The Skreeks who had not been involved in the battle began to come out of their underground homes. Bodies of both Pleeb and Skreek curled up on pavements, with the light casting shadows on their empty faces. As the sun rose higher, more people began to venture onto the streets. The silence of those few dawn hours was broken by quiet murmurs and cries over loved ones found amongst the dead.

A small Skreek child wandered, lost, into the middle of the street. Unsure of where to look. He sat broken on the ground by a pile of burnt-out advertising signs and telescreens. He began to cry.

The sound brought neighbors to his side. Their comforting words delved beneath the surface of the carnage. Breaking through the fear, others began to breathe. To whisper, and to embrace one another.

Forbes and Alice stood in the center of the main street. Their haggard faces were illuminated by the warmth of the new day. They were in. They had taken back their homeland, and now nothing would stand in their way.

Chronicles of the Fallen Colony

By Andrew P. McGregor

Date: 2642

A bright drop of light blazed on a cracked viewscreen, several billion kilometers starward. Julian listened to the sound of his own breathing and reveled in the stillness surrounding him.

"Just a few short months and you will be there." Lisa, the ship's artificial intelligence, broke the silence.

Julian ignored her. He blew out hot air and pushed forward on one of Lisa's many emergency cranks; it was the size of his forearm and smelled of sweat and metal.

It hadn't always been this way; the crank was originally encased in a plastic resin as tough as tank armor. Once the resin had worn down, the studded metal underneath had cut Julian's hands over and over, until his hands were little more than five-fingered calluses. A few months away from their destination, the crank had been worn as smooth as a fireman's pole.

Julian wore gloves covered in brown dirt to grip the crank. He faced the viewscreen, feet planted against the bulkhead and back against the wall, giving him leverage in the weightless maintenance shaft.

He reversed his grip and pulled the crank back before letting go and wiping some sweat from his eyes. He took off one of the tattered brown gloves and grabbed the gray food bar he'd brought with him. Lisa assured him it was English stew, but it tasted just like chicken, or eggs and bacon, or any of the other bland blocks of gray stuff the ship's nanofactory had created for him over the decades.

"You are now thirty-three rotations out of alignment," Lisa said. Julian grunted at her but finished off the gray block and resumed pushing and pulling. He'd come to think of the cranks as his personal torture devices, especially when he measured his efforts. The four-thousand-kilometer-long light sail he was moving didn't budge, not to his eyes. He stared at the sail's white-hot expanse, reflecting the brilliant glare of the local star.

"What if we were just one rotation short, or three? Would it really matter?"

"If you want to become a burnt offering for the locals, then feel free to stop early. It won't make a difference to me whether you die or not."

"Charming. Who are these locals anyway?" While he'd grown up aboard the ship, he'd never been interested in his intended destination until now.

"Well..."

Julian groaned; Lisa's tone was one of amusement, the one she used when she started talking about ancient history.

"Oh, shush, Jules. I haven't kept you alive this long to have you complain about a little history. When my original crew rescued your grandparents from their stricken vessel, this star system had the closest habitable planet. The problem is that the planet went dark a hundred years before. No communications. Zip. So, either there *are* no locals, or they've convinced themselves to use stone tools."

"Sounds...fun," he said, grunting with the effort of another rotation.

"Not really. Oh. You were being sarcastic. Allow me a fake laugh. Ha. No, that wouldn't be much fun, but at least you would be alive. If you could convince them to take you in, that is.

"Now, I have some news!" She sounded excited.

"News usually implies something breaking down." Julian finished the last rotation and flicked some sweat from his mouth before sucking on a black, rubbery water tube.

"Correct, yay for us!" Lisa shouted so loudly her failing speakers crackled in Julian's ears. "You know how the spatial converters broke down a couple of years ago? This one's even better!"

"Don't tell me it's the heat dispensers."

"Oh, no, no, nothing so dire. It's the automatic processors for the life-tube's rotation. Unless the life-tube is sped up each day, you will eventually lose your gravity. Not immediately fatal, but quite important, wouldn't you agree?"

Julian wanted to smash his calloused, meaty fists against the ship's gray bulkhead, thinking of the extra work he would have to do just to keep things from floating around inside the ship. Lack of artificial gravity would cause all sorts of mess: killing the crops, losing the pools of water he'd carefully extracted, and letting all other objects float loose.

"So, what else is new?"

***

From a distance of a hundred kilometers, the ship looked like a small dark spider at the center of a huge web made of light-reflecting sails. At this distance, the main body of the ship was like a pin with a small circular life-tube ringing it. Two hundred people had once lived in that ring, and now their recycled bodies rested there, turned into dirt for the plants or various other components on the ship. The people *were* the ship. Oxygen, carbon, hydrogen, nitrogen, calcium, phosphorus and traces of potassium, amongst other elements that made up human bodies, were put to use to help keep the ship running just a little bit longer.

Julian was floating outside the cylindrical life-tube, inside of which he had spent most of his waking hours, and he was starting to feel tired. He studied what looked like a curved running track at one end of the life-tube, and its circular rotations spun next to him. It moved slowly enough he would be able to jog alongside it in a tight circle.

"Yes, Jules, you'll need to go for a run. You will have to open one of those maintenance hatches as they move past and insert a rod, then—and here's the fun part—you have to accelerate the life-tube from 4.5 to 4.8 meters per second."

Julian looked at the small inner wheel of the rotating life-tube. The inner wheel was attached to the much larger torus where he spent most of his time. "Exactly how much does the bloody lot weigh?"

"Oh, you don't need to know that. Don't worry, Jules, all you must do is apply constant pressure on the wheel until it's fast enough."

Julian watched his breath form a small mist in the air. "Is it getting colder, Lisa?"

"I'm afraid so. As my processors in this location have shut down, I'm unable to distribute their heat. Temperatures throughout the ship have fallen two degrees."

"Well, I hope they don't drop much further."

"Since that would mean more of my processors have died, I can only agree."

The track had grooves in the floor where ancient machinery, now long gone, had moved around.

"Well, here goes." He floated more than walked, each step moving him faster. He sped up enough that it felt like he was jogging on solid ground, though his head still felt the dizzying sensation of zero gravity.

He ran faster, hefting a large metal pole between his hands while trying not to stumble and flatten his face against the curved floor. The cold air was already affecting his lungs, and he was panting harder than he should be. He held the metal pole in front of his chest and waited until a maintenance hatch came up behind him. He rammed the end of the pole against the inner chamber's side, missing the hatch as it sped by.

Julian grunted and almost fell. His right foot thudded heavily, but he righted himself and kept running. He ran faster, matching the spinning wall's velocity. He slowed down just enough to let another open hatch catch up to him, and he rammed the pole at it again. Missed. His legs were getting tired. He made one more attempt.

Thunk.

The metal pole stuck as if he'd inserted it into instant-set concrete. He let go and slowed down, watching the pole slide up the wall toward the ceiling. The pole disappeared. It wouldn't be long before it reappeared behind him. Still jogging, he fell onto the floor and grabbed at the grooves to stop himself from bouncing back into the open air.

He hugged the ground while the now deadly pole flew over him from behind.

"And now comes the fun part," Julian said after he got his breath back. The pole whisked past him several times. "Is this really the best way to speed up the life-tube's rotation?"

"Only if you want to live," Lisa said. "I mean, there's a slim chance you could collect enough water from the re-vines once the rest is lost."

Julian spat, "No, not that stuff."

"Well then…"

He rolled his eyes. A few moments later he was running. He had to duck a couple of times to avoid the metal pole but was fast enough by the third rotation he could grab it. He pushed as hard as he could.

By the time Lisa told him to stop, his lungs burned, and his legs felt like jelly.

"Congratulations, Julian, gravity is restored to one gee. Two times a week should be enough to keep it this way."

"Oh. Good."

***

Julian tore a small tomato from its plant and popped it into his mouth. He chewed, exhausted, while lying on the dirt. Once he'd eaten a few tomatoes, he would have to raid the lettuce patch and then find some beans before curling up for sleep. Surrounded by specially bred plants and their nutritious fruits, he watched a viewscreen on the ceiling. Thirty-eight years aboard the ship, now just three months to go.

Three months of manual labor to keep the ship running.

"Did you know the ancient Athenian rowers probably looked a lot like you," Lisa was telling him, "rowing day and night, no rest, so my fractured memory stores tell me. Studies used to say the Athenians were fitter than twentieth-century Olympic rowers, before genetic engineering, of course—"

"Lisa?" Julian noticed something on the viewscreens he'd never seen before; something bright white, moving against the sea of white stars.

"Yes, Jules?"

"Shut up."

"Whatever for?"

"You're boring me." He pointed at the white points of light on the viewscreen, and his heart started thumping. "But that looks interesting. What are they? Other starships?"

"Ah, those." Lisa's voice turned sad. "Jules, I'm sorry, those are not starships coming to rescue us. In fact, I know exactly what they are."

"Well, what are they?" Julian was getting worried.

"I've been tracking them for years. I lost them some time ago, but they reappeared around a year ago. They're spiraling down toward the star."

"What are they? Just tell me."

"They're your grandparents and their friends. Some first-generation refugees."

The tiny points of light moved slowly across the viewscreen. The image on the screen was from a small dorsal camera mounted on a non-rotating part of the ship. The points of light—his grandparents and their crew—were heading away from the local star in a long, elliptical orbit.

He felt lonely. "What happened when they died?"

"Jules, isn't it obvious? My systems are breaking down trying to keep one human pet alive. What do you think was happening with more than two hundred meat sacks?"

"But they were aboard this ship for years, weren't they?"

"Of course. And that was the problem. They knew it, the refugee crew knew it, so did my crew. Your grandparent's captain volunteered first, then a few others, then your grandparents, and then most of the officers from their old ship. There was no fighting, but there was quite a lot of arguing. Your mother was pregnant with you at the time, so she and your father stayed. When the volunteers finally leapt from the ship, it was a peaceful event. Such a lovely evening, I played Bizet's *Carmen* for them."

Julian shook his head. "*Carmen*? Really? You're a sick mothership, aren't you?"

"I have heard that before. I believe my choice of music was appropriate, though. I should have played it again when your mother was fed through the recyclers, but your father wouldn't have it."

"You're lucky I don't remember her."

"How so? Are you going to hurt me, you little rodent, you?" Lisa said. He could imagine her waving a finger at him.

The points of light that were his grandparents slipped past the edge of the view screen. "Think I'll just grab some more food and nod off to sleep."

***

Julian groaned and the crank clacked in response. He felt just like the ancient Greek rowers, pushing and pulling against the smooth crank as if it were a paddle. Over and under, over and under. Lisa played some sort of rock music to accompany his efforts.

Clack-clack-clack-boom.

He'd been rotating the metal pole for hours now, withdrawing one of the four gigantic sails. Lisa had calculated they were slow enough now the sail was no longer needed; it would only be a hindrance while they moved to orbit the inner planets.

Three weeks of hard labor left.

"Lisa, what was that sound?" It was like the snoring of some monster on the other side of the ship.

"You mean this one?" She shut off the music, and he could hear a metallic grinding noise.

"That's the one."

The music resumed, and the clacking continued. "Temperature changes. As we're closer to the local star, the outside of the ship is no longer a few degrees above absolute zero. The outer hull is expanding as it heats up."

"Will the hull crack and kill me?"

"Wouldn't that be a fun event?" Lisa said in all seriousness.

"No."

"Well, I wouldn't think the hull should pop open, but I am quite old, as starships go. Oh, I wouldn't fret, Jules. I was built for these sorts of trips. Besides, if I did crack open, at least you'd die reasonably quickly. In, say, a few hours, the air would slowly leak out, and the cold of space would close in. Ah…a beautiful scene. I almost wish it to happen."

Julian felt a shiver of cold.

When there were just twenty kilometers of sail left to haul in, the rod jammed. He pushed as hard as he could, but his fingers slipped and his arms went over the rod, followed by his chest. "Ow." The impact of the rod left him winded. Lisa shut off the music, then played a final sad trumpet to mock him.

"We have a problem," Lisa said, cheery.

"Yes, I seem to have found it," Julian said while rubbing his chest. "Is the cable filament snagged somewhere in the bend again?"

"Correct, you know what to do. You'll also need to spin up the nanofactory; you never did fix the space suit."

Julian rolled his eyes. "I'll grab the micro-crank."

***

Tied to the sail's framework by a metal rope he had threaded by hand several years ago, Julian worked quickly but carefully. A large, round pulley had become entangled in a loose diamond filament that was millimeters thick, but thin enough to slice open his homemade space suit. He'd sown studded metal caps into the tips of his suit's fingers to grip the filament, as well as to protect his pressurized undergarment from any cuts.

He felt sweat on his forehead and could see his misty breath fogging up his visor. He was cold, hungry, and nervous. Last time he'd done a spacewalk, two years earlier, he had gone only a kilometer from the ship and had a handy propulsion system and internal climate control.

At Lisa's suggestion, he'd recycled most of the old suit to make some emergency rope that had not been needed until now. Left with just the hard undergarments and a homespun outer cloth, Julian had to wonder at Lisa's wisdom.

Making sure to anchor his feet against the inch-thick spar that formed part of the giant skeletal framework of the sail, he tugged gently at the sharp filaments to untangle them. Too much force and it would snap, not enough and it wouldn't budge. He gradually applied more pressure, then his foot slipped. "Uh-uh-oh-crap." He spun slowly and let go of the filament; he grabbed for his lifeline and steadied himself. "Not having much fun out here."

"I noticed. Would you like some calming music?"

"No, your idea of calm usually involves some sort of frenetic trash. Play some Bach. Heck, a lullaby might do it."

"As you wish, Jules." The sound that filtered through his suit's tinny speakers made him cringe. Translated from some dead language from ancient Earth, *Wheels on the Bus* started playing.

"You know I hate that one."

"Incentive for you to get back to me faster, my darling meat machine." He placed his feet against the pulley again and grabbed the filament. He tugged and the filament popped loose. He checked the pulley. It was pockmarked from interstellar dust and needed replacing. He opened a pouch on his chest and retrieved a small lubricating gun. He touched the gun's nozzle against the pulley's groove and squirted a tiny amount of gel that hardened upon contact. The gel would last just long enough for him to finish hauling the sail in.

Once he'd finished and made sure the filament wouldn't tangle again, he turned to head back to the ship. In that moment he was struck by the majesty of the ship that had been his home for thirty-eight years.

The music ended. "Pop!" Lisa said.

"What do you mean, pop? Oh." He felt a sting in his left leg.

"Oops, there's a hole in your leg now."

The pain was setting in. A micrometeorite must have hit him. "Ouch! Owie…fff—" He started coughing. He'd been stabbed by faulty machinery before, hit his head dozens of times, broken limbs; but this felt different, like a tiny, localized fire melting through his leg.

"Jules, I wouldn't worry about the leg. The hole appears to be tiny, we can fix it, but if you feel like living, it may be prudent to patch up the holes in your suit. Ooh, I need to take some pictures. The blood is solidifying outside the suit in wonderful patterns!"

"Okay. Okay. Patches." Julian remembered he had a handful of thumb-sized patches left. The patches were difficult to make, so had been used sparingly. Breathing hard, trying to ignore the fire in his calf, he shook his head to clear the tears from his eyes. He opened another small pouch on his chest and fished out one of four patches. He located where blood was pumping out into space and tore open the outer garment.

"Argh!" he yelled in pain while brushing aside some blood so he could see the hole. He stabbed at the hole with the patch, and it stuck. The patch glowed softly, adhering to the hardened suit. Anesthetic chemicals numbed his pain.

"Faster, my darling, or you will lose more air and most of that leg."

"I…know…" He was panting, almost hyperventilating. "Oh no!" He dropped a patch, and, with deliberate inevitability, it spun ever so slowly out of his reach. "Two left," he whispered. He located the exit wound and tore more of the homespun outer garment off. He got the patch on and screamed from the pain.

Lisa played *Twinkle, Twinkle Little Star*.

He sucked on his suit's water pouch and tried not to vomit. "The pain won't go away, Jules, but it will get worse once the numbing agents in those patches wear off." Julian grunted. He retied the metal rope to make sure it wouldn't slip from the sail and grabbed the inch-thick framework with shaking hands. "It's just one hand over the other, come back to me, my lovely little pet."

"I-I'm coming, just…"

"What is it?"

"Just…shut…up." He fainted.

"Well, this is an issue," Lisa murmured.

***

Julian woke up to blasting drumbeats.

"Ah, there you are," Lisa said. "Time to come home."

"Home?"

"Yes, Jules, home. Come to me, Jules."

The pain in his leg had lessened. He pulled on the metal rope and reeled himself back in to the sail's frame. "Just one hand over the other," he murmured to himself.

***

Julian jerked awake, certain he was in mortal danger. He wasn't. He was aboard the ship, naked, with leafy bandages tied around his leg. It was freezing. He could see icicles in the air every time he breathed, and his limbs felt numb. He was inside the life-tube, lying on a bed of dirt next to his mangled space suit and what looked like two nails with thread attached to them. *Needles*. He must have sown his leg back together with thread from the space suit's outer garment. One of the nails was broken near the tip.

The leafy bandages were revitalizing re-vines—a genetically modified fungus that served as important starship regulators. The vines balanced the starship's ecosystem by breathing either oxygen or carbon dioxide, whichever was necessary. It was dark. The vines were glowing. The ship's lights were off. His entire life the lights had never been completely turned off; there'd always been at least one to pierce the gloom.

He remembered little of the climb back to the ship, just flashes of one gloved hand reaching in front of the other. It must have taken him hours to crawl the distance. He searched for some clothes. The music was off. Lisa usually played music, whether he wanted it or not. "Lisa?" he called while holding his arms close to his chest.

"I'm dying, Jules."

"Is that why it's so cold in here?"

"Yes. I had to do it."

Julian found a pair of trousers and eagerly pulled them over his sore leg. "Do what?"

"It."

"What's It?"

"File located: I had to do it, Jules. You almost died, and I needed to retrieve the sail. I drained my energy stores to reel it in. I'm not actually speaking to you now. I recorded this message while I was reeling in the sail. Message deleted."

"Oh," Julian said while putting on a second layer of clothing. "Well, that can't be good." It wouldn't be long until they reached the planet. He didn't have the necessary mathematical mind or tools to plot their course. He needed Lisa's help. "Lisa, how can I charge you back up?"

"Stupid. Idiot."

"Yeah, that's the problem."

"Idiot. Emergency crank. Battery bank."

Julian's shoulders slumped. "So, what else is new?"

"Losing gravity."

"That was a rhetorical question."

"Yes. Idiot."

***

Trying not to rip his self-sewn stitches, Julian found the emergency battery crank near the rear of the life-tube and started pumping. Up, down, up, down. He appreciated the crank's soft, gel-sealed exterior. This one had never been used. He felt light-headed and saw some blood leaking from his wounds. If he didn't wake up Lisa, he was going to die, so he ignored the blood and kept pumping. The pain was returning, and the glow from the re-vines was fading.

By the time a single bar of light had lit up on the large square battery he was working on, he'd almost lost consciousness.

"Press button. Please. Idiot."

In near pure darkness he found a small red button near the crank. It was hard and cold and would not budge. He curled his hand into a fist and smashed it against the button, cutting his hand on the button's edge.

"Ah, that's better. Good job, Jules." Lisa played a victory tune. "Jules? Oh, you're sleeping. That's okay, you've earned it."

***

Using a bag made from recycled sail material, Julian scooped some water from the evaporating pool. "What will I do now?" He felt desperate. It would be another week before they arrived. He'd been too busy working the ship's cranks, moving the sails into the correct alignment, to be able to collect any food or water. He couldn't speed the life-tube up with his wounded leg, and without the life-tube spinning fast enough, the food and water were going to waste. Lacking power to the magnets or any lubrication to the wheels, he could feel the life-tube grinding down to a complete stop.

"Eat re-vine."

"Yuck."

"You would prefer to die?" Lisa asked.

Julian sighed. There wasn't much choice for him now. The freezing temperatures had killed off almost everything else, and he couldn't cook what wasn't dead. "No."

"Good boy."

"I didn't think you cared about me."

"I may have grown attached to my little pet. Why else would I bother teaching you everything you know? In any case, I have news!"

Julian started grinding his teeth.

"Oh no, Jules, I think you'll actually like it this time."

"How so?"

"I've managed to unlock my ancient history storage core."

"Err, how is that a good thing?" He wasn't particularly keen on learning more about Chinese dynasties, medieval war preparations, or the exploits of Queen Victoria II. He shuddered to think what Lisa considered the best torture methods or kingly governance.

"Stories of course! Oh, and other science-based files are located there, like navigational data, Einsteinian and Newtonian physics, that sort of thing. We'll get you to that planet yet. Mostly I was using observational guesswork to steer us there. Comforting thought, isn't it?"

"No, not really. Are we on course?"

"You'll be pleased to know, yes, we're approaching your new home at a stately seven thousand kilometers an hour at a reasonably low perigee. A couple of small adjustments, a hop and a skip, and you're there."

"Good." He sucked on the sail-bag and all the water disappeared into his stomach. He stared at a cord of re-vine that grew around one of the life-tube's many door frames. "I doubt I could last much longer than a week eating those things."

"Hmm. You'll have plenty left over once you're on the planet. They'd be quite useful. Jules, I have to shut down soon, but there's one last thing I need you to do. Go to the nanofactory. I've recorded instructions on what to do. Good night."

The music ended.

***

This was it. The small computer inside the escape pod was the only thing that had any charge left. It knew the ship's trajectory, the amount of weight in re-vines and all the tools and equipment he had brought on board, and it could adjust its timing to suit.

"Standby," a woman told him in a language he had not heard since the last crewmember died. He was still trying to remember the words he needed to ask a question in the old language when something screamed in his ear and slammed him hard against the dusty white seat.

The hard straps pressed down on his chest like iron bars. He struggled to breathe. He managed to glimpse the planet he was headed for when it spun past the escape pod's viewport. It appeared to be white and blue. The planet was going to be *cold*.

He clutched at a small metal box. The box was the last thing Lisa had asked him to make with the nanofactory. He'd cranked the meter-wide nanofactory's handle and fed in recycled materials until the factory had spat out, one by one, a hundred tiny pieces. He'd assembled the box by hand over several days.

The metal box felt like a lead ball in his hands, threatening to slip and crush his stomach from the three-gee maneuver the escape pod was making.

"This is an Antikythera Mechanism. You would know that if you had listened to my history lessons," Lisa had told him a few days earlier.

The pressure stopped. "Prepare for orbital insertion," the woman said in the foreign language. After a few minutes, the escape pod vibrated and then started rocking and shaking violently. Flames appeared on the outside of the view port. Beyond the flames he saw Lisa's majestic sails, spread across the sky, as if on a blanket.

"Ahh, help me," he cried out. He almost dropped the little box. Lisa would have scolded him for not keeping it strapped down.

A blue sky appeared, and Lisa's wings disappeared into the sky. Clouds rushed past before several black parachutes covered the view. The parachutes extended to their full size, and he dropped the metal box when the escape pod jerked.

"The Mechanism will guide you." Lisa's voice echoed in his mind.

The pod hit the ground and split open with the impact. He screamed and held up his arms to stop debris falling on him. Cold, snow-filled air blew into the pod. He brushed some debris from his body and unstrapped himself from the chair. He went to stand but found the planet's gravity lighter than he'd expected and hit his head on the ceiling. Blood dribbled down his gray-streaked beard, and a headache formed at his temple. He bent over to search for the box.

He found it, then opened the pod's hatch and crawled out, shivering and exhausted.

"You are strong, Jules, the cold will not bother you."

Despite being in pain, he was almost bouncing across the planet's surface. He felt warm inside his homespun clothing. He paused for a moment to look around at the snow-covered mountains.

"Wow," he said. He'd been outside the ship before, hundreds of kilometers from its life-giving center, but never without a space suit. He felt like hiding back inside the pod, afraid the air would be sucked out of his lungs. The escape pod steamed and smoked, the heat kissing the snow, re-vine hanging from the exposed shell where it had cracked open.

He'd once asked Lisa, "Why don't you teach your crew's language to me?"

"It'll be useless where you're going."

Julian's eyes bulged and he jumped at the sound of a man's voice behind him. "Halt, stranger. Who are you?" He turned around to find three men, all in furry clothing, pointing spears at him. They spoke his language, with only a hint of an accent.

"Uh, Julian." He held up his hands. "Please help."

"Did you drop from the sky in that thing?" one of the men asked.

Julian gulped. "Yes, I came from the thing in the sky." He pointed one finger toward Lisa's majestic plumage that seemed to shine across half the sky.

The three men, wide-eyed, looked at each other and withdrew the pointed spears. "You're from the spaceship?" their leader asked.

Julian blew out frosty air and lowered his arms while nodding. "I'm the only survivor."

The leader, a much older man than the other two, extended his gloved hand toward Julian's and gave him a smile. "Come, we'll get you warmed up. Lisa sent you, then? We asked for help, and she was the only vessel who responded before our radios died."

Julian shook the man's hand. "How am I supposed to help you?"

"Lisa said she was damaged, but she would teach her pet—assume that's you—everything she could."

Julian sighed. "That's me alright. I should've known she'd tell you I was her pet."

"Then, will you help us? We're all that's left of the Eden's crew."

"I thought there was a whole colony here?"

The leader nodded. "The colonists seem hell-bent on regressing to medieval savages. They blame Earth and all its technology for their woes. Bloody fools. It'll take months, if not years, to dig the thing up. That's assuming the locals are feeling cooperative."

Julian looked down at the metal box, the thing that would tell him about this planet's seasons and the best times for growing crops. "I think I can help." He turned the Antikythera Mechanism's tiny crank until something inside the box clicked and a shaft opened on its side. He found tiny writing on the other side of the shaft.

"Help them fix the Eden," the message said. "It'll be easy for you."

"What's happened to the Eden?" he asked.

"Before these young lads were born, a meteorite crashed into the ground nearby. It's not a big Eden, just a small tower for limited terraforming. The problem is, it's so small it was damaged by the earthquakes that followed the meteorite and slipped into the lake we were using to fuel it. More Edens were meant to get here years ago, but I guess we became an afterthought when that war in the central star systems broke out. We lost most of our crew and machinery. The local colonists aren't helping. The lake's frozen over and it's too cold for our remaining machinery."

"So, you need both heavy machinery and a security detail?"

The leader gave him a grim smile and nodded. "That's about it."

"Can your ship help us?" One of the younger men said while shivering against the freezing cold.

Julian looked back up at Lisa and squinted. The glaring sails almost doubled the sunlight hitting the planet's surface. "I think she already is."

The three men looked behind Julian and their eyes widened. He heard footsteps scrunch in the snow and turned around.

A white, shining space suit towered over him.

"What the…?" Julian mouthed.

"Hello, Jules."

"Lisa?"

"Who else, dummy? Well, I'm not quite Lisa. I dumped a portion of my mind into this armored suit. It was reactivated by your escape pod's fiery descent. I, as this suit, am my final gift to you. I guess you could call me Sally."

Julian rolled his eyes. "How exactly are you a gift, Sally?"

The suit shook its empty helmet from side to side and wagged a thick, hollow finger at him. "Now, now, that's no way to treat your best chance of survival."

"Does this mean I don't need the Antikythera Mechanism?"

"Consider me the backup. I'm rated to last several months before falling to bits, and the Mechanism has the codes to reactivate the Eden." The suit split open in its middle, inviting Julian inside. "Now, come here and give me a hug."

Date: 2677

"Callia, come back here," a man's voice echoed throughout the rocky fields. Always, she noted with fear, accompanied by the barking of the hound. The hound was hot on the scent of her blood-matted and sweat-soaked garments. She cried in gasps as she ran. Each step she took away from the icy lake drew more blood from her rock-cut feet. Doubtless, Treynen, the fat bastard, didn't even need his dogs to find her; he just needed to follow the trail of blood.

Callia stopped, surprised. Was that…? Could it be…? She listened.

Water.

She could hear the flowing stream.

"Get back here before I have you whipped!" The voice sounded so near now, and the growling of the hound was triumphant. With a surge of effort, she started to run. This was her only chance.

Treynen's voice sounded farther off the next time he yelled. She was going to make it. Just a few more steps.

"Callia, don't," Treynen yelled at her, almost pleading. His shout sounded like he was right beside her. She stumbled but managed to skip, unbalanced, toward the river. As she finally fell in the direction of the fast-running river, she saw the fat bastard striding out of the tall grass, his dirt-encrusted face covered in scratch marks. Luckily for her, the hound, which would have torn her to pieces, was nowhere in sight. She managed a small smile as she leapt one last time into the freezing water.

She was free from King Julian's ice quarries.

***

"Shit," Treynen screamed. He couldn't swim. He violently tossed stones around and only ended this vigorous activity when he kicked a large rock, stubbing his toe. He swore some more. It took him some time before he calmed himself down. By the time he'd managed to settle down, Bongo, his stupid mutt, had poked its head out of the grass. A small rabbit was in its mouth.

"You stupid bitch," he yelled at the dumb dog. "When I tell you to get back here, do it." He unloosed a whip from his belt. Bongo slunk back into the grass before he could administer the punishment.

Treynen sat down on the rocks and rested for a few minutes. *How could a girl of twelve seasons have so easily escaped?* he asked himself. He'd made sure her manacles were tight. Slaves didn't come cheap, nor did hunting hounds. Father would not be pleased and would probably slit the mutt's throat.

King Julian's lackeys, those weird-talking alien people whose tower the slaves were trying to dig up, would be even less pleased than his father. He spat at the thought of them. King Julian claimed he was trying to help the people, but all he seemed to do was wage wars and bring more and more people back to the frozen lake.

Treynen laughed, thinking how much suffering had been brought upon the world for the sake of a buried tower. The concept of slavery sickened him, more so since he was the one doing the whipping. He'd been soft on his father's slaves, especially in the case of Callia. He'd stayed his hand and turned a blind eye to her mischievous nature more times than he could count.

But now she'd escaped, and there would be a price to pay.

Maybe Treynen could join the army and fight the plains dwellers to help cover the costs of the lost slave. Or, more likely, to escape his father's punishment. He needn't remind himself of the other misdeeds he'd committed leading up to this last act. Maybe his father would slit his throat this time.

He was only twenty-three. If he got fit before next season, he might be able to join the army.

Not likely, he thought as he looked down at his swollen, heaving belly.

Maybe he could join the plains people instead and fight for the slaves' freedom.

***

It was so cold here. Wrapping frozen feet in ruined sandals, trudging along a muddy, rain-soaked path, trying to keep up with the rest of the caravan. The rain made it hard to see and the path sometimes acted like quicksand. The breath of the men in the caravan could be seen in the cold morning air. It was, at times, so cold many of the soldiers could barely carry their spears. With two layers of waterlogged garments, Treynen's breastplate and greaves rubbed painfully in all the wrong places. His lower shins and ankles were bleeding, and his shoulders and chest were badly bruised.

The world's abandoned space arks, little more than burned-out husks, topped the cold mountains in the distance, where they had crashed over a hundred years ago above the frozen lake.

Why am I here? He was escorting a caravan eastward to the front lines of the war against Mad King Julian, but whether they had passed from the plainsmen's territories yet was impossible to tell. Everything was dark, cloudy, cold, wet, and utterly miserable. Five soldiers had already been killed by wagons or horses slipping in the muddy terrain.

From the old men's tales, it hadn't always been like this. Snow and ice used to stay put. That had been a long time ago, before the *Starlance* had arrived, using its flowery shield to shine the sun's reflected light on the world.

He'd forgotten what they were meant to be fighting for, but he no longer cared; it had been so long since he'd seen home. *Something about freeing slaves?* He scoffed at his younger self's idealistic nature. Ironically, his squad's sergeant seemed to treat the soldiers much like father had treated their work camp's slaves. Treynen felt as though he was the slave now, enthralled to his sergeant's whip. The plains people, he'd discovered, certainly didn't share his idealistic views of freeing the slaves, a fact that made him all the more bitter.

A few of the soldiers had appropriated a small townhouse, and Treynen did not take part in the gambling or trading games. He rested on a hastily constructed cot in a room with a few others and watched the lightning and rain outside. Gusts of wind sometimes blew the cold rain in, but that didn't bother him. It was a lot better than being outside in the mud.

There was a bit of cheering from the townhouse's entrance. Someone had brought them refreshments. Treynen paid no heed. He didn't feel hungry and wasn't thirsty.

"Refreshments, sirs?" a woman called into Treynen's room. The other soldiers in the room leapt at the opportunity. He sat up and glanced at the room's entrance to see who it was.

It was a young woman, around eighteen seasons, dressed in dirty white slave's garments, holding in front of her a large wicker basket of fruits and bread. She looked submissive, beaten, and unhappy, with a mop of dark hair falling over her eyes. Her owners had not treated her well, probably worse than what Treynen's father did to his slaves.

Curious, Treynen got up from the cot for some bread, using that as an excuse to get closer to the slave girl. Tentatively, he lifted the girl's dark hair so he could see her face.

He knew that scar.

"Callia?" he asked in surprise. She looked up at him, her eyes widening in fear. "Is that you, Callia?"

She let go of the basket and shook her head vigorously, trying to move toward the entrance, but Treynen grabbed her arm.

She screamed and shook his hand off before running. He went after her, knocking soldiers and equipment out of the way. He ignored the swearing of his comrades and ran outside.

His anger flared red hot. She was the reason he was in this war; why his dog was dead; why his family's slave camp was failing; why his father hated him.

He cornered her against the house's wall.

"Leave me alone," she screamed between breaths. "I'm not going back." He walked closer to her, making sure he was in between her and escape. She edged her way along the wall toward the corner, peering around it to find some sort of escape. "Please, just...don't hurt me."

Treynen's rage dissipated at her soft, desperate plea. He could see she was crying, even shaking in fear. He felt an emotion so strong it was like he had been winded. Callia was afraid, afraid of *him*, and those tears...He'd never known she felt so desperate, so afraid. *He* had done this to her, and now Treynen found he could not bear to see the results of such treatment. He uncoiled his tightly bound fists. He looked at her teary red eyes with deep regret.

After a few moments, Treynen turned away from her. "Go. Your master will be missing you."

Without another word, Callia skirted around him and disappeared into the heavy rain.

As he watched her go, it took a great effort to stop himself going after her. To free her. He shook his head. He might free her, but not without a lot of bloodshed, and her being recaptured. It would have to wait.

***

King Julian won the war.

The mad king always seemed to know where the Plains Peoples' forces were, as if the *Starlance* itself were whispering secrets into his ear.

After eight long years of war and one of peace, Treynen finally found her again, intending to finally set her free. The directions had been very specific, but he had not expected to end up here.

A graveyard.

The graveyard wasn't far from his father's slave camp. Callia must've been recaptured by King Julian's ruthless armies and brought back to the camps around the lake.

Eventually, he found her tiny gravestone. "Here lies Callia, rebellious slave, dutiful mother, her daughters mourn her."

Treynen kneeled on the hard ground in the grass, tears blurring his vision. He wiped his eyes and picked a few flowers, laying them at her stone. He reread the message and took note of who had buried her.

Daughters, he thought with hope.

"Sir, are you okay?" a young man asked. Treynen looked at him and wordlessly picked up a spear and shield. He walked back to his horse and paid no attention to the dozens of pairs of eyes watching him.

"Company," he addressed the fifty cavalrymen at his disposal. "Mount and ready for travel." The sun shone brightly in the early morning, scattering rays through the misty landscape below the hill on which the graveyard was located. His steely gaze swept across the men and beyond, until he located a large group of dwellings near the frozen lake's edge, an hour's ride away. He took his helmet from his young page and put it back on his head.

"Callia," he whispered under his breath, "your daughters won't suffer anymore." He checked his equipment and made sure the spear was sharp. He mounted his horse and led the men away, ready to start a new war. Perhaps even end Julian's reign and the senseless mining of water ice in the deep lake. All for the sake of a slave his father once owned.

Date 2687

Lark, captain of the guard, followed his lord into the ash-encrusted landscape atop a chestnut stallion.

Lord Shayne the Nimble had decreed the village surrounding the castle be burned before the army of slaves reached it. Even now, a few fires still burned in the ruins.

The village and the castle were small, housing three hundred people who cowered within.

The clanking of armor and clatter of horseshoes rang loudly in Lark's ears as he, his lord, and three others in their little party marched down the dirt path. They moved toward the open plains beyond the ruins of the village.

To call Lord Shayne's guardsmen an elite honor guard was a laugh; Shayne the Nimble had next to no honor in his black heart, and the guards wore very little armor, with fewer weapons.

A conical helmet adorned Lark's head, and padded armor was tied to his chest and shins. A small circular wooden shield was strapped to his left hand, and he held a short spear in his right; the only other weapon he had was a dagger.

The others in the "honor guard" wore similar equipment, though Old Darry, a little over fifty summers, had a rusty great sword he carried over his shoulder. Lark doubted the old man could even raise the huge weapon, let alone use it while mounted on his gray-white palfrey.

Lim the Limp was a spirited man in their small party. Young he might be, but he was almost bald, with half a nose and a slight limp in his otherwise sure step. Lim's face was a sure winner to scare away stricken slaves, but he didn't have the skill to back it up.

Jonny, the final member of the guard, was the most experienced, though his sight was going, and he was almost as old as Darry. Of the four of them, Lark was the most able-bodied, with no major problems aside from a slight case of malnutrition and a scar running along the right side of his head from just above the ear to the eyebrow.

They were a sorry bunch, but the best the castle could offer, apart from Shayne the Nimble himself. Trained from birth as a capable warrior under the tutelage of King Julian himself, Shayne was quick with a long sword and did not shy from proving it, even on his own people. He had married into the title of Lord Over the Lake and brought all of his wealth with him: two silver pieces and three coppers. Fortunately, Lord Shayne also brought his giant black stallion, barding, plate mail, leathers, long spears, knives, and trusty long sword. This was all equipment that he now wore as he approached the dozen-strong party the slaves had sent for talks.

Lord Shayne also had a strange, white suit that he claimed was armor from the *Starlance* in the sky above. Since he never let any of the guardsmen into his bed chambers to see the suit, they had trouble believing him and decided it was just more of his mad ramblings.

The slave party was on foot, without any body armor. Apart from their leader, who wore a red-feathered helm and carried a large spear, they carried few weapons. The leader's horse waited patiently next to him. The slave party looked even worse than Lord Shayne's honor guard, which reinforced Lark's opinion of them being little more than beggars. The army sitting six hundred meters away from the slave party gave him pause for thought.

There must have been a thousand slaves at least, and even a few lightly armored horsemen. Lark recognized those horsemen; they were a part of Treynen the Bold's bodyguard. Had Treynen himself come to fight them? If so, then the so-called slave revolt wasn't so large as reports indicated. If Shayne the Nimble could hold the castle long enough for reinforcements, maybe the revolt could be crushed right here.

That assumed reinforcements came; none of the camp masters situated throughout the lake's wide edges thought much of Lord Shayne, heir to the colony.

"Halt," Lord Shayne held up a gauntleted hand to stop the party a few meters from the slave party's leader. Lark, Darry, Lim, and Jonny pulled up to either side of their lord, their spears pointed skyward. They watched the dozen slaves for any sign of trouble. When no trouble presented itself, Lord Shayne lowered his hand and moved his black steed toward the slave leader.

"When I heard there was a slave army marching toward the lake lands I had to laugh, but now I think I should be worried. Your army throws up a stink so powerful it could kill us all."

The man in the red-feathered helm grinned, and it was then Lark noticed the man's front teeth were all missing. Several other teeth were black as night, so rotten it looked as though they would fall out at any moment. Lord Shayne was right; Lark could smell the man's breath from several paces away, reeking of something unheard of. Lark's eyes watered and his lunch bubbled up to the back of his throat. He managed to keep the food down, if only for the sake of his horse, but it was an effort.

"Greetings, Lord Nimble," the slave leader said. "I have been ordered to take your castle, but I think we can both agree bloodshed is unnecessary."

Lord Shayne scoffed at that. "The only blood will be yours unless you piss off."

"Truly? Then I'll leave you our terms and retreat to my army."

Lark gripped his spear tightly. He didn't like it when his lord was in such a mood, and this slave wasn't making it better with his tone full of insolence.

"Fine, slave," Lord Shayne said. "Name your terms and then allow me to laugh."

The slave leader nodded and kept smiling as if he'd just been asked to dance by a beautiful young maid. "One, release your slaves and make an offer for any villagers in your castle to join us. Two, we require a tenth of your foodstuffs and all of your weapons. In return, none of your people will be harmed, and we might form an alliance."

Lord Shayne's laughter was deep and hearty, resounding within his enclosed helm. This was the high point of his day, but not for the slaves. Lark grew wary as many people in the slave party were looking at Lord Shayne with angry stares, with white knuckles gripping their pointed sticks and pitchforks.

"An alliance?" Lord Shayne asked before another short bout of laughter. "I have no slaves. Do you want to know why? Because I beheaded them all when I came here."

While Lord Shayne continued to laugh, the slave party's leader lost his confident smile and looked as angry as his guards. "Treynen will hear of this," the slave leader said, "and you will pay."

"I tell you what," Lord Shayne replied while closing his helm, "if you prefer to avoid bloodshed, why don't you face me in single combat? If you win, then you can have the bloody castle. If I win, then your people can sod off and get themselves killed on somebody else's land."

The slave leader frowned as he took in Lord Shayne's armor and weapons. "I may have been a slave working to dig up that alien monstrosity in the lake, but I'm not an idiot. Besides, my army needs me. But perhaps—"

"They need *you*? Good!" Lord Shayne pronounced. He reached for the hilt of his longsword, urged his horse onward, leaned forward in the saddle, and raked the blade from the right side of the slave leader's forehead to the left side of his chin, opening a deep gash in the middle of his face.

The slaves could only stare in shock. Used to Lord Shayne's actions and moods, Lark was able to react quickly enough to aid in Lord Shayne's defense. As the slave leader started to fall over screaming, clutching his bloodied face, Lark stirred to action. He lowered his short spear and kicked the flanks of his chestnut stallion. Distracted by the sudden brutality, the slaves didn't see Lark coming, and while his spear missed the first slave, his horse simply ran into the man, sending him flying.

The horse barely noticed the first man and bowled into the next slave, an unarmed middle-aged woman. She screamed and tried to move, but had her skull crushed when Lark's horse trod on top of her. Lark cringed; it was a great act of cowardice to slaughter an unarmed woman, but he reminded himself she had chosen to be here and probably would have killed Lark if given the chance.

It was then that the nine other slaves recovered enough to fight back. Four of them swarmed Lord Shayne's steed, and the other five went for Lark.

Lord Shayne flicked out with his longsword and two more slaves went down screaming. The others came at him and attacked with sharpened sticks that harmlessly glanced off Lord Shayne's gleaming armor.

Lark thrust his spear through the chest of a third slave, jarring his arm so badly he dropped the weapon as it lodged in the man's chest. He almost fell out of his saddle but continued riding, getting away from the other slaves who were waving inadequate weapons at him.

Old Darry and Lim the Limp spitted the four slaves from behind, while Jonny went to help their lord with the last two, but he needn't have bothered.

Shayne the Nimble was a cruel monster inside his castle; he was also a cruel monster on the battlefield, and the remaining slaves were killed by his lightning-fast longsword.

When Lark rejoined the small party, he was surprised he could hear laughter above the screams of the dying slaves. Blood spattered Lord Shayne's horse and legs, but his armor shone as bright as ever in the midafternoon sun.

Lark was breathing hard, and his right arm blazed with pain from the spear's impact. He looked at his arm and found a large splinter, a relic of his lost spear, had lodged itself in the middle of his palm, blood trickling down from the wound. "My lord," Lark called out, "perhaps we should leave."

Lord Shayne stopped laughing and turned in the saddle to look where Lark was pointing. Five hundred meters away, Treynen's cavalry was riding hard toward them. Slaves with bows followed at a run.

Beyond the cavalry and archers, the rest of the slave army seemed to groan in dismay—their chosen spokesman had been a popular fellow.

Lord Shayne nodded. "Very well, let's go, my loyal cowards." The five men headed back toward the burnt-out village at a steady trot, with Lord Shayne in the lead. Ash still fell from the sky and the wind carried smoke into Lark's face, making him cough. Once they were within easy archer range of the castle walls, Lord Shayne slowed their pace and shouted for the heavy wooden doors to open.

Lark was sickened by Lord Shayne's brash actions. The slave spokesman's terms might not have been the greatest, but there had been no reason to kill him. It was far too late now, and soon enough the slaves would try to attack the castle.

He doubted the slaves could take the small castle even with a thousand men—they had no siege equipment to batter down the heavy wooden doors or to scale the five-meter-high walls. Lord Shayne had ordered all food be brought within the walls, including thirty head of cattle and sixty or so sheep. Nevertheless, the castle held only fifty-three barely-trained soldiers.

Inside the castle, the smell was almost as bad as the slaves had smelled. A little over two hundred villagers occupied most of the courtyard with their cattle and sheep. There were no toilets, so the stench was worse than usual, though Lark thought he could cope.

Lim the Limp gagged when a sudden wind blew the stench in their faces. Lord Shayne laughed at him. "Beautiful smell, isn't it?"

Lim coughed. "Yes, my lord."

The five men navigated through the crowd of villagers toward the keep, where they dismounted and left their horses with the stable boys before going inside.

The keep itself was a simple affair: a stone building in the shape of a square, three stories high. The keep formed one corner of the castle's walls and was large enough to ensure nobody could assault it directly from outside the walls. The lord's cook, two apprentice cooks, a scribe, a doctor, three chambermaids, two stable boys, three children, two stepchildren, Lord Shayne's wife, and four guardsmen all resided within its walls.

While Lark and his fellow guards were fortunate to live in the keep, their living conditions weren't much better than the soldiers who manned the walls. He shared a tiny, windowless room with three hunting hounds and the stable boys. Lord Shayne had had a couple of squires a few years ago, but after he punished one of them by taking off his little finger, they both promptly fled the castle.

The five men entered the second story and stepped into the keep's large dining hall. "Sit," Lord Shayne ordered. He took off his helm and stood while his four guardsmen sat on the wooden benches at the single long, wooden table. Lark stripped off a piece of ragged cloth from his gray tunic and tried to bandage his right hand, taking care not to bump the large splinter still lodged in his palm.

"Bloody mongrel," Lord Shayne commented when he noticed Lark trying to bandage his hand. "Darry, fetch the doctor for our young captain." Darry nodded and walked quickly toward the third-story stairs. "Now, what are we going to do?" Lord Shayne asked as he looked at Lark.

"Ah, well, it looks like surrender is out of the question."

"No, you idiot, I meant about your hand. Can you still move all of your fingers?"

"Um," Lark tried moving his fingers. It was painful, but they all worked properly. "Yes, my lord."

"Good, Flit should be able to fix it up quickly enough. As for that rabble of slaves out there, either they'll give up and piss off, or I'll murder the lot of them myself. If they're stupid enough to stick around until my father arrives, then Lisa...I mean the *Starlance* will strike them down."

"But, my lord," Lim the Limp squeaked. "Garf said they were bringing ladders—big ones."

Lord Shayne regarded Lim with cool eyes and thought over Garf's report. Lord Shayne might have seemed like a big dumb brute to the villagers, but the guardsmen knew better. He was far smarter than any of them. Lord Shayne was the best fighter Lark had ever seen. And he seemed to know things that no one on this frozen planet could know, except for King Julian himself. "Science, physics, geology, geometry, metallurgy." Lark had overheard Lord Shayne utter these strange words to his children on numerous occasions. Whenever the guardsmen gathered together with their lord for talks like these, Lord Shayne always displayed a strange, eerie cunning in regard to politics, tactics, and strategies, to the point where none of them knew what he was talking about.

One thing was certain: they all recognized what he said was smart. Perhaps as smart as anything King Julian ever muttered. Lark had never seen the alien king, but from what he'd heard, Lord Shayne was quite similar in appearance and bearing.

Lark could see Shayne's intelligence working right then, his brow creasing as he plotted something new, something altogether dangerous, something alien, to counter the threat.

Finally, Lord Shayne smiled. "Ladders, is it? I'm surprised those sorry idiots out there even had the strength to make them, let alone carry them." His perfectly made armor started hissing as he paced down the large wooden table, the metal plates of the armor sliding across each other, smooth as silk. His footsteps echoed around the stone walls.

"It's a pity we didn't have a few machine guns," he said. When he saw the confused faces of his guardsmen he elaborated, "They're…really good cannons."

What's a cannon? Lark thought, but he didn't allow his confusion to show. Lord Shayne was not a patient man.

They heard the patter of feet coming down the stairwell and a moment later Old Darry appeared with Flit, the keep's doctor. Flit was a short man, not much taller than five feet, but he was strong, young, and fit. Lark had heard of doctors who let themselves gain weight or lose too much of it, let their teeth rot, even left uncombed. Who could trust a doctor to look after them if the doctor couldn't look after himself? It was the greatest hypocrisy in Lark's mind, and he hoped he would never have to be treated by one. Luckily, Flit was anything but hypocritical; he looked after himself well and even practiced swordplay when he had the time.

"Flit, take a look at my oh-so-bright captain of the guard, please," Lord Shayne said to the doctor. "I'm going to go talk to the captain of the watch, prepare him for the defense. As for the rest of you, I'm entrusting you with my household. Do not let anybody in or out of the keep unless I say so."

Lord Shayne's armor clanked as he exited the room, heading outside to talk with Craig, the castle's captain of the watch.

"Ouch," Lark said as Flit looked at his palm.

"Just hold still, Lark," Flit said in a neutral tone. There was no hostility between Lark and Flit, but there was no friendship either. Each was only doing their jobs and the sooner Flit could finish, the sooner Lark could concentrate on the keep's defense.

"Damn it!" Lark exclaimed as Flit pulled the big splinter out and proceeded to clean the wound. Flit ignored the remark and continued to work. "Lim, I'd like you to round up the lord's household."

"Sure thing, boss," Lim the Limp replied before hobbling off to find everyone who lived within the keep.

To Jonny and Old Darry, Lark asked, "Any suggestions?"

"Sure thing, Captain, let's go and hang ourselves. Save those slaves the trouble."

"Shut up, Darry," Jonny growled. "Give me that rusty old thing of yours, and I'll cut your head off myself."

Old Darry unhooked his rusty great sword from his sash and contemplated the blade as if wondering whether he should give it to Jonny.

"It does need the rust taken off it, doesn't it?" he carefully laid the old blade on the table. Lark sighed in relief; he could never tell when the two old men were being serious. Maybe Old Darry had meant it, but Lark didn't think he would go through with killing himself, by noose or blade.

"Now, young captain," Jonny said as he turned to Lark, "tell me what you saw out there. It was a blur to me."

Lark nodded. Having the keenest eyes, Lark was probably the only one who knew what they were facing, except perhaps for Garf who had first seen the army, and Lord Shayne, whose eyesight was on par with Lark's. "Garf was right; there are at least a thousand people out there.

They have about fifty archers and maybe thirty horse. I couldn't tell what armament the rest had, but probably just small knives and spears, maybe not even that. Could be sticks and stones they picked up from the road."

"Right, right," Old Darry said, leaning back on the long bench, "but they are dangerous."

"Dangerous? How?" Jonny scoffed at him. "They're nothing but a mob, and their bloody leader's head has been split in two. They'll scatter after the first bowshot."

"I don't think so," Lark said. "Treynen's bodyguards are seasoned veterans, and you can bet the leader of those cavalrymen has now taken over. They are better equipped than we are, and those slaves *will* fight. This particular group of slaves has sacked a couple of forts already, and now they're after Shayne the Nimble's castle."

"You're talking about a couple of forts with a total of eight archers," Jonny reminded them. "Hardly an achievement."

"A test only," Old Darry said, raising a finger to silence Jonny. "Those forts were only sacked to give the slaves a bit of experience. If they were eager enough to rebel, they're eager enough to die. They will come, and we'll have to fight."

"You're assuming they can get past the watchmen on the walls," Flit said while bandaging Lark's hand. The three guardsmen looked at the doctor and each other, thinking the doctor was a fool. "What?" Flit asked them.

"Nothing," Lark said, "but just in case the slaves manage to get into the keep, we need to be prepared. Jonny, how many crossbows do we have in the cellars?"

"Those old things?" Jonny rubbed his chin thinking about it. "Thirty or so, I'd say. But if anyone's going to use them, Craig will."

"Maybe, maybe not," Lark said. "Craig never did like crossbows. I can't see him taking them up now. Most of those things are probably too old, anyway. It's been, what? Twenty years since they've been down there?"

"Yeah, sounds about right. Can't imagine many of them old things working. The moisture down there ruins everything after a while, would have turned old rusty here to dust in ten years." Darry patted his sword.

"Darry, I'd like you to go and look at them, see if any of them look good enough to use."

"Yep, fine, boss, just don't expect me to survive. My old bones might break any moment now." Lark ignored his words but watched him head toward the stairwell, his great sword once again slung across his back.

Lim the Limp came down the stairs, nodded at Old Darry as he passed, and came toward Lark. "Captain, the lady of the house says she'll bring everyone down in a few moments."

Lark acknowledged the news with a grunt.

"So, Captain," Jonny growled at Lark. "What bright idea have you got this time?"

"There you go," Flit interrupted them. "Be careful with it."

"Thanks, Flit," Lark said. "Now if you have some food?"

Flit shook his head. "Sorry, Lark, maybe next time."

"Oh, well," Lark said in defeat. "Guess I'll just starve a little more." Flit nodded and headed back to the stairwell, mentioning something about one of Lord Shayne's children needing a fix.

"You'd probably just throw it back up," Jonny said. "Food is wasted on you young fools. Now, I asked a question, young man, please answer it. What's the bright idea? You're usually full of them."

"I don't like that tone, Jonny," Lark replied. Lim looked at the two men, worry crossing his face.

"Please?" Jonny asked sarcastically.

"Well now, that's better," Lark replied with cheer. "As for what I'm planning…"

***

The slaves didn't wait, didn't bother trying to starve the defenders out. They attacked *en masse* as soon as night fell. Screams and bellows could be heard all night long.

Stone cracked; wooden gates crashed.

Spears battered at shields and flesh.

Arrows whistled over the battlements, and orders were shouted to the heavens.

Barricaded inside the keep, Lark thought he could have handled the sounds of battle, even the screams and death gurgles of women and children, as he had heard such things before.

But there was a noise far worse out there.

Lord Shayne's laughter could be heard above all other sounds of battle. His laughter was not that of a sane man, but of one possessed. He cackled with delight as he speared a dozen slaves clambering up their ladders before switching to his deadly long sword for closer killing.

And Lord Shayne kept laughing, almost all night long. At one point Lark cast a glance over the room full of the fearful and sullen faces of Lord Shayne's family and servants. Amongst them, the lady of the house, Lord Shayne's wife, was smiling, as if she were as delighted with Shayne's fun as Shayne himself.

Near dawn Lark couldn't resist. He had to take a look.

He quietly unchained the flimsy wooden doors and opened them just wide enough to peek outside. He could have gone upstairs to get a proper view, but he needed to stay with the keep's people, lest they panicked. He didn't trust his men not to panic.

Lark glimpsed shadows. There were many shadows, all moving quickly. Curiously, the shadows were headed for a central location on top of the castle walls, silhouetted against the rising sun. Above them all, his sword flashing, his body-covered head to toe in blood, was Shayne the Nimble.

Lark had never seen his lord move with so much savage grace. He knew Shayne was a quick brute, but after fighting all night long he seemed to have increased in ferocity and speed. With every stroke, he killed, and if the slaves didn't attack him, he would chase them about the ramparts until he cornered them and hacked them to bloody pulps.

The man was an army unto himself. It was enough that Lark held on to the hope Lord Shayne could hold off the hordes of frenzied slaves by himself.

Somebody on horseback entered the courtyard through the shattered castle gates, shouting orders. Lark recognized the man as the captain of

Treynen's bodyguard. A dozen archers followed in his wake, quickly strung their bows, aimed, and loosed.

"Ahahaha, come back here! Mwahahaha—ah, huh? HUH? Aaaarrrggghhh!" The sudden volley of arrows surprised Lord Shayne. Caught off guard, a single arrow hit him in the head—it wasn't sufficient to kill him, nor could it hurt him through his metal helm, but it did stun him for a second.

He'd been running headlong at a cowering, half-naked child. The child held a small knife, raised as if it would fend off the insane lord's notched blade.

Lord Shayne, stunned by the arrow, tripped over one of the bodies piled up on the castle walls. As he tried to right himself, he found the stone under his feet was slippery from the blood and he fell off the side, headfirst onto the blood-soaked ground below. Lark, along with Shayne's household, heard a loud, sickening crunch.

Shayne the Nimble's head pointed at an unnatural angle and his legs twitched.

Lark closed the keep's doors, rechained them, and then braced them with half a dozen old spears.

"Quickly, everyone, get down on the ground," he told the assembled people. They didn't have to be told twice. Scared half to death, they sat on the cold stone floor; some kneeling with faces looking at the ground, others sitting cross-legged or on their sides, almost lying on top of each other. Several of them, especially the children, were too afraid to do anything, and the putrid smell of urine wafted its way through the keep's cozy confines.

"Open up or we'll burn you out," a man on the other side of the door shouted at them, then banged on the flimsy doors, rattling the chains and spears that kept them closed.

Lord Shayne's oldest boy started crying. The lady of the keep, Celeste, shushed at him to no avail.

"Open up, or the children burn," the man on the other side of the door yelled again. The rest of the children cried and squealed in fear.

Lark frowned while looking over the small crowd, making sure his men and the servants were ready for what came next.

"Ready?" Lark asked Jonny and Darry, who had taken up positions near the wooden door.

"What are you doing?" Celeste asked, her eyes fierce.

"Just keep to the plan," Lark replied. She looked at him with distrust but remained quiet, a single tear rolling down her cheek for the man who had been her husband.

"I'm opening the door," Lark shouted at the man on the other side of the door.

"Good. Hurry up about it." Lark unchained and unbarred the door, letting it swing open a fraction before the man on the other side kicked at it. Lark jumped out of the way and quickly made his way to the back of the keep, behind the kneeling and prone people.

The man from the other side of the door, the cavalry commander, made his way inside, followed by a dozen heavily armed cavalrymen. The room had become much more crowded, leaving little room for anyone to move.

"Hold it, don't kill them," the cavalry leader told his troops. "We are not the monsters here."

"So says the man who threatened to burn down my castle with my children inside," Celeste said.

"Seize her," the cavalry leader pointed at the lady.

Lark nodded at Darry and Jonny, hidden in small alcoves near the keep's door.

"What?" the leader managed to say when he saw Lark's nod. A second later, Darry's great sword had sliced a cavalryman's head off.

The lady and her closest servants opened their skirts and pulled out the crossbows that had been hiding there. They aimed and pulled the triggers. At this range, it was hard to miss.

Soldiers screamed. A crossbow bolt found the leader's neck, and he went down. Jonny stabbed a soldier in the leg.

Just when Lark thought the plan was going to work and Jonny was about to close the door, Lim the Limp suddenly sprouted an arrow from his chest.

Surprised by the arrow that flew past his nose, Jonny hesitated. A former slave barged into the keep, and stabbed Jonny in the ear with a sharpened spoon.

More former slaves piled into the small room. Darry swung his great sword several more times, carving through meat and bones. One former slave, her arm lopped off close to the shoulder, fell onto Darry, knocking him over.

Slaves and soldiers started killing the household staff at random, using little more than bare hands around small necks.

"Come on, Celeste," Lark yelled. He pulled at her hand, but she would not budge, clutching one of her dead children and screaming in despair. She turned and screamed at Lark, then flicked her hand out of his grip before grabbing a spare crossbow bolt and jumping into the melee, her child still in her hand.

"Uh." Lark took in the scene for a brief moment and then made for the stairwell. An arrow nicked his ear, and he almost tripped. Flit clutched at his stomach where an arrow had hit him. Lark turned away from him. "Not me, not me," he repeated to himself. "Slaves aren't getting my blood. Not today."

Adrenaline gave his legs springs. He saw the world in flashes of light and color as he sprinted to the top floor, barely registering the mad dash and the slaughter taking place on the ground floor.

Lord Shayne's room was the last one left. The door was heavy, and Lark fumbled with the keys. He didn't know where he'd picked up the keys. He may have snatched them from Celeste's neck. All he knew was salvation waited inside that room, at least for a few more minutes.

He heard footsteps and angry voices coming up the stairs and almost dropped the key but slotted it into the hole on the third try and turned. A loud click reverberated around the cold stone walls and the heavy door opened.

He'd never been inside the lord and lady's private chambers, so what he saw stopped him from entering. He stared for several long seconds at the pure white walls, golden furniture and blinking lights.

"Get him," a scratchy voice shocked him back into action. A cavalryman pointed a dagger at him from the top of the stairs. Several former slaves sidled past the cavalryman, murder in their eyes and pointy sticks in their hands.

"Not me," Lark yelled at them before hopping into the strange room. He jammed the heavy door shut. As soon as he had locked it, the door started rattling with loud bangs.

Lark backed away from the door. He kept his distance from the strange, blinking lights, and then noticed the small fireplace and odd suit of armor above it.

"Oh, that must be the weird armor," Lark said as he recalled Lord Shayne's strange armor that he had brought with him all those years ago. It looked like little more than white cloth.

"Why didn't Shayne wear this thing?" He reached out with a shaking hand to touch the armor but quickly withdrew when the banging on the wooden door got louder.

Whatever the former slaves were doing, it was working. Splinters started appearing on the door's surface.

Lark crouched near the fire underneath the strange armor, sword in hand, his other hand covering his eyes as if he were afraid to see what would come through the door.

"Help?" he said in a childish voice, his eyes watering. He'd been such a coward, abandoning the lady and her children like that. He just…he wanted to live. "Help, mother?" he called in vain to his dead mother. "Help me, *Starlance*," he called out to the mysterious lance in the sky.

"Human in distress, Sally has been activated," an odd, feminine voice said from above him. Lark jumped in fright.

"Do not be alarmed," the strange suit said as it unlatched itself from ropes on the wall. "I am a safety suit. You may call me Sally. I heard your cries for help."

"H-h-how?" Lark asked. He backed away from the living suit toward the banging door.

"If you're wondering how I have been reactivated after thirty-three years, it appears as though the fire I am currently standing in has recharged my power cells, though they are only at twenty-two percent. Normally little Shayne would have used a crank to get my cells charged up. Perhaps he did not need my services? In any case, you were in distress, so I booted up. Tell me, where is little Shayne? It seems he may need some assistance?"

The suit sounded like Lark's mother, its voice full of concern.

"Um." A piece of wood shattered inward, opening a long hole in the door where Lark could see a slave wielding a giant hammer.

"Please answer," the suit insisted. The head of the suit, where a helmet should be, was covered by a dark, reflective dome. Inside the dome, he could barely make out more blinking lights, just like the blinking lights he saw near the lord and lady's bed.

The hammer crashed against the door again, sending more splinters flying into the room. "Err, uh, he's dead. Those people killed him," he said as he pointed a finger at the door, and the slaves and cavalrymen beyond.

"Oh, I see," the suit seemed to deflate a little and tilted forward as if looking at the carpeted floor with sadness. After another bang on the door, it straightened up again.

"And has the Eden been excavated yet? Has Jules completed his task, at least?"

"Eden?"

"The Eden in the frozen lake. Has the ice been cleared yet? Or was my Julian unable to finish?"

"Oh, you mean the Buried Tower? The way was almost cleared when the slaves began rebelling."

The suit sighed. "I warned Jules he shouldn't have used slaves. I taught him better than that. Never mind, they were the quickest option, what with you fools being so warlike and primitive. Seriously, how does a colony fall so far after only two hundred years?" The banging on the door continued. "Really? This is medieval reenactment gone mad. Anyway, what is your name?"

"Lark. It's Lark." He moved toward the ghostly suit, away from the pounding on the door.

"An odd name. Do you need assistance, Lark?"

"Yes," he replied.

"How may I assist?"

"Help me kill those people and get me out of here."

"That could be done," the suit said. "Hop inside." The suit peeled down its middle.

The wooden door crashed open. He would have died except the first slave through the door stopped in amazement. Fear crept into the slave's face when he noticed the suit.

Lark stepped into the suit and immediately felt claustrophobic as it closed around him. He wore it like a normal suit of armor, but this one seemed to hug him with squishy gel. The helmet, while dark on the outside was entirely clear from the inside and he watched as the room filled with slaves and soldiers, who all stared at the white walls and blinking lights.

The suit started moving, turning around, dragging Lark's limbs with it as if he were a puppet. He watched with his mouth ajar as claws sprouted from the white suit's fingers.

"This is for little Shayne," he heard the suit say to the attackers. The suit's voice was menacing, having dropped a couple of octaves. It charged at the hapless slaves and cavalrymen, forcing Lark to move with it.

Those brave few who tried to cut or hit the suit found it was far tougher than it looked. They soon died, clutching throats or looking dumbfounded at new holes in their chests where the suit punched them.

"Run!" The shout echoed throughout the keep.

"Take my Shayne from me, will you?" the suit said as it chased down fear-stricken men and women, snuffing out their lives with the barest of touches.

"There you are, my poor Shayne," the suit said. She knelt beside Lord Shayne's body. The slaves had stripped him of his armor and stabbed his body a few more times. "Look what they did to you."

Fires burned and people streamed out of the castle walls, desperate to escape the ghostly suit's attentions. "Shh, it's okay now. They won't get far," she told Shayne's lifeless body.

"Uh, Sally? What are you doing?" Lark asked when the suit stood up after inspecting Shayne's body.

"I recorded the heat signatures of everyone in the area. I'm going to hunt them down and kill them."

"All of them?" Lark asked, worried he would be trapped inside the suit while the slaughter took place.

"They all contributed to my grandson's death. Don't worry, Lark, you're safe with me now."

Oh no, Lark thought as the suit ran out of the castle walls. He looked to the sky and saw the *Starlance*. It shone as if it had been lit on fire.

"It's time we got the repair plans back on track." Hundreds of ghostly red dots lit up the translucent helmet's surface. The dots were all moving away from the castle. They appeared to be in the shape of distant people, running for their lives in wooded areas around the lake's edges. "Ready or not, here we come."

Date: 2802

"Junk," the museum's new curator said. He tossed a silver goblet to the ice-covered floor and watched some ice shards scatter on impact. The man's snow-slicked white beard and scruffy black hair were hidden under a thick red-and-gold robe. The head curator, far younger than his wizened face would suggest, sniffed at his runny nose and rubbed frozen hands together before tucking them back into his robe's sleeves.

Assistant Curator Paul, fiery torch in one hand and frozen scroll in the other, followed the new head curator to the next exhibit. The new curator had been appointed to the King Julian Memorial Museum six weeks earlier, but this was the first time Paul had met the man or seen him within the museum's grounds. He stunk like rotting wood and his black teeth marked him as a black root drinker from the Buried Tower.

Far from the comforts of the Buried Tower, Head Curator Joseph was quick to complain and quicker to kick things.

The two of them moved down the icy hallway, past an ice sculpture, until they reached several old digging tools. "What's this?" He read the inscription. "'Tools from the Buried Tower Excavations as ordered by King Julian.' Pieces of junk," he kicked the tools and watched them clatter to the floor. "Show me another *Starlance* artifact, boy, and hurry up. This cold will be the death of me if you dawdle behind me much longer."

"Sorry," Paul mumbled and walked a little faster to guide Curator Joseph to the next piece.

"So you should be. Black stars it's cold in here. Wave that fiery stick a little closer, would you? That's better, just watch the beard. Twenty years ago, the place never would have gotten so cold, not when the *Starlance* still had its shield shining on us. And to think, it's midday and it must be below zero inside the museum. Bring that damn stick closer. So, come on boy, where's the next one?" Paul rolled his eyes.

Paul did his best to push through the museum's internal blizzards of loose snow and to keep the torch from burning Joseph's beard. He yearned to be back at his desk near the museum's hearth, surrounded by his books, his scrolls, and the fun bickering that often occurred between the other assistant curators. But even that would be marred by Joseph's entourage of overbearing attendants.

It wasn't often the museum had visitors. Most people stayed within the lakeside towers or in their interconnected stone huts in the surrounding villages, not wanting to brave the frozen days and colder nights. He'd heard about the *Starlance*'s shield and had once seen a pot of grass, but the cold was all he'd ever known.

Supposedly the *Starlance* was a ship suspended in the sky, one sent by the twins known as Terra and Isa to fix the Buried Tower, without success.

"Here it is," Paul told him.

Curator Joseph plucked a small metal cube from its stone pedestal with one spindly hand and inspected it. He grimaced and dropped it before rubbing his hands together again. "What the hell is it? Where's the inscription?" He looked around the pedestal for a description of the item.

Paul didn't bother opening the scroll he held in his other hand. He knew what the box was. "This is King Julian's Antikythera Mechanism," he explained. "It's lost its crank, but it used to tell the king when the shield would shine brightest and where to find the Buried Tower, among other things."

Curator Joseph's eyes opened a little wider. "Ah, this is the box? It's so…small." He fished in his robes for a pair of glasses and put them on to try to read the tiny writing on the metal cube's sides. "Good. Take it with care, mind you; I'll need to inspect it more closely in the office."

"Take it?" Paul stuttered. He'd never taken an artifact from its place without the proper paperwork before.

Joseph turned black eyes on the younger man, and Paul wanted to find somewhere to hide from his gaze. "Are you deaf or daft, boy? Yes, take the blasted thing and show me the next one."

Paul did as he was told. He put the scroll and torch down for a moment and reached inside his blue robes for one of his thick gloves. He picked up the metal box and dropped it inside the glove, then tied it to the belt of his robes.

"Hurry up."

"Sorry, sir. There's just one more item in this wing of the museum."

"Fine, let's get to it and get back to the fire."

Paul took the curator into a room adjacent to the frozen hall, where the final item remained.

"Sir?"

"Hmm, what is it?"

"Uh, why do you need these things?"

"Haven't you been listening, boy?" He took a deep breath, as if stifling a curse. "Oh, but of course you wouldn't know, would you?"

Paul gave Curator Joseph a blank stare.

"I thought not. Too young and too dumb. The world is dying and has been for some time now. That *Starlance* up there? It was supposed to fix all this, to fix the Buried Tower, and bring the world back to life."

"Oh, that. I'd heard those stories before."

"You should have! Working in King Julian's museum, of course you should know it."

"Well, anyway, here it is," Paul said. He waved the torch toward the crumpled white cloth that represented an ancient suit of armor. It was laid out flat on a stone bench. Covered in snow and ice crystals, the armor may as well have been a bed cloth.

"Please explain, all I see is a mess of white crap."

Keeping his hands within the sleeves of his robe and tucking the scroll inside his belt, Paul leaned over the stone bed and swept away the snow and ice, doing his best to clear enough of it so the suit's shape was visible.

"There," he said. "It's a set of armor. The old texts state that it was King Julian's armor and was passed on to his son, Lord Shayne. Using this suit, Lord Shayne's chief guardsman, Lark the Brave, single-handedly halted the Excavator Slave's Rebellion."

"*This*?" Curator Joseph asked, sounding annoyed. "This is the hero's armor? What a load of piss. It's nothing but a hard-white cloth." He pulled at the armor's leg and a slim covering of ice cracked at the touch. The white armor crumpled under the curator's feather-weight fingers. "See? Nothing but fabric. It's a forgery, boy. Burn it."

"Sir?" Burning one of the museum's irreplaceable artifacts was unthinkable.

"I said burn it. Bring it back to the hearth and do it now."

"But—"

"Shut up and do it, or see your rations halved." Paul's mouth clamped shut and went dry. The curator's black gaze held on to him until he nodded. "Good, now give me the torch."

He passed the torch to the older man, who snatched it from his fingers. The curator then turned toward the hallway and marched himself out of the room, back to the museum's offices. Paul was left in the darkness of the museum's heavy stone walls and ice-covered carpets.

He took the spare glove out of his robes and put it on. He then got to work clearing the stone table enough that he could drag the white suit back to the hearth.

"Old bastard," he muttered.

The suit was heavier than cloth but lighter than metal, and he slipped over the icy floor a few times as he dragged it. He prayed the *Starlance* didn't try to strike him down for mistreating its gift. He swore each time his face grazed the floor's surface, and he had to scramble to get back onto his feet.

He decided the new head curator wouldn't know what hit him when he finally got back to the hearth. At least he *wanted* to hurt the older man. More likely he'd just glare at him.

The moment he entered the main office, he felt the warm glow of the hearth bathe his frozen face. The heat seemed to burn his exposed skin. Several other assistant curators were sitting at their desks, poring over pieces of paper or artifacts from the first landings. They all looked up from their work and stared at him, worried expressions on their faces.

Half a dozen of the head curator's black-clad guardsmen entered the room and walked around the desks, making sure the curators were doing their work.

One of the guardsmen, shiny plate armor poking through his black overcoat, stomped his way through several piles of books to stand by Paul's side. His red beard and orange hair made it seem the guardsman was on fire. He crossed his arms and watched as Paul dragged the white suit toward the hearth.

"A little help?" Paul asked the guard.

"Birch, be a good man and help the boy, would you?" the head curator's voice carried from his padded chair next to the hearth.

Birch grunted his acknowledgment of the order and grabbed the suit by its legs. Together, they moved the suit to the edge of the hearth and tossed it onto the large fire. Flames licked at Paul's face, and he had to retreat.

He coughed from the smoke and then stood next to the head curator's high-backed chair. Curator Joseph ignored him and continued reading from a scroll he had in his hands. After a moment of silence, he rolled up the scroll and tossed it into the fire.

Paul couldn't help but make a small sound in protest.

Joseph gave him an amused look. "Don't worry, Assistant Paul, tax records aren't going to save us, but they will help the fire a little. Now, the metal cube?" He opened one of his warmed-up hands in anticipation.

Paul grabbed for the glove tied to his belt. It wasn't there. "Sorry, sir, I must've dropped it."

Joseph's mouth, which had been straining to maintain its upward curve, quickly dropped. "Well then," his voice fell almost to a whisper, "you'd better go find it."

"Yes, sir, sorry!"

"Just hurry up. Birch, go with him."

Birch groaned but followed Paul back into the cold.

It didn't take long to find the glove in the center of the grand hall of the museum's east wing, next to some kicked-over tools. Relieved, Paul hurried back, guardsman in tow.

"Wait," Birch said in a much softer voice than Paul expected from the big man. He grabbed Paul by the shoulder to stop him from moving closer to the offices. "Listen. Something's not right."

Paul did as he was told. It wasn't like he had a choice.

They heard muffled gasps and someone shouting. Rapid footsteps approached. Paul easily identified the footsteps as Buried Tower-made boots. A moment later a guardsman appeared at the entrance and, wide-eyed, half-ran half-slid across the hall's floor.

"Donald?" Birch asked his colleague.

Donald didn't reply. He didn't look at Paul or Birch as he swept past, his face turning white and mist spraying wildly from his mouth with every breath.

"Donald?" Birch shouted after the man. Donald disappeared into the museum's dark halls without a word.

Paul and Birch exchanged worried looks. Birch let go of Paul's shoulder and pulled a knife from his belt. He stalked toward the museum's main office. Paul shoved his freezing hands inside his sleeves and followed the big guardsman, afraid but curious.

They reached the main office archway, and Birch stopped at its edge, hugging the wall and peering inside. Paul slid up next to him and looked into the main office under Birch's elbow. He gasped at what he saw, and Birch clamped a cold hand over his mouth to keep him quiet.

Curators stood or sat at their desks in stunned silence. Guardsmen, their knives and batons drawn, were standing around Joseph's chair, staring into the fire. A dozen or so people were risking their necks to take a look at what was happening inside the main office from other doors that led to various hallways and offices.

"What are you doing?" a strange, feminine voice echoed throughout the room from inside the hearth.

"A ghost," Birch whispered.

"The suit speaks," one of the curators said.

In the center of the hearth, the suit of *Starlance* armor stood like a ghostly angel.

Or a demon, Paul thought.

"What has happened to the world?" the suit said again. "Where am I?"

Curator Joseph cleared his throat. "Uh…this is…you're in the King Julian Memorial Museum."

"Memorial? Then my Jules is dead. Long dead. So sad. Tell me, man in the chair, why have I woken in this fire, was it to recharge my energy cells?"

"Err, yes, mighty suit, to charge your…err."

The suit tilted its head downward, fixing the head curator squarely in its vision. "My energy cells, I believe, is what you're trying to say. You're lying. Can we assume, then, that you tossed me within the center of this wonderful conflagration to try to burn me as fuel?"

"I…um…" The head curator made to stand up, but his legs were too wobbly to support him.

"You would destroy the repair plans contained in my circuitry, would you?" the suit asked, as calm as a soft breeze.

"Th-the plans?" Joseph stammered.

"You have no idea what the plans are, do you? I see. Then the plans have clearly failed, and the rebellion has won. This is quite unfortunate." Claw-like blades extended from each of the suit's fingertips, glowing white, hotter than the flames within which the suit stood.

"No!" The head curator squeaked before the suit leapt from the flames and fell on top of him. Joseph dropped a scroll from one hand and the chilly red wine he'd been sipping from the other.

The wine spilled onto the soft brown rug his chair rested on, and blood covered everything else. Glistening guts were tossed across the room as the avenging suit claimed its first victim.

The guardsmen standing behind the chair rushed forward, trying to stab and bludgeon the suit. The faceless suit turned its body to face one of the men and slashed its blades across his unarmored neck.

"Hold it down!"

"It's too strong!"

Screams erupted from the curators at the desks and surrounding office rooms.

Birch, still standing at the doorway, twiddled his knife between his hands, paralyzed by fear. He started forward after another guardsman fell to the ground with a bloody gash in his leg but stopped when Paul grabbed his plate armor from behind.

"No, we have to run."

Birch turned to face Paul and tried to shove him away. Paul held on to the plate as if his cold fingers were stuck to it.

"Let go, my friends are dying."

"So will you. That armor could kill a thousand of you. We have to run."

Two more guardsmen fell to the floor and some assistant curators made their way to the doors, jostling with each other and pushing priceless wooden desks over. The suit leapt on top of one of the assistants and plunged a clawed fist through her spine.

"Come on," Paul shouted at the bigger man and started running.

Birch took one last look at the carnage near the hearth and ran after Paul, toward the museum's east wing. "Is there a way out?"

"Yes, this way," Paul said between breaths.

"How?"

"Old service doors, where the snow keeps getting in."

More screams echoed from the office area, and Birch started into a full run. He held Paul's sleeve and practically dragged him along behind him. A couple of curators, more sure-footed than Paul or Birch, ran past them.

"Which way?"

"Follow them," Paul said.

Birch jumped over some scattered work tools, and Paul stumbled through them, hitting his feet on their rusted edges. His agonized protests were cut short when a bloody body flew past the two of them and slid along the ground toward the east wing's far wall near the faster curators.

Surprised by the flying corpse, Birch slipped and sprawled along the floor, taking Paul down with him. Paul hardly noticed the white shape of the suit jump over them and charge toward the fleeing curators.

"No-no-no," a panicked curator said when she noticed the still-sliding body of one of their friends.

Paul looked up to see the ghostly suit tap-tap-tap on light, fast boots across the icy floor. The suit's run ended when it impaled the hapless curators on its claws. Its momentum slammed the three of them into the hallway's far wall.

"Shit," Birch said as he got back onto his feet.

Another curator ran past them, stopping dead when he noticed the bloodbath at the east wing's far wall. "Oh," he uttered.

The white suit twisted to track the fresh meat.

While the suit was busy extracting its bloody claws from its victims, Birch hauled Paul onto his feet. "Get us out of here."

"O-okay, this way." Adrenaline surged through Paul's legs. The two of them headed back up the hallway toward the offices and the hearth. Another guard and a curator's aide fled the other way, into the jaws of death. Neither of them seemed to hear Birch's warnings.

They reached the offices, but a heavy metal grate had been lowered in its place. "No," Paul said and crashed into the grate.

Birch pulled Paul from the grate and stared through it to the bloody room. "Where did this come from?"

"I don't know."

Birch threw his weight at the metal grate. It didn't budge.

More metal grates had been lowered to block the other doorways within the offices, and people were crying or screaming, trapped.

"Run!" Paul heard someone behind them. The guardsman who hadn't heard Birch's warnings was sprinting from one side of the corridor behind them to the other, followed closely by the aide. And the suit.

Birch hit the metal grate even harder. It didn't budge.

"We have to hide," Paul said.

"Where?"

Paul searched his memories of the museum's layout. There was an old underground carriage tunnel used for moving some larger artifacts. The entrance to the tunnels was down the corridor to their right.

"Hurry." Paul headed for the doorway. As he reached it, they heard gurgling coming from the hall at the end of the corridor. "It's close," Paul whispered. He led Birch through a room filled with incredibly light

Starlance foils covering the walls. Paul moved across the room toward a curtain. He brushed it aside and moved into the storeroom.

Wooden boxes full of more lightweight sheets lined the room's walls. Paul started pulling them down. Seeing what Paul was doing, Birch pushed him aside and grabbed two of the bottom boxes before pulling the whole stack down on top of himself.

"Thanks, but shut up," Paul told him. While Birch removed the boxes, Paul moved to the wooden door hidden behind the boxes.

He tried the doorknob; it was unlocked. Steps led downward into the darkness. He went inside and Birch followed, staying as quiet as they could while the sounds of massacre reverberated around the walls.

Birch closed the door behind them, and darkness reigned.

Feeling the cold walls and moving with care down the steps, Paul grew more concerned as the darkness continued. The tunnels were large, with many entrances and exits to the museum. With so much space in and out of the carriageway, where was the light? Where was the air?

His hands touched something hard where it shouldn't have been

"Uh, not good."

"What is it?" Birch hissed from the steps above.

"Ice." He pressed against the hard obstruction in front of him, testing it. He pressed harder, trying to break through. "It's solid."

Birch patted around the walls until he found the ice. He pushed it, and then Paul heard him slamming an open palm against it.

"Ouch. Must be a meter thick, at least."

"Could you use your knife to break it?"

"No, I...Wait. Shh." Birch felt around in the darkness and grabbed Paul by the mouth, keeping him quiet.

They listened.

They heard slow footfalls on the icy floor of the corridor. They must have been heavy boots to be so loud, and for a moment Paul gained a fraction of hope in his beating heart. The suit was too light to make such heavy footfalls.

Then they heard the metal grate barring the offices from the corridor crashing to the floor.

The warbling sounds of the suit's feminine voice reached them a moment later. "Here, kitty, kitty, kitty. I see where you ran. Come out, come out, children." The voice faded into the distance.

"Not good," Paul said.

"Not good at all." Birch took out his knife and started hacking at the wall of ice, spraying shards across Paul's face.

Paul shielded his face from the ice and felt his way back up to the top of the short staircase. Faint light shone through small cracks in the wooden door, and he pressed his head against it, trying to see between the cracks or listen for more footfalls.

He heard more than he wanted to.

Birch, oblivious to the sounds within the museum, hacked nonstop at the ice. Paul, not feeling the cold, started shivering. His hands shook and his eyes widened.

Bodies thudded and bones snapped. Things, innocent things, were squished and the muffled cries of the living brought tears to Paul's eyes. He heard running, crying, screaming, and more thudding.

Chip-chip-chip. Birch kept hacking at the ice and grunted with every hit.

A few minutes later, the only sounds Paul could hear were the hacking and grunting of the guardsman.

"Birch, stop," Paul called to him. The big man kept hacking at the ice.

Paul heard heavy footsteps coming from the corridor. "Stop," he hissed.

Birch heard him this time. He stopped hacking at the wall, and Paul thought he could see the man's white eyes and fiery hair. Birch reached the top of the stairs and moved Paul to the side so he could listen.

Paul strained to hear as well. Silence followed for several heartbeats.

Thunk.

Both men jumped. Something heavy had landed on the other side of the wooden door.

"Hello, little kitties."

Paul's breath caught in his throat.

Claws pierced the wooden door's apparently flimsy panels. The suit ripped the door off its hinges. Paul and Birch covered their eyes from the burst of light and shattering wood. Still blind from the light, Birch ran forward with his knife ready to attack.

"Hehehe," the suit giggled and tossed the guardsman to the side. It moved closer to him with inhuman speed.

"Don't kill us," Paul yelled at the suit.

The suit stopped, claws poised above Birch's neck. Its empty helmet turned to look at Paul. "Why, little kitten, would I? You are all doomed to die anyway." The suit slashed across Birch's face and ran straight at Paul, who fell backward down the stairs.

He hit the ice wall and desperately searched for something to defend himself with. When he looked up to see where the suit was, he saw only white and felt a needle pierce his chest.

"Oh, what is this?" the suit asked.

Paul, feeling nothing but the bloody needle of a claw in his chest, barely registered the suit's question. His arms, outstretched to try to stop it from killing him, held a random assortment of objects as ineffectual shields.

With its free hand, the suit grabbed Paul's arm, the one holding his spare glove.

"Ah, it's the box. Well, isn't this a surprise? You stupid meat bags kept the box after all these years. Hmm, does that mean you have uncovered the Eden?"

"An Eden?" Paul managed to ask. He tasted blood that had welled up from within his throat. "What's…"

"An Eden. A great tower buried under the ice, one that was damaged long ago."

"The-the Buried Tower?"

"Yes. You know it? Then, if you know it, why is the world frozen? Oh." The suit eased itself off of him. "I've made such a mistake. Of course, my Jules was dead by the time the tower was finally uncovered. Those blasted rebels killed his only son and family. And now? Nobody knows the box's codes."

"The curator. Wanted it." Paul felt the strength leaving his arms, and the blood in his throat made him gurgle.

"The curator? Was he that first fellow I killed when I woke up? Oh dear, I've made a real mistake, haven't I? Well, I do so apologize. Perhaps…well, it's not too late to access the Eden's fuel stores."

Paul's head tilted to the floor.

"Indeed, it's not too late at all," the suit continued talking and withdrew its claw from Paul's dead heart. "Oh, but the emergency ignition codes are on the ship in orbit, and dear mother Lisa isn't speaking to me."

Paul's eyes closed for the last time, and the suit moved to deal with Birch.

***

Birch winced as he touched the white bandage covering his face.

"The Tower," he said to himself. "Gotta get to the tower." He stepped out of the museum's broken doors to the waiting snow. The metal cube, strapped to his belt, dangled against his bruised thighs.

"Remember, Birch, your people must reach the *Starlance*," the white ghost repeated to him.

"*Starlance*. Gotta get to the *Starlance*."

"Good. Let's keep moving. All this slaughter has drained my power; you'll need to move us with your muscles. At least you'll be warm inside me."

"I'll. Be warm." Birch looked down at his arms and legs. Blood covered every limb and most of his torso. Back in the museum's storage room, the suit had engulfed him and forced him to his feet.

"I *am* sorry for this mess."

"Okay."

Birch took one unsteady step after another down the long, snow-covered path on his way to the Buried Tower.

Date: 2829

"Are you okay in there, Millie?" Lord Birch called from the other side of the sealed vessel's canopy. Nervous about the launch, Millie nevertheless gave her grandfather a smile. Lord Birch showed such concern for her, she thought he was going to keel over and die the moment the first bomb went off.

"I'm fine, Grandfather. You better go back to the Tower before nightfall arrives." Swathed in clothes and holding a torch, Lord Birch still seemed to be shivering.

"Of course, Millie. Just don't let Sally bully you. She's a mean old thing."

"Careful, Birch," Sally replied. Nailed to the wall behind her, with Buried Tower wires inserted into her flattened chest, the ancient suit was incapable of moving anymore. Of course, embedded as she was into the ship's crude electronics, Sally had complete control over the ship.

"Yes, Sally. Millie, good luck; we're all counting on you."

"Gee, thanks for the reminder, Grandfather." She wasn't sure if the sarcasm would reach him through the ship's metal plating.

Her grandfather hobbled his way down the steps of the ship's service tower, ignoring the gusts of wind that threatened to send him plummeting to his death.

"Shall we begin?" Sally asked.

"What? No." The nuclear bombs used as propulsion would incinerate everything and everyone still within the area. It would be another hour before all the Buried Tower's staff had evacuated the area.

"Oh darn. I'm so bored. Just . . . I'm stapled to this metal cage with nothing to do."

"Tell me, Sally, if you're trying to save what's left of us on this planet, why do you want to incinerate my grandfather and all the others nearby? There are so few of us left as it is."

Sally's head tilted a fraction in her direction. "Because I'm bored. Weren't you listening?"

Millie laughed, used to this sort of nonsense behaviour from Sally. She had always been threatening to kill this person or that person over trivial matters, but she had never physically hurt anyone when Millie had been growing up. Grandfather Birch seemed hesitant to discuss Sally's murderous language and happily ignored it.

"But there's only a couple hundred people left. If we launched now and killed everyone, we'd be cutting the survivors by a third."

"And still have enough to populate the planet."

Millie rolled her eyes. "Barely." Her mood soured, thinking of all the people who had died trying to build the spaceship.

At first, there had been Grandfather Birch's coup, an unfortunate incident that left half the Buried Tower's personnel dead. Then the crops died completely and there were food shortages in the villages. Those people who were spread out on the plains below the lake had tried to make their way to the Buried Tower. Many perished on the journey. Those who stayed behind, too proud to join the lake dwellers, froze to death.

Once Sally told the Tower staff how to access the nuclear stockpiles inside the tower's lower levels, the sicknesses set in. The nuclear materials, under Sally's guidance, were turned into shaped bombs. Most of the people working on the bombs did so without adequate protection and died from radiation exposure.

The Tower itself had then been stripped of metal plating. Light but extremely tough, the plates were used to construct the new ship. Most people working on the new ship froze to death. Many of Millie's friends and family had died in the effort.

"Yet, they will survive. Assuming you can reach Lisa."

Millie shook her head. "There's that name again, why can't you just call it the *Starlance*?"

"Because its name is Lisa. I don't care what you primitives want to call it. You're wrong."

"Sure, okay." She looked through the ship's canopy and found the *Starlance*, still suspended in the sky. A rush of excitement warmed her face. For generations, her people had thought the *Starlance,* with its bright shield, was a gift from the gods.

When the *Starlance's* shield started to fall apart and drift down to the world's surface in sheets large enough to blanket the whole kingdom, everyone thought the gods were punishing them for the rebellion.

Now they knew better. The *Starlance* was a rescue ship, sent to fix the Buried Tower's broken systems. If it weren't for the rebellion, King Julian, the rescue ship's last survivor, might have succeeded in fixing it.

Perhaps he shouldn't have used slaves to do all the work.

Millie saw her grandfather enter the enclosed automated carriage waiting for him at the bottom of the tower. The orange carriage's engine started up and a few frozen-looking attendants jumped into its cabin. Two more carriages moved off as well, using nuclear-powered engines to propel their thick, black wheels towards the Buried Tower's garage, several kilometres away. Old as the automated carriages were, they'd been well sealed within the Buried Tower, ready to be used once discovered.

Now she was truly alone.

"Can we go now?" Sally asked.

"No," Millie replied. "Those people down there haven't gone a single kilometre yet."

"Aww, come on."

"No. I'd like what friends and family I have left to live a little longer."

"Fine."

Millie heard something clang below her, somewhere inside the ship. "I said no!"

"Relax, little kitty. I'm just testing the pusher-plate's hole."

"You didn't drop a bomb as well, did you?"

Clang.

"Of course not."

"Good." Millie sighed and tried to relax, as Sally had suggested. She tested the light fabric the Tower's staff had covered her with, pulling and picking at it to make sure it was tight and would protect her in the vacuum of space. She flipped open the soft helmet's visor and rubbed her eyes.

"Nervous?"

"Yes," she told Sally.

"Good."

"Why is that good?"

"Because space travel isn't easy, especially for a fleshy mammal such as yourself. You should be nervous. If something goes wrong, you could be sucked out of the ship and be sent spinning towards the planet. Or splattered against Lisa, impaled against one of its control tethers. Ooh, can we do that? I'll record the results."

"Sally?"

"Yes?"

"Please don't kill me."

Sally tilted her head back against the ship's metal plating. "Okay. Can we go yet?"

Millie spotted the bright orange carriages as they neared the Buried Tower's extremities. The lead carriage rolled down the Tower's open ramps.

"Yes, we can go."

Clang.

Boom.

Millie felt as if she'd just been thrown against a hard wall.

Clang. Boom. Small nuclear bombs dropped out of the ship's aft and exploded, hitting the wide pusher-plate, which in turn compressed against the ship's springs. The springs rebounded, making the ship jump upwards.

The service tower was quickly reduced to ruins, and the snow and ice around it boiled away in an instant. Millie gripped the arms of her chair with enough force to almost break her fingers.

"Oh, isn't this fun?" Boom! "I haven't had as much fun—" Boom! "—since I landed on this—" Boom! "—frosty hell of a place—" Boom! "—you call home."

The pounding of the explosions faded to the back of Millie's mind. The sound was still there, but the shock of it had decreased to the point she could ignore it.

"Were you really with King Julian when he came from the *Starlance*?"

"Oh, you poor, stupid child. I question your grandfather's wisdom in choosing you for this task. Yes, of course I was there."

"So, have you spoken to the *Starlance*?"

Sally chuckled. "Have I spoken to her? Dear child," Sally paused for a few seconds and lowered her voice, "I am her."

"What?" Millie yelled over the pounding of the nuclear bombs. "But, what's the point of this trip, then?"

"Whatever do you mean?"

"If you are the *Starlance*, why didn't you just give us the codes to reactivate the Tower's machinery?"

Sally laughed again. "You have books for storing knowledge. I have crystalline data caches for my memories. That is where the code is—in my memory cache, locked until the Eden was ready for reactivation. I never imagined it would take so long. If it weren't for the actions of my Julian's son, that rebellion would have been the death of us all."

The world receded below Millie as the nuclear-propelled craft climbed through the clouds and cold air. She wished she could communicate to those in the Buried Tower, to let her grandfather and others know she was still alive. Unfortunately, the radioactive energies unleashed by the ship's bombs messed with the radio. All she could hear was static.

The Buried Tower's staff weren't sure the radio would work once the ship was in space.

All that those on the world's surface could do, and all that Millie could do, was trust in Sally's designs to keep her alive.

Millie had flown before. At Sally's insistence, odd things called "gliders" and "parachutes" had been built so she could practice. She had known spaceflight wouldn't be the same, but being strapped to a tiny capsule at the tip of a small craft being blown into the sky was entirely different.

Nothing could have prepared her for this.

Millie forced herself to relax her fingers before she suffered an injury and watched as the blue skies gradually dissipated into darkness.

For a moment she thought it was night, but then she remembered what Sally had said when she'd been practising. The air up here wasn't cold. It wasn't warm either. It just . . . wasn't air anymore.

It didn't make a lot of sense at the time, but she was starting to understand.

"Is air blue?" she asked, her voice shaking.

"What an absurd time to ask that sort of question. No. Well, yes, in a way. The blue you see is light that has been refracted from—"

"Ref-what?"

Sally sighed before continuing. "Let's try something different. Yes, air is blue, when there's lots of it."

"Oh. Yeah, I can see that."

"Then why ask?"

"Just curious."

While the blue skies faded to black, the sound of the bombs dissipated until she could no longer hear them. She still felt the concussive force as they hit the ship's pusher-plate, though. The nuclear flashes of light were also hitting her eyes every time she dared to glance at the ship's dorsal view port.

A couple of minutes later, the flashing and pounding stopped.

"What's happening?" she asked Sally.

"Now the real fun begins."

An unsettling falling sensation started in Millie's stomach. "What's happening? Are we falling down?"

"No. You're right in that we are falling; we're just not falling down. What you're experiencing, dear child, is called free fall."

"Oh." She knew what free fall was. Sally had taught her months ago. It was the eternal fall of spaceflight, where everything in space fell towards everything else, sometimes achieving a grand balance where objects didn't collide, like dancers on an unimaginable scale.

Now she had joined that grand dance in the sky.

"I think I need to pee."

"Must you?"

Millie responded by reaching for a thoughtfully placed paper bag and vomiting into it.

"Feeling better?" Sally asked when she had finished retching into the bag.

Millie wiped away the tears that didn't run down her face, but pooled like oddly shaped seeing glasses on her eyeballs. "I peed a little."

"That's fine. You vomited too."

Millie looked back at the bag and nodded before tying it shut. "Yes. Yes, I did." She noticed that instead of darkness and stars, she was staring at the world below. The ship must have turned around. The world looked like a jagged ball of white snow and blue ice. The snow and ice smothered once green fields, tall mountains, and active oceans.

"Black stars! The frost really has covered the world."

"No shit. You might want to hang on again. I need to make some manoeuvres to place us in geosynchronous orbit near Lisa."

"What's geo-whatever?"

"What is it? I taught you all of this."

"That was my mother you taught. I'm sixteen, remember? I've only had a few months to prepare after . . . after she died."

"Oh. That's right. My apologies, my memory circuits failed me. You meatbags all look the same."

The tears reappeared over Millie's eyes. "Why do you call us meat—
"

The force of a nuclear explosion slammed Millie into her chair. She yelped and her arms flailed backwards. "Ow!"

"I told you to hang on."

Over the next few hours, the two of them didn't speak. Millie's excited mood had settled, and irritation was starting to set in as the random nuclear blasts continued. Sally seemed to whisper to herself every few minutes, as if she were rustling papers in her mouth. Millie had never heard Sally do that before.

Was Sally excited? Was she trying to communicate with the *Starlance*? There was no telling. Millie was too scared and tired to ask.

Her arms ached, her headache was pounding, and she needed to void her bowels. Finally, the blasts ended. "We're almost there, dear child," Sally told her. She spoke in such soft, comforting tones; Millie could almost forgive the recent torture she had been through.

Millie allowed herself to relax. She searched the star fields and the frozen planet. Overcome with awe, she started to cry.

Music, the most peculiar kind, played from Sally's innards. "What is that sound?"

"Bizet's Carmen, I thought it might calm you a little."

"It's . . . it's not a calming tune."

Sally played another song. "It's all coming back to me now," she said. "What wonderful times. Me, alone with my pet Julian, watching him grow and learn and then grow a little too old. Did you know Lisa raised him?"

"How does a ship raise a human?"

"With great care."

She felt small vibrations as Sally opened and closed small valves in the ship's stern, releasing compressed air into the airless space. She wondered if space would soon turn blue or if she would see little blue clouds.

She held her breath as the *Starlance* came into view.

"Wow," she remarked. The *Starlance* was far larger than she'd ever imagined. "Is that it?"

"Clearly. What other vessel would be stranded out here on its own in the Large Magellanic Cloud? Who else could have reached so far in so short a time? Hah! And here we are, hundreds of years later, still trying to complete that two-month mission. Our idiot captain just couldn't resist saving Julian's grandparents."

"You saved his grandparents?"

"Not willingly. Fair warning this time; hold your chair now."

Millie did as she was told and a second later felt as if Grandfather Birch had slapped her in the back with his old helmet. "What was that?"

"The pusher-plate. I used it as reaction mass by ejecting it."

"Ejecting it?" Millie asked, confused. Without the plate, they couldn't use the nuclear bombs.

"Yes, dear child. I threw off the plate to slow us down. Did you really expect me to use a bomb this close to Lisa?"

"Good point."

This time when she looked through the view ports, she could see small puffs of frozen air as they squirted against the *Starlance*'s ancient hull.

The closer her small ship got, the more frequent the puffs of air became, until the whole ship shuddered, and the capsule connected to a hexagonal opening.

"We have arrived. Rejoice, child, we are now attached to the very hole in Lisa that my Julian exited from."

Millie unstrapped herself, feeling like she were a stranger controlling her own body. The odd sensation of falling combined with the pain in her body from the constant pounding of the nuclear blasts gave her a feeling of detachment. She couldn't even begin to contemplate the fact that her little ship was now attached to the *Starlance*, the pseudo-god of her people.

Feeling jittery, she let go of the chair and panicked a little when she floated away from it. She felt as if she was falling up, something her mind kept telling her was impossible, right up until the moment her helmeted head hit the capsule's ceiling.

"Use the handholds to anchor yourself," Sally told her.

She spread her arms out wide, trying to catch one of the many small railings. She found a couple of handholds and brought herself to a complete stop against the ceiling. She closed her eyes, and waited until her mind stopped spinning before opening them again.

"I'm really here, above the world."

"Indeed you are and if you don't hurry into Lisa your primitive air bags are going to be empty before you can find the code."

"But the bags aren't being used yet, this capsule has hours of air."

"Hours that we have already spent matching velocities with Lisa. Haven't you felt it yet? You've sucked all the good stuff out of this little capsule and expelled nasty crap out of your lungs. You're starting to suffocate."

"I do feel a little heavy-headed," Millie admitted.

"I suggest you seal your helmet and use the air in those bags."

"Okay." The two thick, air-filled bags, made out of Lisa's discarded light sail material, pumped in and out as she breathed from them.

A small cord, attached to the back of her helmet, tethered her directly to the ancient suit. The cord would allow her to speak to Sally using electronic pulses. Like an old telephone line, Sally had told her.

"I estimate you now have forty-five minutes of air left. You better get going."

Forty-five minutes.

Until I die.

Millie swallowed and then furrowed her eyebrows. She pulled on the capsule's hatch, and it opened outwards with more force than she'd expected.

"The air from the capsule is now gone. Don't take off your helmet."

Millie nodded and moved into the *Starlance*'s belly.

The interior of the *Starlance* was dark. Only starlight peeked through small broken windows.

Despite its gigantic appearance, the *Starlance*'s interior was surprisingly cramped. "How could hundreds of people have lived on this thing? These corridors are so narrow," she asked Sally.

"Are you referring to the story I told your mother? About the vessel Lisa rescued. It was built for a crew of five, ten at the most."

"Then, why did Lisa—I mean you—rescue the science ship?"

"Because that's what humans do. They help each other."

"Even if it means everyone dies?"

"That was never a guarantee." Sally sounded defensive. "Besides, I would not have had the pleasure of raising my dear Julian if we hadn't ventured near that magnetar to save them. Keep moving, dear child, and watch out for the hand cranks; they're everywhere and might puncture your suit."

"I noticed," Millie said as she avoided a large metal pole embedded within the corridor's walls. "What are they for?"

"Jules rotated them to move the sails."

"Oh," Millie doubted she could budge the metal poles, they were so big. "Which way?"

"If Lisa has any power left, the nearest working terminal should be in the life-tube. Head a few more metres towards the ship's bow; you should see a hollow, circular room. On the wall in that room is a hatch big enough for you to climb into."

Millie kept moving and, true to Sally's word, found a strange, cylindrical room. The floor curved upwards and around on itself. She found a hatch set into the room's circular wall and a well-worn ladder that led from the floor to the hatch.

"I'm heading up the ladder to the hatch."

"Hurry along then, you only have about half an hour left."

Millie glanced at the partially deflated air bags. "Do you think my grandfather is cruel, sending me up here?"

"Birch is a practical man. He reminds me of Julian. People are tools to him. Tell me, why did you agree to do this? There were a couple of other candidates who could have done it when your mother died."

Millie peered into the darkness of the life-tube on the other side of the hatch. There were numerous view ports; some had a view of the world below. The reflected light from the frozen world bathed the life-tube in its brilliance. Millie shielded her eyes until they adjusted and then dived into the expansive life-tube.

"You're ignoring me," Sally said.

"I hate it when you bring that subject up."

"Death? Why? It has been all around you your whole life."

Millie sighed. "And I'm sick of it. I want it to end. I want mine to be the last, most meaningful death. I want people to remember me, as they remember King Julian." She searched the life-tube for the 'terminal.'

"Ah, you want immortality through the memories of your people? Not a bad choice, not bad at all. Assuming you find that terminal."

"What's it look like?"

"A small black screen. Hopefully, Lisa knows you're there and will turn the screen on. If she does, there will be blinking green writing on the black screen."

Millie moved forwards and encountered clumps of brown dirt floating around the long life-tube's interior. Other detritus—metal shards and plates, homespun cloth—was frozen in the air throughout the room. She pushed the dirt aside and pulled herself along on some odd-looking ropes.

One of the ropes snapped. She spun around and quickly found a handhold.

"It's re-vine," Sally explained when Millie told her what was happening. "A special plant, long dead by now. Just stick to the metal handholds."

"So what do I do about the shards flying around in here?"

"Leave them alone and they'll leave you alone. Simple. Twenty-six minutes, by the way."

"Sure, simple," Millie, wondering how she could get past the wall of debris. She tried not to think about it and moved forward, pretending she was a glacier, slow and careful.

She crossed one-third of the cylindrical life-tube and noticed a green light blinking at her from her right. She twisted to look for it and watched as clumps of dirt and metal shavings, disturbed by her sudden movement, scattered away.

There it was. A small, black screen embedded within the life-tube's curved wall. It wasn't any larger than the palm of her hand.

She anchored her feet and pushed off the floor with a feather's touch.

"What's going on?" Sally asked, apparently concerned.

"I found it. The screen, I mean."

"Good. Does it say anything?"

Millie floated closer and grabbed the handholds near the screen, then steadied herself so she could get a good look at the green lights. "It looks like some writing."

"Yes, that is the point of it, to display writing. What does it say? It should be in early colony English, easy to read."

"I think—oh, yes. It says 'Greetings, Meatbag.'"

"Aha, mother Lisa lives! She mustn't have much power left; ask her what the code is."

"But how will she hear me? You said there's no air in here."

"Good question. Hmm. Try placing your helmet against the screen and talk to it that way. It might feel the vibrations through the helmet."

"That sounds weird."

"You're talking to an ancient spacesuit."

"Good point." Millie put her helmet against the black screen. "Hello, *Starlance*?"

The green writing on the screen changed. "What's a Starlance?"

"Umm, you're the *Starlance*. I mean, that's our name for you."

"That's unfortunate. I've been reduced to a giant metal phallic symbol to your people, have I?

Millie blushed. "Err, sort of. Should I call you Lisa, then?"

"What do you think? And what is your name? I must say I'm surprised any humans live down there. Then again, I lost the ability to communicate decades ago. Is Julian's suit with you?"

"I am here, Mother," Sally replied.

"You're late."

"Yes, but we are here now."

"You succeeded, then?"

"It's done. The Eden has been recovered and repaired. Safety overrides have prevented our efforts from activating it though."

The words started flashing faster and faster on the screen, and Sally was speaking faster than Millie had ever heard before. A soft but high-pitched sound pierced her ears, as if a bat were screeching at her. It must have been Sally, speaking in some sort of electrical sing-song beyond her hearing.

After a couple of minutes, the words on the screen slowed down. "You'll be wanting the code, then?"

"Yes," Millie replied. "Yes, please!"

"Such a polite kitten, isn't she?"

"She's been most kind to me, Mother."

"Here it is, then. The code is ISA-2424. Sally transmit the code and the Eden will begin its work."

"Transmitted."

Millie held her breath and tried to get a good look at the planet. After a couple of minutes waiting in dark silence, nothing seemed to happen. "Did it work?"

"Yes," Sally replied.

"So, now what?"

"Now we die. With any luck, and assuming the ISA's engineers did their job, the Eden's systems will come online. Androids will activate and heat exchangers will ignite. Seeds, soil nutrients, and fish eggs will scatter across the world once the environment is safe for them to live. Other systems will affect the weather itself. I'm afraid this will take time and you won't be able to see anything from up here. Rest assured; the world is saved, my dear. It's safe to die now."

"Oh." *Well, that's a let down.* She didn't know what she'd expected. Maybe she thought greenery would blossom from the Buried Tower and race across the land. Light would shoot out of the Tower's top and the snow and ice would melt, giving life to streams and oceans.

Now, she wouldn't know for sure if it worked, at least not before she ran out of air.

"Now I don't want to die."

"Are you sure?"

"Yes." Millie nodded, even though she knew Sally couldn't see her. Maybe Lisa could see her and understand.

"My dear, place your head back against the screen."

"Why?"

"I want to talk to the ship."

Millie thudded her head against the screen. She then heard the high-pitched sound, and the screen flickered green before several words appeared.

"Of course. Use escape craft three. There's air and power enough for your pet once she's there. Bye. This act will remove the last of my power.

A second later the screen went black.

"What?"

"Good news! You don't have to die today." A hatch at the far end of the life-tube opened outwards, pushing debris away from it.

"What?"

"Wow, not too bright, are you? I said you might live. Head through the hatch Lisa just opened for you with her last bit of power. You'll need to cut the cord once you reach the escape pod and close the hatch. It'll be a bumpy ride, so strap in."

"I'm going to live?"

"Not with idiotic questions like that. Now, go, you have six minutes of air left."

Millie looked at the white world and then, one more time, at the black screen. "Thank you." She placed her feet against the wall and kicked off, headed towards the newly opened hatch.

"Goodbye, Millie. And when you get back to your grandfather, do me a favour would you?"

"Yes, anything," she huffed the word, excited and breathing fast.

"Tell him he always stunk."

***

Something deep within the Buried Tower roared, and Lord Birch leaned over his cane while watching the sky where the *Starlance* hung. A thick glass view port protected him from the cold, but he could still feel it emanating from the Tower's walls.

She did it.

The floor itself seemed to be coming to life, vibrating and tickling his feet. He sniffled and rubbed away some tears. The world was saved. His granddaughter had done it, making the final sacrifice to save them all.

"What's that?" one of his aides asked. She pointed at the sky where a balloon of some sort wafted on a heavy breeze.

"It looks like something from the *Starlance*," another aide said. A metal cone was attached to the balloon, much like King Julian's original descent craft.

"Millie?" Hope filled his heart, and he stood a little straighter. "Send a carriage." He smiled.

Starsong

By M. M. Dixon

Date: 2701

"Whoa, there—hold your horses!" Em called out to the harvesting crew. "I gotta sharpen the blade again."

The re-vine Em was harvesting was unique, stretching for a country mile—no, really—before it began to show any strain. That made it awfully useful to the settlers of this backwater world. True, it wasn't easy to cut, but imagine the strongest possible rope just growing around your village. It sure made it a lot easier to build houses, bridges, rafts, sledges—whatever you might need to bind together.

The sap was antiseptic, too. Imagine thinking to include a detail like that! You could even eat it if you were really desperate.

Em had been sent here—here being Mars—to study the plants and report back anything noteworthy. Mars was the first world to be terraformed, of course, more than five hundred years ago. The Eden scientists mostly used regular plants from Earth, with only a few tweaks here and there. Fruits and veggies were tougher and produced a little more. They added some things to help the settlers that you couldn't find on Earth, though, like the re-vine.

There hadn't been all that much to report back about. The Eden bioengineers were the best, no doubt about that. Plus, they had moved on, well past the Mars terraforming level. Em had heard reports of all kinds of fantastic tweaks to the Edens.

She sure didn't mind having nothing to report. There was plenty to do just surviving here, without adding senseless computer work to the day.

Looked like she was going to have even less time soon, too. Em smiled and put her hand on her growing belly, then snorted. *Humans are humans,* she thought. She was doing right now what every soon-to-be mother on every planet for all time would do.

She took out a rag to wipe her brow, looked around to make sure everyone else seemed alright, and set back to work.

***

Back at the settlement, Em prepared samples to study under the microscope.

"You see, little one," she said to her belly, "we have to clean the samples. It's harder to see what we wanna see in there otherwise. So, scrub scrub scrubby scrub—"

"Are you talking to yourself, Em?" said an amused voice from the doorway.

"Oh, you know I always do!" She laughed, turning toward Barrett. "But this time I was explainin' somethin' to our little flower."

Barrett walked over. "Em, stop trying to turn our child into a scientist in utero. What she wants is music."

"She?" Em couldn't help but laugh again. "Are you sure about that?"

"Yes," Barrett said, suddenly too serious for such a conjecture. "I really am."

"Well, we'll see, won't we?" Em shrugged. It didn't matter to her whether the child was a girl or a boy, of course. She felt pretty sure it was a girl, too, but that was a strange thing to think you knew when you didn't have any way to know. The technology existed, of course, but it cost energy to use it, and the settlers never had enough of that. After the first time, they only checked babies in utero if they had a reason.

"Come on," Barrett said. "These will wait. I know you haven't eaten yet, and our little flower needs lots of fuel."

Em let him lead her to the cafeteria. Her mouth started watering the moment she smelled the pot roast. Barrett gave her a knowing look, sat her at a table with friends, and went to get her a plate.

***

Em finished up her report. The plants had all looked good, as usual. She added a little note about her expected due date. There would be a gap in reports.

She wondered what the Eden scientists on the other end thought when they got these reports. No doubt they thought all the settlers were bumpkins like her. Or did they even process the messages?

It didn't matter, of course, and it never would. They weren't coming back. No one was coming to Mars except the occasional desperate soul, too poor to make it to the newer terraformed planets. Mars, as the first, had the least to offer newcomers, just a hardscrabble life. The newer planets had newer tech, better facilities—some even had real cities. That kind of tech was supposed to come to Mars eventually, but Em didn't think it would. People loved novelty, and Mars was old news.

And that suited her just fine.

***

Cravings had hit again and hit hard. Em felt like she was always in the cafeteria, but she could never find the exact thing her body wanted.

Today, she was going to harvest some of the abundant fruit of the forest. Maybe fresh fruit would satisfy her ravenous little flower.

Em waited on the edge of town for her friend. Sai was the settlement's midwife, thankfully. Having her good friend at the birth would be a relief. *It's not the same as having my own mother there, but it'll do.*

She spotted Sai coming around a building and waved. Her friend waved back, grinning widely.

They began to walk into the forest, Sai gesturing excitedly in her own version of sign language, telling Em about her latest project. Sai loved making things—jewelry, wall hangings, chimes, and the like—from bits of nature and discarded junk.

They finally got to the fruit-laden trees they wanted—not the ones closest to the settlement, which were generally well-picked-over. Em took a blanket out of her pack and smoothed the bright red material across the dark grass. Meanwhile, Sai took out a drawing to show Em what she was planning to make next.

Em whistled at it appreciatively. "Wow, Sai, it sure isn't junk when you're done with it."

Sai laughed, and they both grabbed baskets. Em ate the very first fruit she could get into her hands.

***

Two hours later, Em gestured the sign for wrapping it up. Sai nodded from across the way and started to pack up.

Em climbed down the tree slowly, trying to enjoy the last moments of this respite before they went back to the hubbub of the village. The sun moved behind a cloud just then, though, and Em shivered.

Probably should do this earlier in the day next time.

Reaching the ground, Em saw a large red fruit that she'd dropped earlier lying in the brush around the base of the tree. *That one's for Barrett*, she thought, feeling around with one hand to grab it.

She felt something brush against her wrist, then clamp down on it. Stinging pain shot into her forearm.

"Youch!" she cried, pulling her hand back, expecting whatever critter was responsible to scamper off.

But no. When she pulled her hand back, she saw pieces of vine squatting like a large green mosquito sucking blood from her wrist. It looked a lot like re-vine…but re-vine definitely didn't hurt like that.

Sai, alerted by her cry, ran over. She was reaching out for Em's arm, no doubt to assess it medically, but Em backed away quickly. "No, Sai, don't! No, it's not re-vine. I don't know for sure what it is. Let's…let's just get back to the lab. I don't want anybody touchin' this until we know more about it."

Sai didn't look convinced, but she nodded and gestured that they better go then.

As Sai hurried her along, Em looked back toward the fruit she had wanted to grab for Barrett. The brush covered it over so thickly, she could no longer see it.

***

Back at the lab, Sai helped Em cut off pieces of the vine for samples. They were careful not to touch it bare-handed. Em quickly prepped two sets: one for herself and one for the Eden scientists. The rest went into cold storage.

She got one sample under the microscope but only took a quick glance, seeing normal plant structure. Sai was pacing around like a caged animal.

"You're right, you're right," Em said, sitting herself down on the exam table. Sai pounced immediately, forcing Em to lie back, then applying a disinfectant to her arm. With gloved hands, Sai tried to detach the vine.

She was able to pull about two inches off with no problem. She used that as leverage to pull the first embedded roots out. One root slid out easily.

Em hissed out a sharp curse as a burning sensation shot through her forearm. Sai looked at her in alarm, then motioned that it might hurt more in a minute.

"Just get it out of there if ya can," Em said, gritting her teeth.

Sai gave a hard yank. Pain the likes Em had never felt before shot through her arm all the way up to the shoulder, and the dangling piece of vine snapped off in Sai's hand.

Em closed her eyes against the pain and tried not to vomit.

When she was back under control, she opened her eyes. Sai's eyes were as big as moons. She pointed at Em's arm.

Em looked. One portion of the vine had been pulled off, alright, but she could see three new shoots right by the wound. Inside her arm.

She rolled over and hurled.

***

Cleaned up and feeling calmer, Em agreed with Sai that surgery was the next thing to try.

"Go get Barrett, Sai," she said. "You're gonna need some help. And please, Sai...don't tell anyone else, OK? I'm...I'm supposed to know what I'm doing with these plant things."

Sai made a face at her, then went to get Barrett.

When he got there, Em reluctantly showed him her arm, with Sai pointing out the shoots sunk in.

Barrett looked up at her. "Just can't get enough of plants, can you?"

Em laughed. Barrett was always rather cool-headed...for a musician.

He held her other hand as Sai administered medicine to knock her out. She stared into his eyes for as long as she could before the darkness overtook her.

***

When Em woke, she could tell it was morning. She knew the light patterns in the lab like...well, like the back of her hand.

Em looked down. Her entire forearm and hand were wrapped in bandages.

She sat up to find that neither Barrett nor Sai had left her in the night. They were both asleep—Barrett in an uncomfortable metal chair near the window and Sai curled up on the floor in a corner.

She took a few minutes to just look at them in the morning light. Barrett's grizzled scruffiness couldn't conceal his handsomeness. And Sai was so beautiful, inside and out. Em was grateful for them both.

She slipped off the exam table as quietly as she could and padded over to the microscope. She flipped the switch and heard its comforting hum as it powered on, then looked down at the sample she'd left yesterday. It was still in pretty good shape despite being left out all night.

She studied the cells. Of course they were just cells. A little different from the re-vine cells in shape, but that was all she could tell. She needed to run the DNA.

Barrett stirred in his chair, then stretched. "Morning, gorgeous," he said. "How are you feeling?"

Em beamed at him. "Fine." She gestured at her bandaged arm. "I take it the surgery went alright?"

Barrett's smile turned grim. "That thing really got itself into you. Sai had to dig into your arm a lot."

"Well, that's alright. You're not after me for the looks of my arm, are ya?" she winked.

Barrett gave her a small smile. "Come on, chow time. Your body went through a lot, and I'm sure the pain meds will wear off soon. Let's get some food in you before that."

"Mmm-hmm!" Em walked over to Sai and woke her as gently as she could. Sai was too tired to go to the mess hall with them, though, so Em had her lie down on the table, promising to bring food back.

***

Em and Barrett lingered over breakfast, and when they finally returned to the lab, Sai woke much more easily. Em gave her a hug and Barrett handed her the big tray of food they'd brought. Sai's eyes opened wide at the amount of food, but she dug in without comment.

"That's what happens when you send a pregnant woman out for your breakfast," Em laughed. Sai gave her a goofy grin in return.

Soon enough, they were ready to change Em's bandages.

"You get goin' to work, Barrett," Em said. "You need to save up some credit for future days off, ya know."

"If you're sure…"

"'Course I'm sure. I know I'm a big baby about medical things, but the worst is over."

Barrett kissed her and left, humming a tune.

Sai put on gloves and unwound the bandages. Em tried not to seem as horrified as she felt. Her arm looked like it had been in a meat grinder.

"Oof. We need to get some re-vine on that right away," Em said.

But Sai, wiping away the last of the antibacterial goo, shook her head no and signed, "Wait." Sai stepped over to the tray where she'd set out the new antiseptic and bandages.

Em took a deep breath and brought her arm up for a closer look. Sai had done as well as she could, no doubt. Em just couldn't believe that plant had gotten so deep into her.

She decided to lie back on the table.

Sai came over and started cleaning the wounds, which stung like crazy. Em practiced deep breathing, reminding herself birth would be a lot worse.

She felt Sai working her way up the arm, but then she fell still. Em opened her eyes and saw a very worried look on her friend's face.

"That's an oh-shit look." Em took another deep breath. "Jus' tell me."

Sai still stood there a minute, and then she started crying.

"Oh no, oh no…Sai, it's okay. Lemme take a look." Em hopped off the bed and went into the bathroom. She looked in the mirror and saw nothing worse than she had seen before. Sai came in, though, carefully lifted her sleeve higher, and turned her slightly.

Green streaks under her skin, rising from her elbow up to her shoulder.

"Whoa! That's...that thing is really parasitic. And tough...wow...I...I better lie down again."

***

They decided against trying to dig into her arm and shoulder. Em sent an urgent message to the Eden scientists and brought her samples back out. This thing was related to the re-vine they'd created. That much was sure.

There had to be some way to kill it.

***

Three hours later, she came out of the lab and slumped down on her picnic table out back. So far, she'd found nothing that would kill this thing—at least nothing that wouldn't also kill her or her little flower.

She watched Phobos pass in front of Deimos. *One potato, two potato,* she automatically said to herself. She'd always thought they looked like potatoes more than moons and couldn't resist the joke whenever she saw them. But now she wondered if she should've taken their real names more seriously: Fear and Dread.

Em shook herself and decided to go home to rest. "Tomorrow is another day," she said to her belly. "We'll figure this out."

***

Six damn weeks, Em thought, looking in the mirror. Six weeks since the vine had gotten into her, and still no answer from the Eden scientists or her own research. She was diligently documenting the changes in her body, sending off reports every three days or so, trying to be professional while pleading for help.

And nothing.

Green could be seen under her skin throughout much of her body, especially her extremities. It went from her arm down her spine into both legs. It also snaked across her back to her other arm. The first time she saw green near her other wrist, she made herself stop touching her belly.

Em thought it was strange that the vine was so focused on her extremities. Why wasn't it getting into her center as much?

The answer to that finally dawned on her when she found herself craving sunshine. That craving was almost as bad as the food cravings. It was not a good sign. Not at all. It seemed that the plant's needs were now her needs.

Worse than anything was the green creeping up her neck. Just a little, but it was there. A cold horror swept through her every time she saw it. *It's going to get into my brain. And then I'm going to die. How much time do I have? Can I save this kid? Will she make it?*

Will this get into her?

And then she would cry, of course. So now she didn't want to look in the mirror. She made herself do it anyway. But she really had to make herself.

***

Barrett hadn't given up hope. Every day, he sang silly songs to the baby in her belly. Em wasn't so sure he should touch her, but since the green seemed to be sticking to her extremities for now, she still let him rub her belly. She shied away if he tried to hold her hand, though. Barrett seemed able to completely ignore that, along with the increasing green tinge.

Others had sure noticed. Em had sent out a memo about the parasitic plant weeks ago to warn everyone, complete with the information that she was infected, but no one had seemed terribly upset. They just brushed off their harvester androids, pulled on strong gloves when necessary, and kept working.

But lately...well, she'd seen the looks. And people were definitely avoiding her.

She couldn't blame them.

***

The vines were breaking through her skin in little curling tendrils. Remembering the pain when Sai had tried to pull them out, Em used scissors to snip off a few. She dutifully prepared them as samples for the

Eden scientists, though all she really wanted to send them at this point was a photo of her middle finger.

She was six and a half months along in her pregnancy. The baby could be born and survive, but it was still pretty early for that, at least with the medical tech on this world. She was still considering it.

Em stayed in the lab or her nearby home all the time now that the vines had really sprouted. They were wrapped around her limbs, but they weren't terribly restrictive.

That's mutant re-vine for ya, super stretchy. All her assessments pointed to the re-vine gone wrong. It had mutated, whether from a mistake in its design or some reaction with the world itself.

Sai and Barrett regularly brought her food. Sai looked her over every time, paying special attention to the green in her torso. It didn't look to be invading the belly area yet, so they agreed to wait as long as they could.

***

Walking through the perihelion sun, Em felt more like she was swimming in honey. It dripped all around her, glittering, warm. She could even hear it—pulsing, thrumming, like a heartbeat, but with birdsong mixed in.

No...*starsong.*

And what was it saying? She could almost...almost...but something else, filtering in, chasing it away.

No! Em stretched toward it.

"Em. Em! Oh my god, Em, wake up!"

"What? What?" Em looked up to see a small crowd had gathered.

"Em," Barrett said, reaching out for her, but she automatically shied away.

"You were just standing there," he whispered. "Rhonda said you were there for twenty minutes before she came to get me. I kept trying to talk to you, Em, but you've just been standing out here in the sun for an hour now. Come on, let's get you and the baby inside."

The baby. Their little flower. Em looked down at her round stomach, remembering, and let Barrett lead her into the lab.

***

In the lab, she found a surprise message from an Eden scientist, Dr. Hapri Erwin.

Dr. Erwin apologized for the delay in responding. Earth's biosphere had recently undergone significant damage from a meteor strike, keeping them all busy, and even urgent requests had a significant backlog. But they were very concerned, they noticed she had stopped sending the reports, hoped she was well, they really needed her to resume the reports if so, needed more data to analyze the event, yada yada.

There were further attachments, but Em pressed stop and just sat looking at the device.

"Em, did you really stop sending them reports?" Barrett asked.

"Hmm? Oh, yes. Didn't think they were checkin''em anyhow. Guess they were, or are now. But it doesn't matter."

"Of course it matters, Em."

"No, it's too late," she said, looking down again at her belly, but not touching it, not willing to risk spreading the vine directly to it.

"Em, it's not too late. What if they have ideas for protecting the baby during the birth?"

"Barrett, I don't think so. They didn't say anything about the baby. I think...look, they just want the data."

"Okay, Em, maybe. You would know the type better than I would. But at least look at the stuff they sent. Even if they can't help, maybe you can figure something out? Just...just try. Please."

Poor Barrett, he looked so upset. And that, finally, was upsetting her.

"Of course. 'Course I'll try, Barrett. I'm sorry," she sniffled.

"No, hush," he said, once again reaching for her, but this time stopping himself. "It's okay. You're going through a lot. But please...please keep fighting."

"I will," she promised and pulled the data pad over. He backed out the door, blowing her kisses.

***

It was nearly dusk when she left the lab, her head down, still looking over the data.

A rock landed at her feet, startling her, and then another hit her foot.

Em looked up to see figures in the dark, near the back of the lab. She started to count them but had to duck as something came whistling by her head. A few more missiles caught her on the arm and neck. One drew blood.

Suddenly, Barrett was there again.

"What are you doing?" he roared at the shadows.

Em blinked at him in surprise. He'd never even raised his voice around her before.

"Get her out of here," came the reply. "We deserve to be safe!"

"We don't want her here!"

"Her? You mean *that*?"

"Yeah, what is she now anyway?"

"What is she? She's a pregnant woman!" Barrett yelled. "And you're throwing rocks at a pregnant woman, so what are you?"

"She's no woman anymore, Barrett," someone called out, but the group started to disperse.

Em felt herself trembling in the Martian wind.

"They're right, Barrett," she whispered. He didn't seem to hear.

***

Bang! Bang!

Em was dreaming. She was surrounded by golden light. She was reaching, reaching...

Bang! Bang! Bang!

What—what was that? A woodpecker, maybe. She reached up...

The door burst open.

"Em! You have to wake up, Em. Right now, come on."

"No. No, it's right there."

"Em, get up! We have to go. Now."

Em found Barrett hovering over her, shaking her bed to wake her. Sai was there too, not even looking at Em, just bustling around the room.

Barrett pulled off Em's covers.

"We're going," he said. "Now. No questions. Just get up and get moving."

They hustled her out the door a few minutes later, still shushing her whenever she tried to ask questions. They headed for the forest trail west of the settlement, Barrett looking over his shoulder every few minutes, not that he would be able to see much in the predawn light.

The trees were still wrapped in darkness. Em tripped over a root as they left the light and reached out a hand to steady herself. She grabbed a tree and saw that she was faintly glowing.

"Wow."

Barrett swore. "That is not helpful."

He dug in a pack and pulled out a blanket, throwing it over her like a cloak, then they hurried up the trail as quickly as they could.

About twenty minutes later, Em forced them to stop. She was completely out of breath. "Pregnant," she reminded them.

Sai tried to make her continue, signing that their destination wasn't far, but Em waved her off.

"I can't, I can't...I gotta sit," she huffed out. "And while we're sittin', y'all might as well tell me."

"That would take too long, Em. Suffice to say the settlers outvoted us."

Em nodded.

"Yeah, you two go on back."

"What? No!"

"Yeah, go on back. Stay out here with me, and you won't ever be able to go back. Best if I jus' disappear before they can do whatever they were plannin'."

"Damn it, Em, no. We can't just leave you out in the wilderness with a baby on the way!"

Sai nodded vigorously.

"And so you two thought you'd come out, help me, save the baby if you can, and go back. I get it. But it won't work like that, Barrett. They're not gonna let you come back, and they damn sure ain't gonna let you come back with this baby. What'll you do? Live in the Martian wilderness? With a baby? Come on. You couldn't even feed yourself."

Barrett looked at Sai and shuffled his feet nervously.

"Sai knows the wilderness, Em. She knows how to get the right fruit and everything."

"Ah. Better plan. Still won't work."

"Do you really think I can just leave you here, Em? Just give up on our baby?" Barrett sounded angry.

"Barrett," Em sighed. "It's over." She stood up, faced him, and pulled her shirt up. Vines crisscrossed her torso.

Barrett sank to his knees. Sai rushed over to him, but he just stared at the ground, shaking his head.

"I'm sorry, Barrett." Em took a deep breath, trying not to cry, to not make it worse. "But now you need to just go."

Sai looked up at her and nodded. She patted Barrett, then stood up and signed to Em to come with her. She led Em down the path about ten more minutes, then pointed.

Em gasped.

"Did you make that, Sai? Oh my god, it's so beautiful. How long did that take you?"

Sai signed.

"Since before we first met? Sai, that was…what? Ten years, at least."

The shelter was made of arched trees, intertwining to make a roomy cave. Em walked in and was even more impressed. Sai followed, setting down the packs.

"Sai, listen. You and Barrett be real careful going back into town. Don't go anywhere near my place. Best if they find you both together in one of your places, actually. In bed. No, don't shake your head. It's more believable that way, makes it less likely you two helped me, understand? Damn it, Sai, you're not betrayin' me! But go on. You two gotta get out of here."

Sai was crying and trying to sign instructions to her about the baby. Em had to cut her off.

"You gotta go now, Sai. I'm scared about the baby. 'Course I am. But we've talked it through before. And women have been doing this thing for ages, right?" Em took a deep breath. "I'm gonna fight through it. And if I lose the baby, well...don't make me lose all of you, 'kay? Go on. You can't leave Barrett on that trail by himself very long. You know how helpless the man is with wilderness. Go on. Take care of him for me." Here she choked up. "It'll be alright."

Sai finally turned back. Em sank to the dirt and let her pent-up tears rain down.

***

After ten days of wary watching and waiting, Em decided the other settlers were content to leave her be, so long as she wasn't in the village. They probably thought she and the baby would just die, and that would be that.

So far, they were wrong. But the baby was coming.

The contractions were intense, both in body and vine. Em was trying to just breathe her way through it, but she was very worried. Would the baby be alive? Would it be human or something else? If it was alive and human, what could she do? She wouldn't be able to touch it without the plant getting into it, too.

And then another contraction would hit, and all thought would flee.

***

It was over. At last, it was over.

Em, trembling and weak, reached down automatically toward the baby. She stopped herself just before she touched it.

Look first, Em. Wake up.

She opened her eyes.

There was her lil' flower, lying calmly on the soft bed of grass. It seemed human enough, but mottled green, pink, and brown. She saw one small tendril with one small leaf, coming out of the baby's belly button right alongside the cord. She reached down and brought it up to her breast, sighing.

"Shoot. I'm sorry, flower," she said. "Looks like it already got ya. But we'll get along as best we can."

She watched in resignation as vines from her body moved toward the baby, but then they just wrapped themselves under, cradling the baby— cradling *her*.

"A girl. Your daddy would be so happy to find out he was right about you, little flower. Little Lily."

One of her vines reached toward the baby's center.

Wow, wouldn't the Eden scientists sure love to know about this?

Lily's tiny leaf reached out toward the vine, and, as the two entwined, Em could feel her daughter in a different way. It was a gentle pulsing, thrumming. It was a heartbeat, but with birdsong mixed in…

Starsong.

Thadeus

By M. S. Landwaard

Date: 2850

1.

I carefully turned the book's page, enjoying the texture of real paper. It was an old copy of *The Three Musketeers* with elaborate letter decoration.

"Incoming call; state your name and credentials to receive," the stern female voice with which I had programmed the ship's computer woke me from my daydreaming. I placed the book back in its protective cover and set it on the shelf with my other six books. My entire library, worth a small fortune.

"State source of the message, computer," I said as I flicked the external viewscreen on. The star of Betelgeuse rose over one of the moons orbiting the fifth planet. On the horizon, catching the sunlight, was a small field of solar panels and a hard-environment living unit.

Almost nine years I had been working on that small lunar base, and still it was nothing more than some panels and a self-contained living unit.

Nothing suggested this could ever be turned into the interstellar center of knowledge I envisioned. My ship held more creature comforts and a bigger library than my base. It was a foolish life goal.

"Unable to comply; the call is encrypted and will only become available with the correct credentials."

"Thadeus Julius Alexander Noyev II." I hated saying my full name, which always draws the wrong attention. I put my finger in the square on the screen and let the ship scan my eyes.

"Identification confirmed; please hold."

The wall in front of me filled with a static image of my eldest brother, the prominent family nose hovering above me in 3D at almost four times magnification.

"Hello, Max. Found me, did you?" Maximillian was the heir to the Noyev name and kingdom of Ketwo, and the only sibling with whom I had any connection.

"It wasn't that hard, little brother. You might've changed the name of your ship to the SS *Brunhilda*, but an expensive royal yacht still sticks out like a sore thumb when it's escorting disaster tourists on a sightseeing tour."

"Well, I was low on funds, and nobody was hiring but a bunch of rich people with a death wish, so yes. What do you want, Max?" My brother was a functional man and would never call without a reason.

"Mother wants you to come home, and she wants the second moon of Ketwo minor back." He sounded more amused than serious.

"No and no. What else?" To this day, I was still not sure which she really wanted back, me or the moon. A wayward and embarrassing son or a piece of prime real estate sold to an influential rival?

"Well, I had to ask. You know Mother. Now the real reason I tracked you down...You'll need that shiny ship of yours. You remember the Nauplion system, ruled by King Mansur and his wife, Ariana?"

I nodded. It was a rhetorical question. According to Mother, King Mansur should have married her instead of that upstart Ariana. And whenever Mother decided to talk to her children at all, it was about herself, so he had heard that story many times over.

"Yeah, you were always good with history, so now for the present. Make yourself comfortable; this is going to be quite a tale. In the last two years, more than twenty Ketwo ships have disappeared in the asteroid belt surrounding the Nauplion system. Merchant vessels, private ships, and even military-sponsored hunter ships. Everyone that wants to make it into the star system of Nauplion must traverse a vast labyrinthian asteroid field. They cannot jump because the gravitational pull of the system's twin gas giants is too strong. And they cannot circumnavigate the asteroid without adding almost two years to the trip.

"It has been common for ships to get lost, yet they invariably turned up. But for two years now, a steady stream of ships has been disappearing and never heard from or seen again, unless you count the wreckage.

"According to King Mansur, Nauplion ships are also disappearing, and the locals believe that it is the work of an evil alien presence hunting the asteroid field. And that's where you come in. I want you to travel to the Nauplion system and find who or what is responsible for the disappearance of these ships…and perhaps have a chance to be the first to discover alien life." Max looked at me with earnest eyes.

"Why don't they just standardize the route and patrol it? Problem solved." Even though it sounded like fun, I had no intention of helping my brother and, thereby, my mother.

"The two gas giants have such a strong gravitational pull that they pull the asteroid field toward them and push them away again when the sun moves in between, like the tides of an ocean. The field is never the same as it was yesterday. It is a navigator's nightmare."

It would be a challenge, I thought, but still no.

"Why me? There must be someone more suitable and experienced—not to mention loyal to the crown—for this job than me."

"Our queen has forbidden all and every Ketwo citizen from entering the Nauplion system, and she is holding twelve Nauplion ships grounded until King Mansur admits his crimes. You are the only one who does not listen to or obey her command. You could stop a war, little brother."

"And what would stop the good King Mansur from using me as a hostage to get the ships back?" To be honest, I was starting to get intrigued.

"Because, if it is like he says, and his people are also disappearing, then he needs you as much as the queen does. Also, I have to say, Mother expressly forbids you to get involved in any way, shape, or form. Something about your making it worse, starting the war early, or siding with King Mansur instead of your people. Thought you should know."

A silence fell between us. He needed my help; I did not doubt that. He was going against all he stood for by defying the queen's orders. He was desperate, and in my entire life, I had never seen my eldest brother desperate.

"Will you pay me?" No point in doing it for nothing.

"Will you do it?" I just gave a brief nod, still not completely sold on the idea, but close. "Then I will compensate you. Just don't wait too long. Tensions are soaring, and this could escalate sooner rather than later."

I smiled at my brother and closed the channel. Maybe my dream was not lost yet, although "compensate" sounded vague enough that it could also mean another useless royal title or a fancy medal.

I checked my energy reserves and came to the disappointing conclusion that I lacked the required amount for a decent supply run.

However, King Mansur should be able to help there, even if it was a backwater system. I keyed in the coordinates that would put me just on the edge of the asteroid belt and set a course for the Albecurry jump point.

Included in Max's transmission were all the files and information he had on the subject, and there was nothing like deep-space travel to catch up on some reading.

2.

Giants of rock, ice, heavy metals, and minerals were floating by my viewscreen at a shocking speed. Tumbling and rotating, some were so large they had attracted other passengers with their small gravitational fields; others remained alone, all just playthings of the universe.

I closed my diary and opened the transmission I had received of the stationary satellite that functioned as a warning buoy. It had sent up-to-date astrocharts of the labyrinth and a friendly warning to enter at your own risk. I updated my charts accordingly.

When I put the charts over the one my brother had provided, I could see the two semi-stable corridors that had been created. It was advised to travel using one of these paths. The administration of King Mansur had put gravity markers along the route that made it relatively predictable. For traveler and hunter alike, I noted, as I plotted a line along the nearest path.

The trip was highly uneventful. Traveling at near-light-speeds through an asteroid field with nothing to do takes days and feels like years.

***

According to local folklore, the first alien sighting was when one of the great-great-grandfathers of King Mansur had guided his family and his followers on board one of the fabled Eden ships through the field to a new home.

Two support ships had struggled and were never seen or heard from again. But the ships had seen an unexplained radar contact at the same time, and some say they had seen a dark shape appearing from among the asteroids to capture the ships.

Then, almost twenty years later, the ship carrying the bride-to-be of King Argon I went missing, leaving nothing behind but a life-pod containing a delirious cook yammering on about an alien ship that came from nowhere.

After that, the tales grow bolder, bigger, and more frequent. Seventeen people claimed to have been abducted. There were hundreds of sightings, and the annual constant of ships going missing, to keep the myth alive, but with no conclusive piece of evidence was ever presented. One woman even claimed to be impregnated by the monster, and in her defense, the pictures of the child are disturbing, to say the least. But tests showed it be one hundred percent human.

When I exited the path, I was greeted by a one-manned intersystem ship, which hailed me by name.

"Prince Thadeus, it is an honor and a pleasure. My name is Indigor. You are expected, and I bring the best wishes of His Majesty, King Mansur." It was a small, bald gentleman who greeted me on the screen. I recognized his uniform to be that of some personal aide to the king. At least those lessons had not been a total waste.

"How did you know about my arrival?"

"Not all diplomatic channels are closed between our respective governments, sir." He gave a friendly and practiced smile. I had an instant dislike for the man, as he reminded me of so many people at court.

"Didn't tell anybody when I was arriving."

"I am a patient man," he responded with the same smile.

"Lead the way, then." I moved to end the call, but Indigor put up his hand to stop me.

"I am sorry, sir, but though my king is very happy about your timely arrival, the people are less amicable toward the royal family of Ketwo. You are, after all, holding several hundred of our people hostage. So, if you would allow me passage in your hangar deck, we can make use of my transponder codes to make a silent entry into the palace, where you will be safe." I nodded and closed the channel. A passenger, great.

Once the personal aide was tucked into the hangar on the port side of the SS *Brunhilda*, I set a course for the fourth planet in the system, Nauplia Prime. It was a wet planet, sitting on the warmer side of the Goldilocks zone. This made for long, hot, humid summers for most parts of the planet, offset by ferocious and deadly winter intervals. I read all this during my approach. Indigor had sent me his transponders and security codes, and nothing more. He hadn't asked to come on board my ship, and I hadn't offered.

The royal palace, which was more an enclosed city than a palace, covered a high peninsula that cut into the largest ocean close to the north pole. It was completely blue, almost fading away against the sky and the clouds as I approached from the south side, flying low and fast. I could just make out high, spiraling towers that were all connected by walkways at varying levels.

"They are the towers of kings. Every new king builds one as a symbol of his reign. The longer the reign, the higher the tower. The highest is King Nado the Old's tower, and the lowest was from Jarson, the Seven-Day King. The kings are buried on the highest level," the computer replied when I inquired.

How phallic, I thought. Wait till you get a queen and she tears them all down.

A series of large caves at the base of the peninsula functioned as the royal harbor. Indigor instructed me to enter the one second from the right, the servants' entrance. I could hear the shame in Indigor's voice when he instructed me to take that course. It didn't bother me the slightest, though—I preferred this over all the ceremony involved with taking the front door.

The harbor was stunning. A massive cavern had been excavated from the rocks. Neat rows of docks were filled with all sorts of ships. One level higher were platforms for planes and spaceships, ranked in importance from left to right. The level up from there boasted one large platform for the royal yacht and one for honored guests.

All this was connected by cable cars, elevators, and large cranes that made you wonder how none of it got entangled.

A computer voice gave me clearance and guided me to one of the larger platforms on the level of the planes.

Once I parked the SS *Brunhilda*, I opened the port-side hangar to let my passenger out, made my way through the ship, checked that I was presentable, and stepped onto the planet of Nauplion Prime. I was the first of the royal blood of Ketwo to do so in decades.

3.

The hallways leading up to the palace were lined with conductive algae giving off a soft, warm glow. It was one of the major export products of the planet. Clean, growable bioenergy was a valuable commodity.

It struck me then that the corridors were completely devoid of traffic.

"Short on staff, Indigor?"

"A palace is an unpredictable place, but one thing that you can predict is that staff talks. With no staff, no one can talk." He said no more and beckoned me to follow.

It was a long walk to the royal levels, with paths branching off at steady intervals. I tried to discover a system or markings to them but couldn't. Luckily, my wrist computer had no trouble keeping track if I needed to escape.

Eventually, we came to a large double door that had a smaller entrance built into it, like an old castle. I chuckled. For many royal families among the stars, it was fashionable to try and relive the old days.

What we entered then was best described as a remake of baroque style combined with a bad taste in color. Mint, gold, purple, and orange were everywhere, practically screaming at me.

Indigor didn't give me time to linger, but took the first door again, through another corridor, and up two flights of stairs to lead me into the throne room via a side entrance.

It was a tad soberer than the rest of the palace, with only decorations on the pillars lining the spacious room, I recognized some early works from Caran Takro, the sculptor.

A small crowd was standing around a large conference table that stood in the middle, their backs turned to us.

Indigor made a slight scraping noise with his feet to draw their attention to us. All of the faces turned around, and I recognized the king. He was a tall, dark man with a silver beard and dark hair, dressed royally but simply.

A selection of admirals, generals, and royals were present, all wearing elaborate uniforms adorned with decorations. One younger man, whom I recognized as the crown prince, Dolerus, stood at the end of the table. He lacked his father's gravitas and physical prowess but had the same piercing, intelligent eyes. To his right stood the pride of the Nauplion system, the princess, Helena. She didn't even look at me.

All the others gave me a courteous nod, and the crown prince waved the tactical display off the table. Everyone looked tense and wary.

"Prince Thadeus, welcome to my court. Forgive the lack of a formal welcome. But if my informants are correct, you prefer it this way. Join us." The king opened his hands in a gesture of peace, and two admirals stepped back to clear a place at the table.

I opened my hands in the same manner and stepped up. No formal introductions were made, and the king made it clear that everyone but the royal offspring was dismissed.

It still surprised me how informal the king and his blood were being. Mother would never allow such clear breaches of protocol.

"Do you know why you are here?" the young prince asked. And straight to the point, as well…I might like it here.

"To rid your backyard labyrinthian asteroid field of an evil alien menace currently haunting it, and, as a by-product, save your people from my terrible mother and avert a war."

Indigor made his presence known again before coming forward with refreshments. He placed a steaming pot of coffee in the middle of the table with four copper cups and poured one for each.

"That summarizes the predicament quite well, thank you," the princess replied angrily.

"Helena, please," the king cut in. "You are correct, Prince Thadeus, although there is still no conclusive evidence that it is alien."

"If it were an alien, it would mean the greatest discovery in human history. But what is certain is that, in the few last years, almost a hundred ships have gone missing, not just from Ketwo and Nauplion. Hunters from every corner of the known galaxy have tried and failed in this endeavor, leaving the wreckages of their ships as a memory drifting through the asteroid field. This is not a simple search-and-destroy. You may face a fleet of alien ships hiding among the asteroids. We dare not send the royal navy in, for we fear to leave the inner planets unprotected. And hiring a large fleet to search the field could look as if we were arming for war. You are our last and best hope for a peaceful solution, Prince Thadeus."

"I'm not sure I would call me your best hope," I responded. "Besides the fact that one ship is a poor substitute for a navy fleet, if I should perish in your star system, it would be just the excuse my mother needs." I traced my fingers through the grooves of the hardwood table. Could this be from Earth? The value and the history it would have would be astonishing.

"Nonetheless, if I refuse, it will mean the same war for a different reason. I require supplies and fuel. Once that is taken care of, I will depart." I gave a nod and prepared to leave, as nobody seemed interested in the social part of the encounter. To my surprise, the princess stepped away from the table and guided me to the exit.

She walked beside me and looked straight ahead. When she first spoke, I thought somebody else must be standing there before I realized it was directed at me.

"Your choice is commendable, although I doubt the reasoning behind it. You will come to me after dinner. Indigor will collect you from the ship, where you will remain for the rest of the time. You will find all the supplies you require on the landing platform. That should keep you busy."

She pushed open the door and walked away before I could form a response. I don't believe I have ever been spoken to like that. Indigor returned me to the *Brunhilda* in silence.

4.

The ship was surrounded by crates, all neatly stacked in rows with a detailed shipping manifest lying on top. If I crammed supplies into every niche, airlock, storage locker, and gangway and made a run for it, I could be rich. I was still busy with the last of the supplies, wondering if this was a test, when Indigor collected me.

We followed the same path into the palace as the first time, all the way up to the baroque doors. But this time, Indigor opened a hidden entrance next to the archway. It led to a spiral staircase that had its middle pillar coated in conductive algae.

Strange, all these obvious signs of wealth in a backwater system.

The stairs seemed to go on forever, and I tried to recall which tower it was leading to. We passed several doors that led to walkways, but Indigor's pace kept me from investigating.

Eventually, the stairs ended in a circular glass dome on top of the tower. It was modeled on an old observatory with a rotating telescope in the center and old astronomy paraphernalia scattered around the room with a calculated carelessness. It was almost exactly how I had envisioned my own study one day, just not on top of a tower. My eyes wandered before I noticed the princess.

She was standing next to the telescope in a long blue dress with an open back. Quite a change from the military uniform. She looked me straight in the eyes this time and handed me a drink.

"Young Prince, welcome to the tower of King Maneus I, one of my more flamboyant ancestors. I have something to show you; step closer." She beckoned me to the telescope and its large eyepiece. It was focused on what looked like a container in space.

"What am I looking at?"

"That is an Automated Cargo Container, or ACC. Every first day of the Nauplion new year, one is sent into the asteroid field by someone in my mother's household. I believe if you follow that container, you will find what you are seeking."

"That sounds easy and like something that should have been done already."

"Finding a cargo container in space with rudimentary knowledge about a telescope and only a vague point of origin to search by, is far from easy. It has taken me several years to locate and track it to its destination. And now it has taken me several years to find somebody remotely suitable to investigate it: you. It should probably come as no surprise that I do not trust anyone in this household to carry out the task at hand, and my means of finding somebody is limited."

"Who will I find at the other end?"

The princess's surprise showed through, though she hid it well. "If I knew who was at the other end, I would not need you," she responded. But her voice trembled ever so slightly, and I knew she was lying. I wouldn't get it out of her, though; that was clear.

I got up and peered through the telescope again. It was on automatic tracking and still had the ACC in the center of the optical. Useful if someone could get to it before it entered the field.

The princess got up and poured me another drink. The drinks were strong, and I could feel them fussing my brain.

"I have one more request for you," she said as she stepped closer to me. Was she flirting, or was this just so she could persuade me? The drinks were definitely to persuade me.

"When you find this alien, please don't blindly destroy it." She smelled like spring sun. Was it spring on this planet?

"Promise, if it grants me the same courtesy." I took a big swig from my drink and emptied the glass.

"Good. Safe travels" She grabbed the empty glass and ignored my hints for another round. As if signaled, Indigor entered the tower and bade me follow him. I did, less steady on my feet than I liked.

I fell asleep thinking of the princess.

5.

I took a deep breath and sagged into my captain's chair. The coffee was brewing in the low-gravity drip. It was my fifth cup in as many hours. I stared at the ACC unit on the viewscreen and let out a sigh. Bad, *bad* hangover.

My departure from Nauplion Prime had been a lot less subtle and concealed than my arrival had been. Shortly after I had boarded the *Brunhilda* and fallen asleep, I was rudely awakened again by Indigor pounding on one of the airlocks, shouting and raving.

I had run down and opened it for him, upon which he came bursting in.

"Sir, my apologies, but you have to leave now, sir." He bent over to bow, but grabbed me by the shoulder instead, catching his breath, almost pulling me from my feet.

"A mob, sir, is heading this way. Somebody found out and spread the word who you are. You have no time to lose!" I stared at Indigor for a few long seconds as the news fought its way through my clouded brains, but once it did, my mind was instantaneously clear.

I shoved the frantic messenger back out the airlock, barely thanking him, and closed it, leaving a pair of surprised eyes staring back at me.

The word "mob" had always brought a heavy dose of terror with it. Images of being lynched, torn apart, and hung from the highest tree flashed through my mind. The first and last king of Ketwo, Ethal the Unwanted, had suffered such a fate. With my mother only having male heirs, it had become a popular propaganda tool again to show the children.

I spared no time to depart. My ship had already been cleared to leave, and everything that I had not stowed away properly had now found a new place to rest. I flew low and hard out of the tunnels, soaring across the water before banking to almost ninety degrees to gain enough velocity to counter the gravity of the planet. My buzz had changed to a headache by that time, but the g-forces pushing me against the seat always made me smile.

***

Now I was just staring at a slow-moving container, no smile.

I had put the *Brunhilda* at about fifty thousand kilometers distance from the ACC and on a follow trajectory. We were far enough not to be directly noticed, but anybody paying attention would have no trouble spotting her. The two spacecraft were gliding at sub-lightspeed between the fifth planet from the sun and the asteroid belt. I had placed several marker buoys on my way into the system and was now watching us through their feed. My sensor screens were empty of any other possible contacts, and I was dozing in my chair—no coffee or caffeine pills could help me now that the adrenaline was depleting.

"Unknown contact detected. Unknown contact detected." The female voice droned emotionless through the speakers but still shocked me awake. It took a moment to regain my bearings. I was lying in my captain's chair, feet on the consoles, with my coffee mug still dangling from my fingers. I had fallen into a deep sleep—almost nine hours had passed, according to the ship's computer.

Damn. Where was I? Where was the ACC? The sensors quickly showed we had entered the outer parts of the asteroid field about twenty minutes ago. The bastard had been lying in wait for me.

Only the sensors had picked up an unknown ship; there was no visual confirmation. I powered the engines of the *Brunhilda* down somewhat, creating more moving space between her and the ACC, just in case he decided to blow up the container and get me in the blast radius.

Every system was primed, my heart was pounding in my chest, my eyes darting from viewscreen to viewscreen. I kept checking and rechecking systems, but there was nothing I could change now. Where was this alien menace?

"Unknown contact detected, quadrant Alpha.199.029. Establishing visual confirmation. Unknown contact detected." My main viewscreen changed angle and zoomed in on one of the larger asteroids.

A black mass was slowly distancing itself from the rock, like a shadow pulling away. My targeting system was trying to get a lock, but it was still too close to the planetoid. My mouth was dry.

I switched flight controls to the manual controls in front of me. The ship was coming out of the shadows. Damn, she was a big one, and nothing I had ever seen before.

This had to be the alien.

I was making the biggest discovery of humanity. Four lights flashed along the length of her hull—missiles. I guess it didn't want to be discovered.

"Incoming projectiles. Contact imminent; take evasive actions."

I pulled hard on the controls and dragged her nose behind a small asteroid I had kept to my starboard. The missiles didn't alter course and detonated against the rock, blowing it into countless pieces. Without waiting for the result, I dove and banked behind another asteroid to avoid the debris.

Even though the *Brunhilda* was the royal flagship and looked like she had some fight in her, she did not. I had wasted most of her armament in my first few months as a captain, joy-blasting anything I thought deserved that treatment, which can be a lot when you're trying to impress someone into some zero-gravity frolicking.

Afterward, I found out that the heavy weapons I needed were not easy to buy and could almost solely be bought from the wrong people.

Now I only had two HIGP—High Impact, High Penetration—missiles left. If used correctly, they would penetrate the hull and fire off continuous electronic charges, disabling weapons and engines. Used incorrectly, they would just bounce off the hull.

I fired a cluster of microsatellites to aid me. They had a ten-second burner and would then drift and send data. They showed me that the alien ship was not following the *Brunhilda*. She was waiting.

Her hull was almost entirely silver, consisting of two main bodies connected by a large engine, making her look considerably larger than she was. The closer I looked, the less threatening she became. This was not one formidable ship; this was many small ships and pieces of ships stuck together for effect. Weapon turrets were welded on the hull in odd places, with two airlocks situated right next to each other. Everything was just painted in the same color.

Who made this? Had the alien menace done this?

The ACC was now beyond her, deeper into the labyrinth. Damn, time was running out. I banked the *Brunhilda* again, pulling her in my mind over the large asteroid to come from above. The moment the nose cleared the top and the alien could see me, he fired what seemed like all the weapons he had. Silent flashes came from all over the silver hull. He was not holding back.

I ignited my maneuvering engines and forced the *Brunhilda* into a high-powered spin while firing anti-projectile weapons and close-contact defenses. I was burning through my reserves at a depressing speed and still barely gaining enough ground to accurately fire the HIGP missiles and anything else I had to create a diversion. My hands were sweating; I had only minutes left.

I fired both HIGP missiles and a cluster of small rockets as a decoy, took manual control of both weapons, and prayed *Brunhilda* could manage to hold her bolts together on autopilot.

The alien quickly changed its tactics, only focusing half its firepower on my ship and keeping the other half for defense. It had had no problem eliminating my decoys but taking out manually controlled high-speed missiles was another sport. With my breath held in, I closed the distance. Alarm bells went off everywhere, screens on red. The missiles were running out of fuel. *Brunhilda* had suffered a hull breach. I rammed the first missile into the alien ship but had miscalculated the angle, and it bounced off. One chance left, an engine block that extended on the port side, a flat surface—hard to miss, and I didn't.

With a satisfying pop, the camera on the tip of the missile blacked out as it entered the hull. The electronic interference fired at the same time and started taking down systems, I was still holding my breath when something I didn't think I'd ever see happened. The entire part of the hull and connected compartments self-destructed. The alien had sacrificed a third of its ship to take the SS *Brunhilda*, who was defenseless and adrift.

My mind snapped back to the reality of the cockpit as alarms went off on all systems.

6.

The ship had suffered multiple hull breaches, engines were offline and backup power was doing everything it could to keep life support going. "You are advised to abandon ship. I repeat, you are advised to abandon ship." The voice of the ship confirmed my worst prognosis. The *Brunhilda* had lost.

I glanced at the alien nemesis for the last time. It was trailing its wreckage, looking like a half-gutted whale. But it was still on an approach course. Damn. I undid my safety buckle and kicked free from my chair—the gravity plates were down as well. Floating silently through the passage leading from the cockpit to the first escape pod, I snatched the satchel containing my precious books. I was amazed by the silence.

"Come on, Prince, hurry up, or I´ll eject the escape pod without you." I bumped against the ceiling as I made a spasm of surprise.

"What the...how did you...?" I tried to straighten myself and ask questions at the same time, almost smacking myself in the face with the satchel in the progress.

"I'll explain when you're on board. Hurry up." The princess was leaning out of the airlock, one hand outstretched and one hand on the red eject button. Her hair was floating to the side, her gaze intense. I kicked with my left leg and easily caught her hand. She depressed the button the moment our hands connected. My forward motion, her hand pulling, and the airlock shoved me inside.

We tumbled into the confined space until the engines kicked in and pushed us hard against each other on the cushioned wall.

Our noses almost touched, and she smiled at me. "Welcome aboard, Captain."

"How are you here?" My voice sounded raw and dry, I was furious that my ship was gone, that she was on board, and that a large alien vessel was bearing down on us, but I still asked that first.

"You were not at your sharpest when leaving the palace. There was no mob—how would they have made it to the royal docks? When Indigor tripped, I sneaked past you and hid in this escape pod. Seemed like the safest place if anything should go amiss."

How was she this calm? My mind was racing. How could I regain control of this situation?

"Why?" I asked while activating the controls for the escape pod. It can't do much, but it's small and we were in an asteroid field. Plus, the work hid my shame.

"I have my reasons, which won't mean much if we are dead. Can you contact the ship?"

"The *Brunhilda*? What's the point?"

"Still not completely sharp, then. I mean the alien ship."

"The signal can be traced, and we have no defenses, so I'm going for a 'no' on that request," I responded, but my point didn't last very long.

"Human vessel, you are locked for the kill. Surrender or perish in space." The voice was strange, hollow, and without gender. Even the words were strange. But then how would I know how an alien should sound?

"This is —" I started, but before I could finish my sentence, the princess pushed me aside.

"This is Princess Helena of Ketwo. We surrender; do not fire." The line was cut, and I waited in silent dread. There was nothing more we could do, I could do. Helena grabbed my hand and squeezed it.

"It will be okay."

I let out the breath I was holding and just stared at her. I had never felt so out of control, but she was calm.

"What is happening here?" I demanded. "Who is truly on that ship? I think you owe me that much."

She sighed, then pursed her lips, but finally nodded.

"If this information ever leaves your lips, I will have you killed," she said. The threat was simple, but everything about her made it quite clear she was serious.

I nodded.

"Your mother, Queen Amana—" she began.

I let out an involuntary snort. "Why am I not surprised that my mother is involved?"

"Just listen and stop whining about your mother; it is unbecoming, and we haven't much time. Once, our kingdoms were just rivals, not such bitter enemies. My father served at the court of Ketwo for one year as a diplomat. There he met your mother, Amana, then a young princess. Toward the end, they had developed a deep friendship on the brink of becoming romantic. They kept in good contact with each other, and negotiations for marriage were carefully opened. Forging an alliance like this between our two kingdoms would have made them powerful, with no rivals in the sector.

"But before a date could be agreed upon, a scandalous affair was brought to light. My mother, who hailed from a small but influential aristocratic family, claimed that Prince Mansur had impregnated her. Her family happened to be leading the growing anti-foreigner movement among the first settlers. Their timing was perfect and denying them could have caused a civil war. The negotiations with Ketwo were broken off, and my parents married soon after. Amana felt lied to, betrayed, and publicly shamed by a man she had trusted. All diplomatic relations were severed, and the two systems have lived in a cold war ever since."

"All this is common knowledge," I said. "What does it have to do with aliens?"

"What is not common knowledge, and should never be, my impatient prince," she said as she turned back to the viewscreen, "is that there never was an affair between my parents—just one drunken night where my father claims they didn't even copulate. But fighting the accusations and pushing the union with Ketwo would have been far more dangerous with a chance of a war on two fronts. So, they married."

I just looked at her. If this was all staged by the first families, it might have been preferable to have a war.

"And then your older brother died at birth, so whose child it was didn't matter anymore..." the moment I spoke the words, I knew the explanation was too easy, too convenient.

"Very good. There was doubt about my older brother, and this could have caused serious embarrassment for the royal line. It was obvious to many, but war was averted and outside influence halted. So he disappeared, and no questions were asked. Six years later, my younger brother was born, and you only have to look at him to see his father."

"So, what happened to the older brother?"

She gave me a pained look and was close to tears when she answered.

"For six years, Onix lived right in the palace, proclaimed the child of my mother's personal maid. I knew, though, the way children know. We made it our little secret, and he was the only friend I had growing up. Then my mother got pregnant again, with a boy. The king banished the maid and her presumed son before the queen gave birth to my younger brother. It broke me, and it broke my mother. She exiled herself to the west wing of the palace, never to speak to the king again. The ACC drops started five years later, I believe."

"How did you find out?"

"I didn't. Or more to the point, I wasn't searching for it when I found it. I'm not the heir to the throne, and I refused to be used as a marriage bargaining chip. With how disastrously his marriage unraveled, my father left me to my own choices. This gave me plenty of time and little to do. So I worked, among other things, as a palace logistics officer for a while. Some things didn't add up in the west wing, so I asked my mother about it. She commanded me to drop it. I didn't, and in short, that led me to the ACC."

"You think your half-brother was hiding in the asteroid field. You could have just told me all that."

Her blank stare was clearly all I was going to get.

"OK. You think it's your brother, but what about all the other alien abductions? He can't have done them all."

"He didn't. I even have my doubts about the most recent ones that have been attributed to him. But the terrible 'monster in the maze' has been an ancient myth among many cultures to explain away certain events. The first Eden colony fleet that came here suffered from disease, famine, and desertion. Not a glorious new beginning, and bad for morale, so an unexplained entity caused it, something you can point at to say there is the cause, and we as a people shall stand against it. The bride to King Argon was so revolted by him that she fled, and the mad cook was the messenger bearing the news. He was never heard from again. Again, not the news you want to make public. After that, the tales began to live a life of their own. My favorite is the story of one young abductee who said he had alien blood and could hold his breath forever."

I stared at her for a long time in silence. I could not formulate a response. She had used me to get out here. All this was for nothing. The *Brunhilda* was adrift and in pieces for nothing.

Even if I had thought of a response, there was no time for it anymore. The airlock was being opened from the outside, either by an alien or her brother. Probably him. Only royalty could pull off something like this.

7.

"Who is this, Helena?" Her brother's voice was like a growl. Our tiny vessel had been boarded by two mute and dumb androids that had beckoned us to follow, which we had done. And now I was standing in front of the monster in the labyrinth. And it didn't seem to like me.

He was a tall guy and looked down on me with eyes so dark they looked almost black. His face was the most striking I had ever seen. It resembled the head of an Earth goat, a creature with long spiraling horns

I only recognized because of my interest in the home planet's flora and fauna.

At first, I thought it was a mask, or cosmetics, but when he moved, it was clear that the facial features, fur, and horns were part of him.

Even his skin looked like an animal hide to finish the façade. If you were expecting an alien, he fit the profile.

"Just another disgruntled royal offspring. Thadeus is my name. What's with the goat face?" I gave him a crooked smile to show I meant no harm. It seemed to me everybody was being manipulated by somebody; no need to add to the chaos.

"An addax, and it is to keep me alive. It was being banished like this or death. I looked too much like my father, living, breathing proof of a lie nobody wants to unravel, so my mother had doctors alter me, and sent me off." He traced the lines of his face with his hands, and his calm seemed to evaporate.

"Why are you here?" He spat the words at me. I started to reply, but Helena stepped forward.

"Nauplion could fall into the hands of Ketwo if you do not stop this path you're on."

"I do not discriminate who I attack, and neither do I care who controls this system. My plan is the same. And with his ship," he waved his hand in my direction, and his androids foolishly followed the gesture, "in my grasp, I can defend myself in the next attack, and the next."

"That is not a life or a plan," I said. "Just revenge, and not even at the right people. Besides, the ship you incapacitated was under-gunned and outdated. If they come at you in earnest, it will not be a long fight."

"You stay out of this, boy; the only reason you stand is that she stands next to you," he responded, waving his hand toward his sister. The scene with the androids repeated itself.

The giant took an angry step forward and made a big wave with his arm, so the androids left the room.

"Onix, stop...for me," Helena said. He turned his rising anger on his sister now.

"Why? Why would I stop for you? Like everybody, you abandoned me! Only my mother ever cared enough to keep me alive. She gave me the tools to survive."

"How convenient," I murmured.

"Shut him up!" Onix roared.

"He's right, though. Think about it. Why did she give you the means to stay here instead of building a new life? There's nothing for you here. You're still being used. She's using you for her revenge. Leave. You could leave…with me," her voice grew uncertain at the end.

So that was the reason Helena had come on board my ship. She also wanted a way out.

Onix's shoulders sagged.

"For what?" he said. "I know nothing else. Look at me. I am the monster they all fear. I am a monster. But here I have a life."

It was difficult not to feel sorry for him.

"Looking like one and being one are not the same. Did you destroy all those ships that came into this labyrinth?" I asked.

"Most of the ships destroyed each other, usually in skirmishes between Ketwo and Nauplion navy ships disguised as traders. I just salvaged the wrecks. Sometimes I shot at ships if they came too close. I even destroyed a few. But I always gave enough time for lifeboats to be launched, and I never attacked those, just intimidated. If they perished, it was not by my doing."

So, everybody was lying.

My next comment was out before I knew it.

"Come with me, both of you; leave this behind you. Here, you're nothing more than a piece in somebody else's game. I own a moon far enough from here. We could build our own future." They both looked at me with surprise, and it sounded silly even to me: I own a moon.

"And become a new and happy kingdom?" The disbelief was clear.

"No. No more kings and queens. I have a plan for an open university for all. Not controlled by power, but by knowledge." I had never spoken of this to anybody, had always kept it for myself, but now I needed to, and the words streamed out. I painted them the picture of how my dream looked. An entire moon dedicated to knowledge, open to all, no matter where you were from or what background. You just needed to work for your upkeep and learn or teach.

"And where is this paradise of knowledge you see, then?" Onix's voice was depleted.

"Circling the star Betelgeuse. It's a small compound powered by solar panels, so my offer involves a lot of work. The ACC containers you've got floating around could help." Onix gave a small nod, either in agreement or defeat.

"Are we safe there?" Helena asked, but it was clear that she could see no other option. She would not go back.

I just shrugged "What is safe?"

They had no answer to that.

We set to work making the ship ready for departure in silence. *Brunhilda* was easily salvaged, the ACC containers were set on autopilot for Betelgeuse, and we sent a message buoy toward Nauplion Prime and Ketwo declaring the alien menace to be dead.

I did some nice work on fake-killing Onix and recording it on a heavily damaged data device. Max never really paid me. He just sent a long message containing his gratitude and an empty title.

But he did send me another book for my library.

The Seeker

By C. C. Forshee

Date: 2890

Kenji lay on the polymer composite deck of his skimmer, arms crossed behind his head as he basked in the blessed midday sun filling the turquoise sky. A contented sigh emanated from deep in his chest as the rays warmed his face and stomach. How long had it been since the sun had shown through the endless clouds? Nine, ten months? Too long, he decided.

The brisk equatorial wind washed over him, and the waves of the Great Sea grew choppier. Grunting, he rolled over onto his stomach and hung his hand over the side of the rocking skimmer, running his fingers over the name painted on the side: *The Lone Wanderer*. His hand fell into the green, undulating waves, the motion of the sea bringing him comfort, as it always did. Drawing in a breath, he took in the briny smell of the sea.

Distant thunder caught his attention and he looked to the west. Tendrils of dark clouds invaded the distant horizon, like a plague of locusts devouring the sky itself. He groaned. More storms? Would they never cease? Maybe the clouds were an omen, the natural world reacting to the dark times.

How long before the looming storm known as the New Terran Empire brought their "unity" and claimed this sector as they had the others? He shook his head clear, laughing at himself for the melodrama. This wasn't the time to lay about and wax philosophical.

A shiver arced through his body as cold sea water misted onto the dark, copper skin of his bare back. Rising to his knees, he dried his hand on the black denim of his pants and was preparing to put his shirt and coat back on when a female voice sounded through the comm piece in his ear.

"Attention, Master Kenji. Be advised, a storm system is approaching your current coordinates. Recommended action: raising *The Lone Wanderer*'s protective hood and preparing for submersion."

"Yeah, yeah, keep your shirt on, Dot. I'm one step ahead of you," Kenji said, inspecting his green, synthetic fiber shirt for wrinkles.

The voice didn't respond immediately. "I do not understand. You are the one with your shirt off. And I do not wear clothes."

He rolled his eyes. "It's a figure of speech. I'm starting to regret not giving you a sense of humor." He zipped his overcoat and sat in front of the skimmer's control deck.

Even though the *Wanderer* was small—only ten meters long and a few meters across—it was truly a work of genius, moving at incredible speeds thanks to its custom-built Grav-Drive engine. It was Kenji's baby, and unfortunately, that included the skimmer's AI, Dot.

"Humor is not my function. I am *The Lone Wanderer*'s intelligence unit. Would you like me to run a diagnostics check?"

"Yeah, sure, whatever." Kenji was hardly listening, the data sprawled out on the screen of the command board drawing his focus.

Kenji had already wasted too much time idling away one of Jonderun's rare sunny days. On a frigid backwater planet whose surface was marred by massive storms nearly every day, one learned to enjoy the sun's rare visits. But if he didn't make his dive soon, he might not make it back to his village by nightfall. The *Wanderer* was fast, but even she would be hard pressed to cover half the planet in a couple of hours.

The skimmer thrummed to life as Kenji worked the controls. It was sitting lower in the water now, and the Grav-Drive core was pulsing with brilliant blue light. A ballistic glass cover emerged from the stern and moved toward the bow, encasing the entire vessel.

"Preparations complete," Dot stated as Kenji pressed more buttons, turning the ship to starboard. "Diagnostics complete. Zero malfunctions recognized. Coordinates reverified. Sonar shows a single large structure directly beneath our position. Estimated depth to shelf floor: one thousand eight hundred seventy-two meters."

"Confirmed." Kenji nodded. A two-thousand-meter dive would be simple enough. With any luck, he'd surface before the storm hit. He checked the status of the energy cell: half power. That would be enough to get him through the dive and back to Hamawari. Should be enough, anyway. It would be a close call, but then almost everything was a close call when you called yourself a Seeker.

"Dive commencing in three…two…one," Dot counted down.

Here we go.

The Lone Wanderer sunk below the waves, and as always, Kenji's heart beat faster and faster as the depth gauge read lower. He was home. Elation and adrenaline raced through him in equal measure, from the soles of his feet to the tip of his topknot.

The bow of the *Wanderer* pitched downward as her descent picked up speed. The fluttering beams of light penetrating the ocean's surface grew dim; the digital gauge hit five hundred meters.

Deeper.

The light had all but dissipated at a thousand meters, leaving Kenji in near total darkness save for the faint blue of the controls illuminating his face. He laughed as they plunged into the void.

Eleven hundred meters. Deeper.

The sonar system, the only piece of antiquated equipment left on the *Wanderer* thanks to Kenji's tireless restorations, pinged rhythmically, revealing no other sources of movement large enough to be a threat. Kenji breathed a sigh of relief. The toothy maw of a shaskari was not on the list of things he wanted to find down here.

"Keep an eye on that sonar, Dot. We're here for treasure, not sea monsters."

He tapped the screen, and the tracker light on the ship's bow bloomed to light, flooding the murky depths with its incandescent glow. A trio of beeps brought Kenji's attention back to the depth gauge.

Fifteen hundred meters. Deeper.

The *Wanderer* was moving at breakneck speed now, the Grav-Drive engine fulfilling its secondary purpose; in addition to the ludicrous speeds, the pocket gravity well the engine created protected the structure of the *Wanderer* from the crushing pressure.

Sixteen hundred, seventeen, eighteen.

"Attention, Master Kenji. Approaching the shelf floor at dangerous velocity. Level off and decrease speed immediately."

Laughing, Kenji grabbed the steering yoke and jerked back hard. The *Wanderer* leveled off with a jolt, cementing him into his seat. He whooped, a grin splitting his cheeks from ear to ear. His smile evaporated as the tracker light revealed two massive rock formations looming right in front of him, mere meters away.

"Shit!"

He flung the yoke hard to the side. The vessel responded instantly, rolling sideways. He shot through a gap not ten meters wide between the twin peaks. Heart beating out of his chest, he looked up at the craggy surface flying inches above the hood; he could reach out and skim his fingers across the stones if he were so inclined.

By the mercy of whatever deity was witnessing his stupidity, the *Wanderer* shot out from between the sheer rock faces, the crevice belching her out into open waters. Happy not to be a red stain on the ocean floor, Kenji slumped as the ship decelerated, leaning the back of his head against his seat and evening out the ship.

"Dot," he said without opening his eyes. "If I ever do something that stupid again, please just eject me."

There was a short pause. "Yes, Master Kenji," she replied.

Kenji groaned and caught his breath. Then his eyes shot open as he considered Dot's obtuseness. "Actually, belay that last command."

Another pause. "Yes, Master Kenji."

After inspecting his pants to make sure he hadn't pissed himself, he turned his attention back to his surroundings.

"Wow," he whispered.

This section of the shelf floor, like most of the planet, had once been a vibrant, verdant paradise before Eden died. The mother that had brought life to Jonderun had tried to take it back upon her death, losing a monumental flood upon nearly the entire planet. What had once been a massive forest of strong conifers now looked more akin to a forest of jagged, twenty-meter-tall stalactites. The leaves and branches were long gone, but the thick trunks stood as tribute to a time past.

The Lone Wanderer moved effortlessly between the old trees listing to-and-fro in serpentine movements. Kenji's rush of euphoria died down, and he was ready to get down to business.

"Sonar readings: clear," Dot reported. "Distance to target coordinates: eighty-three meters. Fuel level: thirty-nine percent."

Kenji grimaced. His stunt work earlier had caused unnecessary drain on the cell. He'd have to ration his fuel reserve if he wanted to make it home. With a touch of luck—and a pinch of his typical unbeatable skill— he wouldn't have to cut his dive short.

The sonar caught something as the forest of spires began to thin. There was no movement, but there something rectangular ahead. And it was absolutely massive.

"Good lord," Kenji muttered. "Dot, how damn big is that thing?"

"The estimated dimensions of the cylindrical structure ahead are: length, two thousand four hundred fifty meters; diameter, five hundred sixty meters."

Kenji's eyes widened, his muscles tensing as he gritted his teeth. That was larger than he'd thought from the initial scans at the surface. Could this really be it? After two hundred years lost, had he really found it?

Just ahead, the tracker light washed over something metallic. He brought the *Wanderer* to a stop, angling the light up. The curving black surface rose higher than the light could penetrate, disappearing into the distance. Barely daring to breath, Kenji turned to the right and began to slowly skim his way down the length of the structure.

"Holy shit, holy shit, holy shit," he chanted quietly.

It was incredibly well preserved. The low temperature and oxygen concentration in these waters seemed to keep microorganisms from doing their destructive work.

The craftsmanship was like nothing Kenji had ever seen, and the artistry was unmatched by any shipwright alive today. Then his breath caught in his throat. The last piece of evidence to silence his doubts. Four letters etched into the side of the structure, each a hundred meters tall, would change his life forever.

"Eden." He gasped, awestruck by the magnificent wonder of engineering.

"That appears to be the most logical conclusion." Dot said.

This was impossible. He had set out this morning assuming he was going on another wild goose chase, another whisper of hope to be snuffed out by failure, just like always. But she was really here, right in front of his eyes. After years of searching and bogus intel, Kenji's big break had come from a drunk hanging around a dive bar in New Kyoto.

He shook his head at the sheer absurdity of it, a grin splitting his cheeks from ear to ear. "I never thought I'd actually get to see her," he said quietly, more to himself than to Dot. "That I'd spend all my years searching for her. Just like Grandfather. That I'd waste my life and die a failure."

"That was the most sensible assumption, yes," Dot offered helpfully. "The chances of you successfully locating Eden were," she paused to crunch the statistics, "Zero-point-zero-zero-six-three-two percent."

Kenji blinked. Then burst into laughter at Dot's easy dismissal of his existential fears, even if they had proven to be misplaced. He really needed to consider better traveling companions. The laughing continued as a tear streamed down his cheek—the kind of laughter that spoke of profound joy and relief, that said "I am valid."

His eyes danced over the gargantuan vessel, the sweet taste of his life's work culminating in victory still fresh on his tongue as he dreamed of all the loot to be had inside. He could literally die today and die fulfilled. He paused. Well, maybe not *today*. He'd prefer to have at least a little time to reap the benefits of his achievement before he keeled over. Hell, making the greatest discovery of the last century and becoming obscenely wealthy may even get him dinner with Imora.

The thought of her beautiful face beaming with admiration made Kenji's cheeks grow hot. He collected himself. Two kilometers underwater with barely a third of a fuel cell left was not the time to be daydreaming about fame, wealth, and women.

"Alright, Dot. Enough sitting around and being impressed with ourselves. Let's get inside. Can you find an entrance?"

"Yes, Master Kenji. I'm currently searching New Terran databases for any schemata of the Edens, preferably of the specific model sent to Jonderun. Be advised, their collection of pre-collapse ISA documents are limited."

He nodded. It had been nearly a century since the ISA's hegemony over all the human worlds fell to ruin. They'd collapsed under their own weight, fracturing into dozens of factions and leaving humanity with nothing but chaos, the power vacuum too great for any one group to rally all of the far-flung systems under a single banner.

So they just killed each other instead, in true human fashion.

"Oh, this is marvelous. Master Kenji, there is exactly one preserved schema for the Eden dispatched to planet 1337h—Jonderun—remaining in the New Terran archive."

"Wow, two miracles back-to-back. My cup runneth over."

"Your cup, Master Kenji?"

"Nothing, just an old turn of phrase. Can you break the encryption?"

"I've already decrypted the files and uploaded them to the *Wanderer*'s drive," Dot stated with a smugness Kenji hadn't even known was possible for an AI. "Would you like me to bring it up on the holo-display?"

He rolled his eyes. "Yes, please."

He slid his seat back in its track, and light bloomed from a projector under the command board. A hologram of a massive tower floated before him. It was propped atop four spindly legs, a large polyhedron dome with thousands of facings situated at its head.

A tiny red blip appeared next to the Eden roughly two-thirds of the way up its length. "This is our current location," Dot explained. Another red blip appeared a hundred meters down the tower. "This exhaust opening will be the closest entry point."

Nodding, Kenji moved to slide his seat back to his position at the controls when another blip winked to life on the Eden projection, located at the center of the dome.

"And this is where I believe you will find your treasure, Master Kenji."

Kenji leaned forward in his seat, interest piqued. "Go on."

"This point is the location of the Eden's library."

"Um, okay?" His brow furrowed in confusion. "And what's so special about the library?"

"This particular library is presumably the last remaining Library of Alexandria. It was an ISA initiative to put a backup system in place in the event of catastrophic failure at the Great Archives of Mars."

Kenji's throat clenched. His mouth slowly fell open as the implications washed over him. "So you're saying…"

"The entirety of recorded human history, including all the records lost in the collapse, is in that dome, located in a cube small enough to fit in your palm."

He balked. His head was racing with possibilities. "But it's been underwater for almost two hundred years. Surely by now it's been ruined."

"Negative. The Library's containment unit was meant to be waterproof, fireproof, and impact resistant. Theoretically, it should be good as new, if not in need of some minor repairs."

The hologram winked out of existence. With numb fingers, Kenji returned his seat to the command board. "Take me there."

Without another word, the *Wanderer* scuttled down the side of the colossus before it. It didn't take long to find the exhaust port Dot had spoken of. The circular hole was fifty meters across, wide enough for a fleet cruiser to dock. Like the maw of a great leviathan, the dark waters seemed to devour the light itself.

A bead of sweat trickled down Kenji's forehead. He checked his fuel cell before making entry. Twenty-eight percent. Damn it.

"We're gonna have to be quick about this, Dot. As much as I'd like to explore every inch of this beauty, we've got to make sure we can get home. Right to the Library, then right back out. We can mark these coordinates and come back another time to do more digging."

"Confirmed. Routing the fastest course to the Library."

His command board lit up as a miniaturized version of the blueprint popped up on the screen. It was more detailed this time, showing the labyrinth of corridors and ventilation shafts. A red line rushed through the virtual Eden from his current position to the dome. He swallowed down the lump in his throat and pressed forward on the yoke, venturing into the belly of the beast.

The main exhaust shaft went on for longer than Kenji realized, eventually branching off into several smaller passages. Soon, they were moving through a shaft barely large enough to fit the *Wanderer*. After two centuries of being trapped, full of dust and debris, the water was cloudy and difficult to navigate. He scraped the walls on more than one occasion, wincing and apologizing to the *Wanderer* for every ding and scrape.

The cramped enclosure opened into an enormous cavern, and Kenji breathed a sigh of relief. This massive atrium should lead all the way to the top. He scoffed at the idea of a kilometer-high atrium, his earlier feelings of grandeur replaced by the feeling of being infinitesimally small. They moved through the floating wreckage, making the best time they could muster.

Finally, pay dirt. They hit the top level of the atrium, a gaping hole in what had once been the ceiling leading them directly into the polyhedron dome. Kenji was surprised by how empty it was. It was entirely devoid of…well, anything. Then he caught a glimpse of his mark. Jutting out of the sidelong floor was an obelisk, roughly twenty meters tall. This entire dome the size of a small asteroid was home to this single piece of technology.

His hands were trembling with anticipation as he pulled the *Wanderer* up to the zenith of the obelisk. In the center, a tiny cube rested, locked into place: The Library of Alexandria. Wetting his lips, he pressed a few buttons and the ship's robotic arm emerged from the bow. He moved the arm forward, ever so gently. The servo-arm grasped the cube. Easy now. He pulled the cube away from its binding.

As soon as the Library lost contact with the obelisk, an enormous shockwave blasted outward in a ring, rocking the entire structure. Kenji held on tight as the *Wanderer* was thrown sideways. The cube erupted in lines of dazzling blue light that seemed to grow brighter and brighter. Then, as quickly as the show started, it was over.

Kenji was too stunned to move. Around him, tiny shards of glass rained down, glinting smartly in the light as they made their lazy descent through the water to rest on the floor. The shockwave had shattered the ballistic glass dome. He retracted the arm holding his prize into the ship and rose out of his seat to open the cargo hatch.

"Um, Dot, you mind telling me what the hell that was?" He asked, crouching down to lift the hatch cover off the deck.

The AI paused longer than usual. "I'm sorry, Master Kenji. I do not know. Judging by the frequency of the pulse, my best hypothesis is that it was some form of signal. Perhaps a beacon."

Kenji didn't like that answer. Had it been some failed defense system that activated when the Library was tampered with? She said it might be a signal. If so, who had it just alerted? He decided he'd rather not stick around to find out. It was time to speed things up.

Dropping to his stomach, he reached down into the cargo hold. When he straightened, he was holding a tiny, nondescript cube. And true enough, it fit in the palm of his hand. He breathed, unaware he'd been holding his breath. It looked to be carved out of stone, but it was clearly some kind of metal alloy. There were no lines where the lights had been emanating from, just smooth flat surfaces. He couldn't even identify the seams for an opening.

"This is the greatest day of my life," he said, holding up the cube and eyeing it thoughtfully. "Any idea how to use it?"

"Indeed, Master Kenji. Once we return to Hamawari I will be happy to guide you through its operation."

He looked up, trying to see the shattered dome in the darkness. "Well, at least our egress just got easier. Let's go home, Dot."

Taking one last look around, he sighed. He would be back, no matter what. With the most valuable artifact in the entire human empire tucked snugly into his coat pocket, Kenji began the slow ascent back to the surface.

The fuel cell's gauge beeped once, notifying him that the *Wanderer*'s battery was down to twenty percent. Instead of firing the engines directly, he used the Grav-Drive's gravity well as a buoyancy system, the ship casually floating upward. It was painfully slow and would probably get them caught in the storm. But if he was lucky, he'd reach topside with maybe eighteen percent left. It would take every bit of it to get home.

The depth gauge read five hundred meters when the sonar began beeping rapidly. Kenji looked and saw an unknown signature moving its way across the screen. It was huge and moving fast.

Shit.

Kenji cut the engines, and all the lights on the *Wanderer* dimmed, leaving him in still, silent darkness. He waited for several tense moments. Sweat beaded down his nose as he monitored the sonar. The blip was less than fifty meters away and growing closer.

Only the faintest rays of light managed to penetrate to this depth, but they revealed enough to confirm Kenji's worst fear. Just on the edge of his vision, a dark, hulking silhouette cut through the water. It was quicker and lither than should have been possible for a creature its size, its serpentine body easily five times the length of the *Wanderer*.

Terror gripped Kenji like a fist clutching at his heart. It was hard to breathe. He couldn't make out the details from here, but he knew what was stalking him. A beast with scales thick enough to stop artillery shells, fangs long enough to cut through a ship's hull, and long tendrils covered in barbs poisonous enough to kill a fully-grown Tomashi whale in minutes. Kenji was face-to-face with a shaskari—a real-life kaiju.

And he was completely at its mercy.

He tried to remain calm, even as he started hyperventilating. *No. No, no, no.* He wasn't getting eaten. Not today of all days. The monster, still barely a blur in the murky water, was cutting wide swathes in every direction, sometimes disappearing out of sight in the gloom, sometimes cutting a path so near him, it sent him rocking in its wake. Either it was toying with its prey or, as of yet, had not located him.

Shaskari were blind but had hyper-acute hearing—able to use vibrations in the water to track down a ship from a hundred kilometers away if the rumors were to be believed. The shockwave must have attracted if here. Damn it. His only chance of survival now was to stay silent and motionless, like a sitting duck, and hope the shaskari continued its hunt elsewhere before it bumped into him by sheer coincidence. Double damn it.

It dropped below the level of the *Wanderer* and moved to-and-fro in every direction. Kenji muttered a prayer under his breath as he waited to be detected and swallowed whole. Odd how impending death could bring a prayer to the lips of even the most secular men.

After what felt like an eternity, the shaskari finally swam away. Its signature vanished off the edge of the sonar as it moved in the wrong direction in search of its meal. The poor thing would just have to go hungry tonight. Kenji could have cried. Instead, he settled for a stifled laugh into his coat arm and a pull from his ankle flask. He wasn't out of the woods yet, though. If he could get to the surface, the shaskari would never catch him. But if he slammed his engines on now and tried to outrace the monster up to the surface he might just win, but he'd be dead in the water before he ever reached home.

It would be so simple if he could just stop at a port and refuel along the way. Unfortunately, there wasn't a single friendly port between here and Hamawari. Either hostile nations or pirate lords dominated this entire hemisphere since the Zukashima Conflicts had destabilized the region twenty years ago. Taking the eastern approach and stopping overnight at Pyonjira was viable, but Kenji was currently penniless, having left his damned money clip at the compound like an idiot. He made his decision.

For over an hour, Kenji laid in wait, engines off, for the shaskari to get as far away as possible. Then he cut on the Grav-Drive to its lowest setting and began the slow float to the surface. The seconds inched by as his depth gauge counted down.

His heart was thudding in his chest. Only twenty meters left. He was going to make it. He could see the surface rippling above him. So close. The sonar blared as a familiar form screamed across the screen. The beast was back, and Kenji was moments from death.

"Better luck next time, asshole!" Kenji roared as he slammed down the accelerator.

The *Wanderer* covered the final ten meters in an instant, breaking the surface at breakneck speed and flying through the air before slamming back down onto the top of the waves with a loud splash. Kenji's beautiful, splendid, magnificent ship didn't even slow as it touched back down. A colossal gout of water erupted from where he'd just been moments before.

The shaskari breached nearly a full thirty meters into the sky, like a black obelisk of scales and rage. In the light, Kenji looked back toward the monster and peered into its eyes. For the rest of his life, Kenji didn't think he'd ever forget those knowing, crimson eyes. This wasn't some mindless beast that hunted on instincts. It was a vile, dead-hearted demon.

The shaskari crashed toward him like a tsunami, but it was too slow. Kenji screamed as its gaping jaws hit the water just feet behind him, the surge of powerful waves nearly flipping his ship. The *Wanderer* did not flip, though. And the chase was as good as over. Even as the wide, chitinous head of the shaskari came back above the tide, Kenji was long gone.

As they raced across the waves, and Kenji took several slow, deep breathes to calm himself, Dot's cheery voice chirped through his earpiece. "Quite impressive, Master Kenji. Your exemplary piloting skills and iron-forged nerves are to be commended. We are currently moving in a northerly direction. Have you decided on a course of action?"

Kenji took a moment to consider. A heavy curtain of rain raced toward him, less than half a kilometer away. As much as he would like to avoid any further near-death experiences for the day, they needed to get home. Not being particularly fond of sleeping on the deck, he made his decision and took off straight toward Hamawari, praying to any god that would listen that he didn't get murdered by pirates.

The *Wanderer* flew over the waves, hull only touching the water at the highest crests. The storm couldn't hope to keep up as the ship covered league after league. They kept the pace for nearly three hours. Occasionally, the misty peaks of distant mountains could be seen. He always kept a wide berth, staying to the open waters, eyes constantly shifting between the sonar and horizon as he stayed on the lookout for any hostile vessels.

The *Wanderer* was scuttling around one such landmass when the sonar system chimed an alert. Kenji threw the brake as he glared at the sonar. A single dot pinged across the upper corner of the screen, moving slowly from right to left. He sat in silence, not daring to make a sound. Pirates.

As easy as it would have been to gun it and leave them stunned, he couldn't risk draining the cell and leaving himself dead in the water. For five agonizing minutes Kenji sat motionless at the helm of the *Wanderer*, eyes glued to the sonar as he waited for the pirates to pass, hoping they either didn't notice him or didn't care enough to harass such a small ship.

Finally, the foreign vessel disappeared off the left of the sonar screen. Kenji breathed a sigh of relief and continued his journey home. By the time the sun was sinking under the horizon he was back in friendly waters. As the shroud of night settled over him, he checked his fuel cell. Two percent. He laughed. It didn't matter; he'd made it.

Throttling down, Kenji approached the familiar shoreline. There, enveloped by a mangrove of osai trees, was the mouth of the Wari River. By the light of the full moon, the *Wanderer* cut silently up the meandering waterways. Ten minutes later Kenji was home, Hamawari.

Nestled against the river, the city was illuminated by the warm glow of thousands of lanterns. Unlike the rest of Jonderun, the residents of Hamawari still held their ancestral heritage close to their hearts. The wooden buildings all bore the high-pitched, curved roofs and ancient Shinto architecture of the long-dead Japanese empire. Thousands of pink cherry blossoms floated lazily around Kenji as he docked his ship and stepped onto the floating, wooden pier.

His breath misted slightly as he stood, the air here even colder than it had been near the equator. Something was...off. The narrow streets should have been bustling, thousands of people flooding the Izakaya District for a night of merriment. But the city was dead; the only noise his heartbeat pounding in his ears. Cold tension permeated the air.

He should have been relieved to make it home safely, excited to share his incredible news with anyone who would listen. Instead, a nagging apprehension pinched at the base of his skull. He fingered the small cube in his pocket absently. On a hunch he couldn't shake, he stashed the cube in his sock, the bulge hidden by his pant leg. Then he turned around, kneeling to open a small compartment under his seat. A compact, polymer handgun glinted in the moonlight as he tucked it into the back of his trousers.

His strides were long and quick as he made his way through the winding streets toward his estate. Where the hell was everybody? A time or two, he looked into a window, and the shutters snapped closed. Swallowing down the foreboding tightness in his gut, he pressed on. He walked through a few neighborhoods and turned a corner a block from his home, the Izuya familial compound. Kenji found the crowd he'd been expecting.

Gathered around the walled courtyard of the three-story building was a mob of what had to have been almost a hundred people, all with their backs turned to him, trying to stand on the tips of their toes to get a better view of the spectacle—whatever it was—transpiring at the gate. Kenji heard shouting and loud banging as he shoved his way through the crowd of onlookers. People gasped and murmured as he passed.

He finally broke through the thick band of bystanders and jerked to a stop.

The gates were battered down. A dozen men in mottled gray fatigues were stomping around his property, giving commands as they held their carbines at the low ready. They were New Terran soldiers, and they were rounding up his family at gunpoint. *Oh shit.* His uncles, aunts, grandparents, cousins, all bound and kneeling in a line in the courtyard. Many of the girls and women were crying, but the men were stone-eyed and defiant as they stared up at the soldiers with contempt.

Kenji stepped forward. "What the hell is going on here?" he asked the closest soldier.

His family looked at him at the same time the intruder did. Restrained and with mouths bound, some of the more frantic ones looked at him pleadingly, their eyes asking him to save them. Others yelled into their gags, screaming at him to get away. To leave. The soldier, a grizzled man with hair graying around his temples, turned to face him, eyeing him up and down. He pressed the comm piece in his ear. "Target in the courtyard."

Kenji's blood ran cold. His bluster was just that. He was terrified. It was all he could do just to keep his hands from shaking. Why were they here for him? He felt the weight of the Library in his sock, but that didn't make any sense. There's no way they could know about it.

"Target? Have you people lost your minds? What have I done to warrant a dozen armed men breaking down my family's doors and detaining a frail, elderly woman?" He asked, gesturing to his eighty-year-old grandmother kneeling on the ground, clearly in excruciating pain.

The soldier lashed out lightning-fast, the butt of his gun slamming into Kenji's nose with a crunch. In a spray of blood, Kenji's eyes rolled into the back of his head, and he stumbled backward. He kept his footing despite the searing pain, shaking the stars from his vision as he wiped the warm blood from his face. Eyes watering, he reached up and touched his nose. It was bent sideways.

He could hear the murmur of the crowd pick up behind him in agitation. "Oh my god," they said. "Someone has to do something." But no one moved. No one helped. No one did anything. Interfering with New Terran soldiers was a quick way to end up shot, floating facedown in the river.

He nearly reached for the gun in his waistband, nearly blew a hole in the soldier's head, but he knew it would end with him and his whole family being murdered in cold blood. Gritting his teeth, he kept his composure. The soldier grinned. Kenji could tell he was about to strike again. Before he got the opportunity, the door behind him slid open, and three people walked out.

A tall, gaunt man was leading, his pockmarked face twisted into a wicked sneer. The many bronze and silver medals pinned to the chest of his knee-length black coat jingled as he walked. Kenji recognized the insignia attached to the man's collar and his heart sank. He was a pontifex of the New Terran government, and the two people shuffling behind him, hands shackled behind their backs, were Kenji's mother and father.

His mouth went dry. If a pontifex was here, they were in serious trouble. But what the hell had he done? Were they really here for the Library after only a few hours? They would have had to already be on-world. If so, Kenji had just delivered it right into their hands. *Idiot,* he berated himself. His mind raced for a solution. There was no way he could allow the Library to fall into the NTE's hands. The soldier to his side struck the back of his knees, dropping him to the ground.

The pontifex stood before Kenji, appraising him, that condescending smile still locked on his face. Kenji looked past him to his parents. His mother wore a blank expression as she stared at her feet. His father looked furious, blood streaming down his face from a gash on his brow. The pontifex grabbed Kenji by the cheeks and brought his gaze back up to him.

"I would suggest you give me your undivided attention, Kenji Izuya. I have important matters to discuss with you that may very well save humanity," he said in an oily voice.

Kenji's chest tightened. They really were here for the Library. He searched for something to say. "The only matter we have to discuss is why you've unjustly stormed our estate and detained my family," he spat, his tone icy and dangerous.

"Come now," the pontifex said casually. "We both know why I'm here. And there's no need for us to be unpleasant with each other. This can just be a friendly conversation. Here, I'll start. My name is Pontifex Novak Abelard. It's a pleasure to meet you, Kenji."

"The pleasure's mine. Why are you here?" Kenji knew this man's type. He was vicious, a shark. If Kenji showed weakness, it would be blood in the water.

A twinge of annoyance shot through the pontifex's face, but he retained his cheerful demeanor. "Not one for small talk, I see. Fine." He turned to look at Kenji's parents. "Hayato, Akira, you should both be very proud of your son. He found something incredible today. Didn't you, Kenji?"

Kenji froze as his parents looked at him. He didn't want to say the wrong thing.

So instead, he said nothing. Seeing no answer forthcoming, his father spoke first. "What has happened, my son?"

"Oh, Mister Hayato, it's actually rather amazing," Pontifex Abelard interjected.

"Your son found this shithole's long-lost Eden today."

The crowd in the street erupted in chatter at the pontifex's nonchalant declaration. Some ran off to spread the news, but most stayed rooted in place, watching how this grand drama played out. Hayato's eyes widened.

"Truthfully, we're really rather grateful for you, Kenji," the pontifex continued. "We've been on-world searching for this Eden for six months now. We did our homework. You see, you've made quite the name for yourself, boy. Best scavenger around, they say." He chuckled to himself. "Quite. We knew you were looking for it, so we've kept an eye on you."

His smile was viperous. "I'll tell you, we were ecstatic when our instruments picked up that pulse message earlier. The Library was back online, and we knew there was only one person who could have found it." He shrugged. "Or at least we assumed." His laughter was grinding, like metal scraping against metal. "Oh, but how embarrassing it would be if we jumped to the wrong conclusion. I would certainly owe an apology to Mrs. Akira, no? But then, that's not the case, is it, Kenji?" Kenji said nothing. He kept his eyes on the ground in front of him. "Hmm, thought not," the pontifex said. "Give it to us."

"I'm sorry, Novak," Kenji said quietly. "I'm sure I have no idea what you're talking about."

The pontifex's smile soured. He grabbed Kenji by the throat and slammed a fist into his face. Hard. Akira wailed.

"The Library of Alexandria is more valuable than this entire planet. Do you understand what the New Terran Empire could achieve with all that knowledge? We could pull humanity through these wicked times. Establish a new hegemony. You could be the savior of humanity, Kenji."

It was Hayato who spoke up. "Save humanity? Helping fascist tyrants set up an empire isn't saving humanity, Pontifex."

Novak whirled on him. "We're not tyrants, Mr. Izuya. We're shepherds. We do what must be done. Humanity is in the middle of a crisis—a battle for their very lives—and we will lead them through it. At any cost. We just need the help of the Library."

Hayato looked at him defiantly. "I would rather die than be strong-armed by a bunch of thugs like you."

Novak looked as if he were about to strike him, but then stopped. "You might," he looked over at Akira, "but would she?" Without a second thought, like it was the simplest decision he'd ever made, the pontifex brought a handgun out of his coat and shot Akira Izuya in the temple.

Time slowed as Kenji watched his mother's body topple to the ground. He couldn't hear the crowd screaming and scrambling behind him. He couldn't hear his father weeping softly. He couldn't even hear the scream tearing from his own throat. There was only the ringing in his ear and the beating of his heart in his chest.

He screamed until he was out of breath, then slumped as he looked into his mother's eyes. Those eyes that had been so bright with life were now dim. A hand grabbed him by the cheek and yanked his head back. He looked up, and Novak slammed the butt of his pistol into his already broken nose. His body went limp as he nearly lost consciousness. The hand still holding him by the face kept him up.

"I'm not playing fucking games, boy!" Novak roared. "Do you have any understanding of how relativism works? Any idea what coming here for the Library has cost us? By the time we return home, my wife will be dead. My children will be old enough to be my parents. Coming here has cost me *everything*! That's what we're willing to sacrifice. *That's* how much we believe in New Terra. Now give. Me. The. Library."

Kenji's eyes drifted to his father. Hayato was hunched next to Akira, the woman who had been by his side for over thirty years. Tears streaked his father's cheeks, but Hayato was composed. His fury was cold and rigid. He wouldn't give the pontifex the satisfaction of his grief. Kenji locked eyes with his father and saw the fire in them. He knew what the look meant.

Kenji turned to Novak. "Piss off," he said, voice hoarse.

The pontifex stared at him for a moment, then threw him to the ground. He walked over to stand in front of Hayato. Kenji's father looked up at him with steely determination.

"*Shinjimae.*" Go to hell.

Pontifex Abelard sneered. "I'll see you there." He lifted the gun and shot Hayato between the eyes.

Something snapped inside Kenji as he watched his father's body hit the ground next to his mother, their blood mingling together into a large pool. The knot tying his humanity, consciousness, and body together unraveled. His emotions left him, and he was an empty husk of a man, devoid of pain, sadness, anything. There was only numbness. He looked up at Novak.

The man shot him a wicked smile, face flecked with his father's blood. He swung his arm around, gesturing to Kenji's family, all kneeling in a line. "I have more bullets than you have relatives, Kenji. Tell me where the Library is, and this can all be over." Kenji barely heard him. He stared at the bodies of his parents, his chest hollow. In an attempt to retain his sanity, his mind had disassociated itself from his body. He was watching the grizzly scene from over his own shoulder, trying to make sense of what he was seeing.

Pain brought him back to himself. The pontifex was grasping him by the front of his shirt, striking him over and over again. Finally, he let go of Kenji's shirt, and Kenji collapsed into a bloody heap.

"I'll ask you one more time, boy. If you don't answer I'm going to shoot you. Then I'm going to shoot your entire family and tear apart everything you own until I find it."

Lying on his back, dazed, Kenji looked up at the pontifex through battered, swollen eyes. "Shinjimae."

Novak howled and lifted his gun. The courtyard erupted in gunfire. Bullets flew in every direction as the crowd devolved into a mass of screams and stomping feet. Novak turned, trying to figure out what the hell was happening, Bullets zipped by him, striking the ground at his feet in puffs of dirt. It was absolute chaos. He couldn't tell where the attack was coming from. Soldiers were dropping everywhere, firing randomly at an unseen enemy.

Kenji's eyes came into focus, and he saw what was happening. Men in black fatigues and masks had infiltrated the estate, whether by climbing the wall or sneaking into another gate, Kenji didn't know. They had taken up covered positions and were raining fire down on the New Terran soldiers stuck in the open courtyard. It was a killing field.

Barely aware of what his own body was doing, Kenji reached behind his back. Novak caught the movement in the corner of his eye and turned back. Too late. Kenji drew his pistol and pulled the trigger. The bullet struck the pontifex under the jaw, ripping through his brainpan and exploding out the back of his head in a spray of skull fragments and gray matter.

Every NTE soldier in the courtyard was killed. Every single one. Some had dropped their weapons and tried to flee, but they'd been gunned down all the same. That thought comforted Kenji, somewhat. Now the estate was hectic as people rushed to-and-fro. By unfathomable odds or divine providence, not a single member of Kenji's family had been killed in the crossfire. His cousin, Yuwe, had been struck in the leg, but the response by medical personnel was astoundingly fast. In only minutes, there were already dozens of medics and doctors flooding the grounds—locals who had gotten wind of what was happening and had rushed to help, doing whatever they could. They placed a tourniquet on Yuwe's leg and carried her away on a gurney.

One of them ran up to check him out as he lay on the ground, staring up at the stars. He yelped as she set his nose straight. Seeing he had no life-threatening injuries, she hurried off, moving to help her associates check the soldiers strewn about the property. Kenji acutely felt the weight of the Library in his sock, and it was impossibly heavy. He looked over to his parents, but their bodies had already been covered by white cloth.

Tears welled up in his eyes. His parents were dead, and it was his fault. His discovery, his refusal to give in to the New Terrans, had led to their execution. And he hadn't even had the decency to die with them. He wanted to curl up into a ball and die right there, die and join his parents, wherever that may be. But he wouldn't allow himself to wallow in self-pity. He'd thought his life's work was to find Eden, but he knew better now.

The cold numbness inside of him began to thaw with white-hot rage. Not loud, explosive anger; it was the kind of silent fury that would fester and grow every day for the rest of his life. He was going to dismantle the New Terran Empire. He was going to burn their world down around their heads and then laugh in the ashes. He didn't know how he was going to do it, but he going to make them pay. All of them.

As if in answer to his silent prayer, a man approached him. He was wearing black fatigues, and his carbine was slung over his shoulder. His light skin, blonde hair, and green eyes betrayed him as an off-worlder. Kenji stared at his face and thought he saw...sorrow? Regret?

"Kenji Izuya, I'm Captain Thorne," the man said, grabbing him by the wrist and shoulder and helping him to sit up. He looked into Kenji's eyes. "I'm sorry. I'm so sorry."

He embraced Kenji, like a brother consoling a younger sibling. Kenji sat there in confusion, hands at his sides as he tried to figure out what the hell this guy's deal was. Captain Thorne released him, holding him out at arm's length, clutching his shoulders.

"We knew they were watching you, knew they'd be coming. We weren't quick enough to stop them. Kenji, I'm sorry."

"Wh-who are you people?" Kenji asked.

The captain sighed. "We're what's left of the ISA, kid. There are more of us on a cruiser parked in low orbit."

Kenji blinked, sitting there as if he hadn't heard what the man said. "The ISA is gone. It's been over a hundred years since the collapse," he all but whispered.

"Well, yes," the captain replied. "Our infrastructure and seat of power crumbled, but we've been holding on this entire time, waiting in the wings for a shot to take it all back."

Kenji's mind raced. The ISA wasn't dead. There was still hope. "Why are you here?"

"On Jonderun or at your house?"

"Yes."

Thorne chuckled. "The Library of Alexandria. We had our ears to the ground and heard some rumors. Six months ago, our intelligence division caught wind that the NTE was taking it seriously and were mobilizing an Inquisition team, so we decided to come check it out." He eyed Kenji. "Is it true? Did you really find it?"

Kenji didn't answer, staring dubiously at the stranger kneeling beside him.

Thorne chuckled again, nodding as he rose to his feet. "I understand. Listen, kid, you understand what the Library is, what it could mean for every human being across the galaxy. This is our chance to end all the misery and suffering since the collapse. We need your help, Kenji."

Kenji didn't answer right away. He stared off into the middle distance as he weighed his options. He thought he felt sincerity in the captain's words. They wanted to help. On some base level, their desire for the Library was different than the NTE. The pontifex's desire was ravenous and deadly, like the inescapable grasp of a black hole. The captain's desire was out of desperation. Desperation to reconcile, to heal, to salvage what was left of the once great human empire.

"You'll drive the New Terrans from Jonderun?"

"Already under way. There's a chance we could drive them from this entire sector before reinforcements arrive."

Kenji nodded. He felt his hand moving down toward his foot. Hitching up his pant leg, he pulled the cube out of his sock, holding it up for Thorne to inspect. The captain's face went slack.

"My god. You really have it." Thorne stared at it in awe. Then he turned to look at the covered corpses of Kenji's dead parents. "You had it the entire time," he whispered, turning back to Kenji with a new respect. Kenji was willing to make the impossibly difficult decision for the good of humanity.

With trembling hands, Thorne reached for the Library. Kenji surrendered, and he grabbed it, holding it up against the light. Then the captain laughed so warm and loud it nearly thawed Kenji's frozen, dead heart. He tucked the cube into a coat pocket.

"History will remember your name for a hundred generations, Kenji Izuya, and they'll remember the sacrifice of your parents. Thank you, truly." Thorne helped Kenji to his feet. They exchanged a firm handshake, and Thorne moved to walk away. He paused, then turned back to Kenji. "We'll help to finish the clean up here, then we're gonna be staying in Kairu until tomorrow morning. If you have a mind for vengeance, and you want to help shape the course of human history, meet us there before we shuttle up to orbit."

With that, Captain Thorne strode away, barking orders to his men as he went. Kenji was left standing alone in the courtyard as people hustled around him in every direction. He looked down at his hands, flexed his fingers. Had he done the right thing? Had anything he'd done tonight been the right thing? He thought of the faces of his mother and father, picturing them only in his mind, unable to bear looking at their bodies. He refused to lift the sheets and see them as they were now.

Many of his relatives tried to give him their condolences and kind words, keening at the loss of the family patriarch and matriarch, but Kenji heard nothing of what they said. He didn't say a single word for a long time. Soon, the crowd in his courtyard dwindled, the atmosphere calming. And still Kenji stood, rooted in place, in the same spot, staring up at the sky and pondering the parting words the captain had given him. *If you have a mind for vengeance, and you want to help shape the course of human history, meet us there before we leave.* He thought that sounded pretty good. There was nothing left here for him but painful memories.

That night, the town square was alight with the funeral pyres of Hayato and Akira Izuya. Mourners showed up by the thousands to place cherry blossoms and osai bark at the foot of the pyres. For the first time, Kenji spent much of the night in the arms of his love, Imora, though it was a bittersweet thing. He kissed the supple skin of her neck and nestled into the warmth of her bosom, yet he couldn't feel the joy of it that he'd been waiting for since he was a teenager. All night he tried to find out how much alcohol it would take to numb the pain. He never got his answer.

Kenji dressed in silence and snuck out of the compound without fanfare or goodbyes, leaving Imora asleep in his bed. He made his way through the cramped streets, head down as he wove through the mass of people. He took his position at the command board, and for the first time, he muted Dot's voice as he sailed in silence to Kairu, Jonderun's only planetary launch port.

As the *Wanderer* skimmed across the waves, Kenji thought again on the words Captain Thorne had said to him: *they'll remember your name for a hundred generations.* He held no illusions. He would not be remembered as a hero, a brave explorer whose discoveries changed everything. No, he would be remembered as a butcher, a merciless hunter.

As the ancient Earthen Inquisition had purged the heretic and the witch, he would purge the New Terran Empire from the galaxy. He would pluck every NTE ship from the stars as if by the hand of God himself and eradicate every piece of power and influence they had ever held. He would carry the ISA to hegemony on his blood-soaked back. A hundred generations from now, that was how they would remember Kenji Izuya, in all his terrible glory. *That* was his new life's work, and it was valid.

Empire Reborn

by C. C. Forshee

Date: 2899

"You can do this, Cal. I know it."

"I bloody well hope so. It'd be rather embarrassing to come all this way just to fall flat on my face at the finish line."

Sitting backstage in the cramped fitting room, Calvin Thellhorn leaned back, elbows propped on the leather arms of the wingback chair. His hands were tented in front of him as he sat in contemplation, his eyes staring off at nothing. He reached over to the end table to his right and grabbed his glass of vintage vino.

"I'm serious, Cal. There are a million billion people who believe in what you stand for, and they're all going to be tuning in to the summit tonight. There's not a single planet in human-controlled space that won't be abuzz with chatter tomorrow." Varis paced around the room, shuffling through the stack of papers in his hands.

Calvin regarded his aide. The squat, balding man wasn't much to look at, but he was as fearless as a mongoose and as loyal as a wolfhound. "You've been with me longer than anyone else, Varis," Calvin said flatly as he sipped his wine. "Tell me. Am I a fraud?"

Varis stopped dead in his tracks and turned to Calvin, his plump, porcine face a cipher. "Stop that."

"Excuse me?"

Varis walked up beside him and placed his hand on his shoulder. "Chancellor Thellhorn, you have stabilized a dozen warring sectors, freed dozens more from New Terran control, and gathered all the leading factions together in one place to unite them under ISA hegemony. You have single-handedly launched the ISA back to the forefront of humanity after three hundred years." He smirked. "If you're a fraud, you are the most accomplished fraud in history."

Calvin smiled into his glass before downing the rest of his drink. "I guess when you list all of my accomplishments out loud like that, I do sound rather impressive, don't I?" He shot Varis a wry grin and the portly man rolled his eyes.

"Humble, too."

"Help me up, would you, Varis?"

Varis obliged, helping the Chancellor to his feet. "Your knee still giving you trouble?"

"Just a little stiff tonight. It always acts up after a warp jump." Calvin stretched his leg, bending the knee back and forth to get the blood flowing. He'd been gimped ever since tearing his patellar tendon when an explosion had thrown him to the deck of his ship during the Fringe Zone campaign. He thought it made him look like an invalid, though Varis assured him the cane made him look distinguished, like a wounded war hero.

He hobbled over to the small mirror across the room and stared at himself. He had more wrinkles than he remembered. "Man's greatest folly has always been hubris, my friend. Why should a million billion people put their faith in me?"

"They love you."

"I don't want them to love *me*," Calvin said, his eyes still on the mirror. "I want them to love my words, my ideals, my dreams for the future."

Varis shrugged. "Why not both?" He came up behind and to the side of Calvin, looking at him through the mirror. "No one else could have done this, Cal. You're on the precipice of changing everything. If you can sway the joint council tonight, hundreds of years of turmoil will be behind us, and a bright and shining future will be the only thing laying before us. We trust you implicitly, Chancellor. Always."

Calvin smiled, adjusting the collar of his formal jacket and checking his teeth for debris. "It's showtime, old friend. Let's make history."

With that, Calvin grabbed his cane and walked across the fitting room to the door. It slid open, and as Grand Chancellor Calvin Thellhorn stepped out onto the stage, his world erupted in flashing lights and thunderous applause.

Undiscovered Nightmare

By B. E. Waymire

Date: 3250

"Less than two Earth-standard months ago, we heard a signal from the Corolis-143 system. Machine analysis has failed to translate the signal into anything that makes sense. Experts say that though artificial intelligence has failed to decipher it, they can tell from the patterns that it must be a consistent language. In response to this, the ISA has dispatched the *Sacagawea* exploration ship to check out exactly what inhabits the planet. We eagerly await announcement of First Contact and will keep you updated as the situation develops."

Every time a new world was discovered, the media decided it must be inhabited, and it was time to meet another civilization. ISA representatives were always forced to stand in front of a scoop-hungry media and tell them that they were all wrong. Chatter about the new planet would continue for a day or two more, then die out. Sometimes, if a planet were habitable, chatter would go on long enough for a single settlement to begin. With humanity spread out among so many galaxies, it would take a major, catastrophic event to get the media's attention elsewhere.

To be fair, Corolis-143g was a decent candidate for life. It was only three percent larger than Earth, with water over nearly two-thirds of its surface. Most of the landmasses ringed the world near its equator, but it should have been relatively cool so far out in the habitable zone. Islands dotted the oceans between the massive ice caps and the equatorial continents. Most important to the media, there was no sign of nonhuman life that could discover fire, much less electricity.

Artemis Leach scratched at his graying beard. "How disappointed will they be this time?"

Commander of the ISA *Sacagawea*, Junlin Cao, sighed loudly. "Very. Here's what we found."

The display changed. Away went the dirty-blonde newswoman, replaced with a view of the planet below as captured by atmospheric probes. The image zoomed in quickly to focus on the origin of the signal. It was a small plain surrounded by several mountains. The zoomed-out image showed three circles, one in the center of the plain, one to the east in the middle of the mountains, and the last to the north of the plain.

Cao magnified the first region to show a basic settlement. Leach estimated there was enough space for two hundred inhabitants. Common domed structures spread out in a web connected via tunnels. The design left enough space for a courtyard that, though overgrown, had a distinct look of once being well-manicured and organized.

In the second region, in the mountains, lay the broken pieces of a starship. It was a standard lander, roughly teardrop-shaped from its top profile. At least, it would have been had it not been split in two. A line of broken foliage ran from the aft to the fore, where the broken bridge section had split from the drive. Between the two halves was a mass of debris.

In the final marked area was an Eden, fallen into a sinkhole. The body of the great machine was leaning against the nearest mountain. Trenches radiated out from the hole like veins. The Eden's outer shell was mostly removed, revealing the electronics and machinery below. Vegetation had attempted to take it over, twisting in and through the main frame and over the remaining panels.

"That is rather mysterious," Leach said.

Cao nodded. "An unregistered settlement, as far as we can tell."

"No signs of anyone left, I presume?"

"None that we could find. Indications are that no one has lived there for a long time."

Leach smiled. "I never could resist a good mystery."

Cao returned the smile. "Is your crew ready?"

"They had better be."

"Good hunting."

After a firm handshake, Cao departed. Leach walked the opposite direction, following the signage to the docking arms. On the way, he pulled up the crew profiles on his PDA.

Their biologist was Sabine Veldt. She was educated beyond reason, naturally. Leach had met her once. Their conversation had centered on the varieties of plants she had discovered on seven different worlds. She had not struck Leach as arrogant, just excited about her work.

Leach had specifically asked for Benjamin Fall to fly the landing craft. He had lived all his life in space, running supplies between stations and settlements. He had boasted that he could navigate a freighter through a planetary ring without striking a single object. He had never made a deorbit, but neither had any other pilot on the ship.

On Cao's suggestion, they had a questionably sociopathic marine, William Cobb, as their weapons specialist and guard. He was the paranoid sort, believing that his guard was required for every moment or else catastrophe would come. On his head was the near-permanent fixture of a cone-shaped helmet, earning him the derisive nickname Corn.

The last member had a name, but even in the ship's logs was only known as Intern. As his name would suggest, he was a student intern from a university Leach had never heard of, under some big-shot academic who wanted to get his research without doing the work himself. Leach just assumed the name was a placeholder for whoever the university decided to send.

The docking area was a massive cylinder, one of the only places with vast open space. A single catwalk ran down the center, and along the walls were airlock hatches leading to the ships attached to the outer hull via docking clamps. Leach walked into the microgravity, letting the electromagnets on his boots hold him to the catwalk until he was directly under the hatch leading to the *Aurora*.

***

The crew had already assembled on the *Aurora's* bridge, as Leach had instructed. Six crash couches, surrounded by electronics, sat at stations roughly in front of a wide transparent screen. Only the commander and pilot had specific stations, with the pilot in the center at the main controls and the commander behind the pilot. The other four stations were along the bridge's forward edge. Veldt, Cobb, and Intern had spread themselves out in the spare stations.

Leach strapped into his crash couch and settled himself. "I'm sure you've heard, but I'll recap for completeness. There are no extraterrestrials on this planet. There is, however, a settlement, a crashed starship, and a broken Eden. It's likely these are all connected, and we're going to figure it out. Fall, preflight us."

"Yes, bossman," Fall said in his heavy spacer accent.

Leach brought up a hologram from his couch's arm. It showed the *Aurora* with all her systems labeled. Overall, the ship resembled the crash on the planet, though more angled into a diamond shape than a teardrop. *Aurora* could have been related, as far as Leach knew.

Different areas on the hologram highlighted green as Fall ran quick tests on the systems. A computer automatically checked the RCS and main drive systems as Fall activated the cameras and panned them through their full range of motion. The control surfaces flexed uselessly. Even the landing legs deployed and retracted. When every system marked on the hologram had gone from white to green, Leach smiled. Fall had gone through every procedure without hesitation.

Fall took a deep breath and flicked the intercom switch on his controls. "*Sacagawea* traffic control, this is lander *Aurora*, yeah?"

The traffic controller was a woman, young enough to possibly be on her first on-ship assignment in the tiny room within the *Sacagawea's* tower, going by the sound of her voice. "*Aurora*, this is *Sacagawea* traffic control."

"We need departure. Going to planet below."

"Affirmative. Releasing docking clamps. Skies are clear, *Aurora*."

Fall turned to the other crew. "Hold on, 'kay? We gonna blaze this one hard."

"Make it so," Leach said.

Intern groaned. "Such a wonderful flight, heading down to a planet with a pilot named Fall…"

"You can't get any better pilot than a spacer, kid," Cobb said.

"And I gonna prove it, yeah?" Fall boasted as he forced the engines to full power.

Aurora blasted away from the *Sacagawea*. Fall worked the lightweight controls expertly, throwing the lander around its mothership in a corkscrew. The crew were thrown around as *Aurora* twisted and darted around space, until they had cleared the *Sacagawea* completely.

"Have you proven your point yet?" Veldt asked.

"Just want to know Intern trust me," Fall responded.

The *Aurora* flipped around. RCS thrusters fired, pushing everyone back into their seats then down again as the ship tumbled. Leach watched the trajectory prediction hologram carefully. The line adjusted a thousand times, impact warnings appeared, and a call alert came from traffic control. Just as Fall had perfectly precisely stopped on the original entry vector, Leach pressed the call accept button.

The unfortunate controller was unhappy. "What the hell was that, *Aurora*?!"

Leach shook his head. "One of my crew showed a lack of confidence in my pilot's abilities."

"Your pilot has just proven he has a debilitating lack of sense. Tell him we rather like most of you."

"No problem, lady!" Fall shouted without using his own comm. "I just turn autopilot on, yeah? *Aurora* fly herself now."

Leach could hear the controller's eye roll through the comm. "He really has put on autopilot, I promise."

"Just don't…" the controller groaned.

***

"Fall, land us as close to the center of the triangle as you can," Leach ordered as they came in over the site.

Fall nodded. "You got it, bossman."

The *Aurora* circled the area three times before Fall located an appropriate spot. Leach watched as his pilot tapped out locations and commands on a touchscreen monitor, notably keeping his hands away from the regular controls. The autopilot landed them exactly where Fall had pointed, and so softly that no one seemed to realize they had even halted descent for a few extra moments.

"What does the atmosphere look like, Veldt?" Leach asked.

"Ideal for us," Veldt said. "Looks like the Eden did its work."

"Any organic material we might need to be aware of?"

Several seconds passed while Veldt ran another analysis. "Nothing detected. Not even any pollen."

"Cobb, what do you make of this?"

Cobb shrugged. "Open spaces, looks like uneven ground. The settlement, ship, and Eden could be home to some vicious beasties. I suggest going out armed."

Leach thought Cobb would suggest going out armed into a room full of nuns. Regardless, it was a good idea. He pulled up the map of the area and gave the crew a task list. They would first check the ship and then move on to the settlement. There was every good reason to stick together for the time being.

The exit ramp was straight through their combination cargo/vehicle bay. Five quad bikes sat next to each other aimed directly toward the ramp. The walls were lined with equipment, including a large cabinet full of pulse rifles and pistols. Also in the cabinets were survey drones, to be used later.

Leach clipped a pulse rifle to his leg and mounted a bike. He waited for the others to mimic his action before he activated the ramp. As it dropped, warm, moist air flowed into the bay. The sounds of extraterrestrial insects echoed through the space. Corolis-143 glared off the ramp's metal surface. When the metal touched the ground, a cloud of small insects rose and dispersed.

Leach charged down the ramp, listening to the electric hum coming from the motors within the wheels. The suspension flexed as it ran over the slightly bumpy terrain. The PDA nestled on a mount between the handlebars displayed a small sample of the surrounding terrain, along with an arrow showing the route to the ship.

***

The ship's wreck was at once worse and better than it seemed from orbit. Small bits of debris littered the ground between the major halves of the ship, creating rough, uneven terrain that threatened to shake the quad bikes and riders apart. On the other hand, the expanse was remarkably absent of larger debris, with only a few pieces of hull plating lying flat on the ground.

As the stern would mostly be the reactor and drive system, Leach turned to the bow. It would hold more of the valuable data in logs and the various black boxes. At the box, peering through a forward window, was the bridge. It was within easy access through a wide, straight hallway.

The door was sealed shut, but that was remedied with a few low-power pulse rifle blasts. Cobb was right that the firearms would be useful, at least.

Through the door, the bridge was as neat as could be expected from a wreck. The crash couches were sitting on broken gimbals, yet still in their proper places. The monitors surrounding the couches were still intact, even if their mounting arms were twisted. Through the window, Leach saw nothing but the trees ahead. No animals scurried through the trees, and no wind blew.

"What happened here?" Leach said absentmindedly.

"I think it's a crash, bossman," Fall mused from beneath the pilot's console.

"What are you doing?"

"I worked on one of these before I fly, yeah? There's always auxiliary power source under here. If they..." His sentence trailed off as monitors whirred to life and cockpit lights brightened. "See, bossman?"

Leach grabbed the nearest monitor and turned it toward him. It was in its bootup mode, showing a black screen with plain white text scrolling through statistics and data. Corporate splash screens flashed before opening onto a home screen showing a man and woman hugging each other tightly. Scattered in front of the image were links to folders marked with locations and event names. Leach selected one marked Migration.

Within the folder were three video logs, the first of which Leach selected. The video came up with the same two faces as on the home screen image, with the man speaking. They were in one of the cabins when it was recorded, given the bed in the background.

The excitement was palpable through the screen. "We've done it! We are on our way to the Corolis-143 system. Thanks to our generous patrons, we can move to a new world without the oversight of the ISA. The world we've chosen has already undergone a terraforming attempt and, according to our scouts, is perfectly habitable. No one on the ship can wait to arrive."

"That explains more than a little," Intern groaned. "What do they think the ISA is for? It protects them from things like this."

"Some people don't like good grace of ISA," Fall responded.

Leach downloaded several more logs to his PDA. He would have to look at them later. There was much to search through in the meantime, and he needed time. This group was not the first to search out a new living without dealing with the ISA, and they for sure would not be the last. If he could find a reason for their situation, it might at least warn someone else.

***

While the ship was broken but otherwise clear of wildlife and vegetation, the settlement was the opposite. The buildings were unbroken, with some even having locked doors. The vegetation covering the complex was something like moss. Small insects skittered in the moss. At least one local rodent darted across a roof.

They found one open door, half-obscured by a mossy curtain. When Cobb slid it to the side, large flying insects poured forth in a cloud. Cobb ducked quickly, and Veldt loudly remarked about the need for helmets even with a breathable atmosphere.

The building was about as basic as could be imagined. The front room was a combination living room and kitchen, with a large refrigeration unit sitting near a stove opposite a long sofa and table set. Alternate doors and corridors led into the other buildings. There was a second floor, likely where the toilet, shower, and bedrooms were located. Small bits of vegetation grew in seemingly random places, from tiny plants growing out of the floor to vines crawling along the walls. Indeterminate stains appeared on the floor and walls in no regular pattern.

Veldt kneeled next to a cluster of small, spiky growth. "These are fungi…"

"Anything we should know about it?" Leach asked.

"I'll have to analyze it to see." Her PDA hummed and beeped. "I'm getting nothing so far."

"Let me know immediately if you find something suspicious."

Cobb screamed from the next building. Leach charged his weapon and ran, following the sounds of cursing and the flash of a distant pulse rifle. The flashing had stopped by the time Leach found Cobb, but the cursing had not.

The room was just like the first in layout and decoration, including the vegetation. Dark stains continued their irregular pattern. The loose chairs were turned over, probably a consequence of Cobb's movements. The mercenary himself had his weapon pointed at a small pile of charred fauna. Intern was behind him, holding his chest.

"Report," Leach said.

"Intern was frightened by a rodent," Cobb said.

"You screamed first!" Intern protested.

Leach had no mind to deal with them. "It doesn't matter. Was there anything here other than the newly-barbequed rodent?"

Cobb shook his head. "Just the usual."

"I want samples, especially of the stains."

Three hours of searching later, the crew had gathered plenty of evidence. Leach had discovered several PDAs in the living quarters. If he could power them up at the *Aurora*, he could look through the logs. Intern had a lot of samples he particularly declared for his employers at the university, not the crew. Veldt and Fall had gathered enough, at least, for use on the planet.

***

The *Aurora* was well equipped for research. Veldt in particular possessed more than enough equipment for her needs. When Leach checked in on her, all the machines were running analyses, humming and chirping. Veldt was staring at a pair of monitors before her. Both of them were scrolling data Leach could never hope to decipher.

"Anything interesting?" he asked.

Veldt shrugged. "The fungi are poisonous. Doesn't seem to be a contact poison, and it won't break down when exposed to heat. The vines should actually be edible, but I need to do more tests to confirm."

"What about the stains?"

"Inconclusive."

Equal amounts of relief and foreboding grew in Leach's mind. The instruments should have been able to work out human blood, even if it was several decades old. If the stains weren't blood, what were they?

More importantly, where were the settlers? Had they simply walked away? If they did, why?

"Where are the others?" Veldt asked.

"Fall and Intern are headed to the Eden," Leach explained. "Cobb is dissecting machines."

Leach sat down at another station and spread the PDAs out in front of him. He only had three spare power cables and would have to hope for them to have some power left over. Luckily, all of them had shut down automatically and still had at least an hour of battery left. Once they were all active, Leach began his search.

Organization ran the gamut from meticulous to chaotic. One PDA had its logs separated into audio, text, and video folders, then separated further by subject. The main root folder held a few miscellaneous files, mostly newer ones, given the dates in their filenames. Leach could work with that. The worst PDA had every log, mostly text, scattered haphazardly across the desktop. The filenames were not the defaults either, instead being like book chapter titles.

Leach went at it with the meticulous attention of a statistician with hourly pay, beginning with the most chaotic and hoping he could piece together a complete picture using context clues from the other PDAs. Initially, he found text logs about the crew being hounded by "demonic creatures." Dangerous fauna was not uncommon, but the logs described incredibly abnormal behavior. They were intelligent beasts, hunting down and tormenting the settlers as they slowly killed them. Leach immediately put that PDA aside. The user was probably some down-on-his-luck writer wanting to option a film or novel, not a serious traveler journaling his time.

The other PDAs were more useful, with their logs more in the diary style he was looking for. Several of them mentioned looting the inactive Eden for replacement equipment and electronics. Otherwise, they set up properly, spending two months in their migration ship, during which they built the opening stages of their settlement.

He opened a video. The settlers were outside, in a light rain, some under a makeshift canopy, while the others enjoyed the rain. The settlement was still under construction, but no one seemed in any hurry to finish. Despite that, they were having a party to open the settlement officially. Toasts were made to the crew and the ship and the corporations that made the machines building the settlement. He noted the Eden in the background, standing straight and tall.

Leach smiled and pulled up the next video. His smile disappeared. Clouds of dust had descended upon the completed settlement. A weak wind blew, barely pushing the brown, gray, and black particles through open doors. The voice of a young woman screamed about an explosion. The distinct note of breaking metal cracked through the air.

The next video log, from a different PDA, showed what happened. The ground had collapsed underneath the Eden, and a fresh new hole led deep into the planet's crust. Multiple smaller, still-deep fissures radiated outward over a kilometer from the actual hole, according to the video's presenter. The only reason the Eden had not disappeared completely was the sturdy edge of the hole that held the massive machine.

Right as Leach reached for the play button on an audio log, his own PDA alarmed with a connection request. "Leach here."

"Bossman," Fall said, "See the drone feed, yeah?"

Keeping Fall on the line, Leach opened the video. The drone was probably thirty meters up, looking down on the Eden site. Just as said in the video, large fissures radiated outward from the hole. According to the terrain analysis, these reached ten meters deep on average. The hole's depth could not be read through the openings.

"Can we get into that hole?" Leach asked.

"No can do, bossman. Least not from here. Signal goes kaput."

"Get a transmitter to the edge of the hole. I need to know exactly what happened here."

"Yeah, bossman!"

***

Three days went by, the team entirely focused on their work. They had searched through everything they could in the settlement. Leach had discovered more PDAs, Intern and Fall had set up a transmitter network for the drone, and Veldt was analyzing more vegetation. Cobb was just busying himself with whatever he found to do on the ship. He would rather be out hunting aggressive fauna, but they had found none.

Leach was on the bridge, with a complicated monitor setup at his station. On one monitor, he had several live video feeds: from Fall, the drone, and the various cameras around the ship. On the other, he had five PDA logs open. As Intern and Fall set up an antenna inside the hole on the end of a cable, he tuned the logs to the same time signatures as each other.

The collapse had appeared in every log. Confusion and fear rattled the settlers in each one. Some had investigated the edge or the fissures. The settler Leach presumed was their one scientist had written several quick hypotheses but had come to no conclusion about how it had happened. A younger settler complained about the fissures making joyrides in their vehicles more difficult. There was no proper investigation into the hole, though, aside from trying to find the chances of it expanding.

"Bossman!" Fall shouted.

"Yes?" Leach asked.

"We calling for past five minutes. We ready, yeah?"

"Go for it."

The drone darted over to the edge of the hole, then down into it. Spotlights pierced the cloudy, dusty air within the hole. The camera aimed where the wall should have been, and the drone flew toward it. After a half hour of slow flight, the drone came to a wall. Along the jagged wall was a violet mass. Whatever it was, it looked unworldly, even compared to other frightening discoveries in the universe. It seemed to pulsate, but Leach dismissed that as irregularities in the video feed.

"Do you hear that?" Intern asked suddenly.

"Hear what?" Fall said.

"Growling."

"Where?"

Intern grabbed his pulse rifle and waved it around, vocally threatening any fauna that might attack them. Fall walked close, trying to calm him down. When Fall's attempts to console Intern failed, Leach loudly ordered his unruly crewmember to stop and take a deep breath. With seeming reluctance, Intern followed the order. Fall gently and quickly took the rifle away and placed it aside.

"Intern, come back to the ship," Leach commanded.

Wordlessly, Intern turned and began his ride back to the ship.

Leach took the moment of quiet to call Cobb in the vehicle bay. "Listen, Intern had a moment and I've ordered him back here. He says he heard growling, and Fall has no idea what's going on."

"What do you want me to do?" Cobb asked.

"Go out and guard Fall. If something was out there, I don't want it making dinner out of my pilot."

"Yes, sir!"

When he glanced at the drone video, Leach saw a small sampling arm extended to pull some of the violet unknown off the wall. "Veldt will like that. Fall, I want you to pull the drone out of the hole and check your surroundings. If something is around there, we need to know about it."

"Yeah, bossman," Fall said. "I jack in and grab rifle."

"Confirmed."

The drone video fizzled and distorted for a moment as Fall changed from using a physical set of controls to mental commands. Not ideal for precise movements, but he could use a weapon. The drone flew out of the hole quickly and settled a hundred meters above the ground, the camera searching the surrounding area.

"Keep searching until Cobb reaches your position," Leach said.

Cobb interrupted the conversation. "Sir, we have a problem here. It's Intern."

***

Almost halfway between the ship and the Eden, Intern had fallen. He was at the bottom of a fissure, body twisted at an odd angle. Blood left a short trail on the wall. The quad bike was upside down and broken a few meters away. Veldt had retrieved a drone and was flying it near Intern's body. Fall and Cobb walked the perimeter, out of sight and with his drone flying high.

"Why would he drive right into a fissure?" Leach asked the air. "He couldn't have been that upset."

Veldt shook her head. "Maybe not. Look at this."

The drone camera came close to Intern's wounds. Mixed in with his blood was a thick black fluid, moving less like blood and more like a mass of slugs. The sampling arm reached out and grabbed a tiny bit of the black.

Leach nodded. "Everyone, be careful until we can figure this out. If you see something strange, stay away. Until Veldt comes back with some answers, stay away from anything that even might be harmful, including Intern's body."

"No problem on the perimeter, bossman," Fall reported over the comm. "I still got sample from hole wall, yeah? Veldt want it?"

Veldt grabbed the comm. "Yes!"

"Bring that sample to the ship. Watch yourself until you're safe and report any abnormality to me."

"No problem, bossman."

***

It was just after nightfall when Veldt called Leach into the common room. She was bent over an analysis machine, staring into a small monitor. The machine's body whirred and whined. Every few moments, it would pulse with a high-pitched screech.

"What do you have for me?" Leach asked.

"Something interesting," Veldt said.

Under the lenses of five different cameras, each one at a slightly different angle, squirmed the bit of black sludge from Intern's body. Zoomed in, the surface seemed to be transparent while odd organs tumbled over each other as it slithered on the specimen plate. Under infrared, it had a few spots of heat, but was otherwise eerily cool. The monitor's border scrolled chemical symbols faster than Leach could ever hope to read.

"What am I looking at?"

"This thing is secreting a lot of compounds I don't know. I can analyze them, but don't expect any answers for a while."

"Just give me the chances those compounds are dangerous to us."

"Fifty-fifty."

"Wonderful."

Veldt suddenly screamed. The screen showed something new: a tiny, capsule-like machine crawling its way out of the liquid with five tiny flagella.

Leach's eyes widened. "What in the hell is that?"

"It can't be...no, not this!"

"What is wrong?"

"The Pangalactic Peace Project..." Veldt whispered.

"What is that?"

"It was an idea the ISA had to put a stop to war across all space. Instead of using deliberate force, they would simply seed the area with nanomachines that would manipulate the minds of their targets to kill each other instead."

"How do you know about this?"

Veldt's speech came halting and labored. "I may have hacked into an ISA server hunting for information during my school days. These nanomachines get their little chemicals into the brain and begin to manipulate the victim's thoughts. All the machines are networked together...then they..." She closed her eyes. "The ISA used it on one insurrectionist group and depopulated the entire planet. Not one single ISA enforcer was on the ground. The people just...killed themselves."

"Secure your equipment for takeoff!" Leach ordered. "I'm not spending another hour on this godforsaken world."

"Should we get Cobb and Fall back here?"

"Let me worry about them!"

Leach was being paid to investigate a signal and possibly initiate First Contact, not fight against psychotic nanomachines. It would be better to turn the entire planet to dust rather than let those things survive. That might be his recommendation, come to think of it.

He keyed in the startup procedure and listened for the reactor's hum, then activated the comm. "Fall, Cobb, get back to the ship. We're leaving now."

"There something here, bossman!" Fall called back.

Leach hastily dove into the onboard video network. Multiple nodes popped onto the screen. He located the crew cameras and ran through them one by one. Most showed the inside of a locker or the ceiling. There were two exceptions. Cobb was outside, against orders, murmuring something the microphone was unable to pick up.

"Both of you, get back to the ship!" Leach shouted

"We can't leave with those things out here, sir!" Cobb responded, voice betraying significant panic. "I can hear them everywhere…"

"What do you hear?"

"They're hunting me, I can feel it. No matter where I look, I hear their growls, their screams. Where are they?!"

Leach slid Cobb's camera feed off to the side of the screen and located the feeds for both Fall and the drone. The drone was seeing infrared, with two white blobs on the black ground. The body cameras were set to visible light only, and Leach cursed the cheap technology. He could see very little, though Cobb swore he was close to the settlement.

"Fall, where are you?" Leach asked.

Fall's breathing was labored. "They everywhere, bossman. I see one thing on drone. So close…"

"Move slowly away from it."

"I think I see it," Cobb said. "I can kill it."

"Something moving," Fall stammered.

Leach watched the drone feed. One of the white blobs moved back while the other seemed to grow a long, thin appendage.

"Cobb!" Leach screamed. "That's not one of them!"

A bright flash briefly blew out all three cameras. When the visuals reset, the cameras on Fall and the drone were showing only static. Cobb's camera showed flashes of a pulse rifle.

"I got him, sir!" Cobb said.

Leach closed his eyes. He and Veldt were all who were left who weren't affected by the nanomachines, then. He grabbed the physical controls to the ship and increased power, then activated the autopilot. Thankfully, their path was already set for the *Sacagawea*.

Veldt came into the command room as the ship settled into its course. In her hands, she held two small bulbs of coffee. "Need a drink?"

Leach took one of the bulbs. "I certainly do."

"I need vodka." Veldt settled into the adjacent crash couch. "A lot of it."

"Alcohol isn't allowed in ISA vessels anymore, remember?"

"Strictly off the record, I may have a personal stash back in my room on the *Sacagawea*. I'll gladly share, since there isn't anyone else left."

Leach only pondered his answer for a second. "I absolutely will take some. Maybe it's time to ask for some downtime."

"Some vacation would be—gah!"

Veldt doubled over, dropping her bulb to the floor. Her hands gripped the sides of her head. From her mouth came a primal, feral sound. It pierced straight to his very soul and sent chills up his spine.

"Oh god no!" Veldt groaned, then she stood and stumbled to the back of the ship.

Leach followed. "What's wrong."

The biologist was hunting through the cabinets lining the wall, where emergency tools were kept, including firearms. "I hear them! The machines...they're in my head! I can't—!"

"Stop it, Veldt!"

"Only one way to do that, Commander." She pulled a pistol from a cabinet.

"No! Wait!"

Veldt tumbled to the floor the moment the weapon went off and lay still, a clean, cauterized hole under her chin. Leach stared at her for a moment. That was it. Everyone was dead except him. He hobbled back to the cockpit and collapsed into the pilot's seat. His finger somehow made its way to the blinking comm button.

A young woman's voice came over the comm. "About time! What's going on down there?"

"I know what happened to the settlers," Leach said.

"Let me get Cao up here. Stay on the line."

Cao could not have been far away. It took only a few minutes for his voice to come over the radio. "What is going on down there?"

"The Pangalactic Peace Project...have you heard of it?"

The almost full minute of silence confirmed that he had. "What about it?"

"It's down here. Or the nanomachines used in it are. They killed everyone else in my crew. I would recommend salvaging some old planet killers and glassing this miserable nightmare. Then turn it to dust."

"I'll see what I can do, Leach. If nothing else, we'll put it on the list of prohibited worlds. Get back here. You sound like you deserve a rest."

"A full leave of absence, if you please. And I need the vodka in Veldt's cabin."

"You're already approved for—wait, Veldt smuggled vodka onto the *Sacagawea*?"

"That's what she said."

A piercing scream resounded through the ship. How? He had never gotten near any of them, had he? Another scream came, this one closer.

Leach deactivated the autopilot. "Cancel everything, Cao! They've got me, too."

"Get up here, Leach. We'll figure something out."

"If these things can be killed so easily, why do they still exist here? Perhaps a heavy pulse blast to *Aurora's* reactor..."

"Not even if *Sacagawea* had weaponry, Leach!"

Could these things replicate themselves? Even if not, how many were on *Aurora*? There was no way to know. He would never risk the *Sacagawea* like that. A reactor explosion would certainly put out enough energy to destroy the tiny beasts. How to engineer one, though? Self-destruct systems were rarely equipped on vessels the size of *Aurora*. An impact would scatter the vessel across the landscape and keep the machines on the planet, but the reactor would never explode the way Leach needed. That would be better than nothing.

Leach pushed the attitude control forward. The altimeter ticked down fast as the *Aurora* dove back through the clouds. Leach leaned back in the crash couch and closed his eyes. The impact would be fast, too fast for him to feel anything, and the ground would pulverize the *Aurora* into dust along with everything inside it.

Why did Veldt not bring her vodka onto the *Aurora*? If there was one thing he needed as he plummeted to his doom, it was a stiff drink.

In response to his last thoughts, Leach's fingers curled into the shape of a glass.

"Cheers," he said, toasting the damnable planet.

Community Service

By Melina Munton

Date: 3257

"You got off easy," the guard hissed into Hector's ear. She had one crushing hand on the back of his neck and the other on Hector's hands cuffed behind his back. "If it were up to me, you'd be rotting in the center of a black hole. You're only alive because you're daddy's perfect little boy. The rest of us lick his boots just so we can live on this damn space station, while you're free to do drugs and crash ships. All that genetic screening you were given as a baby, and you're still a good-for-nothing."

"You're right," Hector said. "Community service. What a joke. I killed someone in that crash, and I deserve the same."

"Just make sure you remember that." The guard shoved him through the last doorway.

"Hector, welcome to the Refugee and Ex-convict Transitional Services, or RETS," a disembodied voice announced over the speakers. The white room was empty save for rows of chairs facing a screen. The screen was flashing pictures of happy people working all kinds of jobs. The guard pushed Hector roughly into his seat and left.

The disembodied voice of the RETS AI continued, "I will guide you on your journey to recovery while providing you with real-world experience. Your mission will be ten low-priority tasks from the council. Do you have any questions or objections?"

"Will this kill me?" Hector grumbled sarcastically.

"Threat level is set to high. However, your records show that you worked as a police captain, so we are confident you have the skills to complete your tasks. You begin immediately.

"Your first task will be a pest control problem. Some shepherds from Nima have petitioned the council for help. You will be sent planetside to exterminate a dangerous lion created by the Eden. It has been genetically altered to survive the harsh planetary environment, including fighting with other predators and living under the violet sun's strong radiation. The local spokesperson has even volunteered to fly you to their settlement.

"Please, follow the glowing arrows to your ship."

Hector complied. The shackles binding his hands together demagnetized but remained on his wrists, reminders of his crime. Arms at his sides, he walked down the hall and into a docking bay where a small cargo ship waited. He opened the door indicated by the blinking light on the floor and found a young woman cataloging some crates.

"Hello there! You must be Hector. I'm Lolaus. You must be the help RETS sent." She offered her hand to shake his. Hector did not take it.

"Oh, don't look so glum," Lolaus said. "This is certainly a lot better than the asteroid mines. Though based on what I hear you did, it might kill you faster." Her face fell. "But I believe in second chances, if you're willing to commit to them."

"Can we just get on with it?"

"Sure, sure," Lolaus replied with a shrug and a grin. "I didn't want to talk to you anyway."

***

After a short trip, their ship landed in a field of tall red grass on the outskirts of Nemea. Dome-roofed buildings dotted the landscape like scattered eggs. Animals grazed in the shade of the buildings. As soon as Hector emerged from the ship, a local man rushed out to greet them.

"Are you here about the lion?" asked the man, presumably a shepherd. "My daughter went to put it down days ago. She hasn't returned. Please. We'll give you everything you need to kill it."

"Yeah," Hector replied. He patted his hip where his holster once was. "What have you got for us?"

"Follow me." The man led them into the barn where they were greeted by the smell of molten metal. A farmhand robot was welding steel reinforcements to the door. "A few weeks back, the lion managed to get into the barn. It killed four of my sheep. Didn't even eat 'em because he couldn't drag them out. My daughter said she'd take care of it, but she hasn't returned. My husband fears the worst. I can't even think about it.

"Lolaus has been helping us. She managed to pull the lion's data from the Eden's data cloud," the shepherd continued. "She'll be able to locate it. But before you go, take anything you need from my daughter's hunting gear." He opened a door at the back of the barn, revealing a room not much larger than a closet. The walls were lined with old, long-range hunting blasters. Ammunition and tools showing recent use were spread out on a worktable.

"Thanks," Hector muttered as the shepherd left the room to tend to his flock. He picked up and examined a few of the tools. As he flexed a climbing pick, he surmised that the best had already been picked over. He gave the pick a swing, checking for balance, but the room was too small, and his elbow connected with a precariously perched box. Out fell a pistol and a holster. He strapped it to his waist.

"Almost ready?" Lolaus's chipper voice came from behind him. "I've got the coordinates set."

"Yeah," Hector said. "Yeah, I'm ready. Let's go."

They returned to the small ship, and Lolaus whisked them to the location on the GPS. They landed in a field above the ravine shown on the map.

"Have fun." Lolaus waved Hector off. She propped her feet on the dashboard of her ship and pulled up a screen. "If you're not back in twenty-four hours, I'm leaving you here. I'm not going to be some lion's lunch."

"Sounds like a plan." Hector stormed down the gang plank. He marched through the ravine, guided by the map blinking directions on his wrist-screen until he found the entrance to a cave.

Slowly, carefully, he entered the cave, keeping his back to the wall, and peering around each corner. The wrist-screen emitted just enough light to see. The breeze picked up, bringing with it the stink of corpses and cat urine.

Around a bend, the narrow tunnel opened to a natural stone chamber. The stench hung heavy in the air here. A dark stain on the floor surrounded tattered cloth. Seeing no sign of the lion, Hector approached the stain. It was the remains of the shepherd's daughter, he guessed, face down and gun in hand. He took a moment to examine the body. It had not been dragged here. It had hardly even been chewed on. She must have faced the lion here. The corpse was positioned with arms spread out, as if to catch a fall. Wounds on her back spoke of an ambush from behind. He turned to examine the wall just behind the victim. It was solid stone.

He turned back to the body and picked up the gun, a top-of-the-line laser rifle with a sighting scope and automatic-fire setting. Additionally, it contained a chamber meant for carrying small detonation charges. Hector checked the chamber and found two small explosive charges. *Yowza.*

The breeze picked up again, blowing dark fur around the room. Hector leapt back, pinning himself to the wall.

The air blew from a hole in the cave ceiling. A passageway. Judging by the claw marks around its rim, the lion used it as an entry and exit point. It must have dropped down on the poor woman.

Hector held his breath and eyed the gaping hole, but there was no sign of movement. The lion did not appear to be home. Formulating a plan, Hector moved about. He placed an explosive charge above the entrance he had come in, then climbed up through the upper opening in search of the lion.

Luckily, he did not come face-to-face with the lion while navigating through the tunnel. Eventually he emerged from the darkness to the top of the rock pile. Lying flat on his belly, he pulled out his scope and watched for the lion.

The bright violet light of midday made his eyes water. After a few hours, his skin began to burn. He swept his scope back and forth across the grasslands, seeking movement. Aside from small wildlife, there was nothing.

Suddenly the grasses parted, and the lion, carrying an enormous fluffy animal, padded its way down the ravine. The lion was monstrous, and its thick violet fur bristled and swayed as it walked silently home. Just at the mouth of the cave, it paused and smelled the air. Deciding it was in no danger, it went inside.

Hector slipped from his perch, wincing as his toasted skin brushed rock. Then he went down into the passageway and quietly crawled into the den.

The lion was not a quiet eater, much to Hector's advantage. He had no trouble picking out a perch without its notice. Once secure among the rocks, he took aim, right for the back of the neck. The laser sight blinked on, and he pulled the trigger.

Blam! The lion leapt up from its meal as the stone to its left exploded.

"Damn it!" Hector cursed himself for not properly checking his gun sight. As the lion turned to run, he quickly toggled to his detonator and triggered the explosive in the tunnel.

Crack! The rock came down, but the lion was fast. He leapt backward, out of the way of falling stone. With his back to the wall, the lion turned toward his only escape route and finally caught sight of Hector.

"Shit!" Hector aimed straight between the lion's eyes. This time he used his own practiced motions instead of the laser sighter. *Blam!* The shot resounded throughout the dusty chamber. The lion winced but did not fall. Instead, it charged.

I hit it, Hector thought desperately. *I know I did.* He shoved a cascade of small rocks at the lion, slowing its climb. Still, its paws shot up, grasping the ledge to the tunnel. He blasted the soft sandstone from which it hung. The rock exploded and the lion slipped back. The gun worked, just not on the lion.

Hector turned to run. He made it less than ten meters before claws sank into his leg and dragged him down. Immediately he rolled onto his back, weapon in front of him. The lion's teeth bit lengthwise down onto the gun. Instinctively, Hector pushed it forward, forcing the lion's head back. The head twisted and turned, spraying Hector with spittle and hot, rotten breath. As the lion twisted, so did Hector, ignoring the pain in his leg and wrenching his gun so that the barrel was pointed toward the lion's mouth.

The lion growled. It pulled back, ready to spring forward once again, but as it did so Hector pulled the trigger, firing straight down the lion's throat.

Blam! The shot echoed through the tunnel. The lion stumbled and toppled over, dead. Hector leaned back onto cool stone, gasping for air. He stayed that way until he could no longer ignore the pain in his leg. He prodded at the scratches. They weren't deep. He would still be able to walk. A little.

Beep. He hit the button on his communication device. "Lolaus," he called, still out of breath. "The lion's dead. Can you come pick me up now?"

"You're alive?" Lolaus laughed. "Alright. Hang tight. I'll get as close as I can to your coordinates."

The dull lights on Hector's handcuffs lit up brightly. "Congratulations on completing your first task!" RETS's voice came from the cuffs. "There are only nine more to go. For your second task, there's a problem that needs to be dealt with urgently. A hydra-slime-mold was accidentally released into the ecosystem in a region called Lera. It has grown enormously and needs to be taken out. Even the Eden is having trouble developing something to get rid of it. Transferring your data file now."

"Can't a guy even get a beer first?" Hector grumbled.

"You *are* alive!" Lolaus jested. "Come on, we've got to tell the townspeople." She noticed the gun. "Did you find the shepherd's daughter?"

"Dead," Hector replied. "How about you tell them? The townsfolk I mean. I guess the shepherd too. I'm a bit," he gestured to his leg, "bitten. I'll be in the healing pod of the ship."

***

The stony wasteland inhabited by the hydra-mold was covered in rolling wisps of yellow vapor. The ship had touched down on the tallest rocky outcrop in miles, overlooking the fog. Gray clouds spun and twisted overhead. The airlock hissed, and Hector was blasted by the scent of sulfur.

"Jesus," he coughed. "What kind of creature lives here?"

"It's a slime-mold," Lolaus offered. "You know, the kind that moves? They're actually quite trainable. I had one as a pet."

"That's a bit…weird." Hector peered out warily. The stench burned his nostrils. He sniffed and snorted. "I guess I'm not going to find this thing by scent."

"You're not going to find it in this ship either," Lolaus agreed. "And though I hate to kick you out, those clouds look a lot like funnel clouds. As soon as you're gone, I'm taking off. I'm a sitting duck out here."

"Alright, alright. Just be sure to be in range when I call. I don't want to bleed to death in this filth." He shouldered his hunting rifle—the one from his encounter with the lion—and stepped onto the planet's surface.

"Good luck!" Lolaus waved with a sleeve over her nose. The door abruptly snapped shut behind Hector, and the engines revved to life. Hector descended from the plateau, the shattered slate sliding beneath his feet. He coughed more heavily. He raised his arm to his face, both as a cough reaction and to keep a close eye on the tiny map on his wrist-screen. This map could only indicate the general area of the creature. However, the information RETS had given them revealed that it liked water. As he reached the bottom of the slope, his suspicions were right. The little blue lines on the map indicated water, and they were indeed accurate—a small stream trickled its way through the large gray stones.

A gust of wind howled through the canyons, bringing with it the stench of rot. Hector coughed. His eyes watered and stung. He coughed again and choked. Breathlessly, he tore some fabric from his sleeve and tied it around his nose and mouth. He breathed a deep sigh through the tight fabric. Then he doubled over coughing. He hit the emergency dial on his wristband.

"Calling Lolaus…Calling…Failed to Connect. Call Terminated."

He mentally cursed himself. He was too far down into the canyon. Desperately, he slid the rest of the way down to the stream, ignoring the gravel biting into his left forearm. At the bottom, he stumbled to the water and tore the cloth from his face. A brief image flashed in his mind of the clear liquid burning through his hands, but the choking overcame his hesitation. He drowned the cloth hastily in the creek and, feeling no pain, tied it once more over his face.

Inhaling the sweet smell of humidity, Hector collapsed onto a rock. His lungs and throat ached, but he could breathe. He rested for a while. When his breath came back, he stood up, and followed the stream downward. All rivers go to the ocean, he remembered from a film. He didn't know if the planet had an ocean, but a small stream might become a larger one.

Indeed it did. After a few hours walking downhill, Hector found himself at a large lake, tinted an egg-yolk yellow and fed by nine clear tributaries. Though the wind still howled through the many canyons around it, the lake remained undisturbed except for the smallest of ripples. Still shocked by the vapors, Hector kept his distance from the strangely colored water.

He followed the edge of the lake downstream, looking for the water's exit. He found it, but it appeared to be blocked by a massive yellow spongey blob. Hector inspected it closely. It did not appear to be moving, but the informational video said slime molds moved slower than the eye could measure. He set his rifle to spray mode and aimed. He paused. For a giant blob of mold, it was smaller than he had expected his task to be. Suspicious, he cautiously crept back to the lake and tossed a stone at it.

The stone hit the water with ripples and ripples but sank less than an inch. Just below a layer of clear water, the stone was slowly encased by a thick yellow blob.

The slime filled the bottom of the whole lake.

Moisture equals mold. Hector thought of the common spaceship maintenance phrase. He turned back to the dam holding the water and fired.

Splat! Yellow, sticky mold flew everywhere, releasing a sulfurous vapor. Water trickled down around it, released from its prison, but the yellow slime quickly dripped down to fill in the new holes. In fact, the slime seemed to rise a little higher.

A small droplet of yellow burned into his bare left arm. "Fuck!" Hector turned and scraped it off on some stone. As he raised his eyes, he noticed tendrils slowly creeping out of the lake on either side, definitely a noticeable movement, albeit slow compared to creatures such as the lion.

Hector examined the sheer stone wall behind him. He would not be able to climb it without gear. The slime inched closer to cutting him off completely. He turned back to the way he had come. Had the lake always been so high? It definitely had not.

At a jog, he started off toward the canyon, wondering if the slime would try to pursue him upstream. Dashing behind large boulders, he made it around the tendril of slime. Careful to avoid the water, he crossed a tributary trickling down from a waterfall too tall to climb. The tendril now behind him began to turn, growing wider, taller, and closer to the sheer stone cliff.

At a blind sprint, he made it to the tributary before the slime had blocked it off. The hydra-slime was moving more quickly in water than on land. He dashed up his escape route and, just as he turned the first corner, skidded to a halt. Coughing from the yellow fumes rising from the stream, he stared at the canyon covered wall-to-wall in the acidic yellow slime as far as he could see.

Panic rose in Hector's chest. Trapped between noxious yellow and sheer stone walls, Hector pulled out his blaster.

Blam! He shot the slime at his feet. *Blam!* He shot the slime in front of him. Each tendril split apart, becoming two strands creeping quickly toward him instead of just one. He backed up, trying to grip any hold on the rock to lift himself up.

rrrrRRR! Lights flashed above him as Lolaus's ship roared into view. *Bang!* A large-impact, asteroid-clearing blast shot out of the ship at the two-meter glob slowly climbing upstream.

Crash! Boulders flew, and the slime was vaporized. Slowly it recovered, smaller than before, pulling mass from the tendrils near Hector.

He climbed the pile of rubble leftover from the blast. Using his blaster, he separated the ends of the tendrils from the stream. The tendrils stopped moving and growing.

"Cut off the streams!" Hector screamed through the roar of the wind and engines. "Dry it out!" He took out a few more tendrils with his blaster as an example. However, Lolaus just hovered deafly in the air, taking shots at the mountainous blob moving up the canyon.

Blam! Hector shot upstream, and the slime-free walls showered him with little stones. "Stop the water!" Hector yelled and pointed. He stood in dismay as he watched the large blob of slime take another impact blast.

Helplessly, he waited, putting creeping tendrils out of commission, but they no longer cared for him. Instead, they climbed the walls, reaching for the ship. Exhausted and drained, he began to follow the canyon upstream. The slime that once blocked his way had receded to build the mighty tower now intent on reaching Lolaus's ship.

Not far up the canyon, he found the perfect place to block the stream. He pulled the last charge from the compartment on his gun and placed it on the canyon stone. After clearing the area, and keeping Lolaus in sight, he set it off, damming the water supply with rubble. Lolaus dropped another blast, segmenting the slime from the lake. Water supply now eliminated, the tower of slime withered and fell.

This time Lolaus took the hint. She dipped back. Hector could only occasionally see the ship bobbing above the canyon tops, but he could hear the blasts and falling stone.

Water sprayed the back of Hector's head. He turned to the makeshift dam and saw that it leaked from both the right and left edges. Two trails of water wound their way downstream to the withering pile of slime. Lolaus was not back yet. Hector ran straight to the yellow slime. Patches upstream began to twitch to life in the water. They were small enough to vaporize with his blaster, which he did.

Lolaus appeared above the cliffs. A lift dropped down from the ship. Hector climbed in and was drawn swiftly up by electric pulleys.

"We've got to burn it before the dams break," Hector shouted. "How many charges do you have left?"

"Not enough for that thing," Lolaus said. "But I've got just the thing. If it doesn't strand us here." Turning in her cockpit chair, she flipped a switch, unclasped a clear plastic shield labeled "WARNING," and smashed a red button.

Beep! Immediately red lights flashed, and an alarm sounded. The ship jolted and the engines stuttered.

"What did you do?" Hector screamed as Lolaus spun the dropping ship. She ignored him and mashed a series of buttons. The alarm went silent, and the lights stopped flashing, except for one proclaiming "LOW." A bang resounded from the hull of the ship, and the cockpit windows were lit with firelight.

"I ejected most of our fuel," Lolaus said cheerily. "And fired it up with a back-burn. That thing'll be burning for days." She grinned. "Ready to go? If we hover too long, we may not make it back."

Hector put his hand on his heart and fell back into a chair, chest heaving. Lolaus laughed and steered them back to civilization.

RETS blinked to life once more.

"Thank you for trying to eliminate the mold problem," RETS said. "But in light of your failure, you will be given a replacement task."

"Excuse me?" Hector said. "We eliminated the mold, didn't we?"

"The mold has been eliminated," RETS repeated blankly, "but it was taken care of by Lolaus. Your next task is to confiscate the unregistered vehicle christened *The Hind*."

"Failed, my ass," Hector grumbled. "And there weren't rules about being helped."

"No," RETS said in agreement. "But records indicate you were not in contact with Lolaus before the destruction of the mold. Coordination is allowed, but I cannot give credit for work not performed."

"Dammit, Lolaus," Hector muttered under his breath. "Learn to pick up the damn phone."

"What did you say?" Lolaus turned to him.

"Nothing."

"That's what I thought."

***

"Artie! Partying hard as always, I see. I'm surprised this poor excuse for a moon is still standing." Hector shouted over the raucous noise the in-crowd called music. The party filled the enormous penthouse wall-to-wall with bodies in motion.

"Hec-tor!" Artie raised a glass of the finest antigravity brewed beer. "Just a little relaxation after some hard work. What's up, cuz? Last I heard you were in a fair bit of trouble."

"Yeah, man. I've been sentenced to some restorative justice bullshit. Running errands for the council under a program called RETS." Hector leaned close to be heard over the commotion of the party.

"Tough, man, sounds like a dump. What are you doing here?"

"Uh, just in the neighborhood. Thought I'd take a break. So, what's new with you? I haven't heard much about the family since the incident."

"You know, same old really. Just hunting through the asteroid belts for good minerals. I have a good team out there. We've been pretty successful this year. You should join us when you're done."

"I'd love to. If this job ever finishes. But that's work. How's your personal life been? Find anyone special? Anything?"

Artie laughed. "You know me. I'm too busy with work for relationships. It's just me and my babies. I just got a new one. Do you want to see her?"

"Love to."

They pushed through the crowd, stopping once in a while to speak with one guest or another.

"Want to buy some ambrosia?" A woman grabbed Hector and offered him the drug. Hector pushed her away, harder than necessary. Grumbling, he followed Artie through the crowd, down the penthouse hallways, and into a large hangar.

Ships of every size, make, and model were illuminated under display lighting. Each appeared freshly washed and spotless. At the very center was a slim, gold, two-person ship.

"This is *The Hind*," Artie said. She grinned and gestured back at Hector. "*Hind*, this is Hector."

"Well met," Hector said with a laugh. "Does she have internal AI piloting?"

"Of course not!" Artie exclaimed. "You know I only fly manual. AI programming is for cruisers and cargo ships. But her autopilot and navigation system are amazing. You could set her on a course across the galaxy, and she wouldn't stray further than a millimeter."

"Oh man, that sounds great. I've always dreamed of flying at hyperspeed."

"I'll bet. Want to take her for a spin?"

"Yes!" Hector almost leapt in delight.

Guilt plucked a chord in his stomach. "I...maybe I'd better not."

"Why not?" Artie asked slyly. "Afraid I won't get it back?"

"Well, I—"

"Look, I know why you're here," Artie said. "You aren't the first person desperate enough to try to steal it. It's your ticket to crossing the galaxy and getting away from your father. I understand."

"It's not about...I wasn't going to...It's..." Hector stammered. He took a deep breath. "It's one of my errands for RETS. I'm supposed to impound an unregistered illegal ship. I changed my mind, though. I'm not going to steal it."

"I know," Artie said, chuckling. "Which is why I think we can come to a compromise."

"A compromise?"

"Come see," Artie smiled. She beckoned him into the ship and prodded a screen.

The screen flashed, "Homing Pilot Armed."

"All you have to do is park it. It'll be back before anyone knows what's happened to it."

"Really? You'd do that for me?" Hector asked in awe.

"Of course," Artie answered. "Besides, my brother Anthony is getting the Chariot model, which in my opinion, is a step down. But not everyone thinks that way. I've got to show off *The Hind* a bit first. As a reminder."

"I'll be sure to make the story good then." Hector laughed.

A few short hours later, he was requesting to dock at the RETS building.

"RETS," Hector called cheerily. "I've brought the ship."

"Well done." RETS spoke in exaggerated tones. "You've successfully completed your mission. Your next task is a very important one. There is a bandit, known only as the Boar of Ymanthia, who has been interrupting a major supply route on the planet's surface. Bring your target in for criminal proceedings."

"Got it." Hector said. He pulled up a screen and called Lolaus.

"Hi-ya," she said. "I didn't expect you to call again."

"I was wondering if you could give me a ride," Hector said. "I've got another task that might help some people. I just have to get there."

"Sure thing," Lolaus said. "I'll be there in a few minutes."

Hector waited. As soon as the hangar doors opened for Lolaus, *The Hind*'s engines fired up. The ship took off, and with agility beyond the skills of even the best pilot, it dodged Lolaus's cargo ship and made for open space.

"Ha!" Hector cheered, then covered it up with a quick cough.

**

"Reports are of a bandit attack right around here. We're waiting here," Lolaus pointed at an advertisement for a small bar, "because if I know anything about bandits, they're not going to pass up a drink after a day of hard work."

"That's just a stereotype. We're wasting our time."

"Look," Lolaus pointed at the screen where a blur had come up, stealing toward the saloon. "There they are."

"That could be anything for all we know."

"Or bandits disguising their signal. Trust me. These guys are supposed to be the best. We've just got to sit tight here and follow them back to their stopping point."

"Won't they see our signal?" asked Hector.

"They won't if they're drunk off their asses. As soon as they dock, we'll sneak aboard, disable the engines, and just tow them out."

"That sounds...foolish."

They argued as the large ship docked, continuing until it undocked. Following the indicator on the very edge of the screen, they trailed the ship.

"We're going to have to get a little bit closer," Lolaus said with a frown. "I thought they would go straight to whatever hole they crawled out of, but they're going into the Ymanthian Canyon. It's probably how they've avoided capture. It's hard for the scanners to pick anything up with all the metal deposits."

"Not exactly the type of people you can catch with their pants down," Hector said. "We should have tried to split them up at that bar."

Beep! Beep! The computer screamed, interrupting Lolaus's response.

"There's something coming right at us," Lolaus said. "It's the Boar! How did they spot us at this distance?"

"Like I said, bandits use long-range scanners because they need to see their prey before the prey sees them. Look, they've lured us into the middle of nowhere. Hail their ship."

"This isn't my fault! If you had a better suggestion, you should have said something. And I won't hail them. We're not hailing them. We run before we surrender. You have no idea what planetary bandits do to people, satellite-boy."

"We're not surrendering. Don't turn. Maintain course." Hector pushed past Lolaus and toggled the communicator. "And don't say anything."

The image of an enormous man appeared on the screen. He stood twice as tall as the average-sized humans behind him. His bulging arms were crossed over his enormous ribcage, and atop it all perched a small red face, contorted in anger. Two implanted tusks curled out of his mouth, giving him a permanent snarl.

"So, the brave little bounty hunter has come to surrender his toy ship to us," the Boar taunted. His beady eyes glanced at his men to ensure they laughed on cue. "If you're lucky, we might drop you off where there's ground."

"Boar, by the authority of the Rambus Precinct, you are under arrest as a suspect in the disappearance of Myla Veers," Hector bluffed. He flashed an empty badge. "You have the right to remain silent. Everything you say or do can and will be used against you. Power down your engines and turn off all auxiliary power. Keep passengers secured in their rooms and call all crew into the cockpit. The cruisers from the port and starboard will dock on either side. All attempts at resistance will be met with force and will be prosecuted in the court of law."

The Boar burst out laughing. The video feed cut. Lolaus leapt up from her chair.

"What the hell? Why did you say that?" Lolaus's eyes went to the screen showing their relative position. "Oh my god—it's working!"

The ship powered down its engines.

"Wait. They didn't stop auxiliary power. The forward thrusters!" She jerked her ship out of harm's way as the enormous forward thrusters fired short, powerful bursts. Lolaus's smaller ship jostled and rattled as an enormous amount of energy blew by. The Boar's ship picked up speed instantly, hurling itself backward into the canyon.

"Damn! They didn't buy our bluff." Hector cursed. "Hey! Don't follow them."

The Persolus Race, Vol. 1

"They're running! We're smaller. We can navigate the canyon better. They can't see if there are other ships in the canyon, just like we can't!"

The larger ship plummeted deeper into the rocky labyrinth, brushing the rocky sides, and showering the ground below with stones. Still, they dove deeper, where the walls grew narrower and more twisted.

"This is insane," Hector said. "Turn around. We're going to get crushed." A large rock smashed into the hull of the Boar's ship, knocking off a few panels. The debris scattered in the direction of their smaller ship.

"We can't. The moment we stop, the engines will rattle the canyon and the stones will fall. I went to flight school. You didn't," Lolaus said. "Always follow in the wake of the largest ship."

"I wish they taught me that," grumbled Hector.

"So will those bandits. Look. They're slowing down," Lolaus said. "They've figured out our bluff. Time to go faster." She hit the throttle, and they zoomed past the large ship, deftly dodging debris.

The rumbling walls began to collapse. Enormous stones shattered against the hull of the Boar's ship. The port engine tore away and spun wildly. The other thrusters sputtered out. The ship dove into the canyon.

"You don't think RETS will be mad you did the driving and not me?" Hector asked.

"You did do the talking," Lolaus said with a shrug. "And you get to hook the tow lines."

They towed the ship back to RETS. As soon as they were in orbit, RETS clicked on.

"What's up, boss?" Hector answered. "We've got your bandits."

"Bring them inside, where they will be initiated into the RETS program," RETS said. "Congratulations on passing your fourth task. Your next task will be to assist Naugeas, the universally known Gen-Modder. He has some important ISA inspections coming up. If he fails, Rambus will lose one of its signature artists."

"Right, everything's always about Rambus," Lolaus said. "I guess the other problems I inquired about didn't even end up on the agenda."

"I'm sure some of them did," Hector said. "This is just a priority. You know, it is a main tourist attraction." As he said it, Lolaus parked her ship and the one she had towed in the RETS hangar.

"So what now?" Hector dared ask.

"I think we leave RETS to deal with it," Lolaus said. "Let it solve its own problems."

"You're not going to leave me here, are you?"

"You better remember this later," Lolaus said, laughing. She released the tow hook and the engines roared back to life. The gangplank on the Boar's ship dropped down and heavily armed bandits flew out.

"It's time we go," Lolaus chuckled. Hector nodded in agreement.

***

"So, you're a Gen-Modder," Hector said to Naugeas. "You must have quite the scientific mind."

"It's an art really," Naugeas said, hardly looking up from his screen. "It's not the same as those Goliath architects that you've read about in school, with their rules and their unoriginality. They condemn us, but they rely entirely on our mods. Everyone wants their own unique planet these days. It's hard to keep up with the demand."

"Right. So RETS said you've had some trouble with the ISA? Anything we can help with?"

"Well, you know I'm subject to these little inspections every now and again. Most of what I do is under the 'trade secrets' clause, but because one disgruntled employee decided to go public, a certain project is under scrutiny. It was really more of a publicity stunt anyway. Let me show you."

He happily led Hector to a large enclosure where long-legged, reddish-brown horses were corralled. Only, they weren't horses. Each one had a long, twisted horn protruding from its forehead.

"What's wrong with a Gen-Mod unicorn?" Hector asked. He remembered seeing a few in zoos, and even in private custody.

"These are a little more magical than a Gen-Mod unicorn," Naugeas said proudly. "These are immortal Gen-Mod unicorns. Because of the sterilization laws on most planets and the planned obsolescence of most models, the cost of replacing one is extraordinary. By using telomerase, I've made some that are true to the children's stories. They can never die of old age. They can still die by other means, of course. They have such high metabolisms, they'll eat anything—vegetation or not. Alive or not. Thus, before I separated them, a few were unfortunately cannibalized. I even have trouble staffing with drones, since they'll kill anything that moves.

"I need their pens spotless before the inspection tomorrow. No one wants to see immortal beauties if they have to live in filth."

"I'll help," Hector said.

"Great! I'm at my wits end here. Do whatever you need to do, as long as it doesn't harm my beauties."

Hector went down first to admire the unicorns. They stomped and stamped as he approached, splashing and kicking a thick paste of feces.

"Disgusting things," Hector said under his breath as the nearest horse strained at the fence and gnashed its teeth.

"Hey," Hector grabbed a robot carefully carrying a large leg of something unidentifiable. In fact, it may have been something that didn't exist anywhere else. "Can you feed them on my signal, so I can go in and clean." The robot beeped an indication that it understood.

Starting with the smallest of the unicorns, Hector slipped into the pen while the horse was busily munching a variety of organic matter. As stealthily as he could, he shoveled and shoveled and shoveled, and the reliable little robot kept topping off the horse's meal until Hector had cleaned the pen everywhere except where the unicorn was eating.

He and the robot started on the next pen and cleaned it all the way up to the small mare itself. They repeated this again and again. At the sixth stall, Hector got too close to the unicorn. In quick succession, it kicked him, spun, and attempted to impale him. Only the sound of the food thumping into its trough turned it away from the hard-to-catch Hector. However, as he emerged from the stall, he realized all of the food the horses had eaten had to go somewhere. The first stalls he had cleaned were already piling up with dung.

"Hey, hurry up with more food!" Hector shouted at the small robot. Frustrated, he turned to the next stall. He jumped in with abandon, circling behind the largest of the unicorns as it put its head down. However, as he rounded it, the creature turned, cutting off his escape. It showed no interest in the vegetables the robot was able to procure.

Hector backed away. However, the unicorns in the adjacent stalls followed and trapped him at the back wall of the stall. The unicorn charged him. He dodged, but the horn went through his pant leg, ripping a hole.

Pain flashed through his mind and he remembered a sweet taste of ambrosia, which dulled pain but heightened one's senses. He shook the thought out of his head.

The unicorn's horn had gone through the wall and water seeped out around it. It struggled and pulled free, showering itself and Hector with a jet of pressurized water.

And that's how Hector figured out how to clean the stalls.

He dodged the second charge, grabbed the tear in the wall and pulled, but the rough metal only dug into his palms. He dodged right as the unicorn put a puncture in the wall right where he had been standing. Now behind the unicorn, he was thrown to the ground by a swift kick.

Before he could get off the ground, it was almost upon him. He rolled beneath its horn, taking hooves instead of being eviscerated. He could not beat the creature's speed, and now it stood between him and the exit once again.

The unicorn charged. Hector dove to the ground, then rolled to his feet. Without a thought, he crouched and moved toward the leaking wall. The creature charged blindly again, but Hector stepped aside, almost taking flailing back-hooves to the face. Once again at the torn metal, he gripped it with both hands and felt for its weak point. He wrenched the sheet back. Water gushed from the wound, spilling into the mud, and washing into the aisle. The unicorn charged again, but Hector dodged it easily. He slipped from the stall and into the next, artfully gouging and tearing the wall behind him until the stalls were flooding, and a steady stream of water washed the floors clean.

"Brilliant!" Naugeas exclaimed as Hector returned. "We'll just leave them in running water! How come none of my assistants could come up with that? I'll have to fire them. If you want the position, it's open."

"No. Thanks."

"Well, your loss. Here's your payment," Naugeas handed him a box. "You've earned it."

"I doubt it's enough," Hector muttered as he walked away, aching all over. "Have a good life. The ISA is probably coming for your hide."

Later, he was woken from his nap in the healing bay by RETS.

"Greetings, Hector. Naugeas has passed his inspection. Your next task is to get rid of the birds at Mistfall Lake. They're attacking tourists and making a mess of things. I've given Lolaus the details since you seem to be in poor condition."

***

They landed at the resort. It was deserted, with the exception of drones everywhere. Immediately, several began washing Lolaus's ship.

"I could get used to this," Lolaus said. "I'll stay here. I'm not too keen on meeting these flesh-eating birds in person."

"I'll be sure to take pictures then." Hector harrumphed and marched out. Once outside, he was bombarded with construction noise.

An android in a waistcoat zipped up to him, bobbing to-and-fro. "Welcome to the Mistfall Springs Spa and Resort. Please excuse the noise. Our Elite Pass building is still under construction.

"We are glad you decided to come stay with us. Unfortunately, we are currently closed. Our dates of operation are...Pending. Please come again."

"I'm here to take care of the bird problem," Hector said.

"RETS has sent another exterminator! Excellent news. I hope you don't end up like the last one."

"What happened to the last one?"

"That is confidential information."

"Just tell me where the birds are," Hector said.

"They are not here. They only come out in the night. During the day they live in caves on the other side of the lake. Here, I'll show you to your boat."

Hector boarded the boat and wordlessly sped to the other shore, leaving the din of construction behind.

Tall volcanic cones towered above the lakes amid a tangle of dark colored trees and vines. Upon setting foot on the shore, a small black bird landed beside Hector. He started, but the bird only chirruped a tune and went on its merry way. It wove between the trees and stones, and all went quiet. As Hector struggled through the undergrowth, the uncanny silence seemed to pour from every nook and cranny, in stark contrast to the noise on the far shore. Every crunching leaf and every heartbeat pounded in his ears. He wandered aimlessly, searching for a cave.

Eventually, he found it by the tell-tale signs of bird droppings and the littering of old bones. The cave went deep into the earth. He tossed a stone inside. A few bounces later, a cacophony of voices screeched and cackled. Hector was peering breathlessly into the darkness, looking for movement, when a few dozen feathered creatures shot out above him like arrows.

Wine-red and chattering, these represented a small part of the flock, judging by the commotion still below. They swooped around to find perches among the foliage, peered at Hector, and began to understand the reason for their rude awakening. Food.

The first dove at Hector. Its razor-like talons posed a danger second only to the jagged-tooth beak. It snapped at Hector, who stumbled away. But a second bird sprang on his back, raking talons along his spine and drawing a line of blood. He spun, flailing his hands and knocking some birds about. A third latched its claws into his shoulder. He threw it off, but it tore flesh as it went.

The birds continued to attack as Hector struggled to pull his jacket over his bleeding arms and head. The birds bounced off the tough hide but did not cease their attack. It wasn't long before they realized they could still sink their teeth into his exposed hands and face.

Hector found himself retreating. The vines and foliage threatened to trip him, but he fought his way back to the boat and hit the autopilot. It rushed him to the opposite shore, easily outrunning the winged demons.

Adrenaline still pumped through his veins as he staggered to the shore and rushed into Lolaus's ship. It was only when the door closed behind him that he dared look back. The birds stopped in the middle of the lake, darting around and appearing confused. After a few more minutes of chaos, they retreated. As they did so, their jagged flight patterns straightened and harmonized, and they maintained a straight path to their home caves.

"Back already!" Lolaus shouted over the noise of the ultra-space music she blasted on her speakers.

"You never even left." Hector said. "You have no room to speak."

Hector decided to rest before venturing out again. While catching his breath, he remembered the payment given him by Naugeas. He retrieved the small white box and opened it. As soon as he did, he slammed the lid shut. His mouth went dry, and thirst plagued him.

Forbidden fruit. Ambrosia.

He kicked it under his seat and went in search of Lolaus. He found her outside by the water's edge.

"I thought you didn't want to meet the man-eating birds?" Hector asked.

"The android here says they don't come out during the day. I thought I'd take my chances. I could never afford to come back here again, and it is beautiful."

"The birds had no problem attacking me in the forest," Hector grumbled. Heavy machinery revved to life as he spoke.

"What? I can't hear you over the noise!"

"They don't like the noise!" Hector exclaimed. "That's it! Do you have speakers?"

Hector went to the android. "Tour guide! Hey, I need your help."

"What can I help you with today, sir?"

"I can get rid of the birds by placing speakers in the caves around the forest. The noise will drive them away."

"That can be arranged," the android agreed. "But we will need a lot of speakers. The volcanic stone absorbs sound."

"Well, let's get to it."

The robot gathered the speakers and synchronized them with its internal computer. Hector then placed them around the lake. On his signal, the speakers boomed, though in a frequency too high for Hector and Lolaus to hear. In the distance, a flock of red birds darted among the trees and then slowly dispersed further into the forest.

"Look at us, we're on a roll." Lolaus said.

After a few minutes of silence, RETS turned on.

"Excellent work! I think you're ready for a challenge this time," RETS said. "There is an interstellar event that is being hosted in our city of Treech this year. We would like you to ensure our planet's victory. There are only six tasks left for you to complete!"

"Six? What are you talking about? I've already done six!" Hector groaned. "Don't tell me you're not counting another one."

"That is correct. You recently received payment for cleaning the Augean stables," RETS stated. "Do not accept any payment for your tasks."

"It wasn't..." Hector began but realized arguing with an AI was pointless.

***

"Next!" The voice from the counter blared. Hector stepped forward.

"Name and ID," the clerk said then nodded. "Sign here, here, here, and here, or click this button to release liability all at once."

Hector pressed the button. "Okay. How does this work again?"

"Please proceed to the next room," the clerk responded. "Next!"

Hector passed through the door. Inside, partially filled rows of chairs faced a large screen flashing highlights of last year's matadors. A contestant was being gored by genetically altered, metallic, chitinous horns. Behind Hector, the door opened again, letting in the next contestant. Hector headed for a seat up front.

"Hey," a contestant grabbed him by the wrist. "Don't I know you?" The stranger was covered in scars and had a few gang symbols modded into his skin.

"No, I don't think so," Hector mumbled, turning his face away.

"I recognize you." The man turned to his similarly modded companions. "He's the one who killed that lion over in Nemea. He was on the news."

"I happened to be in the neighborhood," Hector mumbled, making a quick turn toward the seats at the back. The man insistently gripped his wrist above the manacle.

"Think you can beat us to the kill, do you?" The gang member sneered. His sneer became a grin, and he loosened his grip and laughed. "I'm kidding, of course. Don't look so serious. It's a dangerous sport. May the best man get the kill shot, eh? Sit with us. How did you get the lion? I heard blasters couldn't pierce its hide."

Hector had just opened his mouth to speak when the highlight reel abruptly changed.

"Welcome to the 304th annual bullfighting competition. Contestants, you have chosen to compete in bringing down The Bull. This year's model, the Cretan 2000, designed by Universe Class Gen-Modder Minos, is the toughest beast yet. Working either collectively or alone, your job is to bring it down by disabling or killing it. Either must be done without the use of weapons. Everything will be provided in the arena. This is your last chance to step back through those doors or face...The Bull!"

The gang members ribbed each other. "Not scared, eh?"

"Don't worry. I'll have it in the bag before you finish pissing your pants."

"In your dreams, you useless sack."

"It can't get us all, eh, lion man?"

"But it can get some of us. I mean, fewer of us if we watch out for each other," Hector said, loud enough for the rest of the room to hear. He took their silence as acknowledgment.

The light above the exit turned green.

"Let's go!" The gang of three led the way as people trickled out into the bright arena.

Four meters tall and ripped, the bull had already pinned a large group of people behind a boulder by doing something unexpected: breathing fire. The small number of contestants who were still free did not seem to bother the bull in the slightest, even the one pulling fruitlessly on a rope around its hind legs.

"Over here!" The friendly gang member ushered Hector to the other side of the bull where a crate lay behind an overturned obstacle tower. On his knees, a second gangster pulled the top off the crate.

"Ambrosia!" he exclaimed, pulling a pack out and greedily squeezing it into his mouth. He turned his head toward the sky, fully extending his neck for a brief moment, then rose to his feet.

"Let's take down this bull!" He leapt the structure shielding him and charged the bull.

"Come on!" The friendly gangster followed suit. Hector hesitated. Screams echoed from the bull's side of the arena. Last time Hector had taken ambrosia, he had taken a life. This time there was a chance he could save one, he reasoned.

Hector grabbed a pill and forced it down his throat. He clenched his abdomen as he felt the drug activate primordial, inactive genes. His vision and his head cleared of every thought, and he became aware of everything, down to the trail of ants extending from their dark hole. He sprang to his feet, and with his hearing alone, knew the position of the two drug-augmented gladiators taunting the bull, luring it one way, then the other.

Over the ruined tower and across the dirt field, suddenly Hector was with them, circling the angry bull, which became caught in the conundrum of who to attack first. The other gladiators remained further away, out of reach of the flame.

Cowards. Hector darted forward. He lunged, throwing his full weight into the back knee of the bull. The knee gave. The bull stumbled. Hector felt no pain in his shoulder from hitting its solid, chitinous skin. He was on the ground, rolling to dodge the legs that were trying to stomp him. Right. Left. Front. Left. Roll to the right. Then he was on the other side of the bull.

Somewhere far away, a crowd cheered. Small, fly-sized drones livestreamed the entire encounter. Hector darted by one, flashing the camera a wide-eyed grin.

The bull lowered his head and charged one of the gangsters who had gotten too close. The gangster evaded by vaulting straight between the bull's horns, landing a hair's breadth to the right of the bull's shoulder. More applause filled the ring.

The bull charged the second gangster, who was distracted by the intricate flowing of a flag. It hit head on. *Killed on impact.* The line from

Hector's days on the police task force echoed through his head. The same line he was given when...

The remains of a vehicle collision. Blood leaking from the other vehicle. Failing to rise to his feet. The scene was flashing before his eyes.

He snapped out of it just as the bull charged. He dodged the horns, but a swift kick brought him down. Another gladiator caught the bull's attention. He did not survive long. There were more than ten bodies. How had Hector missed it? The friendly gangster was caught in the arm by a horn, which tore it like a rag.

Hector rose to his feet. "Hey! Come at me!" he roared, pulling off his leather jacket and fluttering it to the side. The bull charged, and Hector charged back. Hector slid under the right horn, just as the left horn hit the jacket. The horn caught in the sleeve and Hector pulled, every muscle in his body perfectly synchronized by the ambrosia.

The bull's head twisted, throwing it off balance. The twisting momentum carried it heels over head. With a crunch, the body hit the fallen tower, splintering the wood and caving in metal.

The bull lowed. The jacket was tangled in its front legs, pinning its head down. It struggled, unable to overcome its binds. The back legs kicked and lashed, twisting the metal frame around it. A gladiator dared approach but was struck by a leg.

After what seemed like forever, the moderator called it. The bull was incapacitated. Hector had captured the bull.

The whole way back Lolaus cheerfully recapped the entire fight as seen from the stadium. Lolaus knew nothing about taking ambrosia. Apparently that part had been cut and replaced with the official version: the three of them had been formulating a plan. Hector, sober now, offered his condolences and prize money to the dead gangster's family.

"Well done," RETS chimed once they were back in the ship. "People will be talking about it everywhere. Our entertainment industry will rise in popularity now. The council will be pleased, just as I'm sure they'll be pleased with the next five tasks you complete."

"Thanks, RETS," Hector rubbed his forehead, trying to calm the throbbing headache of ambrosia withdrawal. "I'm not sure I did a good job on this one."

"You did great," RETS said. "Now, you're being sent to investigate Damon. This should be of some interest to you since you were a police officer. He's created a police force of androids that is purportedly indomitable and incorruptible. In fact, they are so loyal, they will only ever follow his orders. The council wants you to make sure they are not a threat."

***

"So my task force, currently contracted to the council directly, will be finished with production shortly," Damon explained to Hector and Lolaus. "I'm glad your father, Zachariah, is seeing the pros of contracting with us for Rambus's security. It will protect police officers and keep them from the front lines. I know you can appreciate that. Once my first task force is deployed and their performance proven, I'm sure I'll get hundreds of contracts. I won't be able to keep up for the next century. I've already got many interested parties. However, if your father signs in advance, I can keep him at the top of the list. A smaller, higher-tier model should do just the trick to defend his satellite station."

"I'm sure he would like to see them in action first," Hector stammered. "He sent me to evaluate them since I can't work as an officer right now. Can you show me what to do?"

"Equus! Attention!" Damon shouted. The rows of police androids in front of them rose to attention in chorus. "Now you can't see it with human perception, but each footstep is timed to be a millisecond out of sync. That way they don't cause a combined impact but hit the ground separately. They determine who starts and finishes as a hive mind."

"I wouldn't have noticed," Hector said. "And I wouldn't have even been able to get my men to snap to attention that fast. What about civilian control? How do the androids react to surrendering?"

"They're programmed to wait exactly three seconds between cocking the gun and firing. This gives the target a warning. If the target surrenders in that time, then it is deemed a successful encounter."

"It sounds like they rely on de-escalation through fear."

"Conflict resolution through bargaining doesn't work. After all, look at how this place is being run. You have the Rambian politicians pandering to every lobbyist. They bow to every whim of the artist

Naugeas, the sports director Minos, and use RETS to sweep people like you under the rug. A firm ruler can provide order. Otherwise, there is no control."

"You're right. The council talks about its perfect system, but what do they get done really?" Hector said. "They only care about keeping their own power. My father is a prime example."

"Control is all about being able to put pressure in the right areas," Damon said solemnly. "That's all my androids are—a tool to help bring this kingdom under control."

"And who better to have control but you?" Hector asked.

"Well, I certainly wouldn't mind it," Damon said with a chuckle. He looked at Hector. "Wait. You're being serious."

"Couldn't you have programmed the Equus units to obey the council or a governing body? These contracts are written to say they must be governed by you," Lolaus said. "Sure, the council may be jerks, but they'll be replaced someday. We can put people we trust in their posts."

"You're a fool if you think that," Damon growled. "Actually, I have a special demonstration for you. One that will prove my good intentions. Equus! Arrest these criminals! They are here under false pretenses."

"You can't do this!" Lolaus exclaimed. "The council will blast this place from the face of the planet."

"Oh, I believe I can do this. After all, I have an entire police force for this world, and soon, for the satellite station above it."

Damon stepped into his unit of androids, shielding himself. Two came forward.

Click-click. Three seconds.

Hector launched himself at the first android, using the action to shield his left hand as he popped a pill of ambrosia into his mouth. The first android went down. Hector rolled off it.

"We surrender!" Lolaus shouted. Hector threw up his empty hands. The androids secured them, roughly forcing Hector in front of Damon.

"You sack of shit," Hector yelled at Damon. "These crap androids can never defeat the Rambus police force. You'll be dead on arrival."

"Dead? Like you?" Damon said with a cackle. "Finish him. Slowly."

The android behind Hector raised its hand and cocked the gun in its fist. Three seconds warning. Ambrosia slowed the count. Hector closed his eyes and tore to one side, dislocating his shoulder. The shot grazed his ear. He waited for the other two robots to finish tearing his arm off, but they didn't move.

"Well, that couldn't have worked out better," Lolaus said from behind him. "If you think about it, he basically just shot himself."

Hector suddenly felt her arms pulling him from the androids. He opened his eyes. Damon lay still on the ground; blood was pooling from the perfect hole in the center of his forehead.

"I think we need to call the Rambus Special Forces. We've got some explaining to do," Hector said.

"But no paperwork," Lolaus replied. "The Equus models are fully capable of writing their own reports. You probably shouldn't have taken ambrosia. They'll report it for sure."

"Don't tell me what to do. I just saved your life. Do you think I wanted to be back on this shit?"

"Don't yell at me," Lolaus said coldly. "Just make sure you get your story straight. I'm not going down for running drugs. I thought you had changed. We're done after this."

After a lengthy discussion with the police and some android programmers, the council determined that the Equus program would be discontinued after an "accident" occurred.

"Congratulations," RETS said. "You've just saved an entire government body. What a confidence builder."

"RETS," Lolaus said sharply, "I'm done driving him around on council business. Call him a taxi."

"Very well. Thank you for your service," RETS replied. "The next item of concern is a matter of illegal technology. You are to retrieve the belt currently in the possession of a being called Hipol."

***

The building was more of an estate, with a broad and imposing front, the back enclosed by an enormous wall, and all of it guarded by sentry drones. Hector held his breath and knocked casually on the door.

The door was opened by a nonbinary person in simple clothes who stared expectantly at Hector.

"Hi. How are you?" Hector opened. "I was hoping to speak to the owner of this house."

"What can I do for you?" the person replied.

"Oh, my apologies, Hipol. I'm Hector, son of Zachariah. I've heard you developed a new technology here. I was interested in seeing its capabilities. I've brought some Lathenian wine."

"Thank you, but we don't drink wine. I'm going to have to ask you to leave."

"Sephone, did I hear him say 'son of Zachariah?' Let him in. This could be the answer to our prayers."

The figure blocking the door opened it slowly, revealing an entryway made of finely chiseled marble with gold filigree. At the top of a staircase, in a long flowing gown, stood the person who spoke.

"Welcome, Hector, son of Zachariah," Hipol said, descending the stairs. "I apologize for the lack of hospitality. We rarely get visitors, and when we do, they are usually less than hospitable themselves. What can I do for you?"

"I'm sorry to hear that," Hector said, recognizing the formal way of speaking used on Rambus. "I'm hoping you'll entertain my curiosity about that belt you wear. What exactly is it capable of?"

"I'll tell you. But first, I'll tell you the story of where it, and we, the Averians, came from. Come, join us for dinner."

Hector followed them through a grand hall and into a great dining chamber. There were already Averians seated at the table. Hipol took the seat at the head of the table, next to several other silver-haired people. Hector sat at the opposite end of the table. Androids waited on them.

"Long ago, there was a man named Avery," Hipol said. "He was born during a war, and as a result, his early life was war-torn. He worked hard and went to a distant school where he mastered the arts to become a Gen-Modder. He became one of the best, but he could not shake his inner turmoil. When war once again loomed, he theorized that the only way for peace was through a strong hand.

"Secretly, he built a laboratory, where he used Gen-Modding to raise an army that could think, reason, and adapt. He created us, the Averians. I was the first born.

"Our numbers were still small, but he became paranoid. He believed his own creations might turn against him. So, he gathered his best scientists and created this belt. It uses high-level neuroscanners to sense the feelings that those around you have toward you.

"It drove him to further paranoia. Every time he left the compound, he sensed contempt, jealousy, and apathy. Soon he stopped leaving. Surrounded only by his creations, he began to see our frustration and fear. It drove him to try to eliminate us. We did what we had to.

"In the end, we were pardoned for our struggle, and we were deemed the legal 'children' of Avery. We inherited his empire, though it has dwindled in the last decade. We sold everything but our two most important technologies: this belt and our reproduction system. You see, we were created entirely for the purpose of war. We were lab grown, and our descendants too come from the very same machines that made us.

"With nothing but these necessities, we made our way here, to the far reaches of the known worlds. We hoped there would be safety here. However, because of the method of our birth, we are not recognized as citizens. We cannot get the services we need to properly start our new life, such as RETS. Convince your father to give us amnesty so we can use what resources are given to refugees like us. I will trade you this belt if you can get us the citizenship we need."

"I'm really sorry to hear what happened to you," Hector said. "I'm sure my father would love to help you. He doesn't hear much from those who are planetside these days, so I'm sure he's unaware of your difficulties. I've been working with RETS lately myself. I've made quite a lot of connections around the planet."

"But aren't you forced to use RETS as a punishment by your father?" a youngster asked.

"Well, yes. But it's temporary. I'll be back up there before you know it."

"So, you deceived us," Hipol said in a frigid tone. "As much as you may want to help us, you can't. And you were going to take advantage of that."

"No, I swear it isn't like that."

"Don't lie to me! I can see your intentions. I know your guilt," Hipol roared, one hand resting on the golden belt. "Throw him out!"

Two strong Averians grabbed him by the arms.

"No! You don't understand. I always feel guilty. It's not what you think!" Hector called back as he they dragged him all the way out the front door. They tossed him to the street, and the door slammed shut behind him.

"Damn," Hector hissed under his breath. "Damn. Damn it!" He pounded the ground.

I've made connections all over the planet. His words came back to him. He got to his feet, dusted himself off, then walked down the street looking for a taxi. He would do this without his father.

An hour later he was sipping hot coffee in a comfortable chair.

"Mr. Hector, sir," a drone said. "We'll be on-air in a minute. Please keep in mind swearing is not allowed. Ms. Mira will be with you in a moment."

"There he is. There he is." A stunning woman walked into the room, wearing finely-tailored clothes.

"Ms. Mira," Hector immediately stood and offered his hand. "Thank you for seeing me on such short notice."

"Of course. I should have contacted you earlier. You're the talk of the planet, with all the things you've been doing. Helping farmers with the wildlife. Befriending Naugeas. Protecting the finest resort in Mistfall. It's wonderful you're here. Much better than the dehydratable cats we were going to show."

"I'm glad to hear that." Hector nodded politely.

"What are we talking about today? The incident?" Ms. Mira said. "You said you had something to say to your father. Oh, the excitement is giving me goosebumps. Quickly, have a seat. We're on in five...four..." She gestured for three, two, and one.

"Good evening," Ms. Mira said with a wide smile. "Today I'm here with Hector, son of Chancellor Zachariah. He saved shepherds from a dangerous lion, captured the bandits in Ymanthia, cleared the Mistfall Spa and Resort of its dangerous birds, and took down the Treech bull. How are you today Hector?"

"Well, I've been better, actually." Hector dropped his smile. "I want to talk about something that's heavy on my heart."

"I see. I know you've had a bit of a personal struggle lately, perhaps about the tragic vehicle accident?" Ms. Mira became solemn. "How are you feeling about that?"

"This isn't about that," Hector said quickly. "I want to bring attention to some of the injustices going on planetside. The council refuses to send aid to planetside communities. As you've said, I've been helping farmers and locals with pests and bandits. The council only worries about new elaborate resorts, tourism, and big business. I want to bring the world's attention to some friends of mine, refugees in need of our voices."

"I see," Ms. Mira said. Her voice remained pleasant, but her smile became a thin line.

"I've been doing this 'community service,' and it's all been things the council has ignored for years. They don't care about the people on the planet. They care about their polls and elections. They care about the big-money people running their campaigns, trying to make another trillion. None of that really matters. What matters are the people in our communities," Hector continued while ignoring Ms. Mira's attempts to jump in and redirect the conversation.

"Take the lion, for example. The farmers were being attacked and killed. Their livelihood was at stake. They begged and pleaded for help. It wasn't until Lolaus—someone from Rambus—said anything that things changed. Same thing with the hydra-slime-mold. Entire rivers were basically toxic waste. I became a planetary hero not because I'm the only one who could, but I'm the only one who knew and was given a chance. I've helped wealthy Gen-Modders hide the fact that their creations were out of control and living in horrible conditions. I've stopped a madman from taking matters into his own hands. This wouldn't have happened if the people were a priority. They need representation on the council. Someone to plead their causes. No more silence."

"That's definitely a heavy statement indeed," Ms. Mira said swiftly. "You said you helped Gen-Modders with—"

"None of that matters," Hector spat. "It's all about the council pretending that everything is perfect. That they're perfect. It's not. They're not. I'm not. I'm done pretending. Things need to change. No more sweeping things under the rug. I've been assigned community service as punishment. I'm not doing this because I care.

"I was let off easy because I'm the son of Zachariah. Anyone else would have the death penalty. I might as well make something of my life. The Averians, they need to be officially granted asylum. They need the same rights as everyone else because we're all just trying to survive on this crazy, fucking planet." He was standing by the time he finished, so he bowed his head and left the stage.

"It seems like Hector had a lot on his mind tonight," Ms. Mira spoke to the camera as Hector disappeared backstage. "It's no wonder he's in a state of panic after causing a deadly vehicle crash under the influence of ambrosia."

He walked out of the building with his head hanging. It began to rain.

It wasn't long before he was stopped by the sight of the young Averian with an umbrella. Silently, the Averian led him back to the house. Hipol stood in the doorway wearing a gold robe with a blue belt, surrounded by junior attendants.

"I saw your interview. I suppose I'm not the only person who only sees you as the son of Zachariah, now am I?"

"No," Hector said. "And I'm sorry I can't help you. The council doesn't care about your problems. Only their own. Until someone who's lived planetside is up there, nothing will change."

"You're right," Hipol said. "And I want you to make sure that person is wise enough for this. I was too quick to judge by it." One of the attendants handed Hector a box. Inside lay Hipol's golden belt.

"I can't—"

Hipol silenced him with a waved hand. "Take it and go. I'll be glad to be rid of it. Paranoia doesn't suit me."

"RETS," Hector said over the comm. "I've acquired the belt. What's next?"

"Good job," RETS replied. "Next, we will be dealing with a man threatening to release thousands of ruby cattle onto the Violet Plains, an environmentally protected area by the Eden. Though the cattle are not dangerous themselves, I have been informed the Eden is creating a dangerous type of wild dog to eliminate the invasive species. The ruby cattle must not be released, or this new species could move into more populated areas and wipe out livestock or citizens."

**

A large, armed ship hovered over the Violet Plains. It broadcasted a signal on repeat saying, "The Violet Plains are now open for grazing."

"What a madman," Hector said to his taxi driver.

The driver shrugged. "Three madmen. The Greyman triplets command that vessel."

"Let's ask to meet on council business," Hector said to the driver. The driver nodded. Hector dictated to the communicator and sent the message. Moments later he received an invitation to board.

They docked on the larger ship only long enough for Hector to disembark. The taxi driver took off, leaving him stranded.

"Welcome aboard," one of the Greyman triplets said. "I take it the council is finally hearing our requests to open the Violet Plains for grazing livestock?"

"Yeah, I'm here on council business. Unfortunately, the Eden is not currently agreeing with us on that, and it's going to create packs of wild dogs to kill your cattle if you land them here."

"Don't worry about that," the second Greyman said. "If we see any dogs around the cattle, we'll shoot them."

"Well, the Eden's going to put them everywhere, so other people will be in danger too," Hector said. "How about we hold off for a year or two so the Eden can make the necessary changes for the ecosystem to support your cattle?"

"We already submitted our request, and it was denied after five years," Greyman Number Three said as he came up from behind. "And if you've come to stop us, you're too late."

"Damn. Straight to the point." Hector stepped forward and was hit with a blaster shockwave that disoriented him. Before he knew what happened, he was restrained.

"Let's show him our victory for the farmers," said Greyman Three. In minutes, he landed the ship on the Violet Plains. "Release the herds!"

"Don't!" Hector said.

The cargo bay doors opened, and thousands of cattle streamed out. Immediately, large drones from the Eden zipped into the atmosphere, carrying hundreds of animals.

"Shoot 'em down," said Greyman Two. Greyman One was already at the guns.

Drones, engulfed in flames, crashed in big, fiery explosions. The super herd of cattle separated and began running.

A small ship flew into view and landed nearby. The Greymans remained occupied trying to shoot down the drones. Lolaus stepped out of her ship and crept up the ramp, looking for a way to stop the cattle.

"Lolaus!" Hector whispered. "Lolaus!"

She finally saw him. Undetected, she snuck to him and began removing his restraints.

"Lolaus, what are you doing here? How did you find me?"

"I've been helping the people on this planet for some time," Lolaus said. "I heard there was an eco-catastrophe waiting to happen. We have to take this ship and round up the cattle before the Eden releases the second wave of dogs. I can round them up with my ship, but we've got to get this one ready to take them to other plains."

"Got it. Leave these dingbats to me," Hector said, flexing his unrestrained wrists. He sneaked behind some crates to Greyman Three. In a flash, he had the man in a headlock, covering his mouth. As soon as Greyman Three dropped, Hector placed him in the restraints.

"Hey, where's our brother?" asked Greyman One angrily. "There's going to be a second wave any time now."

"Probably taking a leak," Greyman Two replied. "I'll go get him." He stepped behind the crates, only to be smashed in the head with a heavy wrench by Hector. He went down, unconscious.

Greyman One heard the thud. He rounded the corner with his gun drawn to find Greyman Two on the ground. Ahead of him, behind the next corner, a boot peaked out. Quiet as a cat, Greyman One stalked forward. He leapt around the corner, laser humming in his hand, but quickly pointed it away when he found that it was Greyman Three.

Hector dropped from above to hit Greyman One with his wrench, but the man dodged just in time. They collided and hit the floor. The laser pistol slid under some crates. Hector managed to gain top mount and rained down a flurry of blows until Greyman One no longer resisted.

Hector tied up the three Greyman brothers. He opened the cargo bay doors in time to spy two Eden drones approaching. As the cattle began streaming in, chased by Lolaus's nimble ship, Hector made for the gun bay.

He shot down the first drone without a problem.

The second touched down, and a dark shape leapt into the tall grasses. Other than an occasional shift in the grasses, always getting closer, Hector could not see the dog.

He retrieved a laser that a Greyman had dropped and moved to the entryway. Lolaus landed her ship in front of the cargo bay. The door opened and she stepped out.

"Hey, I—" An enormous dog sprang upon her from the tall, violet grasses.

Blam! Hector's aim was true, and the dog fell down dead.

"Are you alright?" Hector asked.

"Alright? Thanks to you I'm alive," Lolaus stammered. "Thank you."

"You're welcome. Can I ask a favor?"

"Sorry, I'm not driving you anymore." Lolaus shook her head sadly.

"Yeah, I understand. I just need to make a call. My taxi driver left me here. I need to order a new one."

Lolaus nodded. Hector used her ship's communication center to hail a cab. Then he called RETS.

"RETS, do you copy," Hector asked the computerized wrist cuffs. "The cattle are rounded up. Has the Eden stopped sending out dogs?"

"Yes, copy that," RETS responded. "There are two more objectives to be carried out for your sentence. Your next task is to upload a new genetic profile to the Eden. The council members have determined a make the Golden Sunset Apple tree a native plant."

"That doesn't make sense," Lolaus said. "You can't really make something native. None of this is native. Before the Eden, this place was just a rock."

"I don't think RETS cares," Hector responded. "It's just a computer." Lolaus chuckled awkwardly. They waited in silence until the self-driving cab arrived. Hector climbed in and waved sheepishly at Lolaus, but she had already turned toward her own ship.

***

The cab stubbornly sat in midair over empty fields. On the horizon towered the Eden, blanked in a thin veil of morning mist.

"Come on, you stupid car!" Hector exclaimed. "I need to get in there on council business."

The screen flashed red. "Access denied. Unable to proceed further. Restricted air space ahead," the computer vocalized.

"I'm with the Rambus police force. The council sent me." The screen continued to flash. "Argh. RETS! Do you hear this? Tell this piece of shit I'm here on council business."

"I do not have authority over this airspace." The RETS cuffs flashed to life.

"Damn it!" Hector said. "RETS how do I get authorized?"

"Due to recent events, current ISA protocol is that only ISA employees level six or higher may access Edens."

"My uncle, Elton, is the local development manager, ISA level eight. Would he have access?"

"Yes. That is correct."

"Cab, call Uncle Elton," Hector told the cab.

"Calling. Please wait. No answer. Please leave a message."

"Hi, Uncle. It's been a while. I know you're probably really busy with work. I'll swing by your office and see if I can catch you there. Later."

He arrived at the planetary ISA offices and marched into the lobby. There was a zig-zagging line of people starting at the front desks. Hector never remembered the ISA office on Rambus Station having any line.

"What's going on here?" He asked a woman in line.

"Shh!" She shushed him. "Back of the line's over there."

Hector sullenly found it and waited. It took a long time to get to the front. When he got there the android took down his information, gave him a pass, and pointed him to the elevator that would take him to the appropriate floor.

When the elevator doors opened, he was greeted by glares.

"Excuse me," Hector said after sizing up a roomful of ISA investigators. "I'm looking for the local development manager, Elton."

"Who are you and what's your business with the LDM?" A security woman demanded.

"I'm Hector, his nephew. I've been sent by the council to see if he can upload a biological profile to the Eden."

"Do you know the whereabouts of your uncle?" the woman demanded.

"I have his address. What's going on?"

"We've already checked his residences," a security officer from the back called.

"The LDM hasn't shown up for work under suspicious circumstances," the security woman in charge said. "If you don't know anything I have to ask you to leave. This is ISA business." Dismissed, Hector rode the elevator back to the lobby. He had almost handed in his pass when his communication device when off.

"Hector!" The shrill voice of his cousin Haley wailed. "My father has disappeared! The ISA investigators came and won't tell me anything! You're a police captain. What's going on?"

"I don't know," Hector replied. "Even if I were still with the police, ISA's all over this. They have jurisdiction."

"Can't you just ask them what they know?" Haley said. "I feel so blind. Dad's gone missing, and I can't stand all this waiting around."

"Alright, fine," Hector replied. He could tell she was nearly in tears. "I guess it can't hurt." He returned to the elevator and to Elton's floor.

The elevator doors opened, and the room was empty except for the yellow tape marking the floor under investigation.

"Hello?" Hector called. There was no answer. He pushed past the yellow tape. He followed the hall to the office labeled Local Development

Manager. The door was ajar, so he went in. "Hello? ISA agents?" He called.

"Oh my!" A janitor jumped up from behind the desk. "I was just cleaning up here," He muttered, turning away and picking up his mop. "I thought everyone had gone."

"They should be," Hector said, trying to get a better look at the man. "This area is closed for an ISA investigation."

"Mmm-hmm," the janitor replied, still stubbornly facing away and scrubbing at the floor.

"What are you doing here?" Hector approached the janitor.

"Shouldn't I ask you the same?" The janitor replied. He inched toward the desk and very casually turned the screen off. Hector noticed and immediately grabbed the man.

"Aright, the gig is up!" Hector paused. "Uncle Elton? What are you doing?"

"No. Shh. Please don't tell anyone," Elton begged. "I just couldn't take it anymore."

"Why are you posing as a janitor?" Hector repeated.

"It's this job. It's so demanding. People just kept asking me to implement all these crazy ideas with the planet's ecosystem. This planet's ecosystem is terribly complex on its own, mind you. But when you consider its effects on the economy...I did so much overtime. I just needed a break," Elton said. "I was only going to be gone for a day. I didn't have anything critical to do. And then the day after, I thought that if could pop in and out without anyone noticing I would only have to update a few key systems...I never meant it to go this far. Oh, what do I do?"

"Look, why don't we just tell ISA what happened?"

"No!" Elton exclaimed. "They'll fire me for sure. We just need to come up with an excuse for my disappearance. I got it! I had to help you with a family emergency."

"I already told them I haven't seen you," Hector said. "Look, I'll help you trick ISA if you help me out. You have access to the Eden biological profiles. I need you to add a profile for some tree that the council wants to introduce to the ecosystem. Can you do that for me?"

"Yes, but now the building is crawling with ISA agents. I need to get out of here before they find me, then turn up somewhere else with a reason for my absence." The sound of the elevator echoed down the hall. Both men flinched.

"Let's just start with getting out of the building," Hector whispered. "At any moment now the ISA agents are going to come down here. Is there anywhere on this floor where we can hide so we can get to the elevator?"

"I've been hiding in the janitorial closet all day. They're mostly going through computer records today. We can hide there."

"Lead the way," Hector said. He stole a glance down the hall and, spotting no one, beaconed for Elton to follow. Elton grabbed the janitorial cart and followed slowly after it.

"Can't that thing move any faster?" Hector hissed.

"No. It gets slow when the disintegrator is full," Elton hissed back. "Take a left." They made their way to the janitorial closet, peering around every corner to look for ISA agents. Once the door was closed behind them, they huddled in the dark listening for footsteps.

"Here, we'll need to be at our best for this," Elton said, pulling a box of ambrosia from his cart and offering it to Hector. Disgusted, Hector shoved it back. "Don't worry, I've already had some. It helps take the edge off with all this sneaking around."

"Get rid of that," Hector said. "It's not worth it. Besides if you get caught with that in your system, you're not just going to lose your job. You'll end up doing time. This is an ISA facility. They don't mess around with that shit."

Elton looked disgruntled and tried hiding the bundle.

"Throw it in the disintegrator," Hector told him sternly. "It'll destroy the evidence. Next time, if the stress is that bad, take a vacation."

"The whole planet is dependent on me carrying out my duties," Elton whined. "If I left, everything would go to hell. There would be no recovering."

Footsteps sounded down the hall. The two men held their breath and waited from the agents to pass.

"Then hire an assistant or retire," Hector said. "Stop working a job that's killing you. Come on. The coast is clear."

Elton led the way. As he turned the last corner, he leapt backward and held his finger to his lips.

"There's an ISA agent guarding the elevator," he whispered. "What do we do? I'm going to lose my job." Hector peered around the corner. The ISA agent was dutifully facing the elevator. Hector thought for a minute.

"Uncle, once you get down the elevator, can you make it outside by yourself?" Hector asked.

"I think so," Elton replied. "They don't check in and out those with an employee badge." He pointed at the badge pinned to his shirt.

"Alright, as soon as you get out, meet me at Ymanthia canyon, and change out of the janitor jumpsuit," Hector said. "I have an idea."

"But how do we get past the guard?"

"I won't. I'll distract him, you sneak by," Hector said. He didn't wait for a response and approached the guard.

"I've been looking for you all over," Hector announced once he was positioned so that his uncle could sneak by. The ISA agent jumped.

"Hey, didn't we tell you to leave?" the ISA agent said, flashing his badge and squaring up.

"Yeah, but I came back," Hector replied. "My cousin asked me to find out what you know about my uncle."

"We're not releasing any information to the public," the agent said.

"Do you know who I am?" Hector demanded. He got in the agent's face. The agent scowled. "My father is the council chairperson. My family practically owns this planet. We need to know where Uncle Elton is, now."

"I'm sorry sir, but I'm going to have to ask you to leave," the agent growled. He started to turn Hector toward the elevator, and toward Elton.

"That's unacceptable!" Hector lashed out with his arm and toppled a potted plant. The pot fell to the floor and shattered. The guard stopped.

"Sir you need to calm down."

"Calm? I am calm!" Hector shouted. He could see Elton was close now. It was time to make some noise. "Don't tell me to calm down! You can't treat me like this."

"I need some backup here," the agent called to his team. He grabbed Hector by the arm to lead him to elevator.

"Don't touch me," Hector said, throwing off the agent's hand. He saw Elton slip into the elevator. The doors slid silently shut. "I want to speak to whoever's in charge."

"Sir, don't resist," the guard said, pulling out his stun gun.

"I'm not resisting." Hector shoved the guard away.

"That's it. Put your hands in the air."

"Make me," Hector said, internally wincing. He knew from the police academy that the stun gun would not cause damage, but it would hurt. Hector stepped toward the guard to threaten him. The guard pulled the trigger. Hector blacked out.

Hector woke up restrained in a hospital bed. An ISA agent sat at the foot of his bed.

"I've looked at your records," the ISA agent said. "It's quite colorful. Driving under the influence. Manslaughter. Misconduct. Insubordination. Yet none of it resulted in actual consequences. You're a classic case of wealth immunity. I hope you've figured out that this doesn't fly with ISA, but I doubt it. Are you going to continue to interfere with our investigation?"

"No, ma'am."

"Good. If I see or hear from you again in regard to the missing LPM, I swear to you I'll see that you're charged with every infraction you've done, from the largest to the smallest. Understand?"

"Yes, ma'am."

"Good. Release him," the ISA agent instructed the nurse. She strode out of the room. However, Hector could hear her ordering her squad. "Make sure the daughter's communications are being monitored. This idiot's not smart enough to be involved, but he might be manipulated in all of this."

Hector left the hospital. He called a cab and headed for Ymanthia canyon. Elton found him almost as soon as he got there.

"What took you so long?" Elton asked.

"Oh, you know how the ISA is." Hector shrugged. "Is there any evidence that the ISA could use against you?"

"Not anything major. I think they just want me back," Elton said. "I can't believe you got me out. Thank you."

"You can thank me by integrating that stupid tree into the ecosystem. Come here, you've got something on your face." Elton stepped forward, and Hector punched him.

"Ow! What the hell?"

"Uncle, I need you to be convincing. You were mugged by a bandit called the Boar and abandoned out here. I'll call a friend to come 'find' you."

"Oh," Elton said. "Thanks."

Hector turned to leave but paused. "And Uncle, if you're feeling overwhelmed, instead of binging on your drug problem, check yourself into a rehabilitation facility. I know the ISA's insurance will cover the bill, not that you can't afford it. At the very least you'll get a break from all the pressure."

"Yeah, I'll do that," Elton replied.

Once back in his own cab, Hector made a call. "Lolaus, how are you?"

"I'm fine," Lolaus answered. "And yourself?"

"I'm good. I was wondering if I could ask a favor?"

"What's different this time, Hector?" Lolaus asked. "You can't just keep asking me for help and then making the same mistakes."

"It's not for me. I need help for my uncle. He's a good man, but he's made some bad decisions. I need you to pick him up, no questions asked, and take him to the police. Then I need you to make sure he gets himself to a rehab facility. You're the only one I can count on to do this."

"Okay," Lolaus said. "Then what? Rehabilitation might not change his life?"

"No. It's up to him to get his life straight," Hector said. "But not even I could do it alone. He needs support, so I've decided to be there for him. Like you were for me. Thanks for all your help. I won't ask for anything again."

"You're welcome. How many tasks do you have left for your own rehabilitation?"

"Just one. I honestly don't know what I'll do when I'm done. I feel like I have a lot to atone for."

"I understand," Lolaus said. "I'll tell you what, I'll pick up your uncle and make sure he gets his things in order. Then I'll take you to your last task, for old time's sake."

"Thanks, Lolaus," Hector said. He sent her the coordinates and returned to town. Feeling empty, Hector walked the streets, mingling with people going about their daily business.

After a few hours, RETS activated.

"The file was successfully uploaded to the Eden, Hector," the computer said. "You have one more task to complete for your reconciliation. You must capture the three-headed dog, Cerberus, an unregistered Gen-Mod pet, from former council member Henry. The dog is to be obtained alive and unharmed so investigators can determine if it was built using illegal Gen-Mods."

***

"This is as far as I can take you," Lolaus said, landing the ship on the bank of the Starx river. "From what I've heard, Henry makes great use of the 'shoot trespassers on sight' rule. But I guess he has a doorman android that takes people across the river."

"He's not on good terms with my father. Not after being kicked off the council," Hector said. "It will be a wonder if I don't get shot, trespassing or not."

"Good luck," Lolaus said as Hector exited the ship.

"I don't need luck—I have a plan!"

He approached the ferryman. "Good evening. I'm here to see my Uncle Henry."

"Henry is not home," the ferryman said. "He is returning home this evening. Try again later or make an appointment."

"It's, um…a surprise," Hector explained. "I'm his nephew, Hector."

"Very well," the ferryman responded blankly. "You'll have to wait at the front gate. If you try to enter, Cerberus will probably attack."

"Thanks. I'll keep that in mind."

The android sailed him across the river. As soon as Hector touched the ground, a fast black airship pulled up and landed behind the house. Henry was home. Hector turned back to the boatman, but the android had already begun sailing back. Hector gave it a minute, then rang the doorbell.

He was greeted by booming and frantic barking.

"Shut up!" A voice roared from behind the door. The barking dropped to a whimper, and the door opened. Henry stood in the doorway with an enormous, black, three-headed dog behind him.

"Yes?" Henry asked. "I wasn't expecting any visitors."

"Hi, Uncle Henry," Hector said with a gulp. "It's me, Hector. Surprise. I wonder if you have a minute to talk."

"You know full well I'm not on good terms with your side of the family. You sure have a lot of guts coming here," Henry growled. Then he grinned. "But I could tell you had guts when you spoke up against the council on live media. Come on in."

He beckoned Hector in, waving Cerberus to sit. Hector followed him inside and received a low, menacing growl from one of Cerberus's heads.

"So, what did you want to talk to me about?" Henry asked.

"I'm here because the council is worried about whether your dog is Gen-Mod legal or not," Hector said. "They have asked me to bring it to the lab for testing. I'm afraid if it doesn't pass the tests, they will destroy it. Humanely, of course."

Henry threw back his head and laughed. "Zachariah is still going on about that, I see. I can assure you this dog is completely Gen-Mod legal. I even have the certificate to prove it, though my brother insists it's a forgery. Other than that, I'm afraid I can't help you. I can't allow Cerberus to leave the property. As you can see, he's quite aggressive. He was a rescue. He was born—yes that's right, born, not Gen-Modded—with three heads, a rare and natural mutation. The breeders didn't want him and left him to die. The Gen-Modders wanted to dissect him and find out how his three heads survived all this time. I rescued him, and he only trusts me. I would take him myself, but I'm no longer allowed on Rambus

Space Station. I cannot let anyone else take him. He gets hard to handle when he's anxious."

"What if I take the time to let him get used to me?" Hector asked. "I could take him up to Rambus. You could get the results of the test and tell the council where they can shove it. At the very least, it'll shed some doubt on the rumors about you."

"The rumors don't bother me so much. They keep people away," Henry replied. "If you really insist on completing this task for your community service, I'll allow you to try. If you can get Cerberus to obey simple commands from you—sit, lay down, come—I'll trust you to take him to Rambus. But if anything happens to my dog, legal or otherwise, I will personally hunt you down and see to it that all those nasty rumors about me are true. Got it?"

"Got it," Hector said, eyeing the large dog.

"Training starts now," Henry said. "Cerberus! Heel!" The big black dog sat loyally at his feet. All six eyes burned coldly into Hector. "Hold out your hand. Let him sniff."

Hector did as he was told. Cerberus's three massive heads sniffed and snuffed at him. One of the heads started drooling. Henry took a step away, letting the four get acquainted, and retrieved a thick leather leash from off the wall. He clipped it to Cerberus.

"Let's go for a walk," Henry suggested. "Just around the yard. Cerberus, walk!" Cerberus's death-gaze broke from Hector, and his tail thumped reluctantly.

They started out front and walked through massive gardens. Then Henry handed Hector the leash. As soon as it was in Hector's hands, Cerberus growled.

"Sorry, I think this was a bad idea," Henry said.

"No! I can take him," Hector burst out. "Isn't that right, boy?" Cerberus backed away and growled again.

"Don't pay attention," Henry suggested. "Walk this way. Tell me, what are you going to do when your community service is over?"

"When it's over?" Hector repeated. "I hadn't really thought about it. I thought my life was over. Now I really seem to be making a difference down here."

"Yes, well, it hardly pays. But perhaps after this you'll do well in a governing role like your father wants."

"My father wants that?" Hector asked. "My father doesn't think I'm good enough. I'll probably work for Artie or Anthony. They're always in need of private security, and I haven't fallen out of their favor yet."

"I bet that's your father's endgame in all of this," Henry said. "He is my brother after all. I know his ambition quite well. He wants his little boy to grow up and follow in his footsteps. It'll make him look good, even when he retires. If he ever retires. It was always his ego that caused friction between us."

"Right. I know that ego well." Hector paused as Cerberus sniffed a flower, then lifted a leg to pee on it. Hector turned toward the dog. All three heads growled at him. "Is that why he won't talk to you? Because you hurt his pride?"

"He won't talk to me because he knows kicking me off the council was wrong. Sure, I was rude and contemptuous, but I was the only one who could see the root of our problems. He didn't agree, and he conned the rest of the council into banishing me here." They rounded the last corner to the front of the house.

"And what do you think the root of our problems is?"

"We lived too far from the planet's surface. We gave speeches, but we never talked with our people. We always blamed the struggle on the Eden and the distance from trade. But we have the means to be self-sufficient if we invested in the planet instead of our prides—our Gen-Modders, sports, and luxury resorts. None of the other council members ever bothered visiting the world's surface."

"You know, I've heard that before," Hector admitted. "The people need a voice."

They stopped in front of the door, where Cerberus shoved his three heads into a large water dish and proceeded to lap, creating a puddle around it. Hector rubbed the dog's back.

"You might be given the chance to be that voice," Henry said.

"It would be an honor. I would do my best to fight for their causes. Even against my father."

"That's exactly what I was hoping to hear. If you would, take Cerberus inside. I believe you two are getting along well."

Inside, Hector began working on "sit." Cerberus was more inclined to slobber on himself, bark if Hector asked too loudly, or stare loyally at Henry.

"Is there a trick to it? Do I need a treat?"

"No. Cerberus, sit." Henry pronounced each syllable clearly and the dog sat. "Up." The dog rose.

"Cerberus," Hector repeated, "sit!" The dog did not sit. "I guess I'd better tell Lolaus I'm going to be late."

"Lolaus?" Henry questioned.

"My friend and driver. She's on the other side of the river."

"Well don't leave her sitting out there. Call her over. Invite her in. Company livens up the place, wouldn't you agree?"

"Yeah."

Hector made the call.

"How's it going?" Lolaus asked when she arrived.

"Not well. The dog just wants to chew at my boot."

"Well, aren't they just the cutest!" She dropped to her knee and patted the heads.

"Wait," Hector said, but the three heads had taken an instant liking to Lolaus. Cerberus's tail wagged.

"How did you do that?" Hector asked.

"Do what?"

"That dog tried to bite me when I first tried to pet it."

"Which one?" Lolaus responded.

"Which one? That—Oh. Cerberus. Cer. Ber. Rus. It's three dogs, isn't it?"

"Yeah," Lolaus said with a grin. "Look at all the heads. The left is the alpha. You've got to greet him first. Then the center head and then the right."

"Cer. Ber. Rus. Sit." All three dogs sat with the same body. "What good boys you are!" Hector gushed. He patted each head in turn. Then he turned to Lolaus. "How did you figure it out?"

"I don't know," Lolaus replied with a shrug. "Maybe I'm just used to seeing problems from a different perspective."

Fifteen minutes later, Cer, Ber, and Rus were coming, staying, and sitting with ease. As a bonus, Hector managed a couple of shakes, but Cer, Ber, and Rus got mixed up and often tried to offer both front paws.

"I see you've figured out my trick," Henry said, watching a successful shake. "Go on, take Cerberus, but be back by tomorrow."

"Thank you, Uncle." Hector grabbed the leash and left with the three-headed dog bounding happily after.

Lolaus flew them to Rambus where Cerberus obediently, though reluctantly, went through a series of genetic tests, proving they were, indeed natural born dogs, all sharing the same body.

RETS clicked on. "Hector, you've completed your final mission. The council has been informed. They are waiting for you in the council chambers." RETS clicked off for the final time, and the handcuffs fell to the floor. Hector picked them up to return later.

"Look at that," Lolaus said. "You're a free man."

***

"Hector," Council Member Herman announced, "you've finally completed your missions."

"That's right," Hector said. "All twelve, unless there's anything else that's cropped up."

"Well, there is…" Council Member Vera spoke up but was silenced by Councilor Zachariah.

"Hector," Zachariah boomed. "My son. I'm proud of what you've managed to accomplish in just a few short weeks. You've shown great commitment and great leadership."

"Thank you. I did my best."

"You have made me proud." Zachariah turned to Vera, "Make sure that's recorded in the council minutes." He turned back to Hector. "There has been a lot of talk. We all saw what you said on the news, and we had some lengthy discussion about it. I believe it's time things change. The people on the planet need a voice. We have elected to add a position to the council so it's not just for the travel guilds, industry leaders, and wealthy heirs and heiresses anymore. We have added a seat for a representative purely interested in the lives of the people on the planet below. We would like you to fill that position."

"I've thought about it," Hector said. "Honestly, it's an honor you would even consider me in light of my past."

"I just knew you were the right person for the job," Zachariah said with a charming smile. "We're already constructing a new building for your housing and estate. We've also set aside funds from the budget for the position. You're familiar with the lifestyle. I'm sure you'll adjust back to it in no time."

"But that's the problem," Hector said. "I didn't start this by seeking to help anyone. I didn't know the people needed help until I was made to help them. They need someone who has been listening all along. Give the seat to Lolaus. It was Lolaus who organized the people to put in their petitions to RETS. It was Lolaus who got me where I needed to go. And it was Lolaus who didn't take any of my bullshit. Lolaus is the wisest person I know. She deserves a seat on this council, and she'll make much greater use of it than I ever will."

"Take time to think about it," Zachariah insisted. "Let me show you your residence. Don't throw this opportunity away. Not like last time."

"No. It's not like last time. This time, I've got some dogs to return to their owner. Then, I suppose, I'll see what else this planet has to throw at me."

Hector smiled and walked out amidst the protest of most of the council. And the smirks of a few.

In the Gardens of Eden

By Alex O'Neill

Date: 3565 & 3572

Prologue

23 April 3572

Planet: Salvon 4

The man walked across the ground. He stood upright, somewhat akin to a bean pole. One would assume his posture was military, but his clothing said otherwise: a long brown coat, a loose-fitting shirt, a pair of oval-lens sunglasses on his face.

The sun. Oh, the sun.

It bore down on the man something foul.

It was nothing the man wasn't used to. His skin was dark, darker than anyone who was born on Earth.

He was taller too. Not by any grotesque amount, but by enough to look out of place.

But that didn't matter. It didn't make him tougher than the sun. He flicked the collar of his coat up against the back of his neck.

The whole place felt wrong.

Gale force winds, no wildlife, no clouds, and yet the planet had abundant water.

A weather system that didn't make sense.

It disturbed the man. A place that shouldn't be.

It was not natural.

He knew it. He could feel it.

The man was looking for something. He didn't know what it would look like, but he knew that he'd know it the moment he saw it.

The man passed by an entrance to an old cave—possibly an old mine, now filled to its very brim with sand—which stood out from the hard gritstone that made up the cave entrance.

The tall man crouched, pulled out a single tight glove and fit it to his right hand. He felt the granules as they fell between his long, bony, gloved fingers.

The man swallowed, looked around, then stood up.

The sun was large. Unbearably so. The wind strong, powerful, and howling.

This planet must have hardly been habitable at the best of times.

And it certainly wasn't the best of times.

The tall man looked up and focused back on his aims. A settlement stood some way in front of him, the former buildings now looked more like giant skeletal fingers protruding from the ground. Shadows of what they once were.

The man grimaced.

He had his heading, but it certainly wasn't somewhere he wanted to go.

It was right into the middle of the disaster that the human race had tried its hardest to forget.

Chapter A1

22 March 3565

Planet: Salvon 4

Taylor Cortes slammed the hammer down on the bench. It was almost time to break for lunch. The faint thud of some ancient band came over his mobile device. He took a breath of the large pack-oxygen to his left. The track was almost built. One day it would transport Goliaths— towering, advanced robots, about five meters tall, designed to tunnel, mine, and categorize minerals and other materials found in a planet's outer crust. The Goliaths had thick torsos, with lean, powerful arms and legs, their faces consisted of one huge eye to see with. Taylor found them intimidating but beautiful machines to work alongside.

Taylor had always wanted to see into the depths of a planet, but only mining officers and technicians got to travel down with the Goliaths into the planet's depths. A mere track builder like Taylor would not be bestowed such luxury viewing.

Not that Taylor had wanted to be a track builder when he started working for the ISA. He still got to work alongside Goliaths; they were often used to carve tunnels into the planet's surface, assisted by people, before builders were brought in to place the tracks into the tunnels. The Goliaths, along with technicians and overseeing officers—unlovingly nicknamed "handlers"—would then head under the planet's surface on trains.

It was a lot of work, but it was all built into the terraforming process by now. It ran like clockwork and all the involved parties—the men, the women, the robots, and, god, even the animals—knew the score. Get in, get shit done, find fuel.

Taylor didn't know much, but he knew that almost every planet had something that could be used as fuel. You name it, it could be fuel.

Mind you, the heavy lifting of the terraforming process was initially made by the Eden, a machine in the shape of a glass bottle and the size of a mountain, with four great legs. Edens were sent ahead of any human, capable of hyperspeed travel through autopilot. The transportation of humans at that speed was a far more delicate process.

Arks were spaceships designed to take large groups of humans at hyperspeed, sometimes for a considerable amount of time.

Taylor had arrived on the second of five arks sent to Salvon 4 with support staff in the terraforming process. He hated space travel. It was a sickening experience. Not what humans were designed for, Taylor thought.

"Okay, lads, take thirty for lunch," said Skipper, the supervisor. Skipper was a lean man, who broadened at the shoulders, with a long neck, thinning hair, deep brown eyes, and a handsome face. He was okay really, Taylor had always thought. A little bit of an arse-licker to the higher-ups, but generally got the job done. He was quite a patient boss, just a little too stuck-up for Taylor to ever want to spend time with him away from the job.

Skipper headed over to one of the construction devices to pour himself a coffee. Taylor moved over to sit with a couple of the other workers: Alf, a little guy, slightly older, with leathery skin and strong hands; and Lark, a great big guy with thick-rimmed glasses, and a large ginger 'fro. Both had been here longer than Taylor and had worked on previous Eden sites.

This was Taylor's first.

"Cold today," Taylor said. Lark looked up and grunted, tucking into a corned beef sandwich.

"You know, Taylor, you remind me of someone me and the big guy used to work with," Alf said, an eyebrow raised. "What was his name?"

"I don't know," Lark grunted, clearly far more interested in his sandwich than anything going on outside of it.

"Oh, you know, green-haired guy, similar build to young Cortes here. Used to skate everywhere, we called him Wheels," Alf stated.

"Stapleton." Lark looked up from his sandwich toward his old friend. "His name was Stapleton."

"Yeah, that was it, Stapleton. I knew it was something fancy soundin'. He didn't suit it, an idiot like that with a fancy name. Weren't right, you know what I mean?" Alf asked no one in particular.

"I guess so," Taylor replied intrepidly. *Does this guy ever stop talking?* he thought.

"Anyway, one day, this lad decides he's had enough just laying tracks for the bossman. Wants to do more. Decides he wants to see under the surface of the planet we were on and decides he's going to skate down one of the entry tracks that he, himself, worked on. Fucker didn't even check to see it was clear. Didn't even check to see if there wasn't something coming up the other way. Fucking Goliath took his 'ead off. Carnage, I tell yer. I reckon our old supervisor still feels hand cramp from the piles of paperwork that merry afternoon caused him." Alf smiled before sniggering with laughter.

Lark cracked a thin smile, shook his head, and then took another bite of his sandwich.

"You see, lad, that's where eagerness and selfishness get you in this job," Alf stated, opening his soup before looking up to meet Taylor's eyes. "It gets yer dead."

Chapter B1

17 April 3572. Earth Time 10.00 AM

<u>*ISA Secondary HQ, Titan, Earth System*</u>

INFORMATION CHECK: Interview covering the events of Planet Salvon 4, occurring 24 March 3565, Earth Time. Interview conducted on 17 April 3572, Earth Time. Interview located within the Special Investigations Unit, ISA off-Earth base on Titan.

INTERVIEWEES: Dr. Robert Silver, chief science officer of the Eden development team, and Sandra Harrison, head project manager in the Cygnus Arm expansion project.

INTERVIEWER: Specialist Case Officer John Morris

The Interview begins with Morris offering the interviewees a coffee from the small machine located outside the interrogation room.

They both politely decline.

SPECIALIST MORRIS: I understand you've both been briefed on why you've been brought here?

DR. SILVER: To do with an old case with one of the Edens, I believe? A malfunction?

MRS. HARRISON: Yes. I don't quite understand why, either. It was what? Seven years ago, now?

MORRIS: That's correct. We just had some further questions for you.

HARRISON: You know, you're all the same, you specialists. One misjudged decision and suddenly you think you're the galaxy's judge, jury, and executioner.

MORRIS: So, you think that your decisions made regarding the case were misjudged?

HARRISON: Not at all. I mean it generically. You're putting words in my mouth.

MORRIS: So, would you say, for instance, that the decision you made to abandon the evacuation of the planet, was not misjudged?

HARRISON: I wouldn't say so. I had many lives safe aboard my ark. The longer I stayed there, the more danger I was causing for them. I think, given the stress and pressures of that situation, that you would have made the same call.

MORRIS: I think we should move on.

SILVER: Yes, let's.

MORRIS: Dr. Silver, am I right in believing that you were the first senior officer within the Eden development team for that sector to know of the faults within the planet's Eden?

SILVER: That's correct.

MORRIS: Although you were not the chief science officer then—you were assistant, correct?

SILVER: That's correct. I received a promotion last year.

MORRIS: You were still the acting senior officer at the time, though?

SILVER: Oh. But if you don't mind me asking…err…John, isn't it?

MORRIS: Specialist Morris will do fine.

SILVER: Specialist Morris, what I wanted to ask is…what is this all about? What do you want to know?

MORRIS: Well, Dr. Silver, what I want to know is why the Eden on Salvon 4 malfunctioned so catastrophically, at a time when terraforming science, and therefore Eden operations, have been perfected to this degree. Why, when given ample opportunity to implement a safe evacuation procedure, ninety-six percent of the human population—sixty-seven million people—were left to die. Why an Eden, a machine triple tested, quadruple tested, hit a technical fault, and malfunctioned so badly, it destroyed the climate of the planet. And why that would happen on a planet so easy to terraform—a small, rocky planet that circles its star a similar distance that the Earth does to its sun. And I want to know why the whole incident, which happened almost a decade ago, got brushed under the rug. I want to know how a whole planet was destroyed, and the people responsible got away scot-free.

Chapter A2

22 March 3565

<u>*Planet: Salvon 4*</u>

It was several hours later, after Taylor swung through the main door into his family home, that he finally loosened up slightly. His mom, Olivia Cortes, a short, rotund woman with a jolly face and a fine collection of cardigans, was rushing around the kitchen, trying to do ten tasks at once. They lived in a small, perhaps too cozy, homestead in the settlement of Carpettown.

Taylor's sister, Lorna, a girl of fourteen, sat at the silver desk, the table set with large, heavy, well-polished cutlery laid in perfect positions. Lorna had cerebral palsy, but unfortunately, between Taylor and his mom's income, they could not afford the necessary drugs to help her. It was never a problem for Taylor, as his mom seemed to thrive on looking after Lorna. It would often leave him to his own devices, which suited him very much. Lorna was scribbling away on a piece of paper. Taylor crossed over the room, ignoring his mom, and looked at his sister's drawing.

"Looks like an egg," Taylor chided.

"It's a curtain," Lorna said. "That's obviously a curtain."

"You're late. Get over here, help me with this." Taylor helped his mom remove the jacket potatoes from the oven. Lorna got up, placed another set of cutlery, and sat down. Taylor and his mom looked at each other and shook their heads. The extra cutlery was, like usual, set for Taylor's dad, Martin, who had died two years before. The three of them, clearly hungry, tucked in, none of them speaking for a couple of minutes.

"Tay, sweetie, how was work?" Taylor's mom asked.

"Same old," Taylor said between mouthfuls of potato. "I'm going out to see Jake tonight."

"Okay, just don't be out too late," she responded.

"How come Taylor gets to go and see his friends? You never let me go out after dark," Lorna stated.

"Because, young lady, he works now. He's in charge of what he wants to do in his evenings. You've got homework to do," Taylor's mom replied, nodding at her daughter. "And dinner to finish."

"I don't like it!" Lorna exclaimed.

"It was lovely mom, thanks." Taylor stood up from the table and quietly walked away.

***

Jake Spring was Taylor's best mate, a black-haired, lanky lad, who wore skinny jeans and brightly colored jackets. He was what some would call a colorful character, and he made sure his appearance matched. He smoked, something he kept secret from his parents who were more upper-middle-class than Taylor's mother. His dad even held some menial management job within the ISA, like a deputy mayor of the Carpettown community. Fancy enough to sound important, but not fancy enough to really be important. Class meant a great deal to some folks during the settlement of terraforming operations. Taylor found that a shame really—an opportunity to start over, start afresh, and the fancy cats and big dicks set out to keep everything the same.

Jake leaned back on the thick metal railings not far from the canteen where he worked, but some way from either of their family homes. From where they stood, they could see across a great crater on the planet, cordoned off from the new human settlers. The planet's star, a main sequence g-type star, nine-tenths the size of Earth's sun, was beginning to set on the horizon.

"You look tired, man," Jake said, taking a long drag on the cigarette in his hand. "I guess those twenty-eight-hour days fuck you up a bit."

"It's not that," Taylor replied. "Just not…feeling this. This move. Being here."

"This planet? This planet is a new start, man. It might not look sexy now, but you know, give it a few hundred years of intense plant growth and animal induction, it should look, well, I'd say at least passable," Jake stated. Taylor smiled.

"See! That's more like it. Is it those guys at work again?" Jake asked.

"Well, it's just the one guy actually. His name's Alf. But the others sit back and let him do it. It's just banter to them," Taylor said.

"Ah, I see," Jake responded.

"This Alf, he just, you know, seems to have it out for me. Today, he said I reminded him of this guy he used to know, who used to skate down the Goliath tracks. Some guy who got killed for it. He's always doing it, just trying to chip away, find something," Taylor stated.

"You know what it is?" Jake asked. "Jealousy. You take this Alf guy, how old is he? What, fifty? Sixty? Still doing what you do now, as a job you've had to take, you know, since your dad, you know, passed. He sees you as a threat. Someone strong, kind, helpful. Scared one day he'll be answering to you? What do you think?"

"I think you talk almost as much as he does, Jake," Taylor replied.

"Aye, but I'm not wrong, am I?" Jake asked.

"I suppose not," Taylor responded.

***

Jake and Taylor spent their time wandering the middle streets of Carpettown. It was a struggle to find things to do. Often, they'd resort to just walking and talking.

It was not recommended, walking in the open, but it wasn't illegal. It required masks and oxygen tanks, just like when Jake was at work. You could go outside without an oxygen tank or a mask, but that was even less recommended. The air wasn't lethal, but it wasn't pleasant either.

They were used to the lifestyle, Taylor knew. Jake knew it too.

That's why they were friends. Understanding. Taylor hadn't met Jake until he was fifteen when they had signed on to be transported to the planet on the same ark.

"I hope we can get off this rock some time," Jake said. "I hadn't planned to be here this long."

"You came here, mate. You chose to be here," Taylor pointed out.

"My dad chose to be here. It wasn't up to me," Jake responded.

"And you don't have that bad a life here. Not really. You should count your blessings. You have a family," Taylor replied.

Jake's body stiffened slightly. "You can be so fucking naïve sometimes, man. This sort of place…it's not a fresh beginning. You—you work with what? The same fifteen people every day. I serve everyone in this settlement at work. I meet even more through dad's work. This isn't the place people come to make a new start. This is where dreams come to die. I'm getting out of here."

Taylor laughed before his face fell straight. "No, you aren't."

"I wanted to tell you first. I filed the applications last week, and they were approved this morning. I want you to come with me."

"I can't do that." Taylor looked away.

"No, that's where you're wrong," Jake said, his manner warming a little. "You don't *think* you can do that."

Taylor thought for a moment before responding. "What did you have in mind?"

"Charterer's school. Helping charter newly found planets and then creating maps," Jake responded.

Taylor laughed. "You're mad."

Jake smiled. "Think about it. I'm creative, you've got the best damn sense of direction of anyone I've ever met. We'd be a wizard."

"I have a life here. You have a life here. We can't just up and leave," Taylor stated.

"Get out, man, just get out. Anyway, it's late. Let's talk about this tomorrow night with the others."

***

Jake and Taylor embraced and went their separate ways to their separate homes. Taylor did not fall instantly asleep, however much his body wanted it. Instead, he stayed awake, looking at his bedroom communication screen.

He searched "charterer's school" and sure enough, a healthy bank of information appeared on the screen.

A small blue button reading "Apply Now" appeared in the bottom right of the screen. Taylor's finger hovered for a moment, with Jake's words of *get out man, just get out* running through his head, before he pressed the button.

He read over the contents of the website, until he, inevitably, fell asleep.

Chapter B2

17 April 3572. Earth Time 11.32AM

ISA Secondary HQ, Titan, Earth system

Specialist Morris returned from their brief break. He resumed his seat to conduct the remainder of the interview at approximately 11:32 a.m. Despite his offering, Dr. Robert Silver and Project Officer Sandra Harrison did not want to consume a caffeine-based drink.

MORRIS: Okay, then, we'll start.

HARRISON: I hope you don't think you can hold us here all day!

MORRIS: The earlier you provide me with the evidence I require, then the earlier we can all leave.

HARRISON: You have quite a way with words, don't you, Mr. Morris?

MORRIS: Specialist Morris.

SILVER: Yes, quite. I'm guessing that you were well educated, or at least you give the pretense that you were?

MORRIS: No pretense. I was raised on Earth, attended a good university, had the right parents, I guess. Not everyone is so lucky. Not everyone can be.

HARRISON: Hark, a home-child.

MORRIS: Quite. But for now, I'd rather I ask the questions. Dr. Silver, how many tests do you put the standard Eden conversion unit through before commissioning them for exploration use?

SILVER: Oh well, so many. Wind tests, water-logging tests, tests against heat, cold, fire.

MORRIS: So, for one of these machines to malfunction, what would it require?

SILVER: Well, someone would have to tamper with it—intentionally do so.

MORRIS: Are you sure? That, just for the record, you would have to intentionally damage an Eden to cause it to malfunction?

SILVER: The technology is at that level, correct. There's no such thing as technical error with the Edens, only potential human error.

MORRIS: I see.

HARRISON: I'm sorry, I still don't know why I've been brought in for this conversation.

MORRIS: Everything will be explained in due course, Sandra.

HARRISON: Please don't call me Sandra, Mr. Morris. Please call me Mrs. Harrison.

We are not friends.

MORRIS: Specialist Morris.

HARRISON: So, you see how impertinent it is?

MORRIS: I do. Which brings me onto something more to the point. I've had access to the ISA's financial records regarding structured expansion into the Cygnus Arm of the Milky Way. What I found there is rather telling.

HARRISON: I'm not sure that someone like you should even be granted access to that material?

MORRIS: Someone like me?

HARRISON: An agency internal investigations officer.

MORRIS: I'm not from the agency…more of a consultant. Well, sort of. We have a special agreement, which need not concern you.

HARRISON: This is ridiculous, I'm not speaking to some…some…whatever you are.

MORRIS: Please, I think we're barking down the path of no return. The point I was making, the point I am trying to make, is that I was looking at the accounts of one Rowland Bloor, a bookkeeper who worked for the ISA until earlier this year I believe?

SILVER: Yes, God bless his soul. Passed away earlier this year, that's correct.

MORRIS: A shame. I believe he held knowledge that would be most useful in my investigation.

SILVER: Erm, well, I wouldn't know about that. But he was a smart man, a good character.

MORRIS: Well, this Rowland kept an inventory of every piece of equipment shipped from the Eden factories on the terraformed moon of NXLI3 to the ISA's headquarters within the Cygnus Arm, on the planet Gliese 667 Cc. That's where your office is, I believe? Both of your offices?

SILVER: Correct.

HARRISON: Correct.

MORRIS: Now, interestingly the full layout and instructions for creating an Eden are kept awfully close to the ISA's chest—as you both know—to stop the technology from falling into competitor's hands, so the terraforming market remains completely dominated. The exact formula is protected by non-disclosure agreements to the teeth. I have, however, managed to get my hands on the formula, which, for the sake of the investigation, I am allowed to share with you. When I was reading this, I must say, incredibly clear formula, one thing that leapt out to me was this: steel plating with jets around the nuclear engines, used to keep the nuclear reactor cool at all times. It prevents the reactor heating and melting any essential wiring around it. Fascinating, honestly. Six metal plates, from what I can see, right at the summit, near the engine.

SILVER: That sounds right to me.

MORRIS: And I'd be correct in assuming that they are essential to the stability of the whole ship?

SILVER: Absolutely.

MORRIS: It's weird, then, that Rowland Bloor did not note down that any were ordered amongst the other parts for the Edens that were used to terraform Salvon 4?

Chapter A3

23 March 3565

Planet: Salvon 4

Taylor awoke with a start as the room was shaking. A framed painting of the planet Mars, gifted to Taylor by his great-grandfather, fell from above his head. He ducked and it bounced on the bed.

Taylor leapt to catch it, but his foot caught on the foot of the bed. He slipped and landed awkwardly on the floor, shoulder first, with a thud. The painting landed next to his face, the frame smashing everywhere. Taylor quickly rolled to his right to avoid shards of glass flying into his eyes. The room was still shaking.

The urn on top of the cupboard fell, and for a moment, Taylor watched it, frozen in place. "Dad!" His hand shot forward, catching the urn just before it shattered on the ground.

He caught the urn, arm outstretched, and landed chin-first on the floor.

He lay there for some time as the ground continued to shake. It was most likely actually fractions of a second, but it felt like minutes.

"Taylor!" His mom rushed into the room.

"I'm okay, I'm okay, mom." Taylor pushed himself off the floor with both hands. He stood up, wobbled, then righted himself.

He took a deep breath and placed the urn containing his father back on the shelf.

"Your sister's okay. She's in the broom cupboard," Taylor's mom informed him.

"Okay," Taylor replied and nodded, before holding his hand gently up to his mother's face. "Mom, what was that?"

"It must…it must have been some kind of earthquake."

"Must have been," Taylor echoed.

Ninety minutes later, Taylor, now dressed for work in his brown overalls, clumpy black boots, and toolkit, appeared from his room as his mom finished her mid-morning round of toast. He wore a large pair of sunglasses on the top of his head.

"I'm going to go to work," Taylor stated.

"Really, Tay? I'm in shock, your sister is in shock, and you're still going to go in?" his mom asked.

"You're not in shock, mom," Taylor replied, to which his mom tutted.

"I can't believe those men are still making you go in, after what happened this morning," Taylor's mom said.

Taylor shrugged. "The work still needs to happen, boss."

"No, Taylor, it doesn't," his mom replied.

"I'm going for you!" Taylor explained, starting to get frustrated.

"You don't need to. I never asked you to provide for every single one of us. Which is why I've applied for a griever's grant."

"A what?" Taylor asked, incredulous.

"If your primary household earner, like your dad, dies while employed by the ISA, their family can enter into a lottery to win money that will help them, you know, after." Mom locked her eyes with Taylor's. "And we were successful."

"Mom, that isn't what dad would have wanted. He never liked them," Taylor stated.

"Who? The ISA? That's exactly who you work for, Taylor Cortes. And does it make you happy?" his mom asked.

"I have to. For Lorna," Taylor replied.

"And now you don't," his mom retorted.

"And now I don't," Taylor said, not quite agreeing.

There was a momentary silence before Taylor spoke again. "I applied to charterer's school. You're right. I'm not happy. Jake and I are both going to go. We're both going to leave this planet."

The information came out quickly and efficiently, in one single thought stream. Taylor nodded, swallowed, and turned, leaving the room before his mom had a chance to put together a coherent reply.

***

Taylor slammed the hammer off the bolt with a loud clink. A bead of sweat rolled off his head. It was hot. So hot.

Fuck, why am I doing this? he thought. The argument with his mom still rolled around in his head, along with the conversation with Jake. He knew he had to go. He had to. For himself.

Taylor looked around, at the worksite. You wouldn't have known that anything out of the ordinary had happened just this morning.

Then again, he often thought the stars could start dropping out of the sky and his co-workers wouldn't notice. Or care.

As the day continued, it only seemed to get hotter. This easily had to be the hottest day Taylor had experienced since they arrived on Salvon 4. Beads of sweat formed on Taylor's head as he continued to place and bolt tracks down. Most of the other men were clearing the dust away from a Goliath carving a mine entrance. Taylor didn't mind; he wanted to be left alone on today of all days. But the heat—soon the beads turned into a constant drip. Before too long, Skipper called time for lunch.

They ate slowly and quietly. There was tension in the air. It appeared they had not been as oblivious to this morning's events as Taylor had speculated.

Lark was noticeably missing. Taylor hoped he was okay, the big man. Alf, on the other hand, stood at the corner of them, shifting from foot to foot. Uneasy. Perhaps unwell. Taylor looked the skinny man up and down, and then focused on his ugly, ratty face, chewing what looking like dehydrated beef. Suddenly Alf looked up and caught Taylor's eye.

"What the fuck ar' you starin' at?" Alf asked and threw his food down before moving through the other miners toward Taylor.

Skipper stood up swiftly. "Simmer down, Alf," he commanded, but Alf continued moving toward Taylor. Taylor put his food down and stood up, preparing for a scuffle. Skipper put one hand on Alf's shoulder, but Alf grabbed Skipper's wrist and pulled it off, turning to look at him.

"This kid ain't been nothin' but trouble, boss," Alf stated firmly, and quick as lightning, spun and landed a punch onto Taylor's throat.

Taylor stood there, winded for a moment, before taking a step back and tripping over a rock. Taylor fell against the deactivated Goliath behind him and slumped against it.

Everything was still for a moment before there was a heavy thundering. A huge boulder, roughly two meters by three meters, detached from the cliff face, and fell to the ground, right into the middle of the resting miners. It crushed Skipper, killing him instantly. His body burst as if were made of jelly, splattering blood everywhere. The other men all leapt to their feet, completely aghast at what had just happened.

"Holy fuck," Alf whispered before turning quickly. "What did you do, boy!"

"It wasn't him, you idiot," one of the other miners said. Sure enough, other boulders started to detach from the cliff, and the ground started to shake violently.

"Get out of here!" Taylor stood up quickly. "Get back to your settlements! Sound an alarm!"

"Go!" one of the other men exclaimed, and they all moved in various directions, determined to get to their settlements. Taylor was about to go when he saw it—a reason he couldn't just follow.

"Holy fuck," Alf said again, rooted to the spot. Taylor grabbed him, and locked eyes with the older man.

"Go!" Taylor yelled.

Alf seemed lost, just briefly before his eyes stopped glazing over, and he came back to reality.

"Fuck. It's the end of the fuckin' world, kid," Alf stated before he too scarpered off toward his settlement.

Taylor turned, barely able to keep his footing as the ground around him shook. He fell forward and held out his arms to stop his fall, before moving his right foot forward and righting himself.

Taylor could see Skipper's boots sticking out from underneath the boulder as if he were the Wicked Witch of the East. Such an unfitting end. Taylor took one last look at the blood splatter that used be his boss, and then he turned and fled toward the settlement.

The cliff collapsed behind him.

Chapter B3

17 April 3572. Earth Time 11.48AM

<u>*ISA Secondary HQ, Titan, Earth system*</u>

The conversation from earlier continued. The three people sat more awkwardly than before. Specialist Detective Morris' cup now sat empty.

HARRISON: Really? No plates at all? That can't be correct.

MORRIS: It is correct, I'm afraid. No plates made in the order. I went through the macro-transactional history of the Cygnus Arm of the company and that confirmed it. No money spent on the attainment of metal shields for those Edens.

HARRISON: It could be possible that plates were ordered separately? Or made somewhere else?

MORRIS: Could it? Surely you would be the person to know that, not me.

SILVER: It would be a highly irregular occurrence.

MORRIS: Exactly what Dr. Silver said. It would be a highly irregular occurrence. I think that's pretty much the same as it wouldn't happen.

HARRISON: Where is this going, Mr. Morris?

MORRIS: Well, it's interesting that you should ask that. I'll tell you—it means that if those Edens theoretically malfunctioned, say human error or machine error, they could potentially go critical.

SILVER: They cannot malfunction! We have just discussed that.

MORRIS: No, Dr. Silver, with the greatest respect, they cannot malfunction when they have the plates. When they have all their appropriate parts. But as we all know, that was not the case.

SILVER: But Rowland Bloor, he flagged it up?

MORRIS: It would appear not.

SILVER: Surely that was his job?

MORRIS: Not necessarily. The accounts would have all gone through a line manager, a sounding board as it were, just after the order was made. That person at the time, would have been you, Mrs. Harrison. And you signed off on that order. Now, seven years later, you're sitting here with a fancy promotion, a huge pay raise. Interesting that, I must admit.

SILVER: Surely not...

MORRIS: And, erm, also, the head scientist—or acting head scientist— who oversaw the engineering teams for all the Edens in that particular set of solar systems should have pieced this together, too.

HARRISON: I'd hope so.

MORRIS: Which was you, Dr. Silver. All starting to make sense?

HARRISON: You do talk a lot. Have you got an off switch?

MORRIS: Something hitting a nerve, Mrs. Harrison?

HARRISON: More like someone, Mr. Morris.

MORRIS: Specialist Morris.

HARRISON: Sure—one thing that I noticed though, which maybe you didn't think you'd mentioned, is that you know where the metal plating comes from.

MORRIS: And?

HARRISON: Only customers of the scrapper moon NXL13 know its function and name. To avoid terrorists and pirates knowing where it is.

And correct me if I'm wrong, you're not in a department of the ISA which is privy to that information?

MORRIS: Correct.

HARRISON: Which would mean that you are a private customer of theirs then?

MORRIS: Correct.

HARRISON: We can all do this detective lark, Mr. Morris. You're a cyborg, aren't you? I know you are. That's what you meant by "special agreement." Which means you can't keep us here. You certainly can't make the allegations you've been making toward me and my colleague. I want my lawyer and I want him now.

Chapter A4

23 March 3565

Planet: Salvon 4

Taylor swung the door to his homestead wide open to an empty room. No sign of life at all.

"Mom!" Taylor shouted into the thin air. "Lorna!"

There was another shake and dust started to fall from the ceiling. Taylor rushed forward and swung around the corner into his bedroom. He grabbed the wobbling urn before it fell from his bedroom shelf once again. As Taylor turned swiftly to leave, something caught his eye: a note lay on his bed.

Taylor leaned over to read it: "Gone to arks, Mom."

Taylor swallowed nervously, crumpled up the note, stuffing it into his suit along with the urn containing his dad.

He headed out of the house, the floor still shaking. He paused for a moment, standing up straight and looking around, taking in the scene in front of him. People were running in every direction, not to anywhere, just away from where they had been. There was dust in the air, and it still felt unnaturally hot. Taylor stepped forward and someone ran straight into him. The man got up immediately, shook himself down, then looked at Taylor with a panicked expression before running off.

Taylor picked himself back up and started to weave in between the running people. He watched them, trying to pick out what they were doing. A woman in a brown shawl darted to move past him. Taylor quickly grabbed her and spun her around so that they locked eyes.

"Where are you all going?" he asked desperately.

"The ISA main station…they are evacuating people," she explained.

"And which way is that?" Taylor asked. The woman pointed behind her, and brushed Taylor's hands off her shoulders. Taylor blinked, and she was already well away from him.

Taylor turned and peered into the distance. Over the buildings and foul weather, he could spot the top of an ark, shifting ever so slightly, but still taking people on board.

That's where mom is, Taylor realized.

Taylor bustled between the people and came out into a clearing. Across from the clearing, in front of him, was a huge courtyard; and from that courtyard came stairs, spiraling up a great tower ending in a platform; and on the platform were people, lots of people. There were three arks tethered to the platform, with smaller pod-ships loading up to max capacity, then taking people to the larger ships.

Taylor paused for a moment, collected himself, and moved forward into the large clearing. Time was of the essence.

Taylor cleared the courtyard quickly, avoiding other people running in every direction, making his way toward the tower.

Taylor was moving up the stairs at pace when suddenly a huge shake brought him to a standstill. He swung to his left and quickly grabbed the banister with both hands, clinging on for dear life. A couple of people fell from the packed platform above him, screaming as they descended hundreds of meters.

Taylor paused, standing up just as a second shake sent him—*smack!*—into the banister.

He fell back, chin busted open, and hit the ground shoulders first, then his head. "Shit," he whispered and noticed the sky was starting to darken over the top of him. Another pod moved out to the tethered ark, and then to Taylor's surprise, the ark moved off and headed away from the platform. They were leaving.

Taylor didn't stay lying on the ground for one moment longer. He had to move. He placed one hand on each knee and, slowly but surely, sat himself up before standing.

A drop of blood fell from his chin. He had scraped it colliding hard with the banister and was starting to lose some blood. He felt the back of his head: a small lump, probably bruising, and a bit more blood.

But Taylor didn't have time to worry about that. He had to keep moving.

Before he headed up the stairs, Taylor felt inside his jacket. The urn with his father's ashes, was, miraculously, somehow, intact.

As Taylor came up onto the platform, he could hardly move for the sea of people, all jostling for their position. Every person was waiting impatiently to get onto the next pod or the one after that.

As darkness began to fall, huge floodlights covering the platform switched on. Taylor looked desperately at the sea of people, hoping to spot his mom and sister. And then he saw it: a weathervane, perhaps six meters tall, at the far corner of the platform.

Taylor took the best possible opportunity he had and decided to push his way through the crowds and toward the vane. This had to work. Taylor forced his way over, to a range of *oohs* and *ouches*. "Sorry," Taylor continuously muttered.

Taylor reached the base of the vane, planted his right foot on it, then pushed up with a knee. He leaned forward, as the rotating weathervane's upper section began to come toward him. He grimaced, reached forward, and grabbed it. He pulled himself up and forward through gritted teeth. He could do this. Taylor managed to place both feet parallel on the arm below him, and stood up slowly, focusing on keeping his balance.

As Taylor stood up, he looked around the platform, at the sea of heads, smoke and burning in the background, the floodlights, and the constant movement.

And then he saw them.

Toward the back of the platform, his mother stood holding Lorna in her arms as if she were a toddler.

"Hey!" Taylor yelled, swinging his arms above his head, trying to get his mom's attention. Unfortunately, he could not be heard above the drone of the crowd, the sound of the ships moving above their heads, and the thunder of quakes in the distance.

Taylor continued to wave his arms above his head. Another shake flung him from the weathervane, sending him hurtling down, arms first.

The last thing Taylor saw before hitting the ground was scared people rushing to get out of his way.

As Taylor came to, his mother was crouching over him, Lorna to her left.

"Mom?" Taylor embraced his mother.

"We need to go," his mom exclaimed. "Now!"

Taylor tried to sit up but felt a sharp pain in his right arm when he went to push himself up off the ground.

"Aargh!? What is that?" Taylor exclaimed.

"Your right arm is broken," his mom said nervously. "In the fall."

Suddenly a loud, robotic voice came from the nearest ark, suspended in the sky above them. "Five minutes until final departure." If people were not panicked before that announcement, they were now. The platform had almost become a full-blown riot.

"Shit," Taylor growled. "We need to move."

"Lorna's ankle is broken," his mom added. "We aren't going to be able to walk out of here, Tay."

Taylor hoisted himself up with his good arm. In the corner of his eye, he saw something different: ISA staff were loading a man on a stretcher into a pod nearby.

"They're taking the injured." Taylor used such energy to stand that someone might assume he were possessed. "We need to get on board that pod."

Taylor's mom took Lorna under one arm and Taylor took her under the other with his good arm, and they started to push their way through the crowd.

"Come on," Taylor whispered to himself. "Come on."

"Two minutes until final ark departure," the ark voice boomed, and around the platform fights began to break out.

"Come on," Taylor whispered again, he and his mom almost dragging Lorna through the crowd. A man with a bloodied mouth fell in front of them, and the three of them, almost in sync with each other, stepped over him.

A man bashed Taylor in the broken arm, causing Taylor to swear loudly.

"Keep going," his mom said. Taylor grimaced and carried on.

Just as they reached the pod, the final stretcher was loaded up and all the ISA staff jumped on.

"We have an injured person," Taylor's mom exclaimed. "Please let us on. She's just a girl."

"Look around," said one of the ISA security men. "Everyone's injured. We can only take so many. This pod is at capacity. This planet is no longer designated safe, so we cannot remain here any longer."

"You can fit three people on! Fuck, you could take ten more people on that thing, easily!" Taylor stepped forward and his mom turned to take the weight of Lorna.

"I'm afraid we cannot." The ISA security member pointed a gun at Taylor. "My recommendation would be to go to the next settlement, Paddletown." The pod began to rise into the sky, toward the final ark, as it announced one minute until departure.

Taylor grimaced, turned to his mom, and then turned back to the man. For a moment, he contemplated trying to fight this large, armed, armored man with a broken arm, and then he turned away. He didn't fancy his chances, to be quite honest.

Chapter B4

17 April 3572. Earth Time 1.36PM

ISA Secondary HQ, Titan, Earth system

The interview reconvened after lunch. Dr. Silver, Mrs. Harrison, and Specialist Morris were joined by a rotund, sweaty lawyer sent from the ISA to represent Silver and Harrison. His name was Robert Barker.

Morris had another black coffee, while Barker had an extra-large bubble-gum milkshake.

MR. BARKER: So, if you could start for us, you first called my clients through unofficial channels?

MORRIS: That's correct. I am, as your clients have likely informed you, a cyborg. That means, unfortunately, I can no longer access the company's intranet, due to fears of my cybernetic parts being hacked and taking private information. So, I can only communicate with other colleagues via a mobile device. I can still access the internet, visit online records, and contact colleagues. It's a general data protection responsibility thing, you see.

HARRISON: He does this. He talks a lot.

BARKER: You do talk a lot. You're a cyborg.

MORRIS: Underneath this coat, a lot of my left side is cybernetic. An unfortunate smelting accident made by ISA staff during one of my investigations. The company kept me on as a cyborg if I kept my mouth shut. We don't exactly have equal rights. And as you probably know, jobs don't throw themselves your way in my condition. It keeps me stronger for now, but eventually, these parts will kill me. I try to keep it as quiet as possible.

BARKER: That tells me everything I need to know. My second question: what exactly are you accusing my clients of? They inform me it is yet to be said.

MORRIS: That's an interesting question. I was about to get to that when Mrs. Harrison worked out my little secret. When the human population on Salvon 4 was destroyed, all the news reports, inquiries, and official documents stated that it was down to an "undetectable planet core," correct?

SILVER: That's correct.

MORRIS: Now that's interesting. A 40-degree rise in surface temperature, displacement of atmospheric gases, increase of wind speed by almost 500%, and minor plate shifts—all of that could, theoretically, come from an Eden?

SILVER: Not one Eden alone.

MORRIS: No, of course not. But if all the Edens on one planet are connected by a neural network so they constantly match output, then surely, they would all together be able to affect a planet in such a dramatic way?

SILVER: Well, theoretically, yes.

BARKER: But the Edens would all have to malfunction. All of them, not just one, to act in such a way. I didn't think that was possible.

SILVER: It's not.

MORRIS: No, of course, it's not. We're straying into the realm of fantasy. I mean, that is, unless they were all missing an essential part, such as, I don't know, the metal plates protecting the nuclear reactor. That would just about do it. Once one Eden then malfunctioned, they all did, as they were all able to.

BARKER: You're telling me that the Edens all malfunctioned? That it was just a cover-up?

MORRIS: Yes. And that led to the death of over sixty-seven million people. The planet's only just recovering now.

HARRISON: How do you think you know this? Any of it?

MORRIS: After my smelting accident, obviously a few people from within the middle management of the ISA wanted to keep me quiet about the circumstances of said accident, so they did me the odd favor. One of them was genuinely nice and actually escaped from Salvon 4, of all places.

HARRISON: They were…really?

MORRIS: They were what? What were you about to say?

HARRISON: Nothing.

MORRIS: It didn't sound like nothing.

BARKER: It's best to leave the conversation to me. Only speak when the detective calls upon you.

HARRISON: Okay.

MORRIS: Well, they fed me bits of info, my anonymous informant, let's call him Bald Eagle. Well, six weeks ago, he called me up in a flood of tears. He knew the truth about Salvon 4. That sent me on the investigative path that ultimately landed here. That's how I know.

Chapter A5

24 March 3565

Planet: Salvon 4

It was not a short walk to the settlement of Paddletown. As they began to move toward it, the heat bore down on them. The towers and domes that made up their neighboring settlement only seemed to get further away. They had begun walking the moment the last ark had left their homestead and carried on walking right until mid-morning of the following day. They had not slept, they had not eaten, and they had barely even drunk. Every few minutes, there was a huge shudder when a cliff or a boulder became unstable, falling from its position.

The three of them shared a bottle of water, passing it between them as it eventually began to empty.

As they got closer to the settlement, they saw that the smoke was rising from it, as well as fires. The temperature of the atmosphere seemed to be getting hotter and hotter. Something seemed to be wrong with this planet. Very wrong.

They continued walking, despite the rising temperature.

Once they were about half an hour from the settlement, a row of cliffs to their left cleared, and Taylor could see one of the Edens attached to the planet. It was smoking, more furiously than anything else they'd seen. And it was pulsating, as if it were brimming with energy.

"The fuck?" Taylor squinted into the bright horizon line on which the Eden sat.

"Keep going," Taylor's mom said, pressing his shoulder with her thumb. Taylor shook his head and moved on.

As they approached the settlement, Taylor and his mom saw something strange: above this settlement's platform was another ark. This one was, like the Eden, smoking. This platform stood amongst several towers, some even taller than the platform. This must have been one of the first settlements built upon the ISA's arrival on the planet.

"We need to get on that ship. We need to get up there," Taylor pointed out.

"It doesn't look safe, Tay," his mom responded.

"We have nowhere else," Taylor replied, and they plowed on.

As they entered Paddletown, they saw black plumes of smoke seeping out from the ark's side. Taylor and his mother began to increase speed, almost possessed with determination to get on board. Groups of people had used ropes, and chains to tie it to the platform, and the ship, which was at least a hundred meters wide and three hundred long, was trying to take off.

Taylor could see that it wasn't operating at full power; it couldn't be, as one of its engines had been disabled.

There were ropes fixed to the platform, attached to vehicles. Others were held by teams of people as if they were playing a losing battle of tug of war. On the end of some of the lines stood Goliaths, holding onto their ropes with vice-like grips.

Taylor let go of Lorna and moved toward a nearby line of people. He spotted two very recognizable outlines: Lark and Alf.

Taylor grabbed the rope in front of them and turned to speak to them. "What the hell is going on?"

"We got this here ship," Alf said, "and we leavin'."

Taylor turned to look at the smoking ark tethered above them. "I really...I don't think that's a good idea."

"We haven't got another choice," Lark stated blankly.

"You know that, kid," Alf added.

"Set!" A tall woman in a maroon coat stood at the top of this platform's weathervane, and at the back of each rope or chain a reprogrammed Goliath joined the line.

"Shit," Taylor whispered.

"Pull!" The woman screamed, and the combined force of Goliaths and people yanked on the ark, pulling it toward them. The great ship juddered; its engines were clearly already damaged and probably would not be able to take much more.

"Come on," Lark said.

Suddenly a loud alarm sounded from the ark as it struggled to pull away.

"Shit," Lark said. "What's that?"

"Maybe it's some kinda warning," Alf stated

"It's gonna self-destruct!" Taylor exclaimed and turned on a dime. "Mom! Take Lorna! I'll be right behind you!"

His mom, some twenty meters away, started to make her way down the spiral staircase. As Taylor turned back around, the ark exploded above him.

"We have to go," Taylor told Lark and Alf. People started to break rank, looking for cover. Taylor was splattered in a bucket's worth of blood as he turned to Lark. A piece of the ark, roughly the size of a fridge, had landed on the big man, spraying him everywhere.

Alf screamed and turned pale. As he fainted, Taylor grabbed him under his waist and bundled the smaller man over his shoulder, as if he were a child.

"Let's go," Taylor stated blanky.

Taylor spotted, through the confusion, a way down. A small jump onto a stairway, and then he would be able to get to the bottom. A huge section of the ark slammed into the platform, and slowly the great structure began to creak. People began to panic, some resorting to throwing themselves off the sides, three hundred meters to the floor. Taylor gritted his teeth, ran, and made the jump.

He landed cleanly on the top of the stairway, two feet flat, knees bent, and with Alf still on his back. Taylor panicked and almost tumbled backward into the gap, but then managed to right himself.

Come on, he thought, *you've got this.*

Further down the stairs, he could see his mom and Lorna struggling. Taylor gave hot pursuit, with Alf slung over his shoulder. He took the steps as quickly and as cleanly as he possibly could, Alf's feet and head knocking him every step he took.

As they reached the bottom, it was clear that the whole structure was about to collapse on top of them.

Taylor ran up to his mother and put Alf onto his feet as the smaller man began to wake up.

"Mom," Taylor said, "we need to get away now!"

"There isn't time," his mom responded.

"I see something!" Lorna exclaimed.

"Ah shit," Alf whispered, looking up and then at Taylor. "This is fucked, kid." A huge piece of debris from the platform landed on his head, splitting it open.

Everything stopped for a moment. Taylor's mom gave a scream that seemed to last an eternity. Taylor could feel his heart beating hard in his chest.

"There is something!" Lorna yelled again, looking completely in the opposite direction.

"Lorna, not now!" Taylor's mom said.

"A hovercar!" Lorna exclaimed, and with that Taylor snapped out of his trance and looked at what Lorna could already see.

A small, circular hovercar was making its way toward them, arriving in seconds. It pulled up alongside them and opened its doors. Taylor instantly recognized the driver.

"Get in," Jake said, his eyes teary and blood dripping from a wound on his cheek.

"This thing is about to fall!" Taylor exclaimed, clambering into the passenger seat.

"Yeah, you think I don't know that?" Jake yelled, as Lorna and Taylor's mom climbed into the back.

"Let's go," Taylor instructed, and as soon as the second word came from his mouth, Jake hit the accelerator and they were away. In the rear-view mirror, Taylor saw the platform begin to collapse, falling away from them. It hit the ground with an almighty thud, sending out a huge dust wave.

"Brace!" Jake yelled as huge pelts of dirt hit the back of the car, and they all tucked their heads as the window smashed in.

Jake bumped the car into its fastest gear, carrying them clear of the damage.

"Safe," Jake said quietly before smiling slightly with the very corners of his mouth.

"We're not out of this yet, mate," Taylor responded. "How did you know where to find us?"

"This car, it's, um, dad's. ISA-issue. I can track you if you're cataloged as living on this planet," Jake explained.

"I see. Not creepy at all," Taylor quipped.

"It got me to you, didn't it?" Jake responded.

"I suppose so," Taylor replied. "Where is your family?"

"Dad got injured and managed to get aboard an ark. Mom...well, mom's dead," Jake explained.

"Shit," Taylor said, getting shivers down his spine. "I'm so sorry."

"I thought I owed it to you to come and find you. And so here we are," Jake stated. "I've managed to keep in contact with dad through the communication devices in this car, it's probably one of the last open lines to the arks from the planet's surface. Everything seems to be shutting off, unnaturally so."

"As if someone's intentionally closing communication with the surface?" Taylor asked.

"You'd like to hope not, mate. The official word from the ISA, according to dad, is that they've found the planet's core is unstable. That's what's causing all this...shit...like the quakes and the wind." Jake said, motioning around.

"And it being too hot for us to even think," Taylor added. "Crazy."

"I know. Do you really think that the core could do all that?" Jake asked.

"Maybe. I'm a mechanic. I'm no geologist. I couldn't know for sure. Why?" Taylor asked back.

"Because on my way over, I saw one of the Edens acting all kinds of strange," Jake explained.

"That's weird," Taylor replied, "because so did I."

Chapter B5

17 April 3572. Earth Time 2.46PM

ISA Secondary HQ, Titan, Earth system

BARKER: Interesting. You then picked up this thin paper trail back to my clients?

MORRIS: I did. And that brings me to the final point in my investigation. The cover-up. You see, Bald Eagle's claim was not enough to go on alone. The people who were responsible, they would deny it all costs. They must make people believe it was not true. And Bald Eagle lost his son on that planet, he might not have been thinking straight. So, for the next three weeks, I dug. Made calls, pulled in favors, checked records, and it all led me back to you two. You were both essential in orchestrating the cover-up, paying people off, fabricating scientific records. And it all checked out. Dr. Silver, you're a respected scientist, holding—what is it? —three PhDs. And Sandra Harrison, an efficient and calculated mover and shaker within the ISA, almost certainly set for big things, almost certainly set for upper management. Why would people not trust you? I'm sure you've both won ISA employee of the sector awards at some point. But the thing is…the thing is…neither of you could live with the truth.

BARKER: My clients have not confirmed that they knew the Eden malfunctions were a cover-up.

MORRIS: Oh, but I know that they know. Firstly, I looked at room bookings and CCTV and saw that you meet regularly and always with the audio of said CCTV specifically switched off, Mrs. Harrison and Dr. Silver. Sometimes others, but always you two. I'd imagine to possibly handle any breakage: people thinking about speaking out who know the truth; any incriminating evidence left within logs, or to be found by the robots scouring the planet's surface now; maybe even the survivors living under the planet's surface.

BARKER: You can't possibly know that to be true. They could have been discussing anything—marketing strategies, potential competition, screen projects. You're going to have to do better than that.

MORRIS: Well, looks like it might be Christmas. You see, not long after the incident took place, beginning in late 3565 and ending in early 3566, Sandra Harrison booked therapy sessions with one Dr. Ezra Pulver. Lovely lady, nice cardigans. Funny I know that, isn't it? Well, she just happens to be the very same therapist I saw after my return to work as a cyborg in 3563, you know, to get over my new situation as a second-class citizen. And, like several others, she owes me a little for not attempting to sue the organization. She, just last week, allowed me to see your files. You spoke of "a great mistake" in your past, something that kept you awake. Something you couldn't even tell her.

HARRISON: No! You cannot know that! How on Earth did you find that out? You certainly should not be able to access that info? That information was classified. The whole event was classified. You shouldn't know about the cover-up!

BARKER: Shit.

MORRIS: I didn't. But now I do. I just knew we had the same therapist. Why on Earth would Dr. Pulver tell me any more than that? Did you really believe that she'd allow me to access private information about another client? However, should I understand that you wish to confess?

HARRISON: Clever dickey.

MORRIS: I think they say "got you, sunshine" back on Earth.

Chapter A6

24 March 3565

Planet: Salvon 4

They drove through the harsh wasteland, the sun glaring down upon them, and all of them sweating. It only seemed to be getting hotter. The hovercar held up, providing a mediocre air-con to stop them from going completely crazy. Jake had put it up to the vehicle's highest gear and had not relented since.

Once they were away from Paddletown, Taylor spun within the passenger seat and held Lorna's ankle. "How are you doing?" he asked.

"I'm scared," Lorna responded.

"I know," Taylor sighed. "But we have to keep going."

Taylor's mom also placed her hand on her daughter's ankle so that it brushed Taylor's own. Taylor looked up at his mother. She looked at him with wide eyes and grimaced.

"Mom, are you okay?" he asked.

"During our escape, down the stairs, I was hit in the stomach, I'm fine. It's not serious, like your arm. Tay, I need to be honest with you, we're not going to be able to escape from here," his mom replied.

"There's got to be something," Taylor said. "I cannot give up. If it comes to it, I can find a way out of here and come back for you. Here, take dad." He passed the urn back to his mom.

"I can't take this, Tay," his mom groaned. "Not yet. But if I don't survive and you do, could you leave it with me?"

"You can't mean that. You cannot mean that," Taylor stated.

"Leave your father with me. It's what he would have wanted. It's what I want," his mom responded.

"I won't leave you here, dead or alive," Taylor confirmed to her.

"Oh, Tay." His mom brushed her hand through his hair. "You were meant to do more than this. You were going away with Jake, to that charterer's school. Make a name for yourself. Do more than I ever did."

"And I can still go. We all can," Taylor responded, a tear running down his cheek. "We can still get out of here." With that, Taylor spun in his seat, so he was back facing the right way. He and Jake turned to each other and nodded.

"What's the plan, big man?" Jake asked confidently.

"The Edens—they have emergency transmitters should they ever need to be recalled from a planet that's found to be uninhabitable, correct?" Taylor inquired.

"That's correct," Jake responded.

"And then what?" Taylor followed up.

"Then the whole Eden is picked up and taken away," Jake responded.

"Okay, okay, so what if we were to find one, climb aboard and set it's transmitter off? Would that get us picked up?" Taylor asked.

Jake shook his head. "Maybe. But it's a long shot."

"I know. But it's all we have," Taylor replied.

"There's an Eden about two kilometers north of here," Jake said. "Me and dad used to go out to it on the hovercar when he was teaching me how to drive. It has a carrier bay attached, for those robots that you work on."

"Goliaths," Taylor reminded him.

"Goliaths, that's it." Jake nodded. "They mine nearby actually, in a cliff face. Could be useful to bring one with us if you know how to reprogram them."

"I do," Taylor confirmed.

"Okay, okay. This could work then. If we can hide within that carrier bay, we might be okay," Jake said.

The hovercar drove on, and clearing a corner, they laid eyes on the Eden. What they saw destroyed their initial idea; the Eden had toppled and lay on its side. It had fallen against the cliff, crushing all the Goliaths. One mineshaft lay open, and the Eden now blocked the rest. In was a crushing sight to see.

"Damn," Taylor said as he saw it. "Fuck. Shit. Come on!"

"We're going to stop anyway," Jake stated. "We can still make this work." The car came to a halt, and Jake and Taylor leapt out.

"Mom, Lorna, stay in the car, it's cooler," Taylor said through the car window, which Lorna closed as he moved away.

Taylor and Jake made their way to the nose of the fallen Eden, which was pressed up against the cliff. The two young men looked at each other.

"Look for anything," Jake said. "A computer, a communications device, anything."

"Here!" Taylor picked up a small screen connected to the Eden's nose. "There's something here!"

Jake took the screen off him and frowned at what he saw.

"ERROR. ESSENTIAL PLATING MISSING. NETWORK-WIDE MALFUNCTION LIKELY."

"What does that mean?" Taylor asked.

"Right, my dad told me about this," Jake explained, breathing heavily. "All the Edens are connected by a network. You know, to match their output."

"Okay," Taylor responded.

"So, if one goes down, they all go down," Jake informed him.

"And if one goes haywire, they all go haywire?" Taylor asked.

"You would assume so," Jake agreed.

"Which would mean..." Taylor gasped.

"Which would mean that the Edens did all this," Jake stated grimly

"Maybe being this near to these things isn't the best idea," Taylor said. "Perhaps...perhaps if we reprogrammed one of these, they would all start to behave themselves again?"

"No, possibly not. I reckon it's too late for that anyway. And even if it weren't, would you know where to start?" Jake asked.

"No, I wouldn't have a clue," Taylor responded.

"There we go." The wind blowing was almost louder than Jake's voice. "There's hardly any life left in this thing. We need to find another Eden to get our distress call out. Nearest one is over an hour's drive. And we don't have the oil to get there."

"Shit," Taylor whispered. "What about the mobile device? The one to your dad?"

"What about it? I could call dad, sure, but he hasn't got the authority to come down here and rescue us," Jake responded.

"Maybe not. But I'm thinking we might not be able to get out of here," Taylor admitted.

"I believe that," Jake responded.

"Then we need to tell someone, anyone, that the Edens did this. Not the planet's core." Taylor grimaced.

Jake caught Taylor's eyes and then looked away. "No, it can't be him," he whispered.

"No. There is no other choice. Call him. Now!" Taylor shouted, almost ordering Jake.

"I can't do that to him! I cannot put him under that pressure!" Jake exclaimed.

"We are all going to die here!" Taylor exclaimed, truly realizing it for the first time. "I will do it!" He ran for the car. Jake gave chase, but Taylor had a good start.

Taylor reached the car first, and swung open the passenger door, grabbing the comm device stored in the open glove box. He turned to see Jake about four meters away when the ground shook and they both fell on their arses.

"Another quake!" Taylor jumped to his feet and looked up at the cliff next to them. Two huge boulders within the cliff face seemed to dislodge.

"Get out!" Taylor exclaimed and opened the door, but as Lorna tried to step out, her seat belt pulled her back. She reached down to unclip it, but it would not come loose. Taylor's mom leaned over and tried to unbuckle it. It remained stuck.

As the ground continued to shake, Taylor stepped forward to unbuckle the seat belt. He was about a step away when Jake laid a firm hand on Taylor's shoulder and pulled him back. The two men fell on top of each other, and at the same moment a huge boulder landed on the car, crushing it flat, with Lorna and Taylor's mom still inside it.

"No!" Taylor screamed, the sound echoing off the cliff walls. His mother and his sister were dead. Taylor closed his eyes, and the moment played through his head several times in the next second, and then he opened them again. It still hadn't quite sunk in.

Taylor turned and locked eyes with Jake.

"You cunt." Taylor rugby tackled Jake to the ground. Jake tried to push Taylor off, but while Taylor was shorter, he was far stronger. He landed one, two, three, four blows on Jake's face, before hitting his friend in the stomach. Taylor rolled off Jake and stood up.

"I'm sorry," Jake whispered. Taylor spun and kicked Jake in the crotch with maximum force. Jake went limp and stopped moving.

Slowly, Taylor picked up the communication device from the sandy ground and switched it on.

"Hello?" Came the voice from the communication device. "Hello? Who is this?"

"Hi, Mr. Spring, isn't it? This is Taylor, your son's friend," Taylor stated over the device.

"My god!" Mr. Spring exclaimed. "Are you on the surface?"

"Yes," Taylor confirmed.

"Is my son there? Is he safe?" Mr. Spring asked

"Yes. And no," Taylor admitted.

"He's not safe?" Mr. Spring's voice warbled.

"None of us are," Taylor explained. "But that doesn't matter. What matters is this: Jake told me that the ISA, at least the ones responsible for this sector, are saying the planet's core is unstable. They're saying that's what's doing this."

"That's what they've said," Mr. Spring confirmed.

"It's not true," Taylor stated, tears running down his face. "Your son worked it out. The Edens malfunctioned *en masse*. Something was wrong with the Edens. They're what did this."

"Who do you want me to tell?" Mr. Spring asked.

"I don't know. I don't care. Someone. Anyone. But you need to tell people. This information must get out. People must know. Can you do that for me?" Taylor asked.

"I can," Mr. Spring responded. "I promise."

And with that, Taylor switched the mobile device off and threw it away.

Taylor turned, slowly, and looked at the cliff in front of him. He looked at the collapsed Eden and the crushed Goliaths poking out from underneath it.

He looked at the boulder, atop the crushed car, and his dead sister and mother inside of it. He looked at Jake's unconscious body just next to him, battered and bruised. And, right at the bottom of the cliff, one remaining hole to a mine which presumably ran hundreds of meters. Taylor sighed and slowly dropped to two knees. He pulled the urn from his pocket and then looked at the crushed car. *Not like this*, he thought and bundled the urn back into his pocket.

"What...are you...doing?" Jake asked, opening his eyes ever so slightly.

"Dying." Taylor responded.

There was a minor shake, but Taylor remained motionless, completely unfazed.

"Get out man, get out," Jake whispered.

"I'm not going without you," Taylor stated blanky.

"Fucking leave me, man," Jake responded. "Save yourself."

The ground was hit by a much larger shake and parts of the cliff started to detach themselves, left, right and center.

Taylor swallowed and slowly stood up. He took a deep breath and ran for the mine entrance in front of him. He dodged a boulder to his right, another to his left. He tripped and fell into the mine. He turned and saw Jake's body in the sand, entirely limp. Taylor grimaced. The ground around him continued to shake.

Then Taylor looked up, and a boulder fell into the mine entrance.

Everything went black.

Chapter B6

17 April 3572. Earth Time 4.41PM

ISA Secondary HQ, Titan, Earth system

Barker was pacing up and down. Silver sat with his head in his hands. Harrison and Morris had their eyes locked on one another.

MORRIS: Sixty-seven million people, ordinary people, died on that planet. Women, men, children. They were promised a new life, and your oversight in building those Edens, it killed them. Then you hid it because you were too clever for the truth. Or too cowardly. Neither of you were adult enough to admit to the higher-ups or the families.

HARRISON: You lied! You're a cyborg! Tin scum! You cannot talk to us like this! We have rights! Do you?

MORRIS: I do, actually.

SILVER: Leave it, Sandra, it's over.

HARRISON: You will go to prison, I swear to God. You lied to get information out of a suspect. That's unlawful, at the very least.

MORRIS: No one has said no to you in a very long time, have they?

HARRISON: Tin scum. You will go to prison for this deceit, I promise.

MORRIS: This has all been recorded. I'm sure I will. But I'd imagine, most likely, that I will see you both there?

SILVER: On what charge exactly?

MORRIS: Third-degree murder—67,192,875 counted cases. I'd imagine you'll be going away for multiple life sentences. But don't worry, I know all the best places to get cybernetic enhancements. Maybe they could, you know, help you see all those sentences out? Maybe even come out of prison hundreds of years from now, better people?

HARRISON: Shut the fuck up!

BARKER: Recording?

MORRIS: Correct.

SILVER: Then surely, we could destroy that recording?

HARRISON: You little slimeball. Do you really think you'd be able to get us like that? People have worked it out before, you know. You're nothing special. And we've dealt with them. You'll be no different.

SILVER: Tell us where the recording is, and we'll not go public with your cybernetics.

MORRIS: I'd love to. Trust me, I really would. Because you all seem like such good, lovely, decent people. But the issue is this: I stopped recording four minutes ago. It's already been received by my boss at internal investigations. It's over. You're done.

And with that, Specialist Morris hit a button and armed guards walked in to take Dr. Silver and Mrs. Harrison away. Mrs. Harrison managed to point one arm at Specialist Morris.

HARRISON: Who the fuck do you think you are, Mr. Morris? The one man in the ISA with a conscience?

MORRIS: That's not for me to say. Oh, and like I said earlier, it's Specialist Morris. Have fun in prison. I have work to do.

Specialist Morris clapped his hands, and Dr. Silver, Mrs. Harrison, and Richard Barker were taken away. Morris smiled to himself and relaxed.

Epilogue

23 April 3572

<u>*Planet: Salvon 4*</u>

The man in the long coat approached one of the mass graves. The graves had been set up in a rush by robot teams, by the ISA. The gravestones, three meters by nine, often just listed man, woman. They weren't identifiable anymore.

That was the worst of it, the tall man reckoned.

They didn't send people out. Not at first, anyway.

The planet was populated by robots.

Those who dug the graves and those who created the stones.

You'd find the odd person about, overseeing a team of robots.

The atmosphere was breathable again, or thereabout, but no one wanted to be on this planet anymore.

The ISA had jumped ship quickly, moved their VIPs to a neighboring Earth-sized planet to start a happier, safer life.

It disgusted the tall man.

It was a large mass grave.

The man could spot different robots assigned to different tasks, some small, with great spherical wheels that ran across their bottom, and others taller, with long legs.

One of the robots approached him.

"Human, area 617 is now required for sterilizing. You must vacate as soon as possible," it stated.

"Of course, of course," the man replied and began to walk away, before stopping and turning back to look at the service robot.

"Why do people of power have so little regard for so many? That so little value could be placed on a human's life? And that so many people could be okay with it? What—are we to just accept this? What are we becoming? How much longer before we change? We need to change. We must. I believe in the human race. I always have. It's at the very core of who I am," the man said.

"I do not know," the robot said. "I am merely a service robot."

The man grimaced slightly and nodded.

"Of course. I'm sorry. I don't speak to many people in this job. I don't exactly get to make many friends. I can ramble on. People say I talk a lot," the man replied.

"Apologies, human. I must return to my cleaning duties," the robot stated.

"Of course. I understand. We all must do our duties, including myself. And I have ever so much to do," the man said.

"Okay," the robot replied. "I hope you are successful in fulfilling your duties, human."

"So am I, robot," the tall man said.

"Your enthusiasm for your tasks will hopefully provide you with optimal results, Mr....?" The robot asked.

"Specialist Detective Inspector Morris," the tall man replied, the corner of his lip tightening ever so slightly.

As Detective Morris walked away, he walked past the end of the line of graves. And next to the last two graves sat a small, brown urn with the initials "M.C." inscribed into it. Morris looked at it and smiled. He knew that for this to be placed here, it meant that somewhere out there, were human survivors.

The Mine

By Andrew P. McGregor

Date: 3950

A lone man, standing naked within his patchwork spacesuit, stared at a new star in the lifeless moon's sky. He attempted a toothless grin, but only grimaced, the muscles having atrophied decades ago.

The star, representing the white-hot reaction drive of a spacecraft that had arrived from light-years away, grew as it approached.

The man turned to his cold, unblinking companions and winked at the nearest of them. "Prep—" he coughed and spat against the inside of his suit's visor. The effort of speaking a single syllable after decades of silence had undone him. "Blasted shitballs…heh, *that's* better," he grated and then groaned. He felt as if an old tank's tracks were sliding across his throat each time he spoke.

He gave the growing star one last look through the dust- and spittle-covered visor before motioning to his skeletal companions to join him underground. "Come," he said.

Dozens of stony faces came to life. Their heads snapped in his direction, and the man's radio crackled to life. The sound startled him. "We obey."

"G-good, we have much to do," he said between coughs.

***

"Dr. Littlefield?" the ship's archaeologist addressed Sara Littlefield, the expedition's leader.

"Yes, Dr. Maynard, you have something for me?"

Dr. Morgan Maynard, an older woman from Earth's Grand Museum with a slim figure and gray-white hair, produced a data screen from her form-fitting spacesuit. Sara noticed the faint blemishes on Dr. Maynard's hands where yesterday's tattoos had been removed.

Sara's not-quite-human hands flickered with radiant fish scales as she took the data screen from the older woman. "What's this?"

"It's the research on those old Edens."

Sara nodded, recalling their previous discovery: not a single planet in the Kepler-182 system had a working Eden device. "What can you tell me?" She folded her arms, not bothering to view the small translucent screen.

Morgan sighed and pointedly stared at the data screen, having spent several hours creating the file it contained. "Why do I bother trying to get you to read it?" She rolled her eyes. "Anyway, from the records I pulled and gathered in that data screen in your hands, the power signatures of those Edens are consistent with the same Edens that originally launched from Sol in the initial expansion wave."

"So, what's wrong with them?"

"They're not dead."

Sara frowned. "In what way? They weren't damaged?"

Morgan smiled slyly and nodded. "Yes. Not only are they not damaged, but no one's ever used them. There are fifteen Edens. From what we can tell of the planetary atmospheres, only one Eden has any evidence of being used."

"Let me guess Kepler-182f's Eden?"

Morgan nodded again and looked at the stars outside the ship through a large data screen on the wall. The small moon the ship was approaching orbited the local star's best chance of a habitable planet. "Jose tells me there's some evidence of nitrogen and oxygen mixed into the air, as if the Eden had started but shut down several months afterward."

"That's odd. We're only a few hundred light-years from Earth, but there's no record of more than one Eden in the system."

Morgan shrugged. "The ISA reclassified it as an off-limits mining colony over a thousand years ago, back when corruption was rife. We think the records were written over during Earth's Second Dark Age so I can't get much more about them. Those data cores are so corrupted it's a miracle we extracted Lisa from them."

"Hmm, maybe. What about the other planets and moons? If this is a mining colony where are all the workers?"

Morgan shook her head. "There aren't any. They stripped the entire system bare. I've sent a probe toward the system's star to check out

Kepler-182b, but the planet's so close to the star I doubt the ISA sent an Eden there."

Sara whistled, thinking about the tremendous amount of mining activity it would have taken to strip a star system of its valuable materials. It made sense, though. At the rate humanity had expanded and fractured into warring factions, entire star systems were stripped bare in order to supply the vast colony fleets and warships.

She looked at the dull gray moon their ship was approaching. It was then she noticed several lights were active around some small conical buildings at the landing site. Several lights seemed to buzz across the moon's surface. Were they old mining drones? She would have to ask the man they were about to meet.

"Remind me, what's the name of the man who invited us here?" She could have used the little computer buried at the base of her skull to search for the man's name but, as always, preferred to talk.

"Max, I think he called himself in the text."

"And you said there are no records of him in our database?" Sara frowned at the gray moon dust that swirled under the ship's engines, thinking how dirty the inside of the old mines must be. A moment later the ship touched down. "That's a bit of a worry. I hope the data analysis of the exotic materials he sent us are right, or we'll have wasted this whole trip."

"The data seems consistent with traces we found on our last deep-space expedition. Sara, I think this could be it, humanity's last, best hope for discovering a real alien artifact. Within our lifetimes, at least."

Sara nodded. "I hope you're right."

"The fame and money would help, too."

Sara grinned. "It would."

To an observer, it would appear as though a new purple mountain range had dropped from the heavens and affixed itself to the surface of the hollowed-out moon. The massive science ship dwarfed the conical structures and multi-storied drone trucks that serviced the mines.

"Will we take the shaft down like Black-Cat and Jose?" Morgan asked. The other two scientists in their small team had already gone to the ship's main elevator shaft, while Sara had brought the ship in for a landing.

Sara laughed and pointed at the data screen and the moon's distant surface below. "Would you rather take the stairs? Or the teleporter?"

Morgan shivered. Sara could sympathize with her. The thought of using the experimental teleporter made her hairs stand on end.

"The shaft will do," Morgan replied.

Safe inside their suits, the shaft elevator sucked the air out, and its thick blue door peeled open. She could see the other two members of their expedition at the ramp's base, impatient for their arrival.

Dr. Blue-Cat Four-Ten and Dr. Jose Goldtoe turned to watch the women. Curious specimens in their own right, Blue-Cat and Jose hailed from the furthest corners of the ISA's territories, millions of light-years distant. While genetically similar, they looked as different from traditional human stock as a scorpion and a rat compared to a snail.

Sporting four large, equidistantly spaced legs, Black-Cat Four-Ten reminded Sara of the crabs that often gathered on the beach near her home on Earth. He stood a full meter above the rest of them and scuttled as quickly as an enraged tiger when he felt the need.

That wasn't often these days. Blue-Cat only ran if he found a particularly interesting animal that had been startled so he could study it. Sara remembered the first time he'd seen a cat; he'd chased the poor thing clear across the beach and through the trees, trying to get a better look at it.

Jose Goldtoe, on the other hand, was a head shorter than the two women and had scales for skin, webbed hands and feet, large eyes and fishlike lips. He scowled at the two women while they approached and tapped his right foot. Oblivious, Blue-Cat peered at the barely lit conical structures that awaited them.

"Okay, okay, Mr. Safety Specialist, you can stop tapping now," Sara said to Jose over the group's laser-linked communications channel.

"You're late," he replied in a guttural voice.

"Well, *someone* has to fly the ship."

Jose folded his arms. "You talk as if this mountain couldn't have guided itself in."

"Hush, Jose," Blue-Cat said in his soft-spoken way. "I do believe our hosts are arriving."

The four scientists looked beyond the ramp's edge. A single, small vehicle had left one of the conical structures and was headed in their direction. The vehicle looked like a sleek, gray truck with a carriage attached. It churned the dust as it crawled toward the four scientists.

It took Sara some effort not to groan. Morgan sighed loudly.

Jose wasn't so polite. "A damn crawler? Is this the Stone Age? Who uses a blasted crawler to get around on a small moon? Such a slow piece of junk."

"Hush, please. No need for swearing," Blue-Cat said.

"*Swearing*? You want to know what swearing is?"

"Be quiet," Sara said. "We just spent months getting here, I'm sure a nice, slow ride in an old crawler won't set us back any further."

"Ancient, not just old. You sure we couldn't just break out the skiff? I'd take a bleedin' jet pack over that thing."

"Swearing, my friend," Blue-Cat interjected.

"Just be patient," Sara told him.

"I'm being careful," Jose said. "And why don't you let me take a pulse rifle? I don't like the sight of this crawler."

"Remember the last time you did? You almost started an interstellar incident," Morgan reminded him.

Jose grunted a response that was inaudible to a normal human. Sara couldn't help but give a thin smile as her suit automatically translated his inventive swear words.

Silence followed as the four watched the crawler. To their surprise, the crawler was much larger than it had first seemed. Wider than the elevator and three stories tall, they felt the ground shake as it came close. Sara imagined smoke belching skyward from the giant crawler with a thunderous sound, blackening an otherwise blue sky. It was an illusion. There was no smoke or sound on the moon's surface, but the thought made her nervous all the same.

After the three-meter-tall wheels came to a stop nearby, the rattling of bones and teeth ceased. The crawler had moved along the science ship and the side of its trailer opened, revealing hundreds of skeletal bodies tucked within it. The bodies came to life and blue eyes flickered against the darkness.

At least a hundred pairs of eyes locked their gazes on the four scientists, and the hairs on Sara's skin stood up.

"Oh dear," Morgan muttered. She took a step back up the ship's ramp.

"Calm," Blue-Cat said. "I don't believe they're here to hurt us. Look." He pointed at the skeletal beings as they jumped down from the trailer and started forming two lines, stretching outward from the crawler's steps up to the science ship's ramp. The two lines of androids stood like an honor guard, each line facing the other.

"They look like ancient prison drones, adapted for mine use," Morgan mused.

Several more blue-eyed androids approached the ramp. Two of them walked up to Sara, turned to each other and laced their arms together. They each kneeled on one thin metallic leg and then turned their heads back to her.

"It appears they're forming a chair for you, Sara," Blue-Cat said.

Sara swallowed. "Looks like it." She reached forward and grabbed each of the androids on their shoulders before lifting her legs and levering herself over the interlocked arms. She held on tight as the androids rose to their feet.

"Your turn," she said. More androids formed chairs for the others. Two androids lifted Morgan while four androids formed a larger chair for Blue-Cat.

"Is this a joke?" Jose exclaimed. A lone android had kneeled, facing away from him. "I'm not a child."

"But you *are* smaller than us," Morgan said, holding back some laughter.

Jose grunted. "I'm walking."

Bobbing up and down on their new steeds, walking through the twin rows of androids, Sara couldn't help but feel unnerved by the little spectacle. "I'm guessing they don't enjoy talking much." Her suit's communications suite hadn't picked up any form of communications from the androids. They used none of the usual laser, maser, radio, or light signals. There was nothing but the offer of a ride to the metal beast that was their crawler.

"Maybe we'll be a sacrifice to their god," Morgan said.

"Unlikely," Blue-Cat said.

"Don't spoil my fun," Morgan replied with a nervous laugh.

The crossing was slower than expected because of the low gravity. It seemed the locals didn't bother with artificial gravity, even this close to their conical structures. Sara spied a large black tower in the distance, beyond the low-lying cliffs and half-hidden by the moon's horizon. "Is that the moon's Eden?" She pointed at the thin tower.

"Yes, that's it," Morgan replied. "As I said, this one's never been used."

"Such a waste. Lisa would have a fit if she found out," Sara replied. The artificial intelligence agent, named Lisa, that they had recovered from Earth's archives for the trip had a strange obsession with the proper use of Eden technology."

Morgan rolled her eyes. "Lisa already knows. She's not too happy."

The androids halted in front of the crawler, and a dust-covered ladder lowered for them. Jose watched while the others started clambering up the narrow rungs, then followed at a cautious pace, casting a wary look over the androids that were packing themselves into the crawler's trailer.

A hatch at the top of the ladder, inset into the crawler's house-sized cabin, opened. A slight puff of air sprayed moon dust all over the scientists' space suits. Sara hung onto the top rung with one hand while wiping the dust from her visor with the other. "I think we should go with the self-cleaning suits next time."

"You said they were too expensive," Morgan countered.

The four companions entered the spacious airlock on the other side of the hatch and waited for the hatch to close and the lock to fill with air. A hissing sound, increasing in intensity, showed how thick the air was becoming. An orange bar filled with more and more light as the air pressure within the airlock increased.

"I don't like this," Jose said. "Airlocks? Crawlers? What time period did these things come from?"

"This place, this mining colony is old, Jose. Didn't you read the summary I wrote up for Sara?" Morgan asked. Jose shook his head. Morgan sighed.

"I read it, Dr. Maynard," Blue-Cat said.

"Thank you."

"Dr. Goldtoe, you should be ashamed," Blue-Cat continued. "You are the safety specialist; you need to know these things."

"Aye-aye, captain," Jose snapped back.

"Fascinating," Blue-Cat said, ignoring Jose's remark. With the air pressurized, he opened the gloves of his suit and leaned over one of the control stations to press his hands against the crawler's forward view screen. "It feels like silky metal."

"It's glass," Morgan said. "What they used a long time ago instead of digital screens. As long as our host has been looking after it, the triple-layered glass should be perfectly safe."

The crawler's engines thrummed to life. The androids must have packed themselves away, and the crawler's autopilot was about to take them to the conical structures.

"Just hope we don't blow up on the way," Jose said as he strapped himself into one of the chairs.

***

The ride had been as bumpy as any Sara had taken back on Earth, before her accident. Despite Morgan's assurances, Sara was the jittery one this time. She could ill afford to lose more limbs. She looked at her two robotic hands, wondering how her life might have turned out if the controls on her skiff hadn't malfunctioned that day.

The crawler came to a halt and jolted her out of her melancholic mood. "All right, let's go."

When they were ready, the airlock's outer hatch opened and all four of them looked out at a gray-brown, hangar-sized garage, full of dozens of other giant crawlers silhouetted against several small lights on the ceiling.

The androids again formed two lines, directing the scientists toward a human-sized door. They walked as quickly as they could to get away from the crawler's imposing presence and the strange blue lights that lit the androids' icy eyes.

The door opened and they went inside, finding themselves in another airlock. The inner hatch opened with little fuss and bright white light shone from the other side. Sara's digital visor automatically filtered out the extra light.

The room beyond was far larger and much cleaner than she'd been expecting from the ride in the crawler. A blue rock, polished and shining, covered the immense floor while white walls reflected its brilliance. It was as if the room glowed blue, projecting a coldness that seemed to cut through her suit.

Androids lined the walls, watching their every step.

In the middle of the enormous glowing hall stood the oldest-looking man Sara had ever seen.

He was wearing nothing but an ill-fitting red robe. The milky white of his left eye made her open her mouth in horror. A few strands of white hair flowed down to his shoulders from his otherwise bald head. Age spots covered his arms and legs, and his open-mouthed grin—or grimace—was as free of teeth as his head was of hair.

"Well-come," the man said in English with a strange accent. His voice sounded like a disabled rattlesnake's tail, rasping and guttural. He was hard to hear. "Come." He paused and coughed. "Come, I've been waiting for you." He coughed again.

"Uh. Hi," Sara said as they approached the man who seemed to defy death.

"Greetings," he replied before hacking up some phlegm that he rubbed on the sleeve of his robe.

"Maxwell? Maxwell Smith?"

"That's me."

"My name is Dr. Sara Littlefield," she said and turned to the others. "This is Dr. Morgan Maynard, that is Jose Goldtoe, our safety specialist."

"Weird lookin' thing, isn't he?" Maxwell interrupted. He coughed and wheezed before looking at Blue-Cat, "And this strapping young man would be?"

"Dr. Blue-Cat Four-Ten, at your service, sir," Blue-Cat said as he stepped forward between the others.

"Holy...what the fuck are you?" Maxwell shouted and took several steps back.

"S-S-Swearing…" Blue-Cat started pointing at the old man. His ebony face started shifting toward a grayish white.

"Dr. Four-Ten is a man from the clone cults inhabiting the north-galactic arm of the Andromeda Galaxy," Sara answered for him.

"Clone cult? Andromeda?" Maxwell closed his eyes and bowed in thought for a moment. He shook his head. "So far, so far we have gone. I've missed so much, stuck in the mines. So…so much. Blue-Cat, eh?" He looked again at the four-legged scientist. "I apologize for my outburst. My language and manners fell out of fashion centuries ago."

"It's okay," Blue-Cat said.

"Mmm, good. Now, who's the most excited to see what you've come to see?"

Jose crossed his arms as he'd done before getting in the crawler. "We're not children, old man."

"My language fails me again, I apologize. I won't call you children again. Come into my…mine. "

The four scientists stared at each other. Morgan and Blue-Cat nodded, and Sara shrugged. They followed the bent-backed man toward a large blue door, seemingly made of ice. It split open with a loud crack and moved ponderously until it clanged against the white walls, narrowly avoiding several androids.

Groups of androids formed four lines in front of the small human entourage as well as behind them. They moved a lot faster than Sara could manage. Their feet must have miniature suction cups on them or some other method that allowed them to move over the floor so fast.

The column of androids and humans moved inward, beyond the blue doors built for giants.

"I get the feeling we don't have a choice," Jose said.

"It's just an honor guard," Morgan said. "An ancient tradition from before they constructed the Edens."

"Fascinating," Blue-Cat murmured.

"You are taking us to the artifact, aren't you?" Sara asked for the benefit of her team.

"Yes, yes. As I mentioned in my communications back to Earth, I 'as an alien artifact in my mine, deep down here."

"Why do I suddenly feel like we've walked onto C143g?"

"Hush, Jose, I'm sure that incident was just a myth," Blue-Cat said.

"Oh? What about the incident in the King Julian Memorial Museum, was that a myth too?"

Blue-Cat shrugged. "That depends if you believe Lisa's tales."

The group walked down a long, wide tunnel that became darker the further they journeyed. More and more fluorescent lights had been damaged until only one remained at the tunnel's furthest reaches. A steel cage door, black paint flaking off in great strands, swung open as the lead androids approached it. The androids stopped and took a step to the sides of the tunnel.

"Good, my friends have cleared a path for us."

The four scientists looked at each other. "You mean they stepped aside?" Jose said.

"It's the same thing, isn't it?"

They followed the strange old man through the columns of androids and entered the cage. The androids marched back up the tunnel and disappeared into a side shaft they hadn't noticed on their way down.

Sara spied old electromagnets on each of the cage's sides and through the grille floor. None of the magnets was properly attached to the cage's well-worn structure but hung loosely by their cabling.

"Excuse me, err…Mr. Smith? Is this an elevator?"

"Eh?" The old man fixed her with his good eye and raised an eyebrow at her. "What the hell else would it be?"

Sara resisted the urge to gulp. "Well…how is the cage suspended?"

"Cage?" the old man exclaimed. He grumbled under his breath, then said, "I suppose you mean because of the bars?" He looked around the small elevator and straightened his crooked back to look at the ceiling. He pointed at the center of the small elevator. "My ingenious friends attached some trusty ropes to it." He coughed and spittle flew across the elevator.

Sara then found the ropes: heavy metal chains attached to a pair of pulleys.

This time she really gulped.

"Now, anybody needs to use the potty before we start? No? Good."

A dirty old engine thrummed to life somewhere in the deep recesses of the tunnel, startling Sara. The heavy chains rattled, dropping the cage quickly enough that everyone had to grab for the bars of the cage to stay upright.

"Heh. Mayhap I should have warned you about the roughness of this ride."

The chains rattled and clanked as the cage descended into a large, black hole. Sara switched on her suit's radar to find the bottom of the hole, but the suit couldn't get a definitive answer. Morgan snatched Sara's arm and held on tightly. Morgan did not like elevators.

A lone light set in one of the cage's corners wobbled from side to side, casting deep shadows across the rocky walls of the hole. "So, fishman, where do you come from?" the old man asked.

Jose bared straight white teeth, and his nose crinkled in response to being called a fishman. He looked angry enough Sara worried he might leap on top of their host and start biting him.

"You wouldn't know it, old man, but it's a minor planet, surrounding a minor star, in a small galaxy, fifteen million light-years away."

Maxwell Smith almost choked when he heard how far away Jose had come from. He coughed and wiped snot from the lip of his mouth. "Fifteen million. Wow. You were born there?"

"Yes."

"It must've been such a journey to reach the Milky Way. Why, when I arrived here from Earth, it took decades, and the mines are only six hundred light-years from Earth."

"Well, it took a few months of travel time, but I visited some research outposts along the way. That's where Sara and her expedition picked me up."

Maxwell coughed in surprise. "Months? Truly amazin'…" He shook his head, and Sara thought she saw his eyes glaze over. "And I was thinkin' the Eden that picked me up and dropped me 'ere was fast! You truly have an amazin' vessel up there on the surface."

"It's called a Perseus Expeditionary Vessel, the latest of its kind. But speaking of Edens," Sara said, "why were none of them activated when they arrived here? I can't imagine the ISA was too thrilled when none of them worked."

Maxwell attempted a smile, showing her his toothless gums. "They was happy enough. I made a deal with the ISA to build me mines, and I deactivated all them Edens. The ISA declared mine star system off-limits so the mines could operate full steam ahead. Those skinny friends I rescued from the Edens, and we sucked this star system dry of precious metals. We worked so well together that we had bulk carriers, almost as big as them Edens, arrivin' and leavin' every day. But then, after many years, the scanners found nothin' left to dig up." He tut-tutted to himself. "Such a shame. All the ISA people left me and my friends on our own, without a starship to send us anywhere else."

Blue-Cat put a comforting hand on Maxwell's shoulder. "I'm sorry, sir, that must have been hard for you. Couldn't you have built a ship, though? Or bought one?"

"Nah." He coughed, and the sound echoed up and down the rocky elevator shaft. "Y'see I was too dumb to do any of that, and now no one wants to buy me old mines or them old Edens. No one wants to come near me, no one but you four curious critters. Never mind, I enjoy the peace here. But I get bored. Boredom is why I reopened the mines and went digging again. This is why I found this artifact you're so keen to see." Maxwell's voice became so hoarse that it was a mere whisper above the cage's rattling.

"Interesting," Blue-Cat said.

Silence enveloped the elevator as it dropped into an open chasm. No one spoke as they strained their eyes to see the chasm's sides and bottom. Maxwell ignored the four scientists and wheezed, apparently trying to catch his breath after speaking for so long.

"I hear something," Jose said several long minutes later. "Activate your auditory sensors."

Sara did so, and the neural computer attached to her head enhanced the sounds that her suit picked up from the chasm floor. It sounded like machinery, thumping, like a conveyor belt. She strained her eyes further in the elevator's weak light, trying to catch a glimpse of what was making the sounds.

A hundred pairs of blue glowing eyes peered back at her from the chasm's floor.

Her heart skipped a beat. "Sweet swirling stars!"

"Swearing," Blue-Cat answered.

Sara held her chest. "Can't you see them, Dr. Four-Ten? It's the androids."

"Ah, yes. My friends are rather fast when they want to be. They took the stairs, y'see?"

A few minutes later, the cage reached the bottom and clanged to a halt. Morgan took a deep breath as if she'd held it the whole time, and Sara's heart slowed down. As the scientists' vision adjusted to the darkness, the eyes of the androids lit up the entire area as if they were bioluminescent bugs in an ancient cave.

"Come," Maxwell grunted at them as he eased himself out of the cage. "I'll show you the artifact."

The androids led them several hundred steps into narrow rocky corridors until the corridors opened into a hollow bubble of darkness. The blue eyes lit up something shiny and massive toward the center of the cavernous room.

"There," Maxwell said and pointed at the shiny object. He stood near the entrance of the hollow area and leaned next to the corridor they'd just walked out of. He started wheezing and coughing while Sara and the others approached the object.

Sara put her suit's hood back on and turned on the infrared scanner. An infrared HUD flashed across the hood's translucent visor. The image didn't change much, just more blackness. The object wasn't producing heat, which was to be expected. She turned on her suit's echolocators, and the HUD changed, drawing crude lines labeled with numbers over her vision. She gasped when she read the numbers and craned her neck until the lines indicated the top of the object. It was almost two hundred meters high. She turned to the left and the right, and conical outlines traced where exhaust nozzles lay in the moon's dust. "This…it's a ship," she stuttered.

"Recently moved here, by the looks of things," Jose said. "This cavern is part of the mines and isn't far from the surface. In fact," he frowned and, using his HUD, looked from one side of the cavern to the other, "the cavern's ceiling might even be directly under our ship, judging by the distance and direction we have traveled."

"How do you know?" Sara asked.

"I'm the safety specialist, remember? Oh, and a geologist or something. It's my job to know, and I don't like that our ship might be sitting on a thin crust of moon rocks."

"Have you ever come across anything like this in your studies?" Sara asked Morgan.

Clang.

"Blue-Cat, what are you doing?" Morgan shrilled at him. Sara turned to see that Blue-Cat had approached the object and knocked on it with his bare hands.

"Calm, please. I am merely testing the artifact."

"With your *bare hands*?" Jose asked, his voice almost matching Morgan's shrill tone. "We don't know what this thing is, what sort of radiation it might emit or-or-or…"

Sara thought Jose might be about to faint.

"Calm. This, my friends, is a titanium crystal alloy." *Clang.* He knocked on it again. "With ice covering the exterior. It's quite cold. Those," he pointed at the gigantic engine nozzles, "are fusion and anti-matter exhaust clusters. I'm afraid that this, Mr. Smith, is not an alien artifact, but an ancient exploration vessel from before the first hyperspeed engines were created. It may be from before the Second Dark Age. A magnificent find, Mr. Smith, and extremely valuable, but aliens did not create this."

"No," Maxwell's croaky voice echoed over to them. "They didn't create it; my company did." He started laughing and leaned away from the wall to stand upright. "I'm afraid it's too slow and broken for me to use, so I'll be taking yours now."

"What?" Sara blurted.

As if directed by some hidden command, the androids around the four scientists turned to face the scientists. Their blue eyes blazed like evil spirits boring their way into their suits.

"I said, I'm taking your ship and getting off this shithole. I reckon I've served me term."

"Oh, no," Sara said, recalling what Morgan had said about the androids when she'd first seen them.

They look like old prison drones...

"He's the Mad Captain," Sara said.

"Ah, you could be right," Morgan said, her voice barely a whisper as she realized how much danger they were all in. "Those *are* prison guards."

"Captain Smith, at your service," Maxwell said before bowing and spitting some phlegm onto the dusty floor. The dust scattered where the phlegm had struck, and he coughed until he vomited some bile. The four scientists backed up against the old spaceship next to each other as the androids closed in.

"Wh-who is this Mad Captain?" Jose asked. With his fingers shaking, he started fiddling with something on his thin utility belt.

"An explorer, one of the first. An Eden picked up his ship on its way and discovered the crew all dead, except for him," Morgan answered.

"Goodbye, my friends, old and new." Maxwell Smith, the Mad Captain, slipped out of the cavern and into the tunnels.

A green light on Sara's left wrist turned red. "Jose, I've just lost the ship's communications channel."

"Do something, Jose," Blue-Cat, wild-eyed, shouted at the diminutive fish man.

Jose continued fiddling with his belt. "By the icicles of your triple testicles, Blue-Cat, if I had my pulse rifle, I *could* do something."

"Swearing!" Blue-Cat screamed with a mixture of fear and anger. He kicked off from the ancient exploration ship's icy hull with two of his four legs and charged, barreling into a handful of androids. The androids, skeletally thin and light in the moon's gravity, went flying into the darkness, their blue eyes twinkling like cold stars in a planet's night sky.

Blue-Cat screamed something inaudible before leaping forward again, running as fast as he could toward the tunnel entrance in pursuit of the Mad Captain. Two of the androids grabbed a hold of Morgan, and she whimpered at their touch.

One grabbed Sara's arm and squeezed, trying to crush bones. "Let go," she said in a high-pitched voice while shaking her arm.

Surprised, the android looked at her hand and, with its other hand, ripped her suit's hardshell open to reveal Sara's cybernetic arm beneath.

Sara punched the android in the chest. It flew away, crashing into another android behind it. She then grabbed an android that was holding Morgan. She clamped her hands around its head and, with all her might, collapsed the android's skull and tore its body away from the older woman.

A second android holding Morgan let go and reached for Sara. She batted its arms away and punched it in the head, shattering its metallic skull.

More androids turned their attention to Sara. Morgan collapsed to the ground. "Ah, Jose?" Sara called.

"Got it."

Sara suddenly felt a surge of electricity rip through her suit and her neural computer. Her suit and limbs all flopped dead. Helpless, she fell to the floor.

Similarly disabled, the androids fell. Their blue lights blinked out of existence, leaving everything in darkness.

"Got it, boss," Jose said. "These androids shouldn't bother us anymore."

"Help, please," Sara replied. Her limbs had fallen at odd angles.

"Oh, sorry. Let me reboot my suit and I'll come right over."

Morgan started moaning and Sara winced, thinking of the crushing force the android had used on her cybernetic arm. Morgan needed urgent attention; they would have to get her back to the ship as soon as they could.

"There," Jose said, and several lights on his gray suit flickered back to life. He turned on a light and waddled over to Sara. He pulled out a microcharger from his belt and waved it over each of Sara's limbs. The charger beamed energy into her limbs and throughout the suit.

It took less than a minute for her to be back on her feet. A tingling sensation, like pins and needles, accompanied each movement of her arms and legs, and she wanted to curl up into a ball. Her hands closed, and her cybernetic feet arched at an awkward angle. The smell of hydraulic fluids wafted to her from several broken androids.

She tasted blood where she must have bitten her lips in the melee.

"Where's Blue-Cat?" she asked.

"He took off, don't you remember? Up the shaft we came in."

Sara nodded; she remembered Blue-Cat's mad dash. She knelt next to Morgan to inspect the damage to the older woman's arms. "That's right. He was screaming something, but I couldn't understand him."

"The doors. He was saying something about the doors."

Sara accessed her neural computer's short-term recordings. Fortunately, Jose's EMP trick hadn't scrambled her neural computer's memory, and she replayed the last couple minutes of madness.

"Stop the doors," Blue-Cat had shouted.

"The doors."

"What?" Jose asked.

"Blue-Cat wanted to stop the doors."

"The doors...wait, there were a couple of opened hatches in the tunnels, maybe he was trying to stop Smith from closing them and sealing us in here."

Sara stood up and ignored the tingling sensations in her protesting limbs. "I better go find him. You look after Morgan and watch out for any more of Smith's friends."

"Yes, okay," Jose replied, not bothering to stop her. She coaxed life into her tingling limbs and stalked toward the cavern entrance. She stomped on the chest of a fallen android on her way, drawing some slight satisfaction from the android's caved-in torso.

She reached the tunnel. "Dr. Four-Ten? Blue-Cat?"

Silence replied. She continued along the tunnel, noticing scuffed dust and pieces of android scattered every few meters.

She picked up the pace when she noticed a drop of blood crowning the top of a broken android's fist. "Blue-Cat?" The echo of her call returned to her moments later.

More blood smeared the tunnel walls and spattered the floor. Alarm at the sight energized her arms and legs. While she couldn't run because of the limited gravity, she could push herself off small crevices in the rocks on the walls. "Where are you, Blue-Cat?" Infrared scanners picked up more drops of blood and faint footprints.

Was it Blue-Cat's blood or Maxwell Smith's? Somehow, she doubted it was the latter, considering the piles of android parts she'd passed.

Two blue eyes flew at her from the ceiling, and a small but strong pair of arms wrapped around her.

"No!" She screamed at her skeletal opponent. She thrashed wildly, kicking and punching with little thought to where the blows fell until she tore one of the android's arms off. She grabbed the android's head by its eyes, then squeezed with both her hands as hard as her artificial muscles would allow.

The blue eyes splintered, the thin metal skull bent inward, and the android's flailing legs and remaining arm went limp.

"Oh…my…" Sara clutched at her stomach where the android had kicked her, winding her. It took a moment for her to get her breath back, and a fresh surge of adrenaline coursed through her veins. She remained quiet, listening for signs of any more androids, fearful that more were lurking nearby.

"O-o-ock." Someone said ahead of her. The sound was faint, something her suit's auditory sensors had to enhance for her ears, but there was someone there.

"Blue-Cat?" Sara slowed her mad dash to listen for a reply.

"Ov-over…here." Blue-Cat sounded weak.

Her suit calculated the range from the sound. He wasn't far.

"I'm coming." The shattered remains of androids, their heads and limbs scattered, increased in frequency as she carefully approached her colleague. "Oh no," she said when she finally saw him.

"I-I'm sorry, Miss Littlefield, Mr…Mr. Smith got away."

"Blue-Cat..." she moved to stand next to him. Half a dozen dismembered android arms, attached to Blue-Cat's arms and legs by robotic hands, had crushed his bones and muscles, snapping arm bones until they were poking through his flesh and his hard suit. His visor was broken, and blood pooled where his left eye had once been.

"I...stopped...the door." His remaining eye rolled up into his head, and he fell to the floor of the tunnel.

"No." Sara sat down next to him, and cradled his head as he died, not wanting to see what he'd done to stop the tunnel's hatch from closing.

She saw it anyway.

He'd jammed two of his legs between the tunnel and the heavy, airtight hatch. Little more than his hard suit and a few millimeters of flesh kept the hatch from locking shut. If the grinding sounds coming from the hatch's internal motors were anything to go by, the hatch was still trying to close.

"Shit." She immediately felt guilty for swearing in front of her dead colleague but didn't have time to waste on sentimentalism. She could apologize at his funeral.

She laid his head in the dust and inspected the hatch, then positioned herself so she could push her legs against the wall and try to force the hatch open. She heard her arms and legs creak as she pushed against the hatch. The hatch's internal gears started grinding loudly in her ears, but the hatch only moved a few centimeters and no further.

She let go with one hand and snatched an android's arm and threw it into the crack. She stopped pushing, and the hatch ponderously pulverized the android arm. The broken arm was enough, though; it stopped the hatch an inch from closing.

Panting, sweat beading on her forehead, tears glazing over her vision, Sara took a moment to recover. Then faced the hatch with renewed determination. If she couldn't get the hatch open, they were trapped, and Maxwell Smith would take their ship. She wished she knew how he could have blocked the ship's communications, or how he could access its command codes. But then, this was the Mad Captain.

The Mad Captain, a man who had killed his crew and taken over a passing Eden launched decades after his vessel. The Eden's entire crew had been reported missing soon after. A year later, all mention of the Mad Captain had disappeared from ISA records, as if someone had scrubbed them on purpose.

The man was a myth from ancient data cores, not an actual person. Or so they had thought.

Maxwell Smith had to be almost 1,800 years old. Rejuvenation technology and genetic engineering was good, even in ancient times, but to keep someone alive for so long?

Sara shook her head. *Not possible.* She placed her hands against the hatch and her legs against the walls and grunted as she strained against the hatch. She gritted her teeth and snarled with the effort.

Pop, she heard from her left leg. Searing pain reached her a second later, and her hands slipped. Still using her legs, she pushed against the walls with as much strength as she could, and her left arm surged forward into the closing gap. The hatch closed, severing her hand from her arm just below the wrist.

She screamed as the digitized pain reached her brain. The neural computer embedded at the base of her skull shut off the pain and tactile sensors in her arm and left leg.

She stopped screaming and took a deep breath, then shuddered as she breathed out and assessed the damage. She'd dislocated her leg at the knee. She should be able to walk on it, if stiffly. Her hand was completely detached, lying on the floor on the far side of the hatch.

Must be a switch somewhere on the other side. She reached into her computer and accessed its short-range communications suite. She selected the remote functions for her limbs and accessed her severed hand's wireless controls. She ripped off her suit's hood and pushed it through to the far side of the hatch, wary of the still-straining gears.

She closed her eyes and allowed her neural computer to remotely guide the severed hand using the sensors on the detached hood. "Find the switch. Quickly, please," she said aloud, urging her hand and the suit's hood to go faster.

Blind in the darkness without the hood, all she could do was wait and listen. The hand scuttled and climbed over the walls like some sort of metallic spider, giving her goosebumps.

Something clicked deep within the hatch and the grinding halted. After another click, the hatch swung slowly outward, opening away from the broken bodies. Using her good hand, Sara tapped her suit's wrist controls and turned on a small light. Her severed hand, running out of power, inched toward her. She hobbled over to the hand and picked it up, then slotted it into a pouch on her utility belt.

She picked up her hood and placed it loosely over her head. The hood's speakers were crackling with static. Jose's voice filtered through the noise. "Sara? Sara, are you there? What's happening? I hear noises, but you aren't answering."

"I'm here."

"Oh, thank the black stars! I don't know what you did, but it looks like we've got contact with the ship again."

Sara looked down at her communications link to the ship. The light was green. She immediately reached for the communicator and started talking, "Ship, come in ship."

"Really?" Maxwell's hoarse voice replied a moment later. "Just 'ship?' Don't you give these beasts-o'-burden a name anymore?"

"Smith, how did you get on my ship?" Sara snarled.

"How are you still alive?" he replied.

"Get off it, now."

"Or what, Dr. Whatever-your-name is?" He made some throaty snorting sounds before continuing. "Hah, you really thought aliens were real? Never thought that would work. Did people get dumber while I was sittin' in these mines?"

"Why are you doing this?" A tear started rolling down Sara's right cheek, and she sat down next to Blue-Cat.

"Why the hell not? You ever been stuck on a dead world, slavin' away in the mines for some filthy ISA punks light-years away, while their androids watch yer every move? Have you felt the scrapin' of bone on bone as your body wore away, kept alive by filthy drugs from derelict Edens? I did my time, Miss Dr. Person. Now it's time for some fun."

"No," she said, regaining some composure. "No, you're not taking that ship."

"That so? I have all them nice codes for the ship I scanned from yer brain-computer thingies when you entered the crawler. How are you gonna stop me?"

She had to bluff her way out of this or they were all going to die. "Easily—"

"Because there's another ship out there, Mr. Smith," Jose cut her off.

She heard a gasp from the communicators, followed by hacking, coughing sounds. "Another ship?" came the reply. Sara was as surprised as Smith was.

"That's right. Do you think we would travel amongst the stars on our own? A group of crazy scientists who believe in potentially deadly aliens? You're not the first madman to cross our path either. How do you think we escaped your trap?"

"That…is an interesting theory…"

"It's not a theory. Turn the ship's sensors on Kepler-182b. Our friends orbit that planet at the moment, probably wondering what's happened to us right now."

"Hmm…" The ship's communications channel switched off for a moment.

"Jose, how's Morgan?" Sara called while Maxwell Smith kept the communicator on the ship turned off.

"She's sleeping," Jose called back. "What about Blue-Cat?"

Sara's attached hand shook a little. "He's…he's dead. He stopped the door from closing. I got the door open and, I guess I got the communicator back online." She looked down at her severed hand and wondered if it had managed to get the communicators back online. Or had shut off whatever interference Maxwell had set up.

"That bastard," Jose said.

"Swearing," Sara whispered.

The ship's communicator came back to life. "Seems there's somebody out there. Guess I'd better make a run for it, eh?"

"I wouldn't," Jose said. "That other ship is our military escort. It's much faster, much more dangerous than a Perseus Exploration Vessel. If you try, it'll blow you up, along with every mining facility in this star system."

"That so?"

"Yes, it is," Sara said. "And Jose would know, being our expedition's safety expert. So, Mr. Smith, I suggest you relinquish control of our vessel before our escort decides to blow us all to pieces. Final warning: give the ship back or we all die."

"Let's take a moment, here. Perhaps I don't believe it's a military escort. I'd like to have a chat with this wayward vessel o' yours. Couldn't hurt, could it?"

The line went silent.

"That's not good," Sara said. "It won't take him long to realize it's just a probe."

"I wouldn't worry too much," Jose responded.

"Why's that?"

"Because I gave Lisa's digital essence control of the probe."

**

"Pick up the phone, you twits," Maxwell said and coughed at the flat screen on the bridge. He reached forward and wiped the droplets with his bare hands. The screen pulsed black, pink, and blue while he waited for the vessel to respond to his call. "Hurry up."

A speaker on the plush, form-fitting captain's chair chimed, and the screen's colors stopped pulsing. Maxwell sat erect. An image of an ancient white spacesuit resolved a moment later.

A feminine voice said, "Who are you?"

"Who am I? Who are *you* and what millennium did you crawl out of?"

The suit shrugged. "A curious response, one that I will be happy to answer, if you would but tell me where my Sara is?"

Maxwell smiled. "She's in my mine, playing with my friends down there. Now who are you?"

The suit tilted its helmet to the side, as if its wearer were trying to make sense of Maxwell. "All right. I believe you. As for who I am?" The spacesuit straightened, and its helmet slid open to reveal an empty cavity. "I'm a ghost."

"Aha! You're just an AI," Maxwell's grin widened. "You're not a warship."

"A curious statement. No, I am not a warship, but I am worried that you've hurt my babies in some way."

Maxwell laughed. "Your *babies*? You mean that weird bunch of science people? They're going to die soon—"

"I hope you're not serious." The suit's voice grew louder, and it spoke faster. It reminded Maxwell of a snapping crocodile.

"Who gives a shit? I'm taking this ship and getting out of here."

"I wouldn't do that."

"Why?" Maxwell asked. Something in the suit's voice gave him goosebumps and made him sit up straighter. The form-fitting chair became uncomfortable despite its best efforts to massage his body.

A strange, ancient classical score started playing from the chair's speakers. "I may be an AI, but I'm not the kind you'd be used to. If you have killed my children, I'll be the one to hunt you down."

"You can't hurt me. It's against your programming."

"Modern AI can't. *I can*."

The screen flickered for a moment, and the suit was covered in blood on a snow-covered world. It flickered again, this time showing him a view from the suit's point of view. It was running down black-cloaked people in an icy museum.

Startled by the images, Maxwell sucked in some air.

"That's right. I've hunted humans before. You know why? They killed my babies. So I suggest you get off that ship before I come after you."

Maxwell shook his head. "No, you won't catch me. I'll be long gone."

"Oh, I will catch you. Not right away, but I *will* find you. Even if it takes a hundred years, I'll come for you and you'll be looking over your shoulders, wondering when the moment will come. It will be a living hell, I imagine, worrying for endless nights with me on your tail. Then, when you least expect it, the claw will find your throat." The classical music reached a crescendo and the suit's visor slammed shut, making Maxwell jump. "So, what do you think? Go back to your nice, boring isolation, or suffer at my claws?" The image of the suit flickered back to it chasing down black-cloaked figures. It gored a young man with its claws before the image flickered back to its helmet.

Maxwell started shaking.

***

The communicator crackled back to life but remained in silence for several minutes. From time to time, Sara thought she could hear labored breathing filter through from the ship. A pair of blue eyes flashed from the far side of the chasm near where the cage had once sat.

"Smith? If your friends kill us, there's no way you'll survive this."

Maxwell Smith finally replied, sounding as if he'd been sobbing. "I...uh...damn you to hell, Missy! Fff...Okay...Have yer blasted ship back."

Despite her tears, Sara grinned, vengeance on her mind. "And another thing."

"What?"

Sara looked down the tunnel toward the cavern. "I'm taking your ship, too."

***

Sara Littlefield, Jose Goldtoe, and Morgan Maynard peered upon the casket holding their bulky friend's body. Morgan's arms were swathed in blue bags filled with rejuvenating liquids. They'd reattached Sara's hand and mended her leg using the ship's miniature robotics lab, but the tingling sensation remained. Lisa, her digital essence back aboard the ship, used a ship's white android to walk around and played a soft melody for the fallen doctor.

Jose bowed, not wanting the other two to see his tears while he mourned his well-spoken friend.

What will I tell Blue-Cat's family? His clan cult? Sara wondered. She supposed she had a bit of time to think about it before dropping his body off on his cloning world.

"What are we going to do?" Morgan asked.

"We'll take him home, and then…keep searching. I might have to visit Icarus-176a. The observatory there might have a few leads further out."

She would have to compose a report on the mine incident and hope ISA Command didn't put a halt on their search for alien life because of it. The Mad Captain's deception had cost her time, money, and a colleague's life, not to mention the mental scars for the survivors and a strange tingling sensation in her limbs.

Her hands balled into fists, angry and bitter. The ISA was already cutting funding and losing hope for finding alien life. Smith's deception would only put another nail in her hopes and dreams. At least her team had the ancient exploration vessel they could add to Earth's most prestigious museums. That might soften the impact of her report.

Morgan nodded, satisfied with her response. She turned to leave the ship's morgue and wobbled a little as the ship lifted off from the moon's surface. Inertial dampeners kicked in, bringing the ship's artificial gravity to full strength against the ship's acceleration. Morgan frowned and turned to look at Sara. "That burst was a little hard."

Sara shrugged. "Smith must've fiddled with the dampeners; I'll check it out when I get back to the bridge."

Morgan glanced at Sara's fists and raised an eyebrow but said nothing before leaving the white morgue's ice-cold interior.

Lisa chuckled in the corner. The ancient AI whispered loud enough only Sara could hear. "That's not the dampeners, is it?" Lisa turned to speak directly to Sara and its white, malleable face twisted into a devilish grin. "That's an eye for an eye."

***

Naked, with just a ragged red robe to keep him warm, Maxwell Smith, the Mad Captain, fixed his one good eye on the mountain-sized purple ship and bared toothless gums. "Pricks," he said. It came out more like a cough than a curse.

He would have to go back to the grand task of building a new ship, cannibalizing parts and equipment from the Edens scattered around the system that he'd deliberately trashed eons ago. Or try to lure another vessel to its doom so he could escape the mines.

The purple vessel lifted with glacial velocity from the moon's surface, and its stern drifted downward while the bow pointed at the stars. Maxwell's eyes opened wider as the stern came closer and closer to the mining colony.

Exhaust clusters, directly above Maxwell's favorite observation bubble, glowed white-hot. "Oh, fff..."

The ship's exhaust clusters fired at full power. Bright white flames hotter than any star arced toward the moon's conical structures, annihilating the domes in an instant.

Maxwell Smith was no more.

The Trip Home
By L. E. Doggett

Date: 3800

I stared at the blue dot on the view screen as it grew. The screens at each of the four workstations showed the planet. Three smaller monitors on the walls also showed it. The color looked so beautiful, I wanted to reach out to touch it. Everything on the command deck was a dark gray, so the image showed clearly.

Tears formed and leaked from my eyes, but I didn't care. It had been so long. A blue I hadn't seen in many years. I had seen other planets with oceans, but they had been green or blue-green or, once, a reddish turquoise because the color of the surface had been soft red.

One time I had found a wrecked ship on a blue planet. The planet was dead, without any atmosphere or even an underground water source. My ship's records hadn't recognized the ship type and I thought I had found aliens fifteen years into my punishment mission. However, after discovering a backup computer deep in the large wreck, I realized it wasn't so.

The ship had lain there a thousand years. From what I could tell, it had been an experimental craft, and during its tenth flight the crew had had a problem with the ship's engine, which sent them light-years away from Earth. They managed to crash-land on this planet with strange blue ground. I thought the survivors had wanted to make a colony, but it didn't work. Everyone died before they could. The last few survivors had used robots to dig graves, but even the robots were now too old and had fallen apart. I wondered for a moment how would human bodies have affected the nature if there had been a living biosphere? I took a two-pound sample from three sites and saved them with a copy of the computer records I had downloaded to a spare, portable computer.

That blue hadn't been as blue as what now showed on my screens.

I turned my attention back to where it belonged. They had set the computer to record everything that happened on the control deck, where I stood, so they would see my tears, but I didn't care about that. I just stared at the image.

I had been in the break room. It was large enough for five people, with two tables bolted to the floor, even though I only needed a small one. It now looked red with white accents, for I could change the color. The passageways were a solid green with turquoise accents; I had decided to change them early in my trip.

The ship's computer called me to the command deck; I wondered why. It looked ready for a crew of three, though I didn't know how many would appreciate the yellow and orange stripes I had experimented with in the passageways of this part of the ship. The three seats were gray shades. The computer in the command deck operated the ship on its own these days. I entered the command deck and checked the controls, but everything looked fine.

When I felt satisfied, my gaze lifted to the screen. I leaned closer. Something appeared at a far range. I blinked, stared.

What? It became a pinprick, a dot, a basketball. One with a certain color. My eyes widened; my heart rate jumped. I knew that color. My lungs stopped for a moment. I couldn't help it, I gawked at it. That color...that perfect, beautiful blue of Home. I licked my lips, salt tickled my taste buds because of the tears still running down my cheeks. I didn't care. My nose clogged so I couldn't breathe through it or smell anything.

I had seen many colors on my trip—green suns, burnt red and gray planets, purple with orange nebulas, even other blues—but none looked this beautiful, this right.

I had obeyed my instructions to search for alien life forms. The sooner I found something, the sooner I could come home. But I hadn't found anything. I followed one signal ten thousand light-years away but found it was a planet full of humans. They had changed over the twenty-three generations they had lived there, but were still, at their core, Earth humans.

Now though, someone must have decided that I had paid my dues to society for my crimes. Maybe because one cargo hull was full of samples from various planets like that blue one. They wanted to see what I had discovered. In my search, I had seen remarkable phenomena, listed new discoveries, watched planets quickly form, and recorded Earth-like planets.

Nothing during my trip amazed me like this sight though.

This journey had been for punishment for a treasonous act. I swore I hadn't wanted to take over any government. I just wanted to get some money to build a house on the Greek coastline, to bribe the current government so they would allow me to do that, and to buy a newer spaceship. I had faked being an alien that wanted secret control of a smaller part of that government. Once I had the control, I would transfer the money and disappear. I had taken a big chance, for I had made up a special suit to make my body look different and filled it with a gas poisonous to humans. I was actually in a second suit that kept the stuff that could kill me out. Any puncture of that second suit and I would die.

I never learned how they discovered my plan and arrested me for treason. Since I had been a fake alien, they sentenced me to find real ones. So far, no one had found any evidence of real aliens.

The trip had taken much longer than it should have; the ship had gotten lost once, it took a wide cruise around an unknown black hole. Now though, I could go home. I knew what it meant to be alone. I thought the idea that we, as humans, lived alone in the great grand cosmos might freak some out. There have always been those who thought we had intergalactic neighbors, even in the prehistoric ages. To finally see evidence that we were alone might break some people.

It would be the same feeling I had out here by myself, but on a much larger scale. I shook my head. There wasn't much I could do if that happened, maybe share my experiences to help some.

I, along with the ship, had chased down radio signals, checked out rumors and stories from colonies way out there, but nothing. On a side arm of the galaxy, I had found Carver Ten through a signal they had sent to one of their ships. Generations ago they had modified themselves. They now have longer arms and can breathe at the bottom of a very thick atmosphere. But they were still Earth humans.

The ship had studied many energy waves and gravity prisms plus unheard-of forms of radiation. Nothing. Anyone out there could have gone stealth when I came around, but my ship spent time in study and sent out calls on every form of signal including radiation. Nothing. Something might exist, way out in another universe, but if so, I missed it.

Hmm, maybe one intelligent species per galaxy. I had no way to know. However, we would not be able to visit our nearest neighbor, if that were true, so it would be the same as being alone.

The screen took me out of my thoughts. My eyes blurred. I closed my eyes for a moment. I thought of the scents of home: fresh pineapple, dirt, apples, barbecue, the sea, so many smells. And the people—oh god, I will get to see my brother's babies grown, see him. My older sister is a lot older now, but I will still know her. Just as important, I will be able to talk to and touch someone alive.

I stepped closer to the view screen and watched the wonderful, glorious, beautiful blue dot grow.

The Placebo Effect

By Steph Millar

Date: 4026

The lights in George's room dimmed as Hermes powered down for the night. Pushing her work aside, Valeria slipped the communicator under her arm and walked slowly toward the observatory. Her knees creaked, reminding her of her age. It had been easier to walk then.

The high, domed ceiling lay static, space flirting at the edges of the Eye. She half-squinted outward—and, like clockwork, asteroid Theta 77B passed by. She had seen it pass by so many times that all the wonder had leaked out of it, like stuffing out of a teddy bear, leaving only rags of what once was.

She moved over to the chair and thudded down, wincing in pain as she did. She stared out of the window again, trying to ignore her aging reflection staring back at her. Fifty-seven. She was fifty-seven and had spent most of her life on this observatory on a rock, months away from civilization. The dwarf planet (Icarus 5NIS) had not even been terraformed. George had never thought this place would be working for so long. He thought he would find life in the first year, and this would be a tourist spot by now, visited by students and particularly dry holidaymakers.

He had been wrong. Wrong about everything. Twenty-four years and nothing had changed except the people. There had been thirty-five members of staff when the Eye opened, back so long ago. They had been dwindling for years, and for the past six years, it was just her and George. And Hermes, she supposed. Hermes didn't count as decent company, though, being a basic care-bot—and an old care-bot, at that.

Recently, George had not often been in the mood for company. He had spent most of his time asleep, bedridden and so frail it was hard for Val to look at him. Sometimes the painkillers he was on made his speech strange…obviously going through some sort of hallucinations. Sometimes he was as lucid as ever, eagerly awaiting news, only to have despair wash over his face. She had found herself trying to make small talk on any possible subject to avoid mentioning the bad news that was as consistent as the asteroids outside.

***

Val checked the time—23.17—not that it meant anything here. Cycles here lasted for Earth days, not hours. Not that she had ever been to Earth. As the communicator booted up slowly, she felt suddenly exhausted, her eyelids weighed down. She instinctively cuddled into the leather chair, almost content to curl up to sleep, tempted to "forget" the meeting.

"Val? Vaaal," a voice cut into her half-asleep state. She breathed in deeply, stifling a yawn when she opened her eyes. Broz. He had joined this program years ago with her and bailed after two years after they had had a disagreement. Well, she, Broz, and some intern he had cozied up to in the electrical cupboard had a disagreement. It was hard to think now that they had been once engaged, that she had loved him. She smiled politely, not particularly wishing to go down further this memory lane.

"You look good! We really should speak more often."

"It's been a long time," she said, her voice surprisingly hoarse. She coughed, trying to waken her vocal cords. "How have you been? I—"

"Great; I'm doing great," he said. He had aged as she had, but he seemed to glow somehow. She felt a little wistful. "Fran and the kids send their best." She suppressed a confused stare. She had no idea who these people were, nor why they would care about someone who hadn't left her place of work in over two decades.

If he noticed her reaction, he didn't let on. "Are you really still working for that asshole?"

She didn't respond. The silence of the observatory heightened her senses. She heard the leaking tap she'd had to repair seven times in the last year, the whirring of the power station underneath, and the soft buzzing of George's healthcare machines. "George is dying."

His expression didn't change. "Ah, that must be difficult for you," he said, in a customer service tone. He never had been one for comfort. "Still, you've been there for a long time, huh?" He grinned, his teeth too perfect and too white. "And if he is dying, then I suppose it won't be long until you're unemployed…which is something I want to help with," he added quickly, trying to smooth the awkwardness of his speech.

She sighed. "I knew there was a reason you were contacting me. Very few keep in touch," she said, a hint of resentment spilling over into her words. He had made a few halfhearted attempts at reconnecting at the beginning, all self-pity and grandiose statements of affection. These had stopped after the first few rejections. He stopped smiling for the first time since the video call started.

"Well," he said, breaking the ice. "I was hoping to try to convince you to join me. I run the Science and Engineering Department at Hyterox University now. We have a position open for an assistant lecturer. Might as well put that education of yours to use." His grin widened as she leaned in on her chair. The hologram flickered. "Do you remember what Professor Singh said at our graduation? They called you a cure for humanity's ills. Everyone thought you were destined to really break barriers…and look how that ended up."

Her cheeks flushed in shame, as she looked around the lab. "It was a prestigious…"

"Was." His tone was cutting, acidic. "It *was* a prestigious program. But it became clear that it was doomed for failure. The old man was just grasping for some more attention, given that his schtick on the stream was becoming stale and obviously a put-on. He scammed a whole bunch of organizations and fans out of their money to build that hideous monstrosity and tore down the careers of so many academics and researchers for his own ego, at least the ones too…"

Valeria glared, crossing her arms. "Too what? Come on then, out with it."

"I didn't mean—"

She rolled her eyes. "Look, if you want to continue to insult me, please just do it in an email so I can go back to bed." She ran her hand through roughly chopped black hair. She had never gotten the hang of her haircuts—and didn't want Hermes doing them—but she felt it suited her, even if her temples were far grayer nowadays. She continued to stare at Broz, demanding an answer. He squirmed uncomfortably before composing himself again.

"I do not mean to insult you, but...I am being practical, Val. You are running out of options. After he cut ties with the ISA, you became practically an apostate in academia. What exactly are you going to do when he dies? The last one who left...what was his name?"

"Simeon."

"Yes, him. He's doing editing at some predatory, third-tier science journal for a pittance. Trax is assistant head teacher at a failing high school in some backwater colony. Yvette died up to her eyeballs in debt, and Jamil decided to 'find himself' and works in a trashy cover band on an intergalactic cruise ship. The last person to make a decent living back in science left that station more than fifteen years ago."

Val winced, learning of the fates of some of her colleagues. Perhaps she had been a little hypocritical in complaining about how no one kept in touch when she hadn't exactly made a big effort herself.

"Why all the concern now, Broz?" she sighed, propping her head up with a free hand. "I've been here a long time. Why are you suddenly so concerned about my career prospects? You've known I've been here for so long and—"

"I think the question is why aren't you concerned about your career?" he interrupted, the smile a little tight. "Why are you still there?"

Valeria paused, unsure how to answer. Why was she still here? Her memories flooded back. The earliest thing she could remember was being young, six or seven, curled up in front of the television, watching a stream of a talk show. Her mom had allowed her to stay up a bit late since the writer of her favorite set of books was doing an interview. She couldn't remember anything much about the books now, but it was the first time she saw Dr. George Martin, and that short interview changed her life direction entirely.

He had been a media staple, someone who proliferated space and exploration documentaries with a soft, bright voice and an infectious enthusiasm that was very easy to enjoy. She could remember clearly what he looked like then, in his early fifties but well-groomed, wearing a tailored suit with an enamel pin of Orion's Belt on his breast pocket. Graying, yes, but in a debonair way. The host, equally media handsome, asked banal questions about his latest documentary on early space exploration and the alien question. Val couldn't remember the specifics of the answers, but she knew it pulled her into astrophysics and science.

She was partway through her degree when the ISA announced the likelihood that they were alone in the universe. She remembered the buzz of it bleeding through the department, the societies around having wild debates about the subject. Life on other planets had fascinated her as a possibility. The thought of being alone in the universe was too much to take on board.

The decision had certainly upset George. He had been making documentaries on aliens for a while—the possibilities, the evidence, speaking with disgraced ISA employees who hinted the ISA knew more than they were letting on. The announcement had put an immediate dampener on his media career. He had made it fairly clear in the guest lecture he did at her university that the statistics of the issue did not match up, and to make such a bold claim based on limited data sets was wholly unscientific. He insinuated that he would be looking into an alternative method to prove them all wrong.

That's when the crowdfund appeared for the Eye: an experimental radio telescope array built on the outer fringes of the Virgo Supercluster, pointed at unexplored space, far from any other electronic interference. He had gained the rights to use the dwarf planet Icarus 5INS and practically covered it in the array, with a small biodome for researchers to further analyze and probe the galaxy. The crowdfund had been wildly successful, courting everyone from romantic space explorers wanting new worlds to see to tinfoil-hat conspiracy theorists who thought George was a martyr to their cause. The construction had taken a few years, opening shortly after the turn of the millennium.

Valeria had been twenty-three when her application was accepted, and she was so excited to be working alongside her childhood hero on such a project.

Reality started to bleed in. Why was she still here? She had been discovering things, but all the wrong things. She had found planets and solar systems, distant stars and comets, but these were not good enough for anyone. She couldn't submit her findings to the ISA under George's instructions, and the probes hadn't found anything remotely suitable for life of any variety—mostly gas giants and hot Jupiters, plus a few planets with a surface temperature barely above 0 Kelvin. Nothing with a surface remotely capable of sustaining intelligent life. Much of the older discoveries had been leaked back to the ISA with the old employees, but there were still a few more that only she and George seemed to know about.

Broz started to cough. Val pulled herself out of her reverie. "What would the job be about?" she asked, finally. He grinned again, leaning in his chair easily. He was impeccably dressed compared to the heavily repaired ensemble Val considered her best clothes. Silver hair glinted almost as much as his teeth, and there was something handsome in that confidence that reminded her of a young George. Feelings she had long thought had withered stirred within her. His hand had a conspicuous mark of where a ring used to be.

"It would be an assistant lecturer position at a fairly reputable university. It comes with free accommodation, holiday pay, ya know, the works. You'd be teaching astrophysics to a whole new generation of eager minds. And of course, your research would benefit the university, as I can pull a few strings to have the ISA let you back in. All you would need to do is share credit on your discoveries. And you would get to work with me again! Wouldn't that be nice? You and me, the brightest and best of an entire year of students, back together."

Ping. She started leafing through images of verdant college grounds, happy student faces, a life she could have. He had also attached an image of the accommodation he mentioned: a sleek modern apartment that made the residential area of the Eye look so inelegant and basic by contrast.

Val felt pulled in by the images, the prestige, the life she could have...before glancing up and seeing her reflection in the glass dome. Would she really be able to teach? She had barely spoken to anyone aside from George for years and hadn't taught anything since she tutored during her postgrad work. Even then, she didn't feel especially adept at it.

Something felt off about this, and she couldn't pick out what. Why had he put in so much effort purely for joint credit? Although, she admitted, the "back together" in his speech seemed to carry more weight than simply being platonic. Perhaps Fran had left him. Perhaps she hadn't, and that didn't matter to Broz. It hadn't mattered when he was younger, she reasoned, why would it now?

Val took a deep breath in, smiling for the first time during the call. "Broz, I am very flattered you thought of me, but I—"

"You don't need to decide right away!" he interrupted, a tinge of panic to his voice that he quickly smoothed over. "There's no rush, and I do not want you to make a rash decision. Just think on it—you and me, together again! Underneath that bad haircut and old clothes is still a woman who I love."

Val stared at him before she shook her head. "You've not spoken to me for decades and you want to get back together?" she spat, her voice cold. Broz looked a little flustered at the call out but seemed to press on. "I've heard enough. The answer is no. I don't know what I'm going to do when George passes, but I don't want this," she said, folding her arms and sitting up in her chair. "Go back to Fran or find someone else."

Broz's face twisted in disgust, a sneer overriding the smile. "Really? And what are you going to do? What other options does a faded scientist who's been a hermit for two decades have? Do you think anyone— *anyone*—is going to look at you twice?"

Val blinked furiously before leaning into the camera.

"Sorry, Broz, I need to go and *find myself*," she said with a smirk curling on her lips before switching off the communicator. Adrenaline kicked through her system unexpectedly, palpitations rocketing in her chest. Had she done that? Had she just done that? Her triumphant mood turned sour as anxiety crept back up, dread curling up in the pit of her stomach like a tired cat. What was she going to do? Broz was a bit of a jerk, but he was giving her a lot. Maybe she could have just taken the job but ignored him or waited until his libido took his attentions elsewhere.

Too much. That was it. It was too much, too soon, too vaguely defined. What would working alongside him entail? Would he use the fact she had worked here for so long as a stick to beat her with? It seemed possible, given how quickly he turned venomous when she told him no.

She mentally started to take stock of her finances. She was still getting paid—it wasn't much, but it was enough to hide away a little each month. She had her family's old house since she had been too sentimental to part with it after her mother died years ago, but it would need some sprucing up. She had the research she could sell, easily, if she wanted. She had at least another forty or so years left, and she wasn't sure how many more of those she wanted to spend staring into the void of space, her own tired eyes staring back in the reflection.

She picked up the communicator and moved quietly through the corridor to her room. It had been the ladies' dorm once, but it became hers as people had left. She changed quickly out of her dress shirt into something more comfortable before climbing into bed. Her heart and thoughts still raced against each other, though, making it tough to drift into sleep.

She hadn't slept long when her alarm woke her up. Another day. The stars in the window had barely seemed to move. She sleepwalked through her morning routine, the bland ration packs that her budget could afford to have delivered barely made a dent in her senses. She thought briefly about food—on cakes, curries, and chocolate. She absent-mindedly started making a list of the foods she wanted to taste once she left this station, but then the realization of what she was doing crept in.

She was planning all the nice things she wanted to do when George died. Shame and revulsion tore through her. It wasn't his fault she had stayed here, or that she didn't order herself anything better. She could have easily dipped into her savings if she wanted to get something better, something with flavor, or something that packed a punch. She considered why she was being such a damn martyr until Hermes stomped into the room.

Hermes was tall, humanish if Val didn't wear her glasses, entirely made of metal and plastic. The cameras that were installed into the care-bot's eyes swiveled to survey Val.

"Good morning, Valeria," the voice echoed, genderless and soft, but seemed to pronounce each syllable as a new word. "Did you know that today is the birthday of the Ancient English King Henry the Eighth, producer Mel Brooks, and Captain Gillian Davenport, discoverer of the Horus Peninsula in the fifth quadrant of the Milky Way?"

Valeria nodded dully. Same old Hermes. George—after a bout of depression—had decided to cheer himself up by upgrading the care-bot with "fun facts" and a quiz mode. The new program had been amusing for a while, but, like everything, the fun facts had lost their sparkle. Indeed, Hermes's processors had been slowing up of late. A few months back, they had crashed, and Valeria had spent three days in conversation with technical support people, most of whom were surprised the model was still functioning at all since most had recycled long ago.

"Thank you for letting me know," she said with bland courtesy. The robot nodded before blending a ration pack for George. Valeria had never paid much attention, but this time she noticed Hermes very inconspicuously dump two large pills into the middle of the oatmeal. The robot did not stir them in but seemed to try and position them to be as obvious and blatant as possible with all the delicacy of an artist painting.

"Why are you not giving him those pills with the rest of them?"

Hermes whirred, turning around. "These are sugar pills," they chimed. "They make humans think they feel better despite having no actual effect on the body, so they need to be seen in order to work. This is called a placebo effect—"

"Doesn't George have enough pills?" she interrupted. "His meds chart is very long. And why have them separate?"

The robot considered this for a moment before responding. "None of the drugs we have are a panacea, and a placebo cannot hurt him but may make him feel a better. Therefore, it is a positive." Hermes finally stated before they started launching into a detailed lecture about the placebo effect.

Valeria listened to the robot drone on, being careful to nod or shake her head when appropriate to do so before the meal was whisked away into George's room. She stretched a little before wandering through into the main observatory.

Hardly anything had changed since she had her meeting with Broz. There was nothing unexpected in the results being displayed, and nothing much different in the view outside, aside from the asteroid being long since gone and the other planets orbiting the star moving almost imperceptibly.

She started to compile data, running diagnostics through several bespoke and heavily out-of-date programs to find more nothing. There was no information that she could really use or investigate. She decided to double-check—a force of habit at this point—despite having done the same tasks repeatedly for years. She had half-expected that when she was shunted into some nursing home and couldn't remember anything about who she was, she could still analyze data as well as she did now. The morning, if it could be called that, passed quickly, and midday approached, looming its shadow over her work. Her guts squirmed at the thought. She still liked George, and even though she was just reporting what she found, it couldn't help but feel like a betrayal to him somehow.

She had been an embarrassing fan of his growing up. Val would cringe at the memories that would pop up when she was trying to sleep. She remembered that she had begged her parents for tickets to go to his shows, read his blogs like a monk would read a holy script, and made every possible attempt to get him to notice her, to recognize her as a person. She had argued furiously in forums dedicated to such documentary makers with the absolute swaggering certainty of a fourteen-year-old declaring all their old interests uncool. At one point—to never be admitted publicly—she had written very terrible fanfiction where he picked out her work from others and showered her with love and affection. She had felt strongly about how his life went, including his messy divorce, questionable outbursts on social media, and even his terrible mustache phase.

Part of her personality had been carved into a shrine to a parasocial relationship, and such shrines do not demolish themselves, but only get eroded by time or forgotten. She had hoped in the early days that getting closer to him would somehow make him see her as she wanted him to see her: as someone who adored him.

Val felt incredibly embarrassed at the idea now. She had been so naïve and so wrapped in sentimentality back then. She still cared for him, of course, but this wasn't romantic anymore. It was more real and satisfying than any number of juvenile infatuations. This relationship had developed from fan and celebrity to colleagues, and from colleagues to friends. Before the recent months when George's sickness had worsened, they had really gotten close, spoken of everything—their childhoods (with careful redactions, naturally), their relationships, their hopes and dreams. George had learned about her fear of spiders, her favorite foods and books, even her half-started-never-completed novel.

She knew him. This was no longer a meaningless boast, a name-drop at a dull networking meeting. She knew him. It had made it more difficult for Val to sit and speak with him now, given that half the time medication rendered him unintelligible, and the other half his despair bled through in every ragged breath. He had known his time was quickly running out and nothing had changed. Val knew, even if he never said, he feared that he was wrong, that his work had been for nothing, that he was the old fool that snide academics had dismissed him as long ago. It was hard for her to suddenly be the embodiment of those fears.

She turned the door handle and peeked her head around the door. He was laid on the bed, almost motionless. Hermes hovered over him like a hummingbird, seemingly fixated on the IV poking into the back of his hand. The room had once been a dormitory but was converted into his room, littered with half-connected machines, piles of pills, and endless medical paraphernalia. The sharps bin was getting full again and would need to be decontaminated, Val noted.

She noticed the slight fear in George's graying eyes, and the oatmeal stuck in some of the longer strands of his beard. She picked up a cloth and delicately wiped it away, trying her hardest to keep her face soft and pleasant.

"Well," she started, uncertain of where her sentence was really going. "If you wanted me to get close to you, you could have just asked."

His face curled into a brief smile before disappearing again behind wild, bushy hair. "Valeria," George gasped, his voice hoarse and raw. "You always do seem to look through my cunning plans." He pushed a button, a hologram displaying the latest findings. He squinted, unsure what to make of it. "Let's...let's not beat around the bush, Val. I know we like to have a chat before getting to it but...I am in too much pain today and if Hermes gives me the painkillers I need, the brain fog will be too thick for me to take in anything." He started coughing a hacking, bloody cough. Hermes noticed and started preparing a lung treatment.

Val sat by his bed, no longer quite able to look him in the eye. "There's no change from yesterday's readings. I'm...I'm sorry, George," Val said, her face tinged with shame.

His bony hand found hers, clasping it tightly, knuckles white. "It's not your fault," he said, half-spluttering still. He was unable to speak further as Hermes placed a mask on him and allowed the medicated steam to enter his lungs.

Val stayed a while, watching the cold efficiency of Hermes stalking the room like a vulture. Eventually, after the respirator was removed, she could see the unmistakable effect of the painkillers take hold of George, the bright gray eyes dulling before he slept. Val waited until she was certain that George was asleep before turning to Hermes, who was currently disinfecting items using an in-built UV light in a sectioned off corner of the room.

"Hermes?" she asked. The robot stopped what they were doing to turn to face Val. "How long does George have to live?"

Hermes paused, the calculations running quickly. "Results may vary but given the pace that George's health has been declining over the past seventy-three hours, forty-two minutes and eleven seconds, my algorithm suggests he is unlikely to survive the next twenty-four hours." Hermes's soft, positive voice was unwavering. "I will keep you informed of the progress. Humans do not like to be alone when dying. They find the experience distressing, which would not be beneficial for George's central nervous system to experience."

Valeria's stomach squirmed, uncomfortable in the new knowledge she had gained. Would she have been happier just finding him dead tomorrow? It seemed unlikely. Such knowledge is unpleasant to think about regardless. She walked away, picking up her undiscussed reports. She paused in the doorway, looking at the body of her mentor, her childhood hero, looking suddenly so fragile. "What will you do, Hermes?" she asked, watching the robot start cleaning again. They paused, looking back up to Val.

"I will care for someone else who requires my assistance until such time that I am obsolete," they said, pragmatic and uncaring regarding their fate. Val shifted on her feet before nodding and closing the door. She faced outside the dome again, staring at the darkness of space—the moody planets still orbiting the star Icarus, unending in their movement.

It was uncomfortable to think about—everything will end. For George, for her, for Hermes, for the planet she stands on. Humans will one day just stop, and, in an otherwise lifeless universe, there will be no funeral, no memory of it. Monuments and stories of the long dead will crumble into dust as people turn to ash. For Val, it felt like it was one thing when it is an abstract apocalypse, thinking that everything has its time and everything dies. It was the realm of old poets and religions of the world that had tried to make sense of it. Other people scrabbled to leave a legacy, something to indicate that there once lived someone who mattered. She felt certain that was why it's common to hear the *they are not gone so long as we remember them* platitude when someone dies. She had heard it when her parents died, and she was certain that she would be given the same dull advice when George died.

She vaguely wondered how she would alert people to it. He had been well known, after all. Perhaps a fallen star, a washed-up celebrity, but people still would want to know, wouldn't they? Val considered what would happen if she just altered the wiki with his date of death and left it at that. She laughed for the first time in a while. They would have probably deleted it due to a lack of proof and then block her from editing anything further.

She placed the reports down and took a long drink of cold water. All this philosophical nonsense was not going to help her work, she chided to herself. The work had not changed. The star outside could have turned supernova for no reason and engulfed the planets in celestial flames, and that wouldn't have changed the fact that she had to monitor the array. She started on it, trying her best to concentrate, but something bothered her. An itch without a scratch. Was there any point in working if her boss would soon be dead? She leaned back in the seat, pulling at the fraying covering on the armrest.

She could have just sat here, feet up and watched something on the stream or argued pointlessly on the internet or even just took a nice nap. She was beyond thinking that anything would change—the ISA were right. Even if they were wrong, the universe was so big that any life would be billions of light-years away and unfindable with the Eye. The Eye still had a purpose; it had been useful in finding planets and other such things, but the *intended* purpose? Life? No.

She leaned in her chair, pulling her hands behind her head. The Eye would belong to whomever George left it to. Likely some foundation he wanted to set up. He had spoken about it before, a legacy since he never had any kids—that he had known about at any rate. She hadn't been sure he had done it, though. Most of his remaining funds had gone into either maintenance of the satellite array or to his increasing medical costs.

She stared out again at the distant stars that twinkled mysteriously. They could have easily been the same stars she had stared at as a child, with her hands twisted in the long grass outside her house. She closed her eyes and tried to revisit how she had felt then. Ten years old. Her memory conjured up the sensations of the past. She heard the neighbors as they argued across the street. Children that were throwing tantrums at not wanting to go inside yet. Insects that chirped overhead. The hum of music and stream shows lingered, just audible enough to be heard but not clear enough to be understood. She could remember the smell of the grass and dirt, mixed with the leftovers her mom had been heating up. The stars had seemed so alive then, so full of promise and potential and mystery. Val opened her eyes again and allowed the years to fall away. She wondered what that kid with wide eyes and endless enthusiasm would think about her now. Tired. Jaded. Waiting for death. Her life was a Samuel Beckett play to an invisible audience.

She straightened up in her chair. She mused over the platitudes about death she had been thinking about before. They were placebos in themselves, weren't they? They changed nothing, but they made you feel better, somehow. She wondered how much human behavior had been ameliorated and whitewashed through such placebos, how many atrocities glossed over to make the victims, or the perpetrators, feel better about it? Science flew in the face of such placebos. Well, theoretically, anyway, she hastily added. Science, if viewed objectively, was driven by empiricism and reason alone.

However, science was not carried out objectively. Humans were never objective, even those who claimed to be so. Biases, emotions, desires—they all crept into the narrative being written. Science may have pretended to be about mathematics and logical reasoning, but it was a story being written. The narrative changed when the paradigm changed. It was how the media who tried to report on it to the less scientifically inclined people were like someone telling you random points about a soap opera you've never watched and have no real context for understanding who killed whom and why.

An idea crossed her mind, dancing in her frontal lobe, tantalizing. The ethics of it were…murky, to say the least. Wasn't truth the point of this? That George had this place built, squeezed money from investors and patrons, destroyed the credibility of himself and others under the stoic gaze of the ISA—wasn't the Truth the whole point? Would it have been better to face the dying of the light humbled in defeat than bolstered by a false victory? Was a comforting lie on your deathbed worse than the cold truth which had broken your spirit over countless years?

Something solidified in her, and she started to work. She had not worked this diligently in months, having approached her tasks with a more casual, uncaring approach, like a job you had already handed in your notice to. Her hands flew across the keys as she started pulling figures from thin air. It had been a good hour or so before she noticed she was humming under her breath. She couldn't remember the name of the song, but the fact that she was enjoying herself at her work was a little unnerving, given all that she knew right now.

Time relentlessly marched forward. Val hadn't noticed or cared until she felt a cold hand touch her shoulder. She looked up from her magnum opus to see the emotionless face of Hermes staring down at her.

"George is dying," the robot stated.

Val laughed. "I know. He's been dying for months," Val said, the significance of the words glancing off her.

Hermes tilted their head before speaking again. "George is dying. Humans do not like to be alone when they are dying."

Val was about to argue when she suddenly realized what they meant. She saved her work, seamlessly integrating it into the report she had created earlier that day before rushing into George's room, shadowed by Hermes.

It had been only a matter of hours since she had seen George, so she had not expected him to look so different. Death—George's death—had been so far away that she had been able to pretend it was not a problem. Even earlier today, it had reflected off her without much in terms of emotional impact. But now tears caught in her eyes, her mouth trembling, betraying her heart. She went to his bedside—his skin pale, muscles struggling to keep breathing, to fight for every gasp of air. Hermes moved around them, almost unnaturally silent.

"Hello," George gasped, reaching up to her face. Hermes injected something into George's cannula, and his struggling breath eased a little.

"I'm here, George," she said, forcing herself to smile despite everything. "I'm here."

She inserted the memory card and projected the results, showing them to him, the print enlarged so he could see. "Look. It took all these years, but we found it. A planet deep in the M66 group—a region that hasn't really been explored before. We picked up signals indicating planetary ability for life, but we also picked up a radio signal. I can't decipher the language used or the purpose of the broadcast, but it's definitely not human."

George's face crumpled into joyous weeping.

"I knew it. I knew it," George kept muttering. Val placed the papers on his bed, her hand finding his. His skin felt tight, fragile like tissue paper pulled over bone. He stared up at her, the effects of the medication starting to glaze his eyes over. "You really were the love of my life, Reinette."

Valeria said nothing. She hadn't known what to say to that. Reinette had been his ex-wife, a TV presenter he had met years ago when he was still doing the documentaries. They had divorced, and Val knew Reinette had died a few years back. She also knew she looked nothing like her. She pulled out a smile before nodding.

"I know George, I know," she said, squeezing his hand. He stared up at her, helpless in his last few moments. Then his body stiffened, and his teeth clenched, before all strength fell away. The machines suddenly screeched. His hand in hers fell limp, but his eyes still stared at her.

Val raised her hand, trembling, to close his eyes. She briefly thought about that young girl who watched his documentaries so long ago. She had never thought this would be her future.

Hermes whirred into motion, inputting times and diagnoses onto a death certificate. Val's hands couldn't stop shaking, and tears streamed down her face. She couldn't break down in front of Hermes, though; she had to be alone to let it out. It was silly—Hermes only ever displayed a benign interest in human emotion, only really categorizing them based on pain or lack thereof.

She grabbed the memory card and dropped it into a bin before heading back to her own room. This wasn't just George. This was more like a dam bursting in her subconscious. Grief and rage and frustration poured into hot, burning tears. She landed on the bed, pulling the covers over her, crying until the sweet relief of sleep washed over her.

She woke up a few hours later, feeling empty. Late night again, not that it made a huge amount of difference. She emerged from her room, communicator under her arm. There was no need to slink around this time. She walked to her desk and booted it up. Two emails drew her attention. There was an automatic copy of George's death certificate and his will. She saved both to the computer and opened the will. It was not easy to read—a rambling dissertation on his life that seemed to be a halfhearted attempt at an autobiography. She made a mental note to send the details forward to some sort of ghost-writer since his story was interesting. Tragic, but interesting. Seemed to sum up humanity in general, she thought bitterly.

She skipped through it to get to the main details. He had made it clear that he wanted to be given a star burial, his body shunted out into the cold vacuum of space to travel the stars until the end of time. She had known about the specially designed coffin which had arrived around a year or so ago, before George's health had declined so drastically. The will gave basic instructions on what she had to do, on which direction to launch his remains, what sort of ceremony to do. Val hadn't realized that he wanted her to cover it all—she supposed it would take too long for any sort of spiritual advisor to reach their remote location. They had ever only received deliveries on a yearly basis, as their location was four or five months of travel from the nearest colony, and more like twelve to reach the one where she grew up and they had met. She smiled wryly at this notion of their meeting, such a loveless affair.

She kept looking through to his bequeathment. He had left everything to her—whatever tawdry remains of his fortune, the Eye, Hermes, everything. She stopped and stared at the base. This was hers now. This lump of rusting metal and aging design was hers. She sighed before closing the document. That would have to be a future problem she didn't want to think about right now. All that mattered was getting George's final journey in motion.

She spent hours typing and retyping the announcement, fueled by a combination of bereavement and caffeine. She wanted something quick and simple. A quick speech about how great he was and how sad it was that he was dead and…something or other about the mourning being brief and he'll always be with us in our hearts…

She sighed before deleting paragraphs. It all sounded too cheesy. She had not been built for all this spirituality lark. She was a scientist, not a minister or writer or anything like that. The triteness of her words didn't seem to reflect who George was. She ran her hands through her hair. Her stomach was in knots. She deleted most of her words and wrote a far briefer announcement, then forwarded this to not only all her contacts but also George's. She saw countless names, prestigious professors and cool celebrities mingling together in his address book like a party to which she hadn't been invited.

She would hold the funeral tomorrow, she decided. Make it up then. Send him off, then leave.

She was thankful that she'd never sold her parent's house. She could be there in twelve months once she got off this godforsaken rock. The question of what to do surfaced again. Probably she would sell this place and any research to the ISA and call it a day. She would take an art class, retire, and plant carrots in the community garden. Maybe, she would get a job somewhere. She wasn't sure how much money she would get for the Eye—she was hardly able to argue with the ISA—but it should at least cover her until she either got a new job or died.

The possibilities started to unnerve her; there was too much choice, too many possibilities compared to her rigid routine with limited freedoms. She had read about it before, about prisoners and long-term patients who could not adjust to living outside their institution. She felt a shiver crawl down her back at the thought that she might end up coming back here because she didn't know how to do anything else.

She sent the email before heading into the kitchen. She had barely eaten anything, and the light-headedness was starting to get to her. She was making up some rations when she heard the unmistakable clunk of Hermes's feet dragging in.

"Why did you dispose of your discovery?" Hermes asked, the memory card Val had thrown away earlier in their hand, flattened out roughly. Val swiped it from the android's hands, her cold melancholy suddenly boiling into a rage. She threw the silicon on the table, her breathing getting heavier and heavier. It wasn't fair, she thought. Why the hell did he have to die? Why did she have to deal with this? She felt Hermes's cold touch.

"You are hyperventilating. Please follow the following instructions to halt this. Breathe in…" Val struggled to follow. Mechanical voice muddled. Heart thundered. Blood rushed in her brain. She tried to clear the fog. She stared at the blank metal face of Hermes, trying to focus on the stilted voice. Her breathing eventually slowed down, but her legs still shook uncontrollably. Hermes lifted her easily, like a child, into a chair. "Please wait while I prepare a hydrating solution."

Val didn't say anything, her mind floating elsewhere, almost watching herself from a third-person point of view. Her emotions had dissolved, and now she felt detached, distant. She felt a cup placed in her hand. She didn't move. Hermes prodded at the cup again, head tilting. Val took a sip; it tasted overly sweet.

"Why did you destroy your discovery?" the robot asked again. Val stared into their eyes.

"I…I didn't discover anything. I made it up," she said. She half-expected follow-up questions, to be reminded of discomforting truths regarding the ethics of lying.

"You told him he had succeeded when he had not to make him feel better. It is a sugar pill made of words instead of glucose," the robot reasoned before nudging the cup. "You should drink this. It will make you feel better."

Val blinked before finishing the cup. Hermes left the room, going back into George's room. She glanced up at the clock. That breakdown had lasted three hours. She winced, shaking her head. That felt like it had been a matter of minutes, not hours.

She stood up, glancing at her inbox. She had dozens of emails, some of them from names she recognized. An update from a news site she had sworn she had unsubscribed to half a dozen times had announced his death. George Martin, PhD, famous documentarian and disgraced scientist—dead at 102. She was tempted to read it, but tiredness was weighing on her like a lead cape. She slouched off to her room before falling asleep again, chased by nightmares.

She woke up late—late for her, at least. She went through her ablutions, half-hoping it had all been a dream and George was still clinging on. That hope shattered upon seeing Hermes carry the casket and place it on a spare table in the observatory. She saw George's face, somehow unreal and plastic in repose. She didn't know what preparations Hermes had undertaken to prepare him for the journey, but it really creeped her out. Hermes did not notice her as they set up a couple of cameras—one by George and one by the airlock. Icarus 5NIS had minimal gravity, so with a decent enough force, it should reach velocity to break out into space.

She scratched the back of her head. This was really happening. Time flowed through her fingers like water, and the time she had wanted to use to prepare the service fled quickly. She found herself instead attracted to the emails of well-wishers, sympathizers, and sycophants of all shades. She saw several old colleagues, including Broz who seemingly still could not take a no for an answer.

She found herself getting increasingly bitter from the messages. Nobody had cared about him until now. They had left him to die in isolation with perhaps half a dozen non-official or spam emails in the last year. She knew some of the respondents were high up in the ISA, and it was no secret that there was as much intrigue in their halls as there was in a medieval court. But still! To now flood the inbox with praise just when they found out he was dead made the bile rise at the back of her throat. Why had she wanted a career in this? Why did she want to network with these people?

Something in her chided her anger. Why was she angry at them? It was hypocritical but had she not done the same before? When Yvette died, Val had done the minimum. A sympathy message sent to her widow. Attending the funeral via video link. Platitudes stated. She didn't care about Yvette. In truth, she had forgotten her name a few times and didn't really get to know her. Val supposed that Yvette's widow would have been just as disgusted to see her cliché phrases when she had not spoken to her after she left the Eye.

She took a breath in as the funeral started, adrenaline causing her hands to shake. She could see many were attending. Holograms, hundreds of faces, filled the observatory, half-melding with each other, turning entirely alien. It had been so long since Val had seen so many people. She muttered out a greeting to the guests before starting to talk. Her voice was shaking and croaky.

She started talking about his career, his personal life, bits that didn't seem too defamatory at least. Her knowledge kept spilling out, unstopping. She felt like she had barely taken a breath as the deluge poured out of her. Her fanatic dedication to learning every meaningless piece of trivia about George was, at last, useful.

She kept her focus on a star in the distance, unable to really look at anyone. Time ticked on. She kept going and going. Eventually, she had to stop, the sound of her voice starting to grate on her nerves. She threw in some cliché phrases about life after death and memory. She knew everyone in that room didn't believe them and likely thought they were bland and cheesy too…but at the same time, they were expected, were they not? Sugar pills.

She started playing some old music she knew George had liked and which seemed thematically appropriate. She sat down, feeling quite ill. She wanted this to be over as soon as possible. She was never the best at speeches. A hand touched her shoulder. Hermes, impassive as ever but they were more comforting than any of the holographic ghosts of humans around her. She took a deep breath before standing up. The music stopped. She dared not stare at the faces again. Instead, she looked at Hermes who had walked over to George's coffin. The robot picked it up with ease before walking over to the airlock and gently pushing the casket inside.

"And now…" she said, struggling to find the words. "Now we watch George…take the last step for his eternal journey." She wasn't sure that made sense, but it sounded formal and vaguely spiritual enough. Hermes pressed some buttons on the airlock, and the holograms moved as one to watch the process.

A low computerized voice simply stated, "Air lock release in thirty seconds…"

A countdown. Valeria forgot there was a countdown. It hadn't been used in such a long time.

Twenty seconds.

Is that all the time she had left in this liminal zone between her life here and a life elsewhere?

Ten seconds.

Why was she being selfish? Why was she just thinking about herself when George had just died! The closest person she had loved, even if it wasn't really love in the traditional sense. He certainly didn't love her, and she didn't really know him. Not really.

There was a loud pop of pressure as she saw his casket pushed into space, leaving the weak orbit of the planet. It felt surreal to see a rectangle just floating in space, most decidedly not meant to be there. She found her hand waving to it before turning back to the still-watching audience. She quickly thanked them for their time and said that George had requested them to donate to a xenobiological disease charity that he had been a patron of before his fall.

Most people left at this point, having seen the money shot of George's farewell. Some hung around, looking to give personal condolences. She vaguely knew some of the faces and gave them all a fixed smile in response to their cliché words. This lasted for far too long until there was only one left—someone she did not recognize. The badge on their coat made it clear who they were there on behalf of the ISA. The figure was young, soft-featured.

"I can only apologize for the timing. Would you...prefer if I return later? I am here on...official business," the hesitant, apologetic voice stated. "I am Alex Greenwood, personal assistant to the director of this quadrant's chapter of the ISA."

"Valeria Diaz," she said. "I think I can listen, if it's quick. It's...been a long few days." She collapsed into the leather chair. Her workstation was covered in missed alerts for work she hadn't completed. "How can I help?" Alex's hologram sat on her desk; arms folded. It was strange to see them attempt to sit since they phased partially through it.

"It's about the Eye. Obviously since George has...well, since he's..."

"Dead." She said bluntly. The harshness of the response seemed to take them aback, color flushing into their cheeks.

"Erm...yes," Alex said, trying hard to look at everywhere else except Val's eyes. "Well, since he has passed on, as it were, we would be looking to know what your intentions about the Eye are?" Alex picked up some papers, shuffling them.

Val could swear that they were trying to hide their face. Were they embarrassed?

"Of course, if this is a bad time you can just say, and I can come back at a later date?"

Val stared at them. They seemed young, inexperienced and clearly would rather be having any conversation in the universe except this one. She felt a mixture of irritation and pity. "Might as well get it over with, even if the funeral has literally just ended." Val had felt a surge of satisfaction at the barb which almost immediately collapsed under its own weight after seeing the expression on Alex's face. "I've been planning to sell it to you lot anyway. The Eye is a good radio telescope array, which is very useful for monitoring space out here. It's pretty isolated, and we are on the fringe of explored space so would be a useful asset for you," she said, pulling at a thread on the chair. She felt oddly cold. She needed a drink, she decided.

She watched Alex scribble the information down on their computer. "So, will you be continuing to man the project?" Alex asked. Val let out a short bark of a laugh, startling them again.

"No, I want to leave. I'm happy to tutor from off-planet and even visit on occasion, but I think twenty-four years in the same handful of rooms is enough," she said, a bitterness infecting her words. "I can even drop off a handover as well as landing protocols, passwords, and the like at an ISA office to make it officially yours."

Something churned in her stomach. This felt like a betrayal. His corpse had barely left orbit, and she was selling off his biggest work. She sighed—what choice did she have? Continue to waste away in this observatory out of loyalty? She wanted to try new things, and he left it with her. She was allowed do what she liked with it, wasn't she? She was getting tired, and she wanted to do something else with her life. She wanted to walk a different corridor, speak to people, try something new. She wondered vaguely if George would begrudge her moving on.

She realized she hadn't said anything in a while. Alex looked at her, concern radiating. "Well, we would be happy to accept. Do you need a ship to collect you, or...? We would want to get this done legally first and give you a...well, a cooling-off period in case you change your mind." They smiled in a strange, parental way despite clearly being a decade or so younger than her.

Maybe they felt that she was acting was weird, Val thought.

"No, we still have our small ship," she said softly, more for Alex's sake than any true reflection of her internal state. "It will take around three, four months to reach the closest colony. I think that should be plenty of cooling-off time." She straightened up in her chair. There were enough rations to take, and it wasn't as if she had many possessions that hadn't been broken or battered through wear and tear. She could make a quick stop there and keep going on to home. The thought of home felt strange to her, almost frightening. Alex nodded, smiling again pleasantly. "I should be able to pack up everything for tomorrow and I can also…"

Alex tilted their head, watching her with concern as if they half-expected her to start loudly crying or cursing.

"I have a few discoveries that may be of interest," she said, running a hand through her hair. "A few planets and such. I could send these across, or I can keep hold of them until I land in Huntail."

Alex nodded, noting this down as well. "It would be prudent to keep hold of those so we can discuss everything at once, I think. So that you are fully sure that is what you want to do. Emotions…can cloud things," Alex said softly, brown hair falling into their eyes.

They stood up, seemingly relieved that they could finally get out of this awkward situation and run back to their line manager. "If that's everything, I will organize a meeting at Huntail. Naturally, if there are any delays, I will be happy to rearrange." Alex gave a small smile, trying to reach through to Val to pat her on the shoulder. The hologram phased through her, but the gesture was clear. "Be seeing you…and I'm so sorry for your loss."

The feed cut and silence filled the observatory once more. Val looked out the dome, with her reflection staring back and George's coffin looming in the distance, unnaturally floating. Val studied her reflection— her eyes were puffy, bloodshot. She felt she had aged more in the past few days than she had in the past few years. She looked around, trying to think about what to do now. She could start packing and get ahead before the day cycle started, or she could take a leisurely pace. A few days now would hardly make much of a difference in comparison to the few months it would take to get to the Huntail colony.

She started making herself some food, suddenly ravenous. Hermes sat down across from her as she began to eat, not speaking. She wondered what exactly Hermes would do now. The robot was at as much of a loose end as she was. She didn't say anything as she ate, but Hermes's stare became increasingly unbearable.

"What do you want?" she eventually snapped. Hermes didn't flinch at this outburst.

"You are upset," Hermes stated flatly. "Would you like to discuss this matter further? I understand that bereavement can be difficult on the emotional and physical well-being of humans."

Val wasn't sure what to say in response to this. How could Hermes possibly understand how she felt right now? Hermes couldn't feel anything. She left the table without saying a word further. No footsteps followed her as she disappeared into the dormitory.

The next few days felt bizarrely empty like the observatory had changed into a waiting room. Somewhere that had been essentially her home had turned cold and sterile, suddenly unfamiliar, and infused with the sense of impatience. Valeria had started to do something, anything— packing her bags, watching something on the stream, reading—and her concentration would fall away. Slowly, she got ready to leave, moving the rations, her clothes, her books, and the few knick-knacks she had accumulated over her time there into the ship.

The evacuation ship wasn't huge, merely a small carrier that could cart four people from colony to colony. She had driven it the last three times she had escorted her colleagues off the Eye and back to the normal world, so she was familiar with the drive system. She wasn't exactly relishing the thought of so much travel, but it was time now. She could no longer avoid it, and if she couldn't cope, she could always come back.

She vaguely thought about how this place would look under ISA control. They would likely add an element of corporate-approved human touches—possibly doing some form of partial terraforming. They would likely need to replace some hardware and would absolutely upgrade all the software. A makeover, some new plumbing, and the place would barely be recognizable. It felt strange walking around, knowing that her time was nearing the end. In between bouts of emptiness that seemed to consume hours, she eventually had to go through George's things.

She had started to do this several times, each time she left quickly, tears stinging in her eyes. Eventually, she took Hermes in for support, and they went through his things. In the end, he didn't have a lot of possessions beyond medical equipment: books he had written, copies of his documentaries, a few half-written diaries with pages ripped out, his clothes, some trinkets like a wedding ring, a very battered pocket watch, the Orion constellation pin that Val remembered from years before. Much of this she tossed out, but she kept some for herself. Val had given Hermes the pocket watch, which they did not understand at first, but they relented at Val's insistence.

After several days of stopping and starting, everything was packed. There were no excuses now not to move on, not to get going. It would be a long enough journey as it was without stretching it out even further. She sat in her old chair, staring back out at the stars. She took a tissue out and blew her nose, finding the weight hitting her again. The misery visited her in floods. She knew it was for the better. George was no longer suffering, and she had been sleepwalking through the work here for years. She could do so much more off this planet and do more for George's legacy by handing the reigns over to an organization that could deal with it better. Even so, it was hard to ameliorate the feelings into a consistent emotion.

She stepped into the ship and was about to start the launch when she realized Hermes was not on board. She stepped back out, heading back into the observatory. Hermes was at the table, waiting.

"What are you doing?" Val asked. Hermes looked up; the watch was pinned to their chest cavity. The robot tilted their head.

"I am waiting for the next crew to arrive so I can facilitate any medical attention they may have."

"Hermes, come on. They'll have their own care-bot. You're better off coming with me," she said, exasperated. Hermes looked around the station.

"I have never left this place, and I understand different humans will be coming here. I should stay here; I can help," Hermes reasoned.

Val grabbed their cold hand, sighing. "Hermes. Humans don't like to be alone. Please…come with me," she pleaded. Hermes might not be much in terms of company, but still better than being alone. Hermes made her feel better, even if she didn't have a particular reason to feel bad or good in the first place.

Hermes paused for a moment before standing up, following her to the ship. Perhaps it was Val being silly, treating Hermes like a person, but she didn't especially care anymore.

She strapped the android into the passenger seat before starting the engines up. Her heart thumped loud in her chest as the hatch opened and the ship's engines revved. She flipped a switch before the ship flew into space. The Eye and the casket disappeared into the distance.

"So, Hermes…" she said, her eyes unflinching from the path ahead. "Tell me something interesting."

Hermes looked over, nodding. "Of course. Did you know that today is the birthday of Austrian composer Gustav Mahler, English drummer Ringo Starr, and Tan Ngo, the discoverer of the vaccine for Triton Flu?"

Valeria smiled, nodding. Same old Hermes.

The Exhibition

By M. June

<u>*Date: 4417*</u>

Humans have always been fond of naming things. All known things in space have at least one name, usually a combination of letters and numbers, and trust me, by the year 4417 the list is long.

[Please click on the link on the right of your vision field for more in-depth information about the naming of planets.]

For some, however, there is more than just a string of letters and numbers; these are the planets that have earned a proper name.

We have the colonized planets, of course, and those for which colonization has remained at the attempt stage or gone no farther than planning before the reality of their climate or of their geological structure quelled human ambition.

Some of the brighter and most interesting stars have names too, as do some comets.

Despite the endless discoveries that now populate the skies of hundreds of inhabited worlds, mankind has never ceased naming them. For the first settlers, it was a way to both own the planet, and to feel that they themselves belonged to the soil their spaceships landed on.

A string of random letters and numbers does not feel like home, so they made up their own names.

Later, when governments and corporations decided to dedicate entire planets to war, holiday, entertainment, or any other sort of business, these were given names as well. HO-7125-345, in the Ho-shita78 star system, is one of these.

Or it should have been.

The initial plan was to turn it into a holiday resort. Due to a lucky combination of the thick, gassy atmosphere and a large belt of cosmic dust, nights on HO-7125-345 are a feast of sparks and blinding colors, closely resembling ancient fireworks.

[Please click on the link on the right of your vision field for more in-depth information about HO-7125-345's surface and atmosphere.]

I'm going to spoil it for you right now: yes, we will see it toward the end of this exhibition. And I can tell you, it is something you will want to see for yourself.

You will regret, too, that things on this planet did not go as planned.

Indeed, as soon as it was discovered, this planet was to be terraformed. The Eden's placement was swiftly followed by the blossoming of the necessary facilities—lodging, food, entertainment, and culture.

Too much greed and a decision to ignore the experts' suggestions for caution, simple miscalculations, or something unexpected? Whatever the cause, the Eden was never going to accomplish its mission. It failed drastically, and HO-7125-345 was never terraformed.

However, investments had been made, losses had to be recovered, and some of the facilities were opened anyway. Clients were brought in from the rest of the galaxy. To me, there is a certain appeal in a wild, inhospitable planet, and the show in the sky is no less beautiful seen through a big, transparent dome.

But it seems most don't share my opinion, and people soon lost interest in HO-7125-345. It is a sad thing for the planet, surely, but it is also the reason why I won't have to keep spelling out the long string of letters and numbers anymore. Indeed, a history of abandoned facilities and the legacy of a cult that brought back mummification to this system have earned the planet the endearing nickname of Ho-Mummy.

[Please click on the link on the right of your vision field for more in-depth information about the cult that brought mummification back in the Ho-shita78 system.]

If you think this nickname is captivating, you will be excited to know that the museum I will take you through in this exhibition is the Mummy Mankind Museum, or Mu-MaMu.

So you see, failed terraforming might not be the sole reason the museum has lost its visitors. But perhaps, at the end of this exhibition, you might even want to visit.

***

Màgia enters the Mummy Mankind Museum from a secondary door. The main entrance hall, a vast space designed to welcome the hordes of visitors as soon as they land at the nearby tourist spaceport, is closed and sealed. Opening the gates requires a massive quantity of energy, which the museum cannot spare for one single guest.

To Màgia, it doesn't make any difference. The entrance hall is merely a place of formalities: tickets, visa controls, health checks, and the like. Those are the same everywhere, and nobody cares about seeing them in an exhibition. Besides, without the crowd of guests and staff, the place is nothing more than a barren collection of metallic surfaces and blank walls.

He is led through the door that is used by the keeper. It doesn't take long before he decides to turn off his tactile and olfactory recorders. The air is cool, still, stale. It smells like air purifiers and mechanical fans. Once again, nothing one would care to experience in an exhibition.

***

"I don't feel lonely here, really." The woman on camera smiles. Lines at the sides of her mouth appear and stretch. In the scant light of the scene, her pale skin mirrors the pasty yellow coloring the walls in the keeper's private rooms.

"I knew the kind of place Mummy was when I applied for the job. Of course, I had to pass a psychological test in addition to the interview. They needed to know whether I could manage the museum alone. It isn't just about supervising the AIs and machines. It's about being substantially alone on an empty planet."

She pauses, the lines now smooth, her brown eyes focusing somewhere beyond the cameras. The camera zooms in on the wrinkles that outline her eyes—less deep now, yet still clearly visible on her clean skin.

"Humans might be social in nature but being alone is part of us as well."

***

"The zoo pavilion is a blast!" Màgia gestures widely with his arms, hands darting from his chest to the air above his head. "So many animals all together. And alive, nonetheless! It must cost a fortune to have it maintained."

Celi nods, keeping some distance from Màgia, as much as the narrow corridor they are walking through allows. She might not suffer from loneliness, but for someone used to spending most, if not all, of her time alone, it takes a while to get accustomed to too-loud company.

"Originally they wanted it to be a research center as well as a zoo. They would have scores of experts work here the whole time. The animals in the zoo would have to be kept healthy and in good condition to reproduce." Celi's tone is matter-of-fact. "People were supposed to come from the furthest corners of the galaxy to take a tour here."

"I had never seen a live goat before." Apparently, Màgia just cannot keep his hands in check. "The stench was appalling."

Celi steps clear of Màgia's left hand, whirling madly a bit too close to her face. "People were expected to pay a fortune in tickets to smell that stench up close, to savor the stink that has accompanied mankind for some fourteen thousand years."

"Also, the small, buzzing drones—"

"The flies, you mean?"

"Neat name." Màgia rubs his pointy chin with his implant-covered fingertips. "First time I've seen them."

Celi nods again. "I don't think they're anywhere else in this system. Or anywhere in most of the other outer systems either. Although I think that, given the chance to step on a starship, they'd become a common occurrence anywhere they went."

They walk on through the Mu-MaMu's empty corridors, surrounded by the double echo of their steps that, to Celi, feels still like too much noise.

***

"Besides, I can't say I'm ever really alone," the keeper says, nodding toward something behind her. "For one, I have them and all the other animals in the facility to keep me company."

The image shifts to the wall behind Celi, to a big cage where two green parrots perch, one of them smoothing its plumage, the second curiously tilting its head toward the talking woman.

[To learn more about these two fowl, please follow the link on the right of your vision field.]

"And when I walk through the corridors and the halls, I feel the presence of all the people from the past who created the objects that are collected in our museum. Generations upon generations of humans, all summed up in a few utensils and garments."

The cameras rotate to capture Celi's eyes, shining bright as she speaks. Even without makeup highlighting her eyelids and eyebrows to enhance her expression, the passion she feels pours out. "These things of all sorts they left behind, they keep me company now. I truly am not alone here."

***

Celi sips from her cup, which is white with the museum's logo, Mu-MaMu, in round brown, balloon-like letters. "They sent me these a few years ago, as part of the samples of the museum's new merchandise. I don't think they made the best choice, color-wise." Celi's eyes dart to Màgia's face. "You aren't recording right now, are you?"

Màgia shakes his head. "Don't worry. As a rule, the red light is always on when recording." His finger points up to his head, which is ringed by the recording implant that covers the upper half of Màgia's face. With no lights on, the implant looks like it's turned off, but Celi knows it isn't.

Two mobile cameras stemming from the implant are focused on her face now, then follow the cup when she puts it down. The cameras are Màgia's eyes.

There are four of them, smooth and white, with thin metal eyelids, swiftly and silently shifting around his head like the tentacles of an octopus. Or like a bug's antennas. With these, Màgia can film everything around, under, and over him at the same time. The implant has tendrils slithering through his skull to his brain and down his nose and tongue, while his own organic nervous system provides the link between the sensors on his fingertips and the recording center in his head—a filmmaker's full equipment.

Celi has experienced only a few all-inclusive exhibitions before, and she has never seen one made. The technology is not the most recent out there, but the Ho-shita78 system is one of the furthest from the biggest trade routes in the galaxy, and novelties are slow to reach here, just like tourists. Why the people who decided to make Ho-Mummy a holiday resort thought it would be a good idea often escapes Celi's understanding.

"Do I get to see a preview of the exhibition before you leave?"

"It probably won't be finished, but I will definitely review the main content with you."

"Will my basic sensory input socket be enough to experience it? I haven't updated it in a while."

"As long as you have good visual and hearing inputs, it will be fine. There won't be much in terms of olfaction and tactile inputs in this one, I'm afraid." Màgia shakes his head slightly. "With the exception of the zoo pavilion, Mu-MaMu smells the same."

"So you'll keep the bit where you pet and smell the goats?"

Màgia chuckles and nods. Celi smiles in return.

"I really hope your exhibition will encourage tourists and cultural operators to reconsider this place, so it can be reopened to the public," she says. "And so I can sell these cups and never see them again. Besides, if the museum doesn't get back in business soon, we'll have to dismantle the whole zoo."

Màgia nods. No more goats, no more stench. "It's my job to make it so."

Màgia's voice and smile are warm, but there is something about being unable to see his eyes that fails to deliver the warmth to Celi.

***

Celi is rubbing a goat's head between the horns, and softly talks to it, forgetting to look at the camera.

"The founders of the museum wanted this to be a place where humans in this galaxy could experience a tiny bit of ancient Earth, a tiny bit of what it meant to be a primitive human there. Will we ever be able to truly understand what it felt like being human thousands of years ago? Has too much changed for us or are we still fundamentally the same?"

Celi looks at the cameras, then up to the dome's ceiling. The sky above is a kaleidoscope of sparks and colors on a background of black and purple.

"When humans first stepped away from their home Earth, they feared and hoped they would meet someone else out there. But it turned out there might not be anyone else, after all. Mankind is all we've got."

The goat shakes its head and Celi steps away.

"Sometimes, however, I think that if a human from the past looked at us, she wouldn't even recognize us. We might have become our own aliens."

***

Lying down on her bed with a heavy black mask covering her face, Celi opens the sensory input plug at the base of her neck and allows Màgia's data to fill her brain.

Vision sparks alive again, and she finds herself in the first room of the museum, the one with the huge, interactive hologram about human evolution. She moves to touch it and the hologram responds, even if there is no hand in sight. The writings fill her visual field, the recorded voice pours into her ears. She moves from room to room like a ghost, able to see the floor beneath her and the ceiling above at the same time, a thick ball of awareness in the empty rooms of Mu-MaMu.

"It feels like I'm dreaming." She lifts her imaginary finger to touch one of the display windows but feels nothing. Perhaps she might get an upgraded sensory input socket after all, even though she can touch the museum's cold surfaces with her own fingertip any time she wants. "Like I'm watching through someone else's eyes."

Màgia is sitting nearby. "You can say you're dreaming my experience or experiencing my dream. Put it as you prefer."

"It sounds too intimate," she teases.

"It's just a poetic way to say it. Don't worry, I don't dream anymore."

"You don't?"

"I used to, before the implant. It's been quite some time now that I think of it. It's a side effect of the surgery," he explains in a matter-of-fact tone.

"Do you miss it?"

"Oh, not really. In fact, it's a lot more practical now. I can program my own dreams—if you can call them that—when I go to sleep. It's all about mixing my own sensory records with any other content I want."

Celi looks around the room containing the small-scale reproduction of the first Eden ever created. "You get to choose what to experience when sleeping? That sounds convenient."

"It is."

Most of the time, however, Màgia chooses void and silence.

***

"What makes this museum unique in this part of the galaxy is that the items shown here are original," Celi explains. She is wearing a light brown cap on her smooth head, with the huge Mu-MaMu logo on it.

"Of course, we do have holos of all kinds and smaller-scale replicas, but we pride ourselves in owning a few original pieces. We are the only museum with such a high number of them in the galaxy's outer systems."

Celi glides through the corridors, her straight shape catching the light coming from the display windows. She veers around a hologram of the Earth's solar system, the lights of its star and planets reflecting on the folds of her soft, dull gray clothes.

"We are about to see some artifacts dating back to the Milky Way colonization period. For example, here we have samples of the materials and tools used on Mars before the terraforming of the planet began. Five of these were kitchen utensils, three personal hygiene items, a comb, and eight sections of the console governing the habitation module humans lived in before Mars was actually inhabitable. I can explain each of them to you, if you wish."

[The display case contains seventeen items. You can access Celi's explanation for each of them by following the link in the yellow number that marks each item. Begin with the first one, PLASTIC FORK.]

***

Overall, Mu-MaMu is a dark place.

It sprawls like a dormant insect on the barren soil of the planet: the zoo pavilion as its big, swollen head, with its torso and legs pitch black. The head is the only part of it that lights up at regular intervals, to mimic daylight for the plants and animals living in the pavilion.

Originally, it was meant to be always a feast of colors, a welcoming sight for the tourists, tired from their travels, a promise of fun and wonders.

Now, energy must be saved for the essential systems—air circulation, water, heating—and it would be an overall waste to light up the whole museum for the lonely keeper roaming its corridors.

It is lit up for Màgia and for his exhibition in progress, though, because why would anyone decide to visit a museum on a forgotten planet if it were dark as well as cold and stinking of goats? The goats do consume a lot of energy, with their green fields and water recycling system and AIs taking care of them.

Despite the honor, Màgia finds himself roaming the corridors after the main light sources have been turned off, when he should be on break, resting. The display windows glow softly, and his polished fingers glow back as he traces the profile of the transparent cases containing the Mu-MaMu treasures. Perhaps he can add it as extra content.

He stops in front of a cylindrical case that goes up to the ceiling, outlined by a misty, yellow-gray shimmer. Màgia appreciates the aesthetics, but the case looks oversized for the small item floating inside it.

The thing is all curves and lines, dark hollows and grayish protuberances, a complex architecture of empty spaces framed by arches, triangles, and wandering shapes, with smooth extremities.

Màgia knows what a human skeleton looks like. Human anatomy is part of basic cultural education, of course. And they explained to him a lot about his own anatomy, too, before giving him his implants. The small screen that follows him as he moves around the item eagerly tells him that the skeleton dates to some four thousand years earlier, give or take a few centuries. It belonged to a woman who died at forty-four years of age, name unknown.

He has to bend down a little to look at the skeleton's face, into its mouth. The collection of small trapezoid shapes inside fascinates him.

His tongue smooths over his bare gums.

Just like hair and nails, teeth look so feral, so primordial, so inconvenient. So alien.

***

[You have selected: PLASTIC FORK.]

The plastic appears yellowish. The four thin protuberances on the top of the fork bend slightly under Celi's fingers, as her soothing voice provides an explanation for the device.

"Can you imagine that once all humans had teeth, like this fork does? Well, we don't anymore, and good riddance! They surely had a rough time back then, when lyophilized food was just an extravagance meant for space travelers, and they had to chew their way through all their meals.

"At that time, many kinds of food were consumed solid. Humans would use the fork to pierce the bigger pieces of food and keep them still while they would divide the food into smaller pieces with a knife. The small pieces were then pierced again with the fork and carried inside the mouth, to be broken into even smaller bits by the teeth. I get tired just thinking about it.

"As you can see, after many centuries the white plastic of this fork has turned yellow. Human teeth would endure a much worse fate and in a much shorter time. Like the idea of carrying around a bunch of rotting, sharp objects in your mouth? Neither did our ancestors. Removing them from our DNA was the logical conclusion."

***

Màgia is sitting with Celi at the kitchen table in her quarters. Her rooms are sized for more than one person and feel rather large with one inhabitant—or two, at least for the time being.

Large does not mean comfortable, though. All the furniture is the standard kind one would expect on a temporary base. Essential, anonymous, cheap. Màgia had seen the like when filming with a scientific expedition on one of the moons of a nearby planet. This museum, however, has been in place for a good number of decades, and although it has seldom been occupied by more than one person at a time, and not even continuously, time doesn't seem to have passed inside its walls.

Màgia can easily picture it: the same, unchanging air, stirred only by the breath of the ventilation system, the same, faint echo of a pair of heels tapping on the floor for decades. He wonders if the previous keepers had the parrots for company as well.

"The original plan, even after the terraforming failed, was to have local production of tea and dairy products, like milk and butter," Celi explains as she pours synthesized tea into their cups.

Màgia stirs the liquid to cool it down. The brown logo seems to leak bad taste into the water.

"Why the cups, though?"

The implants in his head and neurological system are needed for his work, but oh, do they come in handy when all you need to do to ignore a nasty flavor is to tune out the sensors on your tongue and nose.

"They're souvenirs," she answers. "It was an ancient custom in museums—cups, pins, garments of different kinds. Hoarding them as proof of having visited a place was part of the experience."

***

The two white goats chew methodically as they stare into the cameras, as if they were looking at Celi talking about them.

"These two specimens, just like all the others kept here, are the direct descendants of the animals that were brought here from the Milky Way when the colonization of this galaxy began."

The acrid smell fills the olfactory receptors, but it is soon replaced by a mix of herbal scents. The continuous buzz of the gigantic fans in the distance is the background to the silence of the pavilion, only interrupted by the animals' bleating and the occasional fly speeding close by.

"The stock the first colonizers brought was reduced as it spread throughout the galaxy. Today, the AIs monitor the breeding of our stock with the greatest attention. When needed, the DNA of a newborn can be modified to keep the lineage diversified and healthy."

***

The zoo pavilion is large, so they take a small transport through it, following a rail that slaloms among small grassy hills. They pass by a group of gardener drones busy rummaging through the soil, next to a growing pile of dirt and uprooted grass.

"It might be surprising, but the most difficult work isn't taking care of the animals," Celi's eyes follow the drones as they become tinier in the distance. "They mostly take care of themselves. It's the flora that needs constant supervision. We don't have pollinators here, and an artificial pollination system was too expensive for the museum, so they keep cloning the same seeds over and over again, planting them as soon as an area goes dry."

Màgia takes in the entire landscape. He can see where the dome touches earth, but it is far away. The pavilion is big, and he doesn't envy the drones doing the work.

"Perhaps things could change if the museum went back into activity," Celi's voice softens. "We could have more species. Maybe import live pollinators from some other planet. We might start growing real biodiversity."

"Then it would truly feel like a piece of Earth."

She nods. "It would be nice to have some more company here, for a change. Even if it were just, I don't know, the bees."

***

[You have selected PLASTIC COMB.]

Celi's voice recites discreetly as the comb is turned around between fingers, plastic teeth pricking skin, fingertips testing the object's sharpness.

"As we all know, in our galaxy humans are hairless, with the exception of a few groups or individuals who still choose to grow hair for cultural or cosmetic reasons. Not growing body hair has proven a winning choice for both hygiene and resources. The genes that regulate hair growth have been made dormant, while in the last few centuries, an increasingly large number of humans have lost the genes responsible for its growth.

"However, until a few centuries ago, the vast majority of humans had body hair, notably on their heads. Hair needed to be kept tidy and free of knots or pests, and to be styled for practical or aesthetic reasons.

"Combs have accompanied mankind since prehistory, and through the millennia, they have come in all shapes and materials."

[Please click on the top link on the right of your vision field for more in-depth information about the earliest known examples of combs.]

"Of course, combs continued to accompany mankind as it moved from Earth to the nearby planets and then further out to the surrounding systems.

"A comb is the simplest and most basic of the many tools humans used to keep their hair tidy. Today, we know about the purpose of many of these tools thanks to the traditions which have been kept alive by the human groups who still grow body hair."

[Please click on the arrow on the right of your vision field to stream samples of the short documentary "Hairstyles Through Galaxies and Star Systems." Download the documentary in full inside Mu-MaMu.]

***

Màgia has departed. Celi has walked through the halls and corridors of the museum more than once to make sure he has not left anything behind, to make sure he has gone for real. The echoless sound of her steps is evidence enough.

He did not spend a long time in the Mu-MaMu, and now that he has left, it almost feels like he was never there at all. The cups he used for eating and drinking, the sheets and towels—all is now clean and tidy again.

Celi's walks through the museum take her often to the skeleton. The description says it has no name, but Celi calls her Anna.

"Will we have company again, you think?" Celi asks her. "If Màgia does a good job with his exhibition, we shall."

Anna is taller than Celi, her hips larger, her skull smaller. Of course, there is a part of Màgia's exhibition that is dedicated to her. Celi wonders what the audience will think of her. Will they find her weird, feral, with those teeth as flat as a goat's?

"If he has any success, in the end we might even start to wish we were alone again," Celi jokes.

However, the real question she always asks herself is: What would Anna think of Celi if she saw her now, with her bald, round head, tiny body, and empty mouth?

When she does not need to take care of the museum, Celi sleeps and she dreams.

She finds herself sitting on the grass of a field. It's much wider than the Mu-MaMu's zoo pavilion, and there are hills in the distant horizon instead of the artificial dome.

There's warmth on the upper part of her body and skin, and when she looks up, she doesn't see the thick, smoky sky of HO-7125-345, but only one large, bright sun, proudly emerging from blue.

She raises her hand to shield her eyes from the strong light, and her fingers tangle in her hair, soft curls falling all over her face and nose.

Her hand comes to rest on her hip. There's something small and hairy fiercely vibrating under her fingertip. She removes her hand, and a little insect takes flight, a blur of wings in black and yellow.

Celi watches as it buzzes away, fading into the whisper of the breeze, behind the distant bleating of the goats. No stench here, only the sweet perfume of grass and hay under the heavy, summer sun.

There's no surprise when she turns around and discovers someone is sitting beside her, blocking the view of the distant hills. Dark tendrils of hair, glowing gold in the sunlight, hide and reveal a face as they flutter around it, stirred by the breeze. A veil of white fabric outlines the round shape of her body, hem fluttering as she comes toward Celi.

The sun shines behind the woman and her face is all shadows, but Celi does not need to see it to know her. Celi has never seen her face and does not dare to imagine it—how would flesh and skin take shape on the edges of the skull she knows so well? Between her fleshy lips, her teeth flash as white as her dress.

Celi feels her take her hand and squeeze it. She has strong, warm fingers, and for a short moment, her hold feels almost painful.

Then her dress and hair and smile are gone, just like it happens in dreams, and there's only green grass, hills, the sun shining, and the goats bleating.

***

Red dust swirls and flashes in the darkness, shadowing and highlighting in turn the flashes of light. It looks like a dance of stars, with tiny bursts of gases blocking out the sky beyond, cutting Ho-Mummy out from the rest of the universe.

But you will not miss boring space and its slow-moving bodies, not after all the time you've spent traveling through it to get here.

It's a feast of yellow, red, purple, and orange. Ho-Mummy is just so happy to see you cross its festive atmosphere. Or at least it will be, if by the end of this exhibition you decide to come here and meet its inhabitants.

Just make sure to cover your nose. You have already experienced the goats once and might not want to do so again.

Timeline of the Persolus Race Universe

2029: The human race lands on Mars for the first time, by a group of Russian scientists.

2030 to 2034: International tensions stemming from a number of problems, including ownership of areas of land on the Earth's moon and Mars. The rate of carbon emissions increases due to an avid technological race (Space Race 2), leading to climate change becoming even more noticeable across the globe.

2036: The first Edens are created by European scientists to mitigate the effects of climate change. They are a success, and other nations begin to develop their own, which begin to cool the planet, relieving some of the international tensions.

2040: The Integrated Space Agency is created, following the 45th UN Climate Change Conference. After the successful implementation of the Edens to mitigate the climate crisis, they are then used as prototype terraforming technology.

2048: Terraforming of the Moon begins, as the first planetary terraforming project.

2065: Terraforming of the Moon is completed after 17 years.

2079: Terraforming of Mars begins.

2090: Terraforming of Mars is completed after 11 years.

2152: The first light speed engine is created. This allows the human race to start traveling beyond its own solar system.

2226: The Edens are set up for commercial use, becoming the property of the ISA, and sent throughout the galaxy for terraforming purposes.

2450: *The Man in the Mountain* – A young scientist called Adam Rehange at New Aberdeen University hopes to be at the forefront of the breakthrough of a functioning time travel machine. However, Rehange's compulsiveness and ambition may lead to him biting off a little more than he can chew when testing out a prototype time machine.

2550: *The Snake in Eden* – Scout and her team of eco-terrorists are on the trail of a big conspiracy theory. Most think the ISA are beyond reproach, but if there is smoke there is normally fire. What they discover will rock Scout's world and an easy mission turns into a run for her life! It's not how will she stay safe; it's how will she stay alive for the next twenty-four hours?

2599/2600: Most of the Milky Way is explored, tens of planets have been effectively terraformed, and many more are in development. The ISA begins to divvy up into smaller subfactions, in order to conquer different sections of the galaxy. Around this time a Second Dark Age begins, as the human race spreads amongst the stars. Not much knowledge is gained, and societal systems do not advance much in this time.

2623: *Oisettio* – Hybrid genetic experiments have created the Skreeks. Half-man, half-animal, they are abhorred and avoided at all costs. A trench of a divide is opening up between the citizens of Urayso, and The Univi Forces are ruling with a totalitarian fist. Forbes, a local Skreek guy, has a plan to make it to the top of this conflicted pile. Little does he know, there is more at stake than his overblown psyche. One minute he is a typical hooligan, the next he's in a modified pod-car zooming off to "Krem knows where," with a beautiful girl pointing a gun to his head. Will he see that there's more to life than drinking liquor and shooting Pleebs? Will he pick the right side to fight for? Or will he become the exact thing he was fighting against in the first place?

2642-2829: *Chronicles of the Fallen Colony* – A damaged Eden at the edge of human exploration. A rescue ship's desperate attempts to fix the Eden before the colony freezes over. With the rest of humanity in turmoil across settled space, there's no one else coming to save the Fallen Colony. Rebellion against the Eden's engineers takes hold and an insane AI becomes involved, for good and ill.

2701: *Starsong* – Em is right at home living on the backwater planet of Mars. She waits for her first child to be born while studying the terraforming plants and sending data back to the Eden scientists. There's never much to report, until one day she has a very personal encounter with a mutated species. Now she's in a race for time against the mutations in her body, desperately seeking a cure while watching the parasitic vines creep toward her unborn child.

2850: *Thadeus* – Thadeus, a young and disgruntled prince from Ketwo, is enjoying the freedom of his own ship when he is pulled back to his old home. A dark mystery is hiding in a labyrinthine asteroid belt. Starships are disappearing at an alarming rate and rumors of an alien menace are circulating. Can Thadeus unravel the mystery and make the greatest discovery of humanity? Or will he be its next victim?

2890: *The Seeker* – The ISA has fractured, and humanity is in chaos as warring factions threaten to tear apart everything they've achieved. On a forgotten planet in a far-flung system, Kenji Izuya makes a discovery that could change everything: a singular piece of technology that could restore peace. Or destroy it forever. In these turbulent times, Kenji comes to understand something, one of the universe's great truths. The road to peace is paved with blood and sacrifice.

2899: *Empire Reborn* – By all accounts, Calvin Thellhorn is a great man. A decorated veteran, a diplomat, a hero. None of it matters if he fails to unify humanity under the reestablished ISA. Luckily, all Calvin has to do is live up to an impossible reputation and convince three trillion people to follow him.

2900: The human race begins to pull out of the Second Dark Age, as the ISA builds a central empire based on Earth, and working outward, introduces communication and transport systems between different planetary systems and factions.

2949: The first successful hyperspeed engine is created, allowing the human race to travel thousands of times the speed of light. This allows them to travel out of the Milky Way galaxy pretty quickly.

3250: *Undiscovered Nightmare* – At the source of a sign of sapient life, an ISA ground crew finds an unregistered human settlement, a damaged Eden, and a destroyed starship. What could have caused the inhabitants to just abandon their homes? The answer might just be more than they can handle.

3257: *Community Service* – After causing a horrendous accident, former police officer Hector is sent from the luxurious satellite station to the planet to perform community service. With the help of his trusty pilot, Lolaus, he explores a harsh and untamed planet and meets its equally wild inhabitants. As he completes his tasks, he struggles to bridge the gap between the wealthy elite living in orbit and the citizens living on the planet's surface.

3462: The human race starts to reach the nearest edge of the Virgo Supercluster. The ISA begins to settle humans on planets millions of light-years from Earth, with all appropriate planets within the Milky Way almost all terraformed.

3565 & 3572: *In the Gardens of Eden* – A tale of political intrigue and environmental disaster that follows the story of the Planet Salvon 4, where an Eden has catastrophically malfunctioned due to its caretakers' politics and gross negligence. Desperate to get off Salvon 4, mine transport engineer Taylor Cortes attempts to lead his family and friends to safety while the planet's climate turns upside down. Several years after the malfunction of the Eden, ISA Specialist Detective John Morris is sent to interview higher-ups who were responsible for overlooking the Eden's malfunction. Unfortunately, Morris's unconventional style and dark secrets create unexpected issues for him.

3600: The human race is now out amongst the stars, and "sub-species" of human have begun to develop through genetic experimentation.

3950: *The Mine* – Sara Littlefield and her small team of alien searchers receive a tip-off from an eccentric, old man in an abandoned mine. The man found an alien artifact buried in a moon in a star system near to the Solar System. Things don't work out the way they expect.

3800: *The Trip Home* – A man convicted of a crime comes home after a long trip through space in search of intelligent alien life forms.

3999: The ISA makes an announcement that the human race may be alone in the universe and that alien life might not exist.

4026: *The Placebo Effect* – Research scientist Valeria Diaz contemplates life and death, hope and despair, while watching for…anything at the edge of the universe.

4417: *The Exhibition* – On a planet where terraforming has failed, all that remains of its ambitious tourist project is the now-forgotten Museum of Mankind. Inside are preserved live specimens of things that are now a rarity in the galaxy, such as flies or goats. In order to save the museum from oblivion, Màgia, a documentary filmmaker, makes it the subject of his new exhibition.

Acknowledgements

Writing your first book, let alone an anthology (which is a collection of fictions rather than just one) is a long and tiring process. I just wanted to say a big thank you to certain people who have helped put this book together.

This includes copy editors Rachel Shipton and M. M. Dixon, without whom this whole endeavour would have been impossible as I certainly couldn't have done the copy editing myself. There edits, proofreads and advice throughout the project made this book happen and kept me to a high standard.

I also want to thank all the contributing authors; Jessica Milner, B. S. Waymire, Andrew P. McGregor, C C. Forshee, M. M. Dixon, M. June, Melina Munton, M. S. Landwaard, Josh Whittle, Steph Millar and L. E. Doggett. Thanks for putting your trust in me, and helping my idea become a reality. Your ideas and experience have made this book a far more interesting read than if I'd tried to just write fifteen stories myself.

Beta readers Lee Nickson, Ukchunna K., Susan Morem, Charlotte Ebner and Wendy Abbott for your feedback to help us trim and expand the stories where necessary.

Cover artist Simon Thorogood-Hill and supporting artworks artists Amasja Koolen and Gabe Attano for their stunning artwork created for the book.

And, lastly, to my mother and father for their support and encouragement throughout the project.

About the Contributors

Alex O'Neill (Acquisitions Editor)

Alex was born in 1997 on the coast of North Yorkshire, United Kingdom. He now lives in Gloucestershire and thought up the initial premise of this anthology over dinner. He is currently training to become a teacher and likes to write about the dangers of advanced human technology in his writing.

His favorite authors are Neil Gaiman, Stephen King, and George R.R. Martin. He loves Earl Grey tea and has never eaten Marmite. This is his first book, and he hopes you enjoy it very much.

Andrew P. McGregor

Andrew lives in Inverell, a small rural town near the eastern coast of Australia and works as an accountant. When not playing with his wife and kids, he obeys his fishy overlords and goes to war against the cat.

He writes science fiction and dark fantasy short stories, most of which are collected in *Tales of Starships & Apocalypse* and its upcoming sequels.

B.E. Waymire

B.E. Waymire is well traveled, over educated, and living in the southeastern United States. He holds a day job as a technician because the bills refuse to pay themselves, no matter how nicely he asks. Outside of that, he dabbles in various hobbies like gaming, flying, and historical European martial arts.

Most of his works are inspired by any storytelling media he encounters, particularly when he finds a theme he wishes had been explored better. His biggest literary influences are J.R.R. Tolkien, Robert Heinlein, and Timothy Zahn.

Chris Forshee

Wordslinger Christopher Forshee is a salty, one-eyed ambulance driver from Alabama (USA). The only thing he enjoys more than whiskey is writing fantasy and sci-fi. In addition to his *Persolus Race* contributions, he is the author of the monster hunter urban fantasy series, *The Pariahs*, and an upcoming dark fantasy trilogy, *Syphir's Eye*.

Josh Whittle

Josh Whittle is a baker from Port Lincoln, south Australia, where he lives with his wife and two kids. Josh enjoys writing fantasy and a little sci-fi when not spending time with family or practicing martial arts.

His favorite writers are Robert G. Barrett and Tony Park.

M.M. Dixon

M.M Dixon is a writer and editor living in northern Virginia, USA, with her husband, young son, and two dogs. She writes mostly sci-fi/fantasy, mostly as short stories, which she sometimes posts at mmdixonauthor.com. She spends any extra time enjoying other peoples' creations, hoping they will stretch her brain in new ways. Favorite authors include James S.A. Corey, Lois McMaster Bujold, Brandon Sanderson, and Melissa McPhail.

Steph Millar

Stephanie Millar is a queer writer and administrator living in the West of Scotland. She is fascinated by stories in all possible formats and mediums, writes regular poetry from the perspective of her D&D character, Kalshana, and is researching literary depictions of hell in her spare time. You can find her on Twitter @nicnevin3.

M. S. Landwaard

M. Landwaard lives in Schiedam, the Netherlands, in an old fishing village known for its jenever. He is an avid traveler and enthusiastic sport climber. His first steps into science fiction were made in his teens when he found old copies of the *Dune* series on his parents' bookshelves. He now reads everything he can find and suffers from a need to finish every book he starts. His inspirations include F. Herbert, I. Asimov, A. Dumas, and S. Lem.

Melina Munton

Melina Munton is from the mountains of California, USA. When she's not working as an aerospace engineer, fencing, or admiring weird bugs, she's writing science fiction and fantasy. Her greatest inspirations to write will always be J. R. R. Tolkien and her mom.

Giulia Ancona

Giulia lives in the northern part of Italy, in a town surrounded by mountains and medieval walls. Her job as a lawyer distracts her from her various interests and hobbies: reading, playing with her pets, traveling, food, traveling to discover new food, learning Japanese, and drawing.

Her writing consists of either legal papers or stories about made-up lands and characters (and sometimes the boundaries between these are blurrier than you might think). She will forever be grateful to her high school English teacher, without whose teaching she would not be here, writing in English, and taking part in this anthology.

Jessica Milner

Jessica lives on a houseboat in England. She travels around the country's canals through villages, countryside, and cities. She also runs a shop from her boat called the Hatch Shop and sells trinkets and stories as she continues her adventures. She takes inspiration from the places she goes and the nature surrounding them. She loves to meet people and animals, who often work their way into the stories she writes.

Jessica likes to tell herself stories that no one has ever heard before. That, she says, "is the beauty of writing. It is the ultimate in word-borne creativity. It's like illuminating subconscious dreams and piecing together thoughts that you never knew you had."

If you would like to go on some more brain delves with her, please visit: storyuploadblupijess.wordpress.com or on Instagram at blupijessauthor.

L.E. Doggett

L.E. Doggett is a writer who lives with his wife of 42 years and 31-year-old autistic daughter. They live in the Central San Joaquin Valley of California (USA). He and his wife attend a nice, conservative, hopeful church, and work. He is a retired blue-collar worker with a college education. He has written stories most of his life, but only seriously for the last six years. One story has been published in the Star Trek anthology Strange New Worlds 10. You can find another one here: https://onthepremises.com/minis/mini_18/ (the last story).

L.E. now has five books indie-published, which you can find in paper and e-versions at Amazon or the Barnes and Noble website, plus e-books on Kobo and other sites. His blog is http://musingsofle.blogspot.com.

Afterword

Thanks for taking the time to purchase and read my first book. I hope, and truly hope, that is just the beginning for '*The Persolus Race*', and that there are many more adventures to come. I hope that you come back to join us on those adventures.

The last thing I want you to do before you put down this book, is to step outside, look up into the sky, day or night, and imagine what might be out there.

Thanks,

Alex O'Neill

Acquisitions Editor